For Jen,
my moon and my stars

'I didn't mean to kill her, Sarah. It just –'

'Happened. I know,' she says in that quiet, soothing voice that made me fall in love with her all those years ago. She swallows and forces a smile. 'I understand. You don't have to explain yourself.'

We've done this dance before – too many times, I'm ashamed to admit. And, while I'm genuinely sorry each and every time, I also genuinely believe Sarah does, in fact, understand. This isn't wishful thinking on my part. We've been together a long time, Sarah and I; there are no secrets between us. Besides, Sarah couldn't keep something from me even if she wanted to. She's not a good actor, for one, but the reality is that she's not capable of deceit. Doesn't have it in her. She's too meek, still wears her heart on her sleeve. One look at her face and I know what she's feeling. Thinking.

We're sitting together on the living-room couch, the place, it seems, where we always end up having this conversation. I knock back the rest of my bourbon – my third – and stare into the fire, wondering, again, if there is such a place as hell.

'It just got away from me. Again.'

'I know,' she says quietly. 'Still, maybe you should have –'

My glare stops her cold. The firewood snaps and hisses.

'Should've what?' I prompt, aware of the heat climbing into my voice. Sarah knows better than to beat a dead horse. I've already apologized. The subject is closed. Done.

She takes another delicate sip of her white wine and stares down into her glass, like there's an escape hatch hiding somewhere at the bottom. I see how I've hurt her, and I take our glasses and place them on the coffee-table. Then I snuggle up next to her and take her hands in mine. Her smile is tight – not out of fear but because even now, after all this time together, she's still embarrassed about her crooked teeth.

'You're beautiful,' I say.

She reddens and stares down at my hands. The skin is still pink and sore from the hot water and the vigorous scrubbing with the brush. It took a good twenty minutes to remove the blood – especially the blood caked underneath my fingernails. I was so angry, so consumed by rage, that I forgot to put on the gloves. I need to be more careful next time.

And there will be a next time. We both know it.

Sarah clears her throat. 'A walk,' she says timidly.

'What?'

'We should take a walk. The fresh air will do us both some good.'

'Honey, it's the middle of the night. And it's freezing out.'

'I don't care.' The tentative smile on her face is as fragile as an eggshell.

My heart sinks when I break it. 'I'm exhausted,' I say gently. 'Maybe tomorrow night.'

She puts on a brave face. 'Whatever you want.'

'Thanks for understanding.'

She nods, keeps nodding.

I cup her face in my hands, fighting back tears. She swallows, nervous.

'You mean the world to me. I love you. You know that, right?'

'I do,' she says.

And I believe her.

I kiss her forehead. 'Everything's going to be okay.'

I smile. Kiss her gently on the lips. She crinkles her nose, like she's caught a whiff of a bad odour.

'What is it now?' I ask sharply.

'It's nothing.'

'No, go on. Say what's on your mind.' I feel the anger, how it's already moved past the point of no return. I can't help it – can't *stop* it. 'Say it.'

'Shower.' Her voice is barely above a whisper. 'You should take a long, hot shower.'

'Because I stink? That what you're trying to tell me?'

'No. It'll relax you.'

'I'm too tired.'

'I know, baby,' she says, and my anger retreats like dirty water swirling down a drain. She knows I love it when she calls me *baby*. 'It's just that you've got blood in your hair again.'

Day One

I

Darby McCormick felt her muscles relax and her stomach unclench when the helicopter's landing skids touched down. She was so happy – so damn *relieved* – she wanted to kiss Ricky the Pilot and his ridiculous *Magnum P. I.*

Ricky had fought major crosswinds since taking off from Denver. An hour later, when he began the descent to the helipad belonging to the Colorado State Trooper's station in Castle Rock, there had been several tense minutes when she was sure the chopper was going to spin out of control and crash into the nearby trees.

Darby thanked him and took off her headset. He didn't cut the engine; he had to fly back to Denver. She opened the side door to a blast of cold, grabbed her suitcase and rolling forensics kit, and stepped outside, ducking underneath the spinning blades. Hair blowing wildly across her face and shoulders, she made her way to a forest-green Jeep Wrangler, the only civilian vehicle parked in the back of the station.

Coop came out of the driver's door and made his way around to the front of the Jeep to greet her. His camel-hair overcoat and navy-blue suit jacket were unbuttoned, and, as the copter took off and the rotor wash blasted against his clothes, she saw the Glock 23, one of the standard side-arms issued to federal agents, tucked inside his black leather shoulder holster.

Coop had been working for the feds for a little over a year now. When his job at the private forensics company in London had been 'made redundant' – polite and fancy British speak for *we've just laid your ass off* – the Bureau had swooped in and hired him. No big surprise there. Coop was considered one of the best fingerprint experts in the country.

What did take her by surprise was the thought that popped into her head: this was the first time she'd seen Coop in well over a year. He still looked the same – hard and fit – but his blond hair was now cut shorter around the ears and neck to conform to federal regulations. As she drew closer, it amazed her how little he seemed to have aged since she'd met him nearly fifteen years ago. Not only had Coop won the genetic lottery (he was often mistaken for the blond-haired Tom Brady, the New England Patriots quarterback), but he had also been blessed with what she called the Dorian Gray gene – he was the kind of man who, like George Clooney, only got better looking with each passing year.

Coop took her suitcase as the helicopter climbed into the air. 'Didn't think you were going to make it,' he yelled over the roar of its engine.

'Didn't think I was going to either. That storm hitting Ohio screwed up flights all over the country. I got out of Florida just in time.' She pushed the aviator sunglasses back up her nose and brushed the hair away from her face as she followed him to the back of the Jeep. 'Why'd you book me a copter?'

'Quicker than driving to Denver to pick you up.' He opened the hatchback and placed her suitcase inside, then her forensics kit beside it.

Coop shut the door. The bright afternoon sunlight highlighted the intensely deep colour of his heterochromatic eyes: one was green, the other blue.

'You're looking a little green around the gills,' he said. 'Bumpy ride?'

'There were definitely a few moments when I was sure I was going to toss my airport breakfast burrito. Try not to hit any potholes along the way.'

He flashed his winning smile. 'It's great to see you.'

'You too. It's been way too long.'

Coop embraced her. She kissed his grainy cheek and hugged him back, surprised at how fiercely she still missed him. She pulled away before it went any further.

'How far to Red Hill?' Darby asked after he'd climbed behind the wheel.

'About an hour.' He slipped on a pair of Oakley sunglasses, put the car in gear and started making his way out of the station's back lot. 'We arrived yesterday, around noontime. Been to Colorado before?'

Darby shook her head. 'First time.'

'Air here's real thin, and it's even thinner in Red Hill. Town has the highest altitude in the state: 9,700 feet above sea level. It'll take a few days for our lungs to adjust, so we've been told to drink plenty of water or we'll suffer from altitude sickness.'

'Noted. Speaking of Red Hill, I couldn't find much on the internet, just that it was an old mining town.'

9

Coop pulled on to the road. 'The place is like . . . You see *The Shining*? The movie, not the TV mini-series thing.'

'I saw the movie when I was thirteen and didn't sleep for a week. Why?'

'You remember the scene that opened the movie? That aerial shot of Jack Nicholson's shitty VW chugging its way across a road that snakes through an immense forest, tall pines stretching for miles in every direction? That's what Red Hill reminds me of. Nothing there except woods and snow – lots of snow.'

'And a psychopath who's killed four families in a year.'

'And that.' Coop rolled his head to her, smiled. 'You're looking good. Nice and tan.'

'Florida sun will do that, even to a pale Irish girl like me. And look at you, dressed in your big boy clothes.' She chuckled. 'Never thought I'd see the day.'

'We've come a long way together, haven't we?'

'We certainly have, Special Agent Cooper.'

He took the exit for the highway. It was half past twelve, and the January sun was hard and bright in a cloudless sky. Everywhere she looked she saw flat lands covered in snow.

'You think you're going to stay there? In Sarasota?'

Darby shrugged.

'Don't care for all that sand and sunshine?'

'I don't like to be tied down anywhere,' Darby said, and then changed the subject. 'I read over the case files you sent. Not much there. Same pattern every time. Guy binds the family with plastic zip ties to the dining-room or kitchen chairs set up in one of the bedrooms. Covers their mouths with duct tape. Strangles the women and suffocates the men with a plastic garbage bag.'

'He uses a glass-cutter on a downstairs window or on a sliding glass door to let himself in.'

'What about evidence?'

'Smooth glove prints. No DNA or fibre evidence.'

'I'd like to read the evidence and lab reports.'

'Copies are being made as we speak.'

'Who handled the evidence?'

'State lab in Denver. Our lab says they're pretty good.'

'And, what, you disagree?'

'Not a question of agreeing or disagreeing. Lab is only as good as its equipment and its people, you know that. Since I haven't seen these techs in action, who knows what they might've missed?

'The evidence from the previous crime scenes – the duct tape, garbage bags and zip ties – was sent out FedEx to our lab yesterday. Toolmarks section asked to examine one of the windowpanes he cut through. That was sent out this morning.'

'One thing jumped out at me,' Darby said.

'The thing with the beds.'

Darby nodded. 'Each attack happened at night, and the vics were found dressed in their bedclothes. When the police arrived, all the beds were made.'

'Could be we're dealing with a new strain of pervert, some guy with severe OCD issues who feels compelled to make the bed, maybe even does a little light housekeeping before he leaves.'

Darby laughed. 'Still, the whole making-the-bed-before-he-leaves thing? I don't know what the hell to make of that.'

'Neither does Hoder.'

Darby straightened up in her seat.

2

Darby turned to him and said, 'Hoder as in Terry Hoder, the head of Investigative Support?'

'Do I detect a note of excitement in your voice?' Coop asked.

'He's very well respected.'

'And a tabloid staple. What's the name they gave him again? "Hoder the Hunter"?'

'They just call him "The Monster Hunter" now.'

'How incredibly original,' Coop said drily. 'If you're nice to me, I'll get you his autograph for your scrapbook.'

'Why didn't you tell me Hoder was going to be here?'

'You've met him?'

'A handful of times, years ago. I took some of his courses at Quantico as part of my doctorate.'

'What did you think of him?'

'For a fed, he didn't strike me as a total asshole.'

'He isn't. A *total* asshole, I mean.' Coop grinned. 'Actually, he strikes me as a straight shooter, no BS.'

'If Hoder's working on this, why am I here?'

'Because he specifically asked for you. He was impressed with the work you and I did in Boston, so he thought it would be a good idea to get the Wonder Twins back together.'

'Worst superheroes ever.'

'I know, right? Guy can transform into anything he wants, and each and every time he chooses to turn into water or an ice cube. Then again, what else can you expect from a guy who wears purple tights?'

Darby laughed.

Coop said, 'In the back you'll find an envelope holding your ID and some forms you'll need to sign – your consulting fee, per diem, all that fun stuff. You also have to sign a non-disclosure agreement. It's standard. FBI don't want you spilling any of our top-secret detective methods should you give an interview or be inclined to write a book.'

'Hoder's got everyone in ISU at his disposal. Why hire me as an outside contractor?'

'Because you're smoking hot?'

'Besides that.'

'Well, it *might* have something to do with the fact that you cracked both of the two serial cases you worked on – one of which, I may add, eluded my new employer for three decades.'

'Both those cases didn't exactly put your new employer in the best light.'

'Sure as hell didn't. And yet the Bureau hired me, and now they want to hire you. Hoder is a superstitious guy; he's hoping you can work your particular voodoo in Red Hill. Course, it didn't hurt when I told him you're the smartest chick I know.'

Darby shot him a look.

'Sorry, I know how much you hate that word,' he said. 'I meant to say "broad".'

'Much better.'

Coop was joking the way he always did – his expression and tone dancing along the edge of a smirk, using sarcasm to cover up his true feelings.

The last time they'd worked together was well over two years ago: the Soul Collectors case. In the aftermath, words were exchanged. Promises made. She returned to Boston, and Coop flew back to London to break it off with his live-in girlfriend.

When days turned into weeks, Coop waiting for his girlfriend to return home from a business trip, Coop waiting for the right moment to drop the bomb, Darby realized that there was nothing to keep her in Boston any more. Her job at the Crime Lab was gone, her parents were dead, and Coop . . . she loved him but she didn't want to own him. She decided to sell her condo and all its furnishings, and then, using a small portion of her considerable savings, purchased the best motorcycle ever made: a Triumph Bonneville T100 Special Edition, inspired by the one Steve McQueen drove in the movie *The Great Escape*. The Triumph was the only thing she owned now, her life condensed into whatever she could fit inside the bike's small rear trunk and pair of hardshell saddlebags. She lived her life out of motels and hotels.

Darby remembered the cloudless autumn day she drove out of the city. She could go anywhere and do anything. She was bound to nothing and to no one. She had the power to choose.

'You know,' Coop said, 'I find it very, very sad that the

only way I can get to see you in person is for me to dangle a sexual sadist in front of you.'

'A very *organized* sexual sadist. I come out only for the best. Coop, when we spoke yesterday, you didn't mention anything about ViCAP.' The FBI's Violent Criminal Apprehension Program was the largest database of violent crimes in existence; it held and analysed information about homicides – especially unsolved sexual assaults.

'That's because we didn't find anything about a killer who ties up families, murders them and makes the bed before leaving,' Coop said. 'Sure, we found some unsolved cases in the state where a family was tied up and/or killed, either shot or stabbed to death. Those, though, were all burglaries – or staged to look like burglaries. No sexual elements.'

'I read the articles posted on Colorado news websites and didn't see anything mentioned about the killer making the beds.'

'The locals kept that detail to themselves to weed out the copycats.'

Good, Darby thought. 'What else did they keep out of the papers?'

'Guy doesn't leave the rope behind. Lab's taking a look at the ligature marks and trying to see if they can ID the type of knot he uses. The locals are calling him the Red Hill Ripper.'

'Your guy strangles his victims,' Darby said. 'He doesn't mutilate them with a knife or a similar weapon.'

'Reporter who broke the first story thought "Red Hill

16

Ripper" would play and sound better than the "Red Hill Strangler".'

'Ah ... How'd Red Hill PD react to you guys being brought in?' The police chief, Coop had told her, had called Investigative Support. But that didn't mean the chief's people would roll out the welcome wagon for the detectives assigned to the case.

'They practically threw us a parade,' Coop said. 'These guys want us here, which isn't surprising, given the incorporation.'

'The what?'

'Red Hill's an un-incorporated town. Means it doesn't have a self-ruling government.'

'No mayor or city council.'

Coop nodded. 'It also means that the town doesn't have any money for schools and other services. Real-estate market didn't recover from the crash, which is great news for the developers, who are itching to come in and buy a whole bunch of properties and level them to the ground to make way for strip malls. I'm not for gentrification, but this town needs something, because it's practically in rigor mortis. No one's moving in because there aren't any jobs – they all went to China or India or whatever – and manufacturing's dead. With no one moving in and without Red Hill having the money to attract doctors and teachers –'

'The town's in a terminal spiral,' Darby finished.

'Which is the reason why the state wants to incorporate Red Hill with the neighbouring town of Brewster.

Sheriff's office is located there.' Coop turned to her and added, 'And it's not going anywhere.'

'So once the incorporation goes through, Red Hill PD will be no more.'

'Exactly. It's a skeleton crew as it is. The police chief called us because he's hoping we can help his people catch the Ripper. You know how it goes with a serial case – whoever catches the bogey man wins the prize. Brewster sheriff's office is staffed with better talent, but if Williams – that's the detective spearheading the task force, Ray Williams – if he and his people net this douchebag first, chances are good they'll have a place in the new regime.'

Darby had worked her fair share of high-pressure cases where the usual assortment of assholes – administrators, bureaucrats and politicians seeking re-election – demanded a case be closed in days instead of weeks, if not months. Oh, and bad news, kids: we haven't budgeted any funds for overtime, so go on out there and catch the bad guy on your own time – and pronto. But she had never worked a case with the Sword of Damocles hanging over her head.

A cell phone rang. Not hers; it was coming from a BlackBerry tucked away in a dashboard cubbyhole.

Coop picked it up and glanced at the screen. 'It's Hoder,' he said, and then answered the call. 'I'm on my way back with the good doctor.'

Darby couldn't hear what Hoder was saying on the other end of the line, but Coop's face had gone slack. You didn't have to read page one of *Detective Work for*

Dummies to know some piece of bad news had just been delivered.

'You're breaking up again,' Coop said, and gave the Jeep a little more gas. 'What? Yeah, I got the address, we'll meet you there in forty.'

Darby watched the speedometer's needle ease its way past eighty-five.

'Can you hear me, Terry? Terry? Goddamnit.' Coop hung up, sighing heavily.

'What's up?' Darby asked.

'They've just found another dead family.'

3

Multiple homicides in Boston were almost always three-ring-circus affairs. Caravans of patrol cars with their flashing blue-and-whites would block off the main and surrounding streets while patrolmen worked crowd control near the crime scene; a couple of blues would shout orders over bullhorns; and everyone would scramble to keep the herds of reporters, TV cameramen and curious neighbours corralled behind sawhorses.

When Coop turned right on to Salem End Road, the address of the crime scene, Darby saw yet another street that resembled all the others she'd passed on the way here: quiet and ordinary, a long stretch of pavement that looked like it had been carved through the middle of the forest, the modest single-family homes sprinkled along a string of big plots, all of which were set far back from the street and were slightly obscured by trees, as if trying to hide.

Darby didn't hear any bullhorns and she didn't see any flashing police or emergency lights. As they drew closer, the GPS, with its mechanical female voice speaking in a slight British accent for some reason, announced that their destination was coming up on the right, a mere 400 feet away. There wasn't a single person, cop or otherwise, out on the sidewalk.

'I don't know, Coop. All this chaos, I'm not going to be able to think clearly.'

'Welcome to Hicksville,' Coop said, as he pulled up against the kerb and parked behind a white Chevy pickup with an extended cab and mudguards. He killed the engine and pocketed the keys.

Darby, stepping out of the Jeep and on to the sidewalk, saw a black Honda Accord with tinted windows parked in front of the truck. The driver's door swung open.

Terry Hoder was as tall and slim as Darby remembered, but his hair, once jet-black, had gone entirely grey, and he wore the full weight of his fifty-six years in his face. In his ill-fitting suit and bland tie, he looked like a tired professor who had been coerced out of retirement to give one last, important lecture.

But his appearance was disarming. Behind his rumpled façade – his drowsy eyes and soft voice that still carried traces of his Texas accent – lurked one of the brightest and fiercest minds the FBI's Behavioral Analysis Unit had ever produced.

Hoder leaned on a cane, and he saw her staring at it as she drew closer to him. 'Had my knee replaced the week before Thanksgiving,' he said. 'Still on the mend, and the cold makes it throb like a mad bastard, to use one of my father's old sayings. Pleasure to meet you, Dr McCormick.'

'Darby.' She shook his hand. 'We've met before, actually. Long time ago, I don't expect you to remember.'

'Where?'

'Quantico. I took your course "The Motivational Models of Sexual Homicide".'

'Well, I hope it comes in handy here, since our man likes rope.' Hoder smiled wryly. 'Thank you for joining us. It'll be good to have another pair of eyes on this.'

Then his brow furrowed, his gaze narrowing slightly. 'There's nothing wrong with the people in Investigative Support. They're all fine men and women.'

Darby was surprised to hear her thought spoken out loud.

'The problem is that, at the core, they're all academics,' Hoder said. 'I don't mean that disparagingly; I include myself in that group. Over the past two decades, ISU has, unfortunately, been denigrated to an advisory role. Law enforcement either visit us or they send us their case files, and then I sit around a big conference table with my people, studying files and crime scene photos, tossing theories back and forth about what kind of offender we're looking for.

'Have our profiles helped? Yes, absolutely. But it's mostly after the fact. Nothing can replace working an actual case. Or field experience.'

Is this a lecture or a sales pitch? Darby wondered. Maybe it was a little bit of both.

'This is my rather long-winded way of explaining that I'm hoping to get ISU to change its ways before I retire – to get more seasoned investigators like yourself into the fold, and to have them actively involved in working serial and mass murder investigations on the ground.'

'So the Red Hill Ripper is, what, some sort of test case?' Darby asked.

'More like a trial run for what I hope will be a new

approach to multiple homicide investigations. By giving law enforcement agencies direct lab access and the country's best and brightest people, I believe we can shorten the duration of a serial investigation and, hopefully, save lives.' Then, with a frown, he glanced at his watch and added, 'Speaking of which, the MoFo should've arrived by now.'

'MoFo? Who's that?'

'What they called the MFU, the Mobile Forensics Unit,' Hoder said. 'Denver office is loaning us theirs, along with two forensics agents. It's a complete working lab, everything we can possibly need. We'll have satellite access to all our databases as well as anything we need at our main lab. I should go back to the hotel and call, see what the holdup is. Coop tell you about the problem with cell signals out here?'

Darby nodded. 'FBI's really pulling out all the stops with this one.'

Hoder picked up on the slight edge in her voice. 'I understand your past experiences with the Bureau have been, shall we say, less than ideal.'

Don't say it, Darby thought. Then she did.

'I was thinking more along the lines of gross negligence.'

Hoder chuckled, his smile wide and bright. It erased a good decade from his face. 'Please don't hold back on my account,' he said.

'Have you been inside?'

'No. Detective Williams wanted the scene secured. He's the only one who's been in there.'

'Good.'

'I know you're anxious to get to it, but before you go . . .' Hoder shifted his weight on his cane and looked over his car roof at the murder house. The front porch lights were on, and the Christmas decorations were still up – a big wreath on the door and tiny white lights wrapped around the stair railing and porch columns.

The afternoon sun warm against her face, Darby took in the windows facing the street. All the shades were drawn. She wondered if the killer had done that.

Hoder said, 'You caught two serials on your own, with no help from ISU – one of which, I'm embarrassed to say, was right under my nose.'

His gaze settled on the faint hairline scar on her left cheek. It was two inches long and it never tanned.

An axe had done that. It had smashed through a door while she'd been protecting a young woman inside a dungeon of horrors. The surgeons had replaced her shattered cheekbone with an implant. She was damn lucky she hadn't lost an eye.

Hoder cleared his throat. When he spoke, he sounded contrite. 'I'm the one who was responsible for coming up with the profile on that particular . . . person.' His tone and voice remained soft, but his eyes had hardened. 'Clearly, I was wrong. In fact, everything I pontificated about in that profile turned out to be, well, complete bullshit.'

Darby found herself being seduced by the man's easy Southern charm. He had used it when interviewing serial killers, getting them to open up and discuss the dark impulses that drove them. In some cases he got the killers to disclose where they had buried certain bodies.

'What I'm saying is, don't be afraid to challenge me.'

Darby smiled. 'Believe me, you got nothing to worry about on that front.'

4

Darby joined Coop at the back of the Jeep as Hoder drove off. He had been unloading their forensics gear while she'd been talking.

'Why didn't you join us?'

Coop pulled out the bulky Alternative Light Source unit. 'I wanted him to experience the full measure of your glowing personality.'

'Mission accomplished.'

'Judging by what I heard, I'd say so.' Coop shut the hatchback, the sound echoing for a beat. 'Never give an inch, do you?'

'Why live a life of half-measures? Come on, let's boogie.'

Having grown up and worked in a city where sirens and traffic and people yelling at one another were nothing more than background noises, as common as birds tweeting, Darby was struck by just how unbelievably quiet this place was. The wind picked up, shaking the towering pines, but after it died she could hear the ticking of the SUV's engine; the melting snow from the home's roof pinging its way down the gutters, which were packed with ice; and the click and scrape of her boots and the suitcase's rolling wheels as she walked with Coop, who was dragging their equipment.

The air here . . . she had never smelled anything so wonderfully clean. Invigorating. She felt like someone who had experienced the world's best night of sleep and woken up clear-headed and energized.

Or maybe it all had to do with her adrenalin – not from nerves. The adrenalin was psychologically induced from something only another cop would understand: the odd, palpable excitement of being on the hunt.

'What're you smiling at?' Coop asked.

'Just thinking about how much I miss this.'

'Working together?'

'Yeah.' She did miss working with him. But that hadn't been her first thought.

'I know it's going to be difficult, but please try not to jump my bones in there. It would be weird, not to mention unprofessional.'

'I'll try to control myself.'

Coop eased open the door. A white tarp covered the blond-wood foyer floor. Bright sunlight flooded through the windows in the surrounding rooms, and the cool air was fragrant with coffee and a tinge of wood smoke.

Hanging on the white-paned wall on her left were five artfully arranged framed pictures of a young brunette woman with a strong jaw and full lips. High school and college graduation photos, one of her as a baby and another as a toddler, the camera capturing her mid-jump on a bed and in a state of pure bliss.

The daughter, Darby thought, removing her sunglasses. *Please don't let her be in here.*

Darby looked to the archway on her left. The walnut

dining-table seated six. The pair of head-of-the-table carver chairs were gone as well as one of the side chairs.

A man in a navy-blue suit appeared at the end of the short hall leading into the kitchen. He wore white booties over his shoes and his hands were covered in latex. He also held a clipboard.

'Darby,' Coop said, placing his gear on the floor, 'meet Ray Williams. Ray is lead detective on the Ripper investigations. Ray, this is Darby McCormick, the forensics consultant I was telling you about.'

Williams was an inch or two shy of six feet and had dark brown eyes and thick black hair that was parted razor sharp on the side. He was also ruggedly handsome – the kind of man, Darby suspected, who chopped his own firewood, was comfortable with tools and drank good Scotch. She felt her pulse quicken.

Even better, he wasn't a sloppy hick cop who didn't know his way around a crime scene. Wary of disturbing any potential footwear evidence the killer may have left in the hallway, Williams hugged a wall as he moved towards them, avoiding the main area of foot traffic along the floor.

He looked her up and down – not in an overtly sexual way, but more with a look of a surprise, as if he'd been expecting someone entirely different. Then she realized that she looked like she'd just climbed off a Harley – snug black leather motorcycle jacket, jeans and chestnut-brown harness boots. *All I'm missing is a helmet and some tats.*

Coop had picked up on it. 'This is how PhDs from Harvard dress these days.'

'Ray Williams,' he said, his voice a deep, smooth purr.

He had a firm handshake and rough, callused palms. He also had about a day's worth of stubble; Ray Williams was in that category of men who always had a permanent case of five o'clock shadow no matter how many times a day they shaved. 'Thanks for coming, glad to have you here.'

Williams sounded genuine. That wasn't always the case with detectives. They were, by nature, as territorial as a junkyard dog, and about as friendly.

Darby nodded to the stairs. 'How many we got?'

'Hoder didn't fill you in?' Williams asked.

Coop answered the question. 'He tried, but the signal dropped out. Again.'

Williams nodded. Looking at Darby, he said, 'Cell phones don't work too well here. Not enough towers.' He flipped open his pad. 'Vics are David and Laura Downes, and their daughter, Samantha. That's her right there.' Williams pointed to the photos hanging on the wall and Darby felt something inside her tear. 'Samantha's twenty-two. Moved back in with her parents last year after graduating from college, works at the one and only bar that's still open downtown – Wagon Wheel Saloon, across from the place where you guys are staying. David's forty-seven. Lawyer, specializes in real-estate law. Laura's forty-eight. Former schoolteacher.'

'Same as the previous four families?' Darby asked.

'Same plastic bindings, duct tape, all of it.'

'Beds?'

'Both of 'em look as though they were made by Martha Stewart herself. Daughter's bedroom is on the first floor, off the kitchen.'

Coop said, 'Who found them?'

'I did,' Williams said. 'Downes's secretary, a woman named Sally Kelly, called the station this morning. Downes didn't show up for work yesterday, didn't call her or send an email. When she still hadn't heard back from him this morning, she asked if we could send someone over. Said she tried calling Downes at home and on his cell – even tried the wife's cell. I was at the station there when the call came in, so I decided to swing by to check it out. Found both cars parked in the garage and the front door unlocked. No tool marks or forced entry, but there's a hole cut in the sliding glass door off the living-room.

'I got about halfway up the stairs when I smelled them. They're all in the main bedroom. Go to the top of the stairs and hook a left. I didn't enter either bedroom and I stayed away from the main traffic areas – not that I think we're going to find any footwear impressions. This guy is too slick. My notes are here if you want 'em, underneath the sign-in sheet.' Williams held up his clipboard and then placed it by the door. 'Until this place has been worked over, I don't want anyone in here besides the three of us.'

Darby said, 'I noticed there aren't any patrol cars here.'

'A couple of units are on their way here to secure the perimeter, but I doubt this place is gonna turn into a sideshow.'

'What I meant was, why don't you have people doing door to door, talking to the neighbours?'

'There aren't any. You're standing in the only house on the street that's currently occupied. Rest of 'em are vacant – have been for quite a while.'

Coop said, 'Brewster's sheriff's office getting involved?'

'I haven't notified them. Don't plan to either.' Williams let his words linger in the air for a moment. 'Hoder told me he's sending up some sort of mobile lab. Said you guys could handle the forensics stuff, which is what I'd prefer anyway. State lab's backed up like a toilet. We wouldn't get test results for weeks.'

Then Williams turned to Darby and said, 'Coop tell you about the incorporation?'

Darby nodded.

'The guy in charge of Brewster's sheriff office, Teddy Lancaster, is of the belief that me and my people, what few of 'em I've got left, are incapable of finding the Red Hill Ripper ourselves – if we had any talent, he said, we would've found the son of a bitch by now. Ted's been heavily lobbying the pencil-pushers with a view to getting the cases pulled from us.'

'Is he conducting his own investigation?'

'Oh, I'm sure he is. He's got access to all the case files – I'm required to forward copies of everything to him. But I'm not required to call him about what happened here, and since this is still my case there's no reason for him to participate. I want to keep it that way as long as possible. I don't know if Coop told you, but if Lancaster finds the Ripper before me and my people do, it'll pretty much seal the argument that none of us Red Hill folk will be needed in the new regime. And the state will jump on it because it'll save them a good chuck of dough. They'll pass some of the savings Teddy's way, so he can promote his people, maybe build a new deck on his house, or whatever.'

'How many homicide detectives does your department have?' Darby asked.

'You're looking at him. I've got to call the ME. Anything you guys need, ask. I could really use a win here.'

Williams left, shutting the door softly behind him.

'No pressure or anything,' Coop said, slipping out of his coat.

Darby pulled her hair behind her hand and secured it with a rubber band as she looked up the stairs. She didn't want to meet the wide-eyed dead just yet. First, she wanted to get a sense of how the family had lived.

5

Dressed head to toe in a white Tyvek 'bunny' suit and wearing a facemask and clear goggles, Darby gripped a clipboard in one hand, the ALS unit in the other, and moved across the hall and into a small kitchen with a cream-coloured tiled floor and white appliances set against cherry cabinets. Clean dishes and glasses were stacked in a plastic drying rack on a black-and-brown-speckled granite countertop, and a glass coffeepot was full.

It must have been set to an automatic timer the night before, Darby thought, her gaze cutting to the edge of the kitchen counter, where she found a prepaid Netflix envelope with an empty DVD sleeve on top of it. It was for the first season of *Game of Thrones.* The disk was probably still in the player. *The mother probably left the sleeve here so it would be in her line of sight when she came into the kitchen in the morning. So she wouldn't forget to collect the disk from the player and then mail it back.*

Three hardwood steps led down into a family-room with soft, buttery-yellow walls adorned with framed oil pictures of seascapes. A soapstone fireplace took up the far wall, the charred remains of a fire still visible in the hearth.

Pictures of the family were scattered around the kitchen and family-room. David Downes was a thin, bald man with a slight overbite and nerdy appearance – a man who probably wore socks with his sandals. His wife, Laura, was a homely woman with curly brown hair and a bright smile. She tried to hide her ample figure with oversized tees and sweaters, all of which gave her a tent-like appearance. Samantha seemed to be their sole child, as she was the only one who featured prominently in the photos.

A big, L-shaped couch faced a flat-screen TV. Darby imagined the family on the brown sofa with its soft, deep cushions, everyone watching TV as a fire popped and hissed, the trio oblivious to the horror that awaited them one night after they went to bed.

Located ten or so feet behind the sofa was a sliding glass door. Wind blew through a rectangular-shaped hole that had been cut into the glass.

In her mind's eye Darby saw a gloved hand reaching through the hole and clicking back the lock. Pictured the faceless intruder carefully sliding open the door and then stepping into the living-room . . . and then what? *What did you do first?*

We know you brought a glass-cutter, zip ties, duct tape and bags. You wouldn't have carried those things in your pockets – at least not in the beginning. You would have stored them in something, wouldn't you?

Darby imagined him setting a backpack on the floor, then pulling out the items he needed and sticking them in his pockets. After that, he would head to Samantha's room: grab the daughter and the parents would co-operate.

Darby was sure the killer had a gun. Even a small revolver would enforce immediate group compliance.

People played hero all the time with knives. They took risks. That wasn't the case with guns.

Darby moved back to the kitchen and down a short hall that led to a dark bedroom. The door was open. Samantha's bedroom. It had a hardwood floor, and the blinds were drawn so there was no need to turn off any lights.

Coop moved next to her, a DSLR camera gripped in his hands, as she knelt and plugged the ALS unit into a socket. She turned on the unit, its fan whirring and a small motor throbbing, and picked up the attached wand. She held the wand at a very sharp, low angle just above the threshold, turning the beam of intensely bright white light to the right side of the neatly made bed.

Visible in the dust were several footwear impressions.

Coop carefully entered the bedroom, evidence markers in his hand. 'No tread marks,' he said. 'He must've been wearing cloth booties over his sneakers or whatever was on his feet.'

'He was wearing something with a soft sole. He wouldn't want to make any noise.'

Darby shut off the unit. Disappointment growling in her stomach, she used her pen to flick the bedroom light switch.

6

Underneath a ceiling light that, oddly, resembled a large breast with a big metallic nipple, Darby saw a framed *Les Misérables* print hanging on a wall above a poster bed adorned with bright cushions to bring out the colours in the old Americana quilt.

The bed was neatly made. Everything in her line of vision appeared orderly and clean, as though Samantha had tidied up before leaving for the day.

Darby entered the bedroom. The corner shelving installed between the closet and the window held stuffed animals, makeup and back issues of *Vogue* and *Cosmo*, and an iPad with one of those foldable covers that doubled as a stand. Darby saw her reflection in the screen.

While Coop took general photos – used to give an idea of the overall condition and layout of the scene – Darby sketched and mapped the area, taking detailed notes. She noticed that there weren't any personal pictures on the walls, bureau or desk. She didn't find any inside the desk either – which wasn't necessarily odd, as Samantha Downes had been raised in the digital age, when every movement and thought, no matter how inane, was documented and captured by a smartphone or tablet and posted on Facebook, Twitter, Instagram, tumblr. – the list of social media sites was endless.

Darby finished her notes and sketch. 'I'm going to check the area in front of the sliding glass door,' she said, unplugging the ALS unit.

Past the glass door she saw a deck made of pressure-treated wood, the floor damp from the melting blocks of ice clogging the gutters. There was more snow in the backyard. Had the killer walked through there and left footprints, or had he simply walked up the driveway and up the back porch?

There was no question he had stood on the back deck while he worked on cutting the glass. If the wood were wet or damp that night, when he stepped inside the house he would have left a footwear impression on the living-room's hardwood floor.

The words *meticulous* and *careful* echoed in the back of her mind as she turned on the unit, holding the wand at different angles against the floor, hoping the oblique light-ing source would find an impression.

There weren't any. And there wasn't any dust.

Coop entered the living-room. 'Anything?'

'No. He definitely wiped down this area here before leaving.'

'Told you we're dealing with a new strain of pervert.'

Darby pictured the killer kneeling on the deck, the upper half of his body leaning inside as his gloved hand rubbed a cloth or towel over the hardwood. Did he bring his own cloth or towel with him? Or had he used one from inside the house? *And where did you dump the cloth or towel and the cut section of glass?* She made a note on her clip-board to check the trash cans.

Darby removed her facemask and leaned her face close to the floor.

'Don't smell bleach or any other cleaning product,' she said.

'We'll check later just to be sure,' Coop replied, placing an evidence marker on the floor. They'd use luminol or, more preferably, BlueStar, a more chemically potent reagent, to check for blood and bleach, both of which reacted to the chemical. Smart killers – and there was no question in her mind the Red Hill Ripper belonged in this category – used bleach to destroy DNA evidence. She wondered what else he might've cleaned up in here as she stood and moved to the window above the kitchen sink.

The rolling hills of backyard snow were pristine. Undisturbed.

Darby returned to the living-room, where Coop was busy taking general photographs.

'Don't see any footprints out back,' she said.

Coop spoke as he angled the camera lens. 'He probably parked at one of the nearby vacant houses. Walked straight up the driveway and right up the back deck. I didn't see any sensor lights on the garage or along the side of the house.'

'I wonder if that's part of his selection methodology – choosing victims who live in remote areas in order to decrease his chances of being spotted by a witness. The other families – did they live in remote or secluded areas?'

'Everyone here lives in a remote and secluded area. This isn't like where we grew up, with houses practically sitting next to each other. A town like this is a perfect hunting ground.'

Then Coop moved the camera away from his face and walked to the right of the sliding glass door. 'Check this out,' he said, pointing to the cut, square-shaped hole.

Darby moved in front of Coop and looked at the exterior glass. It was covered in dirt and grime – except for the area around the hole, which had clearly been wiped down. There was also some sort of film on the glass.

'What do you think it is?' Coop asked.

'Might be kerosene.'

'Kerosene?'

'It ensures a smoother, crack-free cut.' Darby left the room and came back with a pair of orange goggles. She slipped them on and then she moved the handheld forensic light-source device that had been tucked in her pocket around and around the film.

'It's not kerosene,' she said. 'If it was, it would fluoresce a light blue.'

'What do you think it is – some sort of cleaner?'

'Maybe. The film, though, looks like it has an oily residue. Could be cutting oil. If you can isolate the chemical components in your lab, we might be able to pin down a particular brand. Cutting oils are usually specialty items sold in stained-glass stores.'

Darby made a note on her clipboard.

When they finished taking pictures and making notes and sketches and measurements, they moved upstairs to meet the dead.

7

Darby entered the bedroom and stood stock still, an almost electric charge humming through her blood. She ignored the carnage at the foot of the bed and took in the cold, square-shaped room of white walls and blond-hardwood flooring.

Three windows in here: the one next to an ivory leather armchair was cracked wide open and none of the shades were drawn. She could see and hear the trees swaying and rustling in the wind.

To her left was the door to a small walk-in closet. A silver-framed charcoal-pencil drawing of the daughter, Samantha, done when she was a toddler, hung on the wall next to a built-in bookcase, the white-painted shelves stocked with books on art and on country decorating. She also found popular mystery and thriller novels by Dan Brown, Michael Connelly and Gregg Hurwitz.

The nightstand on the left side of the queen-sized bed held an alarm clock and a pile of cooking magazines, the top one an old copy of *Gourmet*. Everything – the white ruffled comforter and blood-red decorative throw pillows – like the daughter's bedroom downstairs, was perfectly in place.

Was it possible the killer suffered from some sort of obsessive-compulsive disorder, or that the act of making the beds was a bizarre ritual that he felt compelled to perform? Sure. But she didn't put much stock in it: Darby believed the act of making the beds contained no significance other than that the killer wanted to screw with their heads, maybe to throw them off the scent.

On the right side of the bed and set against the wall was a bureau made of dark cherrywood. On top, three more framed pictures: Samantha as a toddler, wearing a diaper and standing in a paddling pool; Samantha on a swing, her bony kneecaps covered in Band-Aids; Samantha standing on the grass and looking in surprise at something out of shot. The nightstand on the right – the husband's – held a first-generation Kindle and an iPad, the latter's smartcover, which doubled as a stand, holding the device upright.

Darby made detailed notes, sketched the crime scene and took preliminary measurements, while Coop began the laborious process of taking establishing photographs of the bedroom.

Finished, she moved to the foot of the bed and met the Downes family.

Daughter, mother and father were bound to the dining-room chairs with plastic zip ties. Samantha, barefoot and wearing a pair of old blue sweatpants and a white baby doll T-shirt, was seated across from her parents. The tee had been pulled down to expose her breasts.

The parents were also dressed in their nightclothes – Laura in a heavy red and black flannel nightgown, David in boxers and a dingy white undershirt with perspiration stains under the arms.

Both the mother and daughter had been strangled; their faces had a bluish pallor from oxygenated blood. Darby couldn't see the father's face; it was hidden behind a black garbage bag that was tied around his neck.

Like her father, Samantha had been bound to one of the dining-table's carver chairs, their forearms secured against the wood of the armrests. The zip ties, three pairs used on each arm, had cut through the skin, the result of the victims' violent struggle against their restraints. The zip ties used to secure their ankles to the chair-legs had also cut through their skin. One thing was clear: David Downes had struggled rabidly against his restraints. The zip ties along his forearms and ankles had cut deeply through skin and muscle, with drops and tiny pools of blood collecting around his limp hands and bare feet.

At one point during the struggle the chair had toppled backwards. On the carpet she found a clear pair of smeared, bloody handprints. They overlapped each other, and between them was a crusted, amœba-shaped smear, which suggested the killer had lifted the chair back up rather quickly. Why? Why not leave the husband thrashing about on the floor?

The mother was tied down to a side chair: because it lacked armrests, her wrists had been bound behind her back and secured to the chair's rear legs with zip ties. As with her daughter, a strip of duct tape had been strapped across her mouth. But there was a difference: here, the tape hadn't been removed during the course of the tor-ture. Darby had seen slight abrasion marks on Samantha's cheeks, a clear result of the tape having been yanked off.

The killer had replaced the tape crookedly, all of which suggested that he had wanted the parents to hear their child screaming for help, screaming for the pain to stop. Then, most likely after Samantha was dead, the killer had replaced the tape over her mouth.

Darby thought about the order of the murders.

Sexual sadists usually focused their attention on their female victims. Darby suspected the killer tied the bag around David Downes first and then went to work on Samantha and Laura, most likely saving the daughter for last. Samantha was younger. Prettier.

Darby glanced to her left. On the wall near the doorway to the master bathroom was a dual digital thermostat. The heat for the second floor was on, set at 70°F. The second temperature, the actual one for the room, read 58°. *The parents must've forgotten to shut the heat off before they turned in for the night*, she thought, and poked her head into the master bathroom. It had white tiles and white walls and two windows set over a small jacuzzi. Everything in there looked neat and orderly and clean.

Had the killer cleaned up in the bathroom after the family was dead?

Darby moved behind Samantha's chair and examined the young woman.

'Coop.'

8

Darby pointed to a pair of burn marks along the side of the woman's scalp.

'Look like Taser marks,' Coop said.

'I agree.'

'So the guy sneaks into Samantha's bedroom, and while she's sleeping he hits her with the Taser. During those few seconds when she's incapacitated, he binds her wrists and tapes her mouth shut.'

'Then he goes upstairs and subdues the parents.'

'To get everyone to co-operate, he had to have had a gun.'

Darby nodded. 'Binds and gags everyone in the bedroom, then goes downstairs and brings up the chairs.'

Coop pointed to the red dots covering the right side of Samantha Downes's face. 'We've got numerous petechial haemorrhages, which are consistent with strangulation.'

'Face is cyanotic above the noose imprint,' Darby added.

'Could you explain that?' Not Coop – Detective Williams. He had entered the bedroom, wearing booties, latex gloves and a paper facemask.

Darby said, 'Cyanotic refers to the blueness you're seeing in the face – lividness caused by imperfectly oxygenated blood.'

Darby studied the furrows the rope had left on the young woman's neck. As was most often the case with strangulations, the rope had left its weave imprinted on the skin.

'Weave looks like a braided pattern.'

'My money's on a nylon rope. Look under the chin.'

Darby did. 'Figure-eight pattern.'

'That's probably from whatever knot he used. But here's where it gets weird. Look at the back of the neck.'

Darby studied the mark. 'It's a single, braided twist,' she said.

'And those same figure-eight patterns are underneath each ear.'

'Definitely not your standard noose.'

Darby moved to the mother. Laura Downes had exactly the same rope imprints on her skin, in exactly the same locations.

'For a knot like this,' Darby said, 'our guy had to have used two strands of rope.'

Coop nodded. 'You notice anything else about the furrows?'

'Yeah. I'm not seeing the typical abrasion patterns.'

Williams spoke up. 'You guys mind explaining that?'

Coop put down his camera. 'When you strangle someone,' he said, moving behind Samantha Downes's chair, 'generally you're using a single piece of rope. You stand behind them and twist. Maybe you even go so far as to loop one end of the rope underneath the other – like you do when you tie a shoe – and then you give it a sharp tug to maintain more pressure around the neck.'

'Okay.'

'You're holding on to the rope, tightening it, and the victim's struggling. Doesn't matter if the vic is bound to the chair, he or she is still going to struggle. She's twisting her head this way and that, you're pulling the rope, tightening it – maybe even pulling the rope up towards you, depending on your height. Either way you're going to see abrasions around the furrows – the result of the rope slipping and sliding around during the struggle. With the daughter and the mother, there are barely any abrasions.'

'Meaning our guy wasn't holding on to the rope while she struggled,' Williams said.

'Correct. This knot our guy used, I think it was already in place – meaning the rope was already tied around her throat.' He placed his hands near Samantha's ears. 'Then he grabbed each end of rope and gave it a hard yank.' He jerked his hands sideways and outwards. 'The knot did the rest.'

Williams looked at Darby and said, 'Guys who are into this shit, my understanding is it's the rope that gets them off. They prolong the strangling, wait until the vic passes out and then revive her so he can do it all over again.'

'That's true. Watching them suffocate, though, could be what gets our guy off. You find semen at any of the scenes?'

Williams shook his head. 'Forensics did a thorough job. They checked the floors, the vics and their clothing, nothing.'

'What about the bed-sheets?'

'Sent them to the state lab, figuring he, I dunno, rolled around in them or something. They found dried semen stains but they all belonged either to the husband or to the daughter's boyfriend. If our guy's getting his rocks off in the homes, he's real careful about it.'

Darby moved into the bathroom. The vanity had his-and-hers sinks. She removed her facemask, leaned close to the sink and sniffed. Williams watched her from the doorway.

'What're you looking for?'

'Bleach,' Darby said, and turned to the other sink.

'You think he tossed one off here and dumped bleach down the drain to destroy the DNA?'

'Maybe. I worked a case back in Boston where a guy broke into an elderly woman's house. After he strangled her, he went into the bathroom, ejaculated into the sink and tried to wash it away with bleach. You or the forensics guys find bleach at any of the other crime scenes?'

'No, but I'll recheck the forensics reports just to be sure. Speaking of which, I've got one of my guys making copies for you, pictures and everything. You'll have them later today.'

'Thanks.'

'I don't think our guy would have had his own one-on-one private party in the bathroom. He's got too much restraint.'

'You're probably right. I don't smell any bleach, but we'll take apart the drainpipes and swab them just to be sure.'

Darby ran the blue beam of her forensic light across the vanity and sinks. Nothing fluoresced.

When she turned her attention to the toilet, its seat lifted, the bowl glowed with faint green dip marks.

9

Darby frowned, thinking.

Bleach wouldn't fluoresce unless it had been sprayed with luminol. When that chemical reacted with bleach, it gave off a blue glow. Here inside the toilet she was seeing a dull green glow. Some chemical other than bleach had been dumped inside the toilet.

But what? She doubted the killer had brought his own stuff to clean up with. More than likely he had used something here inside the house.

Darby examined the floor around the toilet. Nothing fluoresced, but she found a residue of a white, powdery substance. It definitely wasn't talc; this was more granular. After she collected a sample, she placed an evidence marker next to it, got to her feet and moved to the linen closet across from the shower. She used a pen to open the bi-fold doors.

Five shelves. The bottom two packed with an array of cleaning products bought in bulk from a warehouse club like Costco. Darby went down on one knee and, with her gloved hands, rooted through the rolls of paper towels, cans of disinfectant, and bottles of Scrubbing Bubbles, Mr Clean, Windex and Clorox.

In the far back of the bottom shelf, tucked against the

wall and hidden behind rolls of toilet paper, she found a blue bucket with a handle.

Darby removed the bucket. It was dry and empty, and it didn't smell of bleach. When she ran the forensic light inside the bucket, dull green patches glowed from the plastic walls.

'Did he use that bucket?' Williams asked.

'Maybe. Why else hide it in the far back of the bottom shelf, behind all the rolls of toilet paper? The bucket and the toilet have the same green glow.'

'Bleach?'

'No. Something else.'

Darby rooted through the rows of chemicals on the shelves and in the cabinets underneath the sink. Then she returned to the bedroom. While Coop set up his camera to take close-up shots of the victims, she ran the forensic light across the hardwood floor and walls, the victim's clothing, the bedding and furniture. The blood appeared black in her goggles.

The wall to the right of the ivory armchair glowed with dull green patches. She found more green patches and smears on the skirting board, and in and around the chair.

'This is where he cleaned up,' Darby said. 'He wiped down almost everything in this corner.'

She told Coop and Williams about the green marks she'd found inside the bathroom.

'Bleach doesn't fluoresce under an FLS unless it's been treated with something like luminol, Coop said.

I found a bottle of Mr Clean in the linen closet,' Darby said. 'That product *does* react to FLS – it glows green. The marks along the wall and floor are faint, which, if I had to guess, means that there was a faint residue of Mr Clean or something similar in the bucket – and he moved the chair to clean behind it. I found a few drip marks along the side and the back – splash marks from when he used a rag or sponge or whatever to wipe down this area. He moved the chair so that he could clean the wall, floor and skirting board with a rag or sponge. Whatever he used, I didn't find it in bathroom trash can.'

'Might have used the Mr Clean, or taken it with him.'

'But not the bucket. Decided to hide it instead.'

Outside, Darby heard an approaching car engine.

Williams had heard it too. 'Probably some of my guys,' he said, shutting his notebook. 'Them, or the coroner. Excuse me.'

Coop was on his knees, his gaze roving across the wall and floorboards.

'What the hell would he be cleaning up here, in this corner?' he said, more to himself than to her.

'I don't know,' Darby replied. 'But we're going to tear this room apart until we find out.'

10

The two agents on loan from the Denver office were a Mutt-and-Jeff pair named Eric Hayes and Victor Ottaviani. Hayes was the short one. He had piercing blue eyes and short and shaggy blond hair, and, while his sharp black suit had been tailored for his pencil-thin frame, Darby thought he looked like a skateboarder who had dressed up for a court appearance.

Ottaviani – Otto, as he liked to be called – was the polar opposite. He was an inch or two shy of six feet and he had a shaved head and a sizeable paunch. His eyeglasses had metal frames that were considered out of style in the eighties, and he wore a drab navy-blue suit that, had it been donated to either Goodwill or the Salvation Army, would have immediately been tossed into the 'discard' pile.

Otto went to help Coop dismantle the bathroom drainpipes and swab them for semen, while Hayes joined her inside the MoFo. Darby had worked in her fair share of vehicles billed as rolling crime labs, but she found them to be haphazard affairs, a desk or two with only basic forensics equipment hastily installed inside the back of a van or box truck.

Not so with this one. It was housed in a long semitrailer, and everything inside, from the worktops to the equipment, had been carefully laid out. Smelling of fresh paint and metal, and with its strong lights, white counters and floors, and glass cabinets, it had a Steve Jobs/Apple store design vibe about it. Everything Darby saw looked showcase perfect, not a scratch anywhere. She wondered if this was the mobile lab's inaugural run.

'MoFo's got pretty much anything you might need stocked in here,' Hayes told her. The soundproofed walls filtered out the dull roar of the vehicle's running diesel engine, but she could feel it rumbling beneath her feet. 'You need any help, just shout.'

Hayes retreated to one end of the trailer to use the mass spectrometer, which would identify the composition of the oil from the sliding glass door and the white, powdery residue she had found on the floor near the toilet. Darby took the evidence bags holding the duct tape to a workstation equipped with a Superglue Fingerprint Fuming Chamber.

For the next twenty minutes Darby oriented herself with the equipment and the locations of the tools and chemical solutions. Hayes was right: pretty much everything she needed was inside the trailer, including a tank of liquid nitrogen. Perfect. She went to work on the tape.

In addition to fingerprints, epithelial cells, hair and dead skin, the adhesive side of duct tape also picks up an array of trace evidence. Darby examined all six strips for hair and fibres. She found plenty, along with a lot of blood. After meticulously collecting and labelling each sample, she made very detailed notes on her clipboard.

Duct tape is notoriously sticky. Even if a killer wears

gloves, often the adhesive is strong enough to pull off a piece of a latex. Tucked into a torn edge of tape she discovered a sliver of latex half the size of a pencil eraser; on one ragged end was a nearly invisible, pin-sized black smear. After marking and photographing it, she used the tip of a knife to carefully prise it away.

Darby examined the smear underneath a microscope. Given what she saw, she suspected it was ink. The mass spectrometer would be able to identify the sample.

She placed black fingerprint powder, distilled water and washing-up liquid inside a glass beaker and mixed everything together using a fingerprint brush made of camel hair. She put it aside and, slipping on a fresh pair of gloves, moved to the nitrogen tank. She released the tank's locking tab, removed the metal dipstick with the cone attached to the end and poured the liquid nitrogen into the stainless-steel container she had placed on the worktop near the sink.

Carefully she dipped the first strip of tape into the container. She separated the smooth layer from the adhesive side. The smooth layer went into the Superglue Chamber; the adhesive side went on a tray, where she worked the fingerprint solution she'd mixed into it. It went on thick and black, and, after the tape was completely covered, she carried it to the sink. The solution would stick to any fingerprints; the rest would wash away.

Darby held the tape under the running water.

No fingerprints. She bagged the tape and then went to work on the next piece.

'That white powder you found on the bathroom floor?'

Hayes said. 'It's an aminoglycoside antibiotic called neomycin. Not the ointment for skin infections – I'm talking about an actual oral pill, which I didn't even know existed. It kills bacteria in the intestinal tract. It's used to treat E. coli infection and a condition called hepatic coma. That's when the liver stops filtering out toxins and they build up in the blood. It's also used to treat something called – I'm going to mangle this pronunciation – hepatic encephalopathy, which is a worsening of brain function that happens when the liver fails at removing the aforementioned blood toxins.'

Darby had just finished hanging the last smooth side of tape inside the Superglue Chamber when the back door opened. It was Otto.

'Cooper wants you in the bedroom,' he called out over the diesel engine.

'I bet he does.'

His face coloured slightly. 'I didn't mean –'

'Relax, I was just busting your balls.'

Hayes called out over his shoulder, 'Hey, Otto, pause the sexual harassment and come on up here and give me a hand with this computer shit. The satellite feed just crapped out. *Again.*'

II

While Darby had been in the MoFo, the bodies had been removed and taken to the medical examiner's office in Brewster, which serviced Red Hill as well as four other nearby towns. The ME's office, Williams had told them, was, because of years of steep cutbacks, woefully under-staffed, and there was a backlog of autopsies. The office had only one full-time doctor on staff. The part-time doctor who had been helping out had retired at the end of last year, and the office's request for a deputy coroner had been denied.

She didn't need to explain the importance of having an autopsy performed before the organs had completely deteriorated. Williams had followed the morgue van to Brewster to plead his case to Ben Stern, the district cor-oner and chief medical examiner. Williams promised he'd beg – on his knees, if necessary – to get the autopsies slated for sometime tomorrow.

Darby doubted Ray Williams would have to go to such lengths. Like Coop, the Red Hill detective had been blessed with effortless charm, someone who could get both men and women to do favours, pull strings and jump through hoops with smiles on their faces.

Darby entered the house. She put on a mask, then signed the log and moved up the stairs. Coop appeared in the bedroom doorway, his head and face covered by a hood and a respirator mask.

'Bad news on the duct tape,' she said to him. 'No prints on the adhesive side. The smooth side, I don't know yet; they're in the Superglue Chamber.'

'Not that surprising. We know this guy's careful.'

'What I did find, though, was a small piece of latex that's marked with what looks like ink. If we can get sweat or some skin cells off it, we might have a DNA sample.'

'Otto and I just finished using luminol. Our man didn't use bleach to wipe down anything inside the bathroom, and he didn't dump it down any of the drainpipes either. We took them apart and swabbed them just to be sure. Now come and take a look at this.'

She followed him to the corner of the bedroom. A square section of flooring had been removed and then taken apart and placed inside evidence bags.

'In addition to using Mr Clean on this area, he *also* used bleach,' Coop said. 'I sprayed it with luminol and everything glowed. The hardwood is old and scuffed – it's probably the original flooring. The poly sealant is pretty much gone, which is good news for us. The chemicals and rag or whatever he used couldn't penetrate the crevices between the boards.'

'You find blood?'

'Yeah,' Coop said. 'A ton of it.'

I find Red Hill incredibly depressing this time of year – grey winter mornings and short afternoons where the wind hits your skin like a drill bit, keeping people off the streets and tucked inside their homes. By 4 p.m., the world is swallowed inside a pitch-black darkness.

And yet it is during this time – what I call my 'black hole hours' – when I feel the most alive – when the part of me that I keep hidden during the daylight is wide awake, throbbing for attention.

Just a glimpse, I tell myself as I drive. *Just a glimpse, and then I'll go home.*

My destination tonight is two towns away, a place called Kelly's Bar and Restaurant. I have no idea if Tricia's working tonight; this trip is a last-minute idea, a way to clear my head and think. Still, my heart sinks into an acid pit of worry and fear at the idea of her not being there. I need to see her tonight or I won't be able to sleep.

When I pull into the parking lot, I spot a white Honda Civic with a battered rear bumper and a University of Denver decal stuck to the rear window. The anxiety caged inside my chest uncoils, and I immediately feel myself start to relax.

The bar's Christmas decorations are still up. A fake wreath hangs on the front door and, secured to a railing with a bungee cord, is a big, glowing plastic Santa that I'm pretty sure was rescued from a garbage dump. It's scraped and stained; a chunk of plastic the size of my fist is missing from Santa's head.

The interior is small, just a handful of tables sprinkled around a U-shaped bar of polished walnut, its edges decorated with white lights shaped like icicles. The warm, fetid air smells of fried food, even though the dining-room tables are empty, and there is only one person seated at the bar, an old timer wearing a red flannel shirt. His ruddy cheeks are peppered with patches of grey whiskers, and the remaining wisps of white, downy hair lie across his liver-spotted scalp like feathers.

Standing behind the bar and refilling his glass with cheap Scotch is the purpose of my visit: Tricia Lamont, a leggy marvel with a prominent nose and jawline, her dark brown hair with its expensive blonde highlights spilling across her shoulders and falling in tangles against the V-neck scoop of a black T-shirt embossed with the bar's name and slogan – KELLY'S. WHEN YOU'RE HERE, YOU'RE FAMILY. The tee barely fits her. Whoever owns this place makes his ladies (he employs only women, each one no older than thirty) wear a tee one size too small so it hugs their firm and perky breasts. Every time one of them bends over or leans forward to pour a drink, as Tricia is doing right now, the bottom of the tee rides up just a wee bit to show a tantalizing flash of belly, every one of their stomachs as flat as a board.

I pull out a corner stool. I'm hanging my coat over the back when Tricia walks up to me, smiling brightly. She doesn't know my name, and she has seen me only once – last month, the week before Christmas. The Connelly family – John, Lisa and their sixteen-year-old daughter, Stacey, who were, at that time, the Red Hill Ripper's latest victims – had been laid to rest that afternoon, and I decided to stop by here for a drink. The family and whatever mistakes that might possibly have been made at the crime scene weighed heavily on my mind.

'What can I get'cha?' Tricia asks, her eyes seemingly alight with genuine pleasure.

'You have Knob Creek bourbon?'

'Sure do.' She smiles. 'You have great taste.'

'Make it a double, neat.'

As she moves to the bottles, I watch her, lustfully conjuring up all sorts of wonderful scenarios of her lying naked in my bed, the soft moan that escapes her lips and caresses my ear as I enter her. The feel of her thighs sliding up against the sides of my chest and the moment when she presses the balls of her feet against the small of my back and pushes, begging me to go deeper . . .

Is Tricia a fighter? Or will she act like the others, mewing and crying and begging for it to stop?

Sarah never fights or cries. Even in the beginning when she first saw the rope, she did what I asked with a smile on her face.

Tricia comes back with my drink and places it on a napkin. She tucks her hair behind an ear, playful and sexy. I suspect – correctly, I think – that Tricia, with her beautiful looks and hard yoga body, belongs to that class of women who view men as walking wallets. A woman who wants to squirt out a kid or two, then hire a nanny so she can drive her new BMW to her Pilates class and then spend the afternoon inside a hotel screwing some young stud.

'Want to start a tab?'

Absolutely. I want to stay here and drink and watch you and feed my growing hate and think about that moment when I slip the noose around your neck.

The phone behind the bar rings. 'Excuse me,' she says, and as she walks away I think about what an odd choice she is for me. The four other candidates I have in mind are nowhere near as attractive or as physically fit, but at least I've meticulously researched their backgrounds. Their routines, habits and schedules. I've been inside their homes and on their computers. I've slept in their beds.

That's not the case with Tricia Lamont. I know she's twenty-two, a graduate from the University of Denver with a degree in business communications. Like the good majority of recent college graduates trying to enter the workforce in this monstrous economy, she's had a difficult time landing a job, which is why she's most likely living back home with her parents, Rick and Jennifer, who own three dry-cleaning stores. Tricia works at one and supplements her income by bartending here. I don't know if she has a serious boyfriend or if she's playing the field or whatever these young whores call it these days. I haven't read her texts or been on her computer yet.

My thoughts shift to the tools sitting inside my trunk. Everything I need to break inside her house is in there. I could leave here and, if her parents aren't home, let myself in and play with her things for an hour or two. I've already cased her house. I know the best way to approach it without being seen, and I know the perfect spot where I can park my car.

It's tempting. As I sip my bourbon, I actually consider it for a moment.

But I know better. Everything comes down to impulse control. That's the key to not getting caught. You don't strike or take any action when you're fevered with bloodlust, as I clearly am right now. You plan meticulously and then you execute the plan so you don't make any mistakes. And I can't afford to make any mistakes, especially now that the FBI are in Red Hill.

The news has been circulating all over town for the past week. That's the downside to living in a place as small as Red Hill; anything out of the norm instantly burns its way like a brushfire across the town's grapevine. Terry Hoder, the famous monster hunter, is here in Red Hill to track down the Red Hill Ripper – it's all anyone's talking about.

I smile and sip my drink. The Red Hill Ripper. What a ridiculous name.

Tricia stands at the other end of the bar, her back to me as she talks on the cordless. I stare at her, marvelling at the way her dark jeans hug her ass, and wonder if she does that hot yoga thing, Bikram. Probably does that with her girlfriends and then they all go out afterwards to Starbucks and order low-cal scones and skim-milk cappuccinos and talk about how they use men.

I have plenty of time to find out. I can wait. Hoder can't. At some point Hoder and his band of merry men will pack up and leave, and then *I'll* decide when to take Tricia or one of the others. They're not going anywhere, my candidates. All I have to do is wait and be patient. Then, when the time is right, I'll choose one.

Maybe I'll bring Sarah along with me. No matter what time of night, people aren't afraid to open the door to a woman.

Tricia laughs. It's a lovely sound.

I wonder what her screams would sound like.

Just a glimpse, I promised myself. And now I've had it. Besides, there's one other thing I need to do before I go home. I knock back the rest of my bourbon and place a ten on the table. I pick up my coat, feeling warm and comfortable and satisfied. Hopeful.

12

By 6 p.m. they had finished processing the master bed-room and bath, Samantha Downes's bedroom, the living-room floor and the back deck off the sliding glass door. Darby's lower back ached and her mind felt cramped from hunger and the fatigue that was working its way through her limbs.

They had collected the usual preliminary evidence found at a homicide – hairs and fibres from the bodies and rooms as well as an assortment of fingerprints, all of which, Darby suspected, belonged to the Downes family. The footwear impressions on the living-room floor were matched to footwear belonging to the family. No finger-prints had been found on either the toilet or the blue plastic bucket, which suggested he had wiped everything down. And he had taken away whatever rag or towel he'd used on the bedroom wall, because they hadn't found it in any of the garbage cans.

Darby had checked the family's medicine cabinets. While David Downes took medications for high blood pressure, insomnia and several anti-depressants for anxiety and depression, Darby hadn't found a prescrip-tion bottle for neomycin belonging to him, his wife or his daughter, nor had she found an empty one in the trash. They'd need a court order to access the family's medical records to see if any of them had been taking the antibiotic.

Coop had also found a 'plastic' fingerprint on the skirting board – a three-dimensional friction-ridge impression created when someone presses a fingertip in fresh paint, soap, hot wax, tar or car grease. In this case, it was in polyurethane. The skirting board had been treated with the polymer years, maybe decades, ago. There was no way the Red Hill Ripper could have left the print, but procedure dictated that Coop process the print anyway. He would use it later, in the courses that he taught at the FBI Academy, where students, forensic investigators and law enforcement officers learned how to identify and retrieve tricky prints from various surfaces.

The mobile lab's satellite was down and could be fixed only in Denver. MoFo Coop, along with Otto and Hayes, would go there to work on the rest of the collected evidence.

Coop had another reason for wanting to go to Denver tonight: the Regional Computer Forensics Laboratory, an FBI-sponsored and accredited full-service digital forensics laboratory and training centre that worked with law enforcement agencies in Colorado and Wyoming. RCFL had agreed to examine all the home and business computers and tablets belonging to the Downes family.

The Denver RCFL facility also had a cell phone kiosk that utilized a newly developed FBI technology called UFED, short for the Universal Forensic Extraction Device. It could download data from any cell or smart phone and collate it into a report, which could then be burned on to a CD or DVD in as little as thirty minutes. Use of the kiosk, however, was by appointment only, and Coop had booked a slot for tomorrow at 11 a.m.

It was now coming up on seven. Darby stood with Coop inside the kitchen, cataloguing evidence. Hoder, who had been on his feet most of the day, balancing his weight on his cane, had returned to the hotel so he could ice his swollen knee. He wouldn't be making the trip to Denver.

'I want you to stay here, in Red Hill,' Coop said.

Darby looked up.

'If Williams can get the autopsies scheduled for tomorrow, one of us should be here. Besides, I'll have help in Denver.'

Darby felt relieved. She wanted to spend the evening going through the evidence files. A long-time sufferer from motion sickness, she had never been able to read or concentrate while in a car.

'Sounds good,' she said, and went back to writing.

'Really?' Coop asked in mock surprise. 'Here I was expecting an argument.' He handed her the keys to his rental and added, 'You must be getting mellow in your old age.'

As Darby wrote, she thought about the plastic bag that had been stuck to David Downes's face like a cobweb, his skin pale and sweaty beneath the bag, the thinning remains of his fine brown hair matted against his scalp and forehead. Several strips of duct tape had been wrapped around his mouth and the back of his head.

But it was the man's eyes, wide and nearly bulging from

their sockets, that haunted Darby; how, after the bag had been removed, they had been locked on his daughter. Intimately familiar with the mechanics of death, she could feel the man's terror – could feel the plastic bindings biting and then cutting through his skin as he thrashed about with the bag taped over his head, sucking in the last few breaths of precious oxygen through his nose and unable to see his wife or daughter but able to hear Samantha begging and pleading and screaming.

Coop was saying something to her.

'Sorry, what's that?' Darby asked as she continued writing.

'I said I hope there aren't any surprises when this case goes to court. You know how lawyers can get.'

'Which is why we should put this guy in a body bag.'

Darby caught Coop's reproachful glare. 'You can't treat, let alone cure, a sexual sadist, Coop. There's no therapy or psychotropic-medication regimen that will bring them anywhere near the neighbourhood of normal, that will allow them to feel remorse or empathy. If you don't want a sadist to kill again, you either lock him up for life or you put him down.'

'And you're for putting him down.'

'Why should taxpayers have to pick up the tab for someone who's the mental equivalent of a rabid dog?'

Coop studied her face.

'You don't resolve evil, Coop. You extinguish it.'

'You might want to keep these thoughts to yourself while you're out in the dating pool. Just a suggestion.'

After Coop and the others left, Darby sat alone in the

house, waiting for the patrolman to deliver copies of the case files, which had been promised by Williams.

The man arrived a few minutes past 7.30. He had a handlebar moustache and smelled of pipe tobacco. The nametag stitched into the breast of his coat read MILLER. He stood on the front porch, and he didn't ask to come in.

Not that Darby would have let him: every person allowed access to a crime scene increased the risk of contamination or the destruction of evidence.

'Evidence files are in my trunk,' the patrolman said to Darby. 'You done in here?'

Darby nodded. 'Does Williams want me to seal the door?'

'No, just lock it up. Mike will seal it.' Miller jerked a thumb over his shoulder, in the direction of the patrol car parked in front of the driveway. 'He's taking the night shift.'

'Williams told me David Downes had a secretary, Sally something.'

'Sally Kelly.'

'Do you know her address? I'd like to talk to her tonight.'

'I don't know it off the top of my head, but I can get it for you.'

Darby grabbed her jacket and the keys to Coop's rental. She placed the time of her departure on the security log, shut off all the lights and locked the door behind her. She carried her box of evidence to Miller's patrol car, where she exchanged it for one stuffed with files.

Miller had written Sally Kelly's address on a piece of paper. Darby plugged it into the GPS.

The faces of the dead crowded her thoughts as she drove through the pitch-black roads. They had street-lights, but they were turned off. She suspected the struggling town had cut the power to save money.

Darby was halfway through her sixteen-mile trip when she realized she'd left her kit at the house. She wanted to use her own equipment at the autopsies that she hoped would take place tomorrow. Not wanting to have to get up early to come and retrieve it, she turned around and backtracked to the Downes home.

Fifteen minutes later, when she pulled up against the kerb and parked a few feet behind the police cruiser assigned to watch the house, she felt her throat constrict, her breath like shards of glass trapped in her chest.

The lights for the master bedroom had been turned on.

13

Darby could see a shadow moving behind the shade facing the street. Then she looked to the cruiser bathed in the beam of her headlights and, seeing it was empty, killed the headlights and the ignition. She pocketed the keys as she threw open the car door, the veins in her temple and arms humming with what felt like an electrical charge.

This isn't your case, an inner voice warned. *You're a consultant, nothing more than a hired hand. Cool it or you'll get bounced.*

Darby walked on to the driveway and saw a silhouette out of the corner of her eye. The patrolman assigned to watch the house stood in the woods to her right, steam rising from the tree where he was relieving himself.

Darby didn't break stride; she continued towards the house.

'Nature called,' he said, fumbling with his zipper as he staggered down the slope of snow. 'You know how it is on a watch.'

Darby didn't answer.

The patrolman chased after her. Then he darted in front of her, blocking her access to the walkway.

'Something I can help you with?'

'You can get out of my way,' Darby said.

The patrolman didn't move. He was her height but wide across the shoulders, probably in his early thirties, and he had the kind of pitted, acne-scarred skin that looked like it had been worked over by a cheese grater.

'You can't go in there until tomorrow,' he said, panting, his breath steaming in the cold air. 'Boss's orders. He doesn't –'

'He in there? Williams?'

'No. Place is locked up, remember?'

'I know. I locked the door myself and shut off *all* the lights. Care to explain to me why the bedroom lights are on?'

'You must've left them on by –'

'Can it,' she said, and brushed past him.

But the patrolman wasn't finished with her yet. He jumped between her and the front door, and his expression morphed into a man who had just discovered his jockstrap had been spiked with Bengay.

'I didn't have a choice,' he hissed. 'This isn't my fault.'

'Who's in there?'

'Someone with the power to deep-six me with a phone call.' His voice cracked and he had to clear his throat. 'If I get shit-canned, I lose my pay and my medical. My wife's pregnant and outta work. I can't afford to get mixed up in this pissing contest between us and –'

'What's your name again?'

'Nelson. Mike Nelson.'

Darby turned the doorknob. It was unlocked, and she saw that there wasn't a police seal on the door.

'This is what you're going to do, Nelson. You're going to park your ass in your car. You're going to sit there and shut your mouth until I'm ready to talk to you, got it?'

'Yeah. Yeah, sure.'

'Next time you need to take a leak, don't do it at the site of a crime scene. Now get out of here.'

Darby entered the house. After slipping on a pair of cloth booties, she picked up the clipboard holding the security log. Hers was the last name on the sheet. She put the clipboard down and climbed the steps, bright red spots flaring across her vision.

Not your case, that inner voice warned her again, only it was growing dimmer, drowning in her growing anger. *You're just a consultant, not your case . . .*

The man standing at the foot of the bed and writing on a clipboard was rail thin and had a squared-off jaw and a chiselled profile. He wore bifocals and tan polyester slacks and a thin black tie draped across a starched taupe long sleeve shirt with epaulettes, and he smelled of cigar smoke.

He was also short. In his thick-soled Red Wing boots he stood no taller than five seven. He wasn't wearing booties or latex gloves – the stupid son of a bitch hadn't taken even the most basic precautions to protect the integrity of the crime scene.

He glanced at her over his shoulder, looking over her person. He had country-boy good looks and cornflower-blue eyes, and his dark blond hair was immaculately combed and parted razor-sharp.

'Can I help you?'

'Yeah,' Darby said, aware of the heat climbing into her voice. 'You can explain to me why you're contaminating my crime scene.'

His eyebrows arched and his mouth opened and he

flinched like a man who had just been treated to a surprised rectal exam. '*Your* crime scene,' he said.

'Who are you?'

'Theodore Lancaster.'

The Brewster deputy sheriff, Darby thought, and then recalled what Ray Williams had said about the man, how Lancaster was angling to take the Ripper investigation away from Red Hill. *Don't give him any fuel.*

'My name is Darby McCormick. I'm –'

'I know who you are and why you're here.' His tone was calm and indifferent, maybe even slightly bored. He sounded like he had been asked to impart information about the day's weather. He used his pen to point at the evidence markers placed in the corner area the killer had wiped down. 'Tell me what happened over there.'

'Detective Ray Williams. He works here in Red Hill.'

'I know who he is.'

'Then you know he's the lead detective and that this is his case.'

'This is a joint investigation between –'

'If Williams wanted you involved, he would've called you here. You wouldn't have had to sneak in.'

Lancaster turned and held his arms behind his back, almost in a military stance, and gave her his full attention. She could hear the heat rumbling through the wall and ceiling vents.

'I noticed your vehicle isn't parked anywhere out front,' Darby said. 'My guess is you parked somewhere close by where no one would see you. After we left, you came over and intimidated a patrolman who's barely out of puberty into letting you in here. Congratulations on reaching a whole new level of spinelessness.'

The skin tightened around his eyes.

Dial it down. This isn't your zip code.

'I need you to leave,' Darby said. 'Now.'

Lancaster made a clicking sound in his throat. 'You don't have any authority here.'

'Neither do you. Time for you to leave, chief.'

Darby saw the beginnings of a grin tugging at the corner of his mouth, and it reminded her of the neighbour who had lived across the street from the house where she grew up – a widower named Stan Perry who had always watched his property with a vigilante's energy and enthusiasm. Once a neighbourhood boy who suffered from some form of mental disability had lost control of his dog, a hyperactive black Labrador, which had sprinted across Perry's lawn and got into his newly planted hydrangeas. The dog was in the process of relieving itself when the boy caught up with it and grabbed its leash.

Perry had darted out of the house, his cheeks and neck the colour of a fire hydrant. But he didn't scream or yell. Instead, he leaned forward, his hands resting on his knees, and spoke rapidly to the boy. Darby couldn't hear the exchange – she watched from her living-room window – but the boy left in tears, and what she remembered was the way Perry had smiled at having found an outlet for the cruelty that lived inside his heart.

Lancaster, though, seemed a bit slicker – the kind of man who never spoke in anger and nursed his hatred and cruelty in private, at home or at a bar, sipping a drink while he plotted ways to leave his mark on those who got in his way or denied his wishes. He looked at her with a smug complacency.

'Well,' he said, a smile playing on his lips, 'far be it from me to argue with a woman so full of *passion*.' He slid the pen back inside his breast pocket. 'By the way: if you want to address your menopausal anger and mood swings, I've got the name of a doctor who will be more than happy to prescribe something.'

It shot up her spine like a flare. Her lips pursed and she felt the muscles in her arms tighten, her right hand forming a fist.

Lancaster walked away.

Let it go.

'Sheriff?'

Lancaster glanced at her from the doorway.

'Make sure you sign out before you leave.'

'Of course. Anything else, doctor?' His eyes flickered with amusement.

'Yeah,' Darby said. 'Speak to me like that again and you'll be taking your next meal through a feeding tube.'

14

Sally Kelly lived with six cats. An 8 × 10 photograph of each one was set in an expensive-looking matted frame, all of which were proudly displayed on her mantelpiece. Each photo had been taken on a Christmas-tree skirt, a small gold bell affixed either to a red or a green bow tied around the animal's neck.

'Lissie's no longer with us,' Kelly said, and pointed to a Maine Coon with a pancake-shaped head and a snaggle-tooth. 'I had to put her down right after the holidays. She was hell on wheels that one, and about as friendly as a cactus. But she'll always have a special place in my heart. Let's go into the kitchen.'

If it weren't for the pictures, Darby wouldn't know that five cats, let alone one, lived here. The woman ran a fastidious household. The pleasantly warm air didn't contain a single whiff of cat litter or urine, and the living-room carpet and furniture showed no sign of any fur.

The kitchenette was also immaculate. Darby sat at a breakfast nook with a wraparound high-back bench, the table covered with a blue vinyl cloth, while Sally Kelly, a petite woman with hair so shockingly white it seemed to glow, shuffled about the kitchen, making a fuss of making tea, even though Darby had declined the woman's offer.

Maybe she just needs to keep busy, Darby thought, her

ballpoint poised over her notebook. David Downes's 53-year-old secretary was clearly still in shock from this morning's grisly discovery. The woman's face was leached of colour, her eyes bloodshot and puffy, and she kept looking around the black-and-green-speckled laminate counters and sand-coloured linoleum floor, blinking rapidly, as though she had misplaced or lost something of importance.

'I explained what happened to the police,' Kelly said, fetching mugs from a cabinet. 'On the second day, when David didn't report to work, I –'

'Excuse me for interrupting, Mrs Kelly –'

'Miss, actually. I've never been married. Please, call me Sally.'

'I'm trying to get a feel for the family. What they were like.'

'They were good and decent people.'

'Mr Downes was a lawyer?'

Kelly nodded. 'Real estate law,' she said. 'I worked for him . . . must be eight years now. He hired me as his secretary. Then he had to let his bookkeeper go, when the housing bubble here burst, and I took over those duties too.'

Kelly placed teabags into a pair of heavy white mugs that sat on the narrow laminate counter and set some water to boil in a saucepan on the stove. She had developed the same unresponsive glare Darby had seen over and over again in the family and friends of murder victims – a thousand-yard stare that begged for someone to release them from purgatory and to return them to a normal life.

'They made –' Her voice caught. Kelly swallowed and cleared her throat. 'They made me identify the bodies.'

'Mr and Mrs Downes didn't have any family in the area?'

Kelly shook her head. She wore jeans and slippers and an oversized grey wool sweater that came down almost to her knees. 'David was an only child,' she said. 'Linda too. They met in high school, here in Red Hill, did you know that?'

'No, I didn't. I'm sorry for your loss.'

The woman's eyes were bright. 'Such horrible things shouldn't happen to good and decent people.'

Darby could hear the faint tick of a clock coming from somewhere down the hall. She waited a decent interval before gently moving forward.

'What can you tell me about their daughter? What was Samantha like?'

'Sammy was . . . solid. A solid person. Smart. Had her act together, never gave her parents a lick of grief – and what a hard worker! You don't see that much any more. These younger generations, they don't want to put in the time and effort. The sacrifice. They just want to click a computer mouse or tap some button on their phone and have everything given to them.'

'Did you know her well?'

Kelly nodded. 'He made me a part of his family, David,' she said. 'I had dinner with them just last week.'

'When?'

'Sunday. Linda made pot roast. She was a very good cook. Took it up after she retired. She was a nursery-school teacher.'

'Was Samantha there? At dinner?'

Kelly nodded as the kettle whistled.

'How did she seem to you?'

'The way she always did, sunny and happy.' Kelly poured the boiling water into the mugs. 'Well, maybe a little the worse for wear. She was putting herself through graduate school. University of Denver. Business, I think. Or economics, one of those.'

'Do you know where she worked?'

'Wagon Wheel Saloon. It's a bar. Downtown.' Kelly picked up the mugs and carried them to the table, walking stiffly. Painfully. She caught the question in Darby's eyes.

'Fibromyalgia,' Kelly said. 'It's always worse in the winter, especially when the temperature keeps jumping up and down.' She placed the mugs on the table and then eased herself into the opposite seat. 'One day it's freezing cold, and then the next day it's in the sixties, and all it makes me want to do is lie in bed.'

'Did Mr Downes ever mention anything to you about his daughter having an encounter with a strange man? Maybe someone who was watching or following her?'

'The police asked me those same questions. I told them no. If something like that had happened to Sammy, David never mentioned it to me. Well, there was – never mind, it's stupid.'

'Tell me.'

'She said he smelled. Like garbage.'

15

Darby had her pen poised over her notebook. 'Who smelled like garbage?'

'This man at Sammy's college,' Kelly replied.

'This man was a student?'

'I think so. I don't know for sure. I overheard Sammy talking to her father about it, when she came to the office to get his keys.'

'When did you overhear this conversation?'

Kelly's face reddened with embarrassment. 'I wasn't eavesdropping, if that's what you're insinuating,' she said. 'The door was open and they were chitchatting about college, how classes were going – that sort of thing.'

'When was this?'

'In . . . September, I think. Yes, early September. College had just started, and Sammy had come by the office to get her father's car keys, because the car she used, Linda's Buick, was having problems again. David told her to take his car to Denver because he was worried about her getting stuck on the road. Sammy said something along the lines of, "Remember that guy who came to class and made the room smell like a garbage truck? He never came back." Something like that.'

'Did she mention a name by any chance?'

Kelly shook her head. 'The way she said it, though . . . She sounded sad. Like she felt bad for him.'

'Did Samantha or Mr Downes ever mention this man again?'

'No.' Kelly casually waved a hand near her face, as if trying to swat away a fly, and added, 'It's probably nothing. Frankly, I feel foolish for even mentioning it.'

'Don't.' Darby placed her hand on the woman's bony wrist and smiled. 'What can you tell me about Samantha's friends?'

'I know she was close to a couple of girlfriends from high school. Jennifer and the other one there . . . Debbie, I think her name was.'

'Last names?'

'I don't know. I do know they're no longer here. They moved away after college. Somewhere on the East Coast, I think. Most of Sammy's friends moved away, there was certainly no reason for them to stay here. She was very close to her parents. Only children are sometimes like that. I wouldn't know personally – the good Lord didn't bless me with children – but I've read articles about how only children have attachment issues. As adults, they like to stick close to their families. Or so these so-called experts say.'

'Did she have a boyfriend? Anyone serious?'

'Not that I know of. She dated, obviously – she was a beautiful girl – but I didn't know any of her beaus – and I most *certainly* did not ask.'

The way Sally Kelly spoke and acted for some reason

reminded Darby of another era: the time of Prohibition and speakeasies, when women wore skirts that covered their knees. A time when men wore fedoras and nice suits and courted women and had the manners of proper gentlemen – opening car and restaurant doors, goodnight pecks on the cheek, calling everyone 'miss'.

Darby closed her notebook and placed her business card on the table. 'If you remember or think of anything else, you can call me on my cell. You can also leave a message for me at the station or at the hotel, the Silver Moon Inn. Thank you for your time, Miss Kelly.'

Sally Kelly gripped the back of the bench and struggled to rise.

'I can let myself out,' Darby said. 'Please, sit.'

'I need to lock up after you leave.'

Darby helped the woman to her feet. 'What's your take on the Red Hill Ripper?'

'My take?'

'You have any thoughts on it?'

Kelly looked like she'd been asked to lick a toilet seat. 'Absolutely not,' she said, as they shuffled into the living-room. 'That is *not* a topic I choose to dwell on.'

'Why's that?'

'Are you married? Live with anyone?'

Darby shook her head.

'I've been on my own my whole life. You reach a certain age and you learn to shut out certain things or you'll spend the remainder of your life in a constant state of paralysing fear.' There was no anger or remorse in her voice or expression, just a sad acceptance. 'I purposefully don't follow the news any more because I find it too upsetting, too violent. I'm not naive, but that doesn't mean I have to invite it into my life. And I certainly don't want to carry such thoughts with me into bed each night.'

They had reached the front door. There was no peep-hole or deadbolt, just a cheap rickety security-door chain that had probably come with the house. It looked old, and the brass plating had chipped away over time.

'It's an exercise in futility, isn't it?'

'What is?'

'Evil. Trying to understand it, trying to stop it. It will have its way with you if it wants, won't it?'

Sally Kelly seemed to be waiting for an answer. Darby didn't have one to give her.

16

The Silver Moon Inn resembled one of those old-time prosperous banks built during the height of the mining boom – three floors of weathered brick and Victorian-style windows, each with a fleur-de-lis above the keystone. Parking was in the back.

Darby stepped inside the dimly lit lobby and felt as though she had just slipped through a portal into an early-nineteenth-century gentlemen's club, the kind where old white men wore three-piece suits and carried pocket watches and sat around discussing politics and the matters of the day while smoking cigars and drinking single-malt Scotch served to them by white-gloved waiters. The ornate chandelier hanging over the well-worn leather club chairs looked like it had been rescued from some dank English castle. The small reception desk was made of old wood. Mounted on the wall behind it was an old-fashioned cabinet of pigeonholes, used to store the individual room keys. A banker's lamp glowed from the corner of the front counter.

Darby placed her box of files on the counter. Apparently the owner wanted to keep the whole *Boardwalk Empire* motif going, because she didn't find a computer, just a thick ledger, and, lying on its top, an antique-looking fountain pen and a small, pear-shaped bottle of black ink with a tuxedoed penguin on the front. The blue and red sticker for 'J. D. Humphrey Ink' had cracked and yellowed over time, and its edges had curled.

Darby found the hotel bell, but there was no need to press it; the door behind the reception counter had swung open. The woman who lumbered out had a braided grey ponytail and wore lots of silver jewellery. She looked exhausted, the bruised skin under her eyes hanging like black curtains. Darby assumed she slept in the back office: she had spotted a cot propped up against the wall before the door shut.

'Welcome to the Silver Moon Inn, Miss McCormick.' The woman saw the question mark in Darby's face and said, 'The FBI told me you'd be coming in sometime today. You're on the ground floor, Room 8.' She reached into a pigeonhole and came back with a key.

'An actual, physical key,' Darby said with a grin. 'I can't remember the last time I was at a hotel that used one of those.'

'The owner is real intent on maintaining the hotel's Old World charm.' The woman stepped aside and, turning, pointed to a rotary phone mounted on the wall behind her. 'That's the hotel's original phone.'

'Does that thing still work?'

'Absolutely. There's a company in Iowa that adapts all the old phones so they'll work with the new technology.' Then with a sly grin, she added, 'But don't worry, everything in the room is completely modern. My name's Laurie Richards. Please don't hesitate to contact me if you need anything, Miss McCormick.'

Darby entered her hotel room, tired and sore, and wanting two things – a long shower followed by a stiff drink.

The stiff drink wasn't an option, at least at the moment. The room didn't have a mini-bar, but there was a bar across the street, a place with a big wagon wheel in the front. As far she could tell, it was the only thing open in downtown Red Hill besides the Silver Moon Inn.

The country's never-ending economic recession seemed to have hit Red Hill especially hard. Taped to the inside glass windows of virtually every business she'd passed on the way here were signs and handwritten messages on poster boards that read OUT OF BUSINESS or CLOSED PERMANENTLY. She hadn't seen a single Starbucks or Dunkin' Donuts; there were no chain restaurants or big box supermarkets, hardware or department stores. Either gentrification had somehow bypassed Red Hill or big business wasn't interested in creating anything here, viewing the town as the equivalent of a toxic-waste dump, a place where nothing would thrive.

Darby placed the cardboard box of evidence files on her bed. Then she went back into the hall to retrieve her suitcase, forensics kit and briefcase, and used her foot to shut the door.

Her room had crimson-painted walls and a headboard and bedframe crafted from birch logs. It had recently been cleaned; she could smell lemon-scented furniture polish, and the vacuum cleaner had left tread marks in the soft carpet. The pair of windows on the far wall overlooked what appeared to be a dense section of woods, but it was too dark out there to see.

Darby hung her jacket inside the small closet and slipped out of her boots. She opened up the box, picked up a random file and opened it – the Connelly family, who had been murdered last month. She flipped through the thick stack of pages, pleased to find that the Denver state lab hadn't skimped on crime scene photos.

Her encounter with Deputy Sheriff Lancaster hung in her mind like an uninvited houseguest. The only way to get him to leave before he took up permanent residence was to focus her attention on something else – something productive. She sat cross-legged on the bed and removed the remaining evidence files.

The first murders had occurred just over a year ago, on 4 January. Eighteen-year-old Cynthia Gardner, home for the Christmas holidays, had stayed the night at a friend's apartment in Denver. When she went to her parents' house the next morning she found them seated across from each other in kitchen chairs placed at the foot of their bed. Her mother had been strangled, the T-shirt that she slept in ripped open to expose her breasts. A black garbage bag had been tied around her father's head. The Red Hill Ripper had waited until spring to kill the Bowden family. The Brazilian woman they employed to clean their house every two weeks had used the key given to her to enter. When she stepped over the threshold, an odour like spoiled meat and sewage hit her like a fist. After she vomited in the bushes, she used her cell to call the police. Martin and Heather Bowden had been killed the same way as the Gardner family.

Talk of a possible serial killer had spread through the

small town. Jim and Elaine Lima had installed new locks on their doors to protect them and their twin sons, Brad and Alex, who were in their senior year at Brewster High. Brad hadn't been home that night; he had been away on a ski trip when the Red Hill Ripper killed his brother and parents the week before Thanksgiving.

Three weeks later, John and Lisa Connelly and their sixteen-year-old daughter, Stacey, were found dead by John's sister, who had arrived from San Diego to spend Christmas and the New Year with her brother's family.

No semen was found at any of the crime scenes or on the bodies. The medical examiner found no evidence of penetration. The breasts of the female victims showed extensive bruising, the result of having been pinched and twisted.

Darby spent most of her time on the bedroom pictures. With the exception of the victims, the crime scenes were nearly identical: same plastic bindings and duct tape; same seating arrangement; and the same black garbage bag tied around the father's or husband's head. The killer had entered the home by cutting a hole through a window or sliding glass door.

Darby arranged the bedroom photographs on the quilt and stared down at them, willing a thought to come to her. She paced around the room, thinking. She could see only carnage and desperation.

Darby pinched the bridge of her nose and blinked her eyes several times, trying to get some moisture into them. Then she arched her back and stretched. She was thinking about heading into the shower when she recalled the bar across the street, the one with the big wagon wheel out front. Samantha Downes had worked at a bar called the Wagon Wheel Saloon.

The shower could wait. Darby picked up her jacket and headed back out.

17

The Wagon Wheel Saloon was one of those local tourist traps designed to give people an authentic old-time cowboy experience: duckboards covered with green sawdust; oak timber beams and wood walls festooned with antique six-shooters; and black and white pictures of cowboys, miners and settlers; wood-bladed ceiling fans; and a long, handcrafted mahogany bar with brass poles, its top polished to a high shine.

The dining area, which made up the entire left side of the room, consisted of a dozen or so tables covered with red and white checked tablecloths. About half were occupied, either by elderly couples eating in silence or by haggard-looking couples who were unwinding after work or enjoying some peace and quiet away from their kids. They all looked like what she called the 'God Bless America Crowd' – people who, she suspected, listened to country music and went to church every Sunday, organized bingo fundraisers and did potluck get-togethers with other couples. An archway in the corner led to a room with a pool table, and, on the other side of it, a jukebox swirling with neon colours.

Darby approached the lone man standing behind the bar, at the far end, loading draught beers on to a waitress's circular carrying tray. He had a bowling-ball-shaped head and greying brown hair thick with some sort of styling product designed to give him that I-just-got-out-of-bed look.

She leaned against the bar, waiting for him to finish, and out of the corner of her eye she saw a group of men seated at a nearby table stop their conversation and take turns checking her out. They didn't go about it surreptitiously, either. All five of them turned and gawked. Three continued to stare brazenly, one pretended to be busy with his phone, while another raised his beer in salute and winked at her. He had cold blue eyes and a promising future as a wife beater.

Had the Ripper sat at one of these tables, watching Samantha Downes delivering drinks and food? Had she ever waited on him? Had they talked? Or had he, like the majority of sexual predators, watched her covertly, circling her like a shark and collecting information?

The bartender stepped up to her. He wore a black polo shirt, the sleeves stretched around biceps the size of grapefruits, and he had a blue and red tattoo of a snake along his right forearm.

'If you're here to eat, you can go on and grab a seat.'

'The owner around?' Darby asked.

'Why, you looking to buy?'

Darby showed him her federal ID.

The man sighed heavily. 'I was wondering when you guys were going to show up,' he said.

'Why's that?'

'You're here to talk to me about what happened to Sammy Downes, right?'

'You already heard what happened?'

'Yeah,' he said sadly.

'From who?'

'Everyone's talking about it. And it's posted on the *Item*'s website. That's our local newspaper, the *Red Hill Evening Item*.'

Then she remembered: a young-looking photographer had snapped pictures of the black body bags being removed from the house while a reporter from the *Red Hill Evening Item*, a chubby man with a full beard and a tweed jacket, got a brief statement from Ray Williams. They had been the only two onlookers who had showed up at the house.

'I *am* the owner, by the way. J. D. James Doherty.'

She shook his hand. 'Darby McCormick. How well did you know Samantha Downes?'

He shrugged. 'As well as an employer can know his employee, I guess. She worked for me for . . . five months? She was . . .' His thoughts drifted for a moment. Then he leaned forward and gripped the edge of the bar. 'Sammy was the kind of kid you're always rooting for, you know? Smart, worked hard, had her shit together. Good kid, quiet, kinda kept to herself.'

'And pretty.'

'That too.' He sighed heavily and then was quiet for a moment, locked on a private thought. 'Goddamn waste.'

'Any guys ever bother her?'

'There were guys who hit on her – guys her own age. If someone was bothering her, she never mentioned it to me.'

'What about an older guy, forties or fifties, who came in here alone and asked to be seated at one of her tables, maybe asked questions about her? Someone who might've given you or one of your employees or customers a bad vibe?'

J. D. was shaking his head the entire time. 'I've been racking my brain about that all day,' he said. 'Is it possible someone like that was in here? Sure. But if he was, I didn't see him. Believe it or not, this place gets hopping, and when it does I'm balls-to-the-wall. You should ask Evelyn. She's one of my waitresses. Evelyn Roy.'

He pointed to a short woman dressed in tight black jeans and a black polo-style shirt who was in the process of transferring red baskets of onion rings and barbeque chicken wings with cups of blue-cheese dipping sauce from her carrying tray to a table where two middle-aged women were seated. Both women had round faces and wore oversized sweaters to hide their ample curves.

'Evelyn can give you a better idea about Sammy,' he said. 'I didn't know her beyond the employer–employee relationship. She was a great worker, showed up on time, never gave me any guff.'

'What about the Red Hill Ripper? What's the scuttlebutt around town?'

'The scuttle-what?'

'The gossip. Your employees and regular patrons, friends, people you talk to, what are they saying?'

'I hear some people are trying to take out home equity loans to get burglar alarms installed. God knows I've changed my locks. I've got two kids. My wife makes me sleep with a baseball bat next to the bed.'

'What about you? What do you think's going on here?'

He shrugged. 'Who knows? I haven't given it much thought. The main thing on my mind is how to keep my head above water, financially. I know that sounds cold, but, well, I'm being honest. Something to drink?'

Darby ordered a Maker's Mark. When he returned with the glass, she gave him her business card, along with a twenty, and told him to keep the change.

The waitress, Evelyn Roy, was twenty-two and wore a lot of foundation to try to hide her blemished skin. She had a degree in English and, like Samantha Downes, was having trouble landing what she called 'a real job'. The young woman couldn't recall seeing any older men who had given Samantha trouble or had come in there alone and watched her.

Evelyn said she didn't know Sammy that well. 'She was kind of . . . not shy but private,' she said. She had a high-pitched nasal voice and a small chip along the bottom of a front tooth. 'I kinda got the feeling she was under a lot of pressure.'

'About what?'

'Money? A boyfriend? Who knows?' The young woman shrugged. 'Like I said, she was private.'

Darby gave the woman her card and then took her glass to a bar stool near the front windows. She sipped her drink, trying to sort out her thoughts about the day; but they were scattered, like pieces of a ceramic jar that had been dropped from a great height. She couldn't find enough shards and fragments to form a coherent thought.

She watched an older couple sitting at a nearby table. They were huddled together, sharing an iPhone and looking at the screen where a toddler was holding up what looked like a crayon drawing. At first Darby thought the couple were looking at a picture; then she realized they were talking via Skype or FaceTime.

Seeing the toddler made Darby think about David Downes again, that moment when he realized that he was going to die listening to his daughter begging for her life. Darby finished the rest of her drink and then went back to the hotel to make a careful study of the case files.

Darby had been going through the files for an hour when the hotel phone rang.

'Hello?'

'We've got a debrief scheduled tomorrow morning at eight,' Ray Williams said. 'Autopsy's at 2.30, in Brewster. It's about a 45-minute drive to the ME's office.'

Darby filled him in on her conversation with Sally Kelly.

'Guy with a bad smell, huh?' Williams said. 'That's a great tip. We'll put out an APB on a fart.'

'I met Lancaster tonight.'

'My condolences. Where did you meet him?'

'Inside the Downes house.' Darby explained what had happened.

A long silence followed after she finished talking.

'Your guy Nelson was scared shitless,' Darby said. 'I wouldn't be too hard on him.'

Williams said nothing. She could hear him breathing heavily on the other end of the line.

'I talked to Nelson afterwards,' Darby said. 'A few minutes after I left, Lancaster came up and cornered him. Told Nelson he was going inside to take a look around, and that if Nelson called you or opened his yap to anyone he'd find himself on the breadline with his pregnant wife. That's a direct quote. Guy's a class act.'

'That he is.' Williams sounded like someone was squeezing his windpipe.

'Bottom line is that Lancaster took advantage of the situation and bullied his way inside,' Darby said. 'If you're going to be pissed at anyone, it should be me. I shouldn't have lost my cool.'

'Teddy brings out the best in people.' Williams sighed. 'Forget about it. You get the copies of the forensics reports?'

'I'm going through them right now.'

'You eaten dinner yet? There's a place across the street from your hotel, the Wagon Wheel Saloon, that ain't half bad. Got good burgers.'

'I was just there.'

'How about a drink?'

'I think I'm going to call it a night,' she said. 'How about a rain check?'

'Sure.' He sounded disappointed. 'You change your mind or if you need anything, call me at the station. I'll be here for at least a couple of hours doing paperwork. You got my numbers?'

'Coop gave 'em to me.'

'Well, goodnight, then.'

'Goodnight.'

Darby hung up. She sat on the edge of the bed and rubbed her face, thinking about Ray Williams, with his strong jawline and soft brown eyes and rough masculine hands. It was her first pleasant thought of the day, the only one that didn't remind her of death.

She also realized something else about the man, another

thing he had in common with Coop: Williams hadn't treated her any differently because she was a woman. That wasn't always the case with male cops – and it was especially true when it came to sexual crimes. Some men were simply embarrassed to talk about the subject in the presence of a woman; they smiled tightly and chose their words carefully and then excused themselves to have whispered conversations with the other males in corners and behind closed doors.

The good majority, though, still carried a deep resentment at the whole politically correct and liberal diversity movement that had allowed women into what was still considered to be, even in the twenty-first century, a boys' club.

She fished Williams's card out of her back pocket and dialled his direct number.

'How about I buy you a drink?' Darby asked.

'What time?'

'I'll meet you across the street in fifteen.'

'See you then.'

Darby went into the shower and scrubbed the stink of slaughter off her skin and hair under the hot water. She kept seeing the faces of the dead.

She reached for something more pleasant and relaxing – Siesta Key. She had been in a motel in Pittsburgh, thinking about going someplace warm, when the name popped into her head. She had never been there before but had heard how beautiful the barrier island was – eight miles long and just offshore of Sarasota, the Gulf water a pale blue and warm, even during the winter.

She had pulled out her iPhone, plugged 'Siesta Key' into Google, and seconds later had an endless supply of links, photos and videos to choose from. A website for a sidewalk café whose name she couldn't recall offered a live streaming webcam for the Siesta Key beach. She remembered lying on her hotel bed, with its hard mattress and stiff, starched sheets, and thinking about how she could reach Siesta Key in just under seventeen hours.

How had the Ripper watched the Downes family?

Darby shut off the water and dried herself quickly. She ran a comb through her hair, pulled her hair behind her head and fastened it with an elastic band as she moved into the bedroom. She slipped into a clean pair of underwear, picturing the son of a bitch parked in some dark driveway and watching them through a pair of binoculars, waiting for them to leave so he could get inside the house. *Did you watch them through binoculars or did you do it another way?*

How else could he watch?

Darby fastened her bra, thinking. There were so many different ways nowadays. You had cameras installed in cell phones and tablets and laptop computers. Like the parents she had seen inside the bar, you could have a face-to-face conversation on your phone with your kid or with someone halfway around the world using programs like Skype and apps like FaceTime and ooVoo. You could watch a beach in Florida, day or night, any time you wished.

Darby was sliding into a pair of jeans when a cold, neutral voice that wasn't her own spoke inside her head: *The Downes family owned two iPads.*

So what? They also owned two laptops, and each family member had their own iPhone.

The iPads were standing upright.

Darby remembered seeing her reflection on the screen of Samantha's iPad.

The tablet was facing the young woman's bed, and it contained a camera.

And the iPad sitting on the nightstand in the master bedroom – that camera was aimed at the three chairs seated at the foot of the bed.

Darby's skin turned cold and her hands trembled as she rooted through the evidence files, searching for the pictures of the bedrooms.

Here was a photo of the Connelly bedroom. A laptop sat on a bureau, the camera above the screen pointed at the carnage of the dead family.

Here was a shot of Jim and Elaine Lima and one of their twin sons, Brad, bound and taped and dead. An iPhone, tilted against a stack of books, was resting on a nightstand, its camera aimed at them.

Darby grabbed the cordless and dialled Coop's number.

'Cooper.'

'He was watching himself and the families and he was probably watching us today.'

'Watching how?'

'The iPad in the bedroom: it was sitting upright and the camera was pointed at the family. Same deal with the other four families. I'm looking at the pictures right now. In each bedroom there's a laptop, smartphone or iPad, and the cameras are aimed at the families.'

'Wouldn't the iPads and the other stuff have to be turned on?'

'I don't know. Maybe. But I don't think this is a coincidence.'

'I'll get the computer guys on it first thing in the morning.'

After Darby hung up, she threw on a shirt and then paced the rough carpet in her bare feet. The Red Hill Ripper had used those devices to watch himself, she was sure of it.

The phone rang and she realized she had forgotten about her drink with Williams.

'Sorry, Ray, I'm running late. I've found something about the Ripper – how he's watching himself and the families.'

Williams didn't answer.

'Ray? You there?'

'You've got really nice tits. And I like those tight little boy shorts you just put on.'

The voice on the other end of the line was deep and guttural, almost a moan. It was also disguised by a voice-changer.

'I can't wait to get you in the rope.'

'Why wait? Why not –'

'*Goooooodbye.*'

Darby was staring at the window when the line went dead.

Day Two

My mother, whose name was also Sarah, was a slim woman with rough hands who wore too much makeup and smoked too much and dressed every day like she was going off to a country-club dance or a thousand-dollars-a-plate political fundraiser. She had wanted a girl and made no secret about it.

Boys confused her, she told me on several occasions. They ate like pigs, shovelling food into their mouths before bouncing outside with the boundless energy of a puppy, and spent each day rolling around and digging in dirt and getting into fistfights and playing sports. They came home covered in filth and sweat and reeked of BO. They wolfed down their supper and they put up a fuss when they were asked to wash their hands or take a shower.

Girls, my mother said, were the complete opposite in almost every way. They didn't come home smelling like they had spent their day swimming in a sewer. They enjoyed taking long baths and they wore clean clothes and they made an effort to look pretty. They were polite and had table manners. The biggest difference – the most important one, my mother argued – was when girls reached puberty they didn't act like unneutered dogs, humping legs and bedposts, pillows, whatever got them off. Girls developed into ladies. Boys turned into monsters of fornication.

I don't know how my father felt about boys or girls or children in general because I'd never met him. My mother told me his name was Roy, just Roy, no last name needed, and the only contact I had with my father was through a small steamer trunk that sat in a dusty attic corner strung with cobwebs. Inside, I found an army uniform and a bayonet and a collection of detective magazines from the fifties and sixties. They had had the word 'detective' in the titles – *Real Detective*, *Spicy Detective* and *Gold Seal Detective* – and each cover featured a woman wearing a ripped dress or a skimpy bikini or just her underwear and bra. All the women were tightly bound with thick rope to chairs, posts, beds, tables and radiators, some gagged, some captured mid-scream with their teeth bared and their lips painted blood-red, every one of them frightened.

The articles were the kind of tripe you'd usually expect – 'THE NUDIST CAMP MURDERS!' and 'HE MADE THEM SLAVES . . . AND THEY LIKED IT!' A few, though, usually the ones that weren't advertised on the front cover, were instructive, explaining the mysteries of women, how they *really* wanted to be treated, their true desires, needs and wants.

When my mother wasn't home, which was often, I would spend long afternoons inside the attic, alone with the pictures. It was the most peaceful time of my life. I was thirteen. Everything ended – changed – when my mother caught me *in flagrante delicto* – the magazines spread over the floor and my shorts and underwear around my ankles, my free hand slowly increasing the tension on the rope I had tied around my neck. She didn't give me a chance to explain. She beat me with her hands, and when she spotted my father's belt, which was conveniently sitting inside the trunk, she picked it up and hit me with it until I couldn't stand without help.

That night she made me kneel on grains of rice as she read from the Good Book. When dawn finally, mercifully arrived – my knees cut and bleeding, the muscles in my thighs and lower back locked in spasm and my head filled with an excruciating, skull-splitting pain that had, at least twice that awful night, caused me to collapse and black out – my mother slammed her Bible shut, convinced that she had fully exorcized the succubus. From that day on, until I left home for good, she'd tie me up every night to prevent the demon from returning, binding my wrists to the headboard and tying my ankles to the bedpost.

I'm startled into wakefulness, the red glow of the alarm clock the only light in the bedroom. In my mind's eye I see my mother staring at me accusingly. She has a smile that says *I know who you really are and I know all your dirty little secrets. Wait until I get hold of you . . .*

She would never speak that way to me, of course. Too many words.

Sarah, my loving partner all these years, gently touches my arm.

'Bad dream?'

She's dead, I remind myself. I swallow, my heart tripping. *She's dead and I buried her.*

'You're shaking,' Sarah says.

'I'm fine.'

'You were crying out for Tricia. Who's that?'

I whip off the covers. 'I'm going out for a run,' I say.

It's coming up on 5 a.m. and the cold air feels like razor blades against my skin, like shards of ice inside my lungs. I want to turn around and go home, but I keep running, pushing myself, because exercise is the only way I can banish my mother. Even now, after all the years she's been dead, it still amazes me in a naive, childlike way how you can bury someone but you can't bury that's person's memory, their connection to you. I spoke about my mother once to a psychologist, years ago, a matronly woman with kind eyes who had once been a nun. She refused to see me again. The woman's secretary never explained why.

I don't need a psychologist to explain to me why my mother visits me in my dreams: she is the embodiment of my fear, specifically the fear of being discovered by the police. I made a critical mistake at the Downes home. If the police don't discover it, Hoder will.

I return home, rubber-legged and sweating, and take a long shower. When I arrive downstairs, the air is warm and smells of coffee and eggs and sausage. Sarah is cooking breakfast and listening to the radio, an old model with a manual dial and an antenna mended with duct tape. It sits on the windowsill above the sink, tuned to the local news. She shuffles about the kitchen, wearing her slippers and the frumpy pink housecoat I've told her to get rid of tied around her body, which has started to thicken with age.

I curl and uncurl my fists for a reason I can't pinpoint or explain.

Sarah hands me a mug of coffee and returns to the stove. I sit at the table and stare out the kitchen window. The exercise and fresh air and shower and promise of another fine morning – the sky above the tall pines is a deep red and gold, cloudless – these things should have me feeling light. Buoyant. Instead, nameless and shapeless thoughts like an army of fire ants crawl through my skull, eating their way through my brain.

Sarah puts a plate of eggs, ham and sausage in front of me and goes back to the stove to fix her breakfast. *My two Sarahs*, I think, picking up a fork. One a demon who visits me almost every night in my dreams, the other a Milquetoast angel who offers up endless and bottomless wells of forgiveness, patience and kindness.

Sarah refills my coffee mug and I'm possessed by the urge to tell her about what happened at the Downes house. About the mistake I made and how the FBI are in town and they're poking around – I want to unburden myself but it would only burden her.

There's got to be a way to fix this, I tell myself, sipping my coffee. *There's got to be a way out.*

As I watch Sarah pick up strips of bacon with a fork and lay them on a plate covered with a paper towel, I feel a tight band of pressure around my head. She sees me watching and gives me a shy smile and the pressure intensifies. I scratch my eyebrow with a knuckle and watch her cook and think about how she does the laundry and washes the dishes and cleans the house and irons my shirts and wakes up at the same time as I do every morning and she doesn't complain and she doesn't ask questions or talk back – so why does my chest feel so tight and why won't my heart stop racing? Why do I feel like I'm suffocating to death?

'Baby?'

I look up and find Sarah staring at me in alarm.

'You're burning up,' she says.

I drink my coffee. Sweat pours in rivulets from my brow. My armpits are soaked.

'You feeling okay?' she asks.

STOP ASKING ME THAT.

'Fine,' I reply, gripped with a sudden, inexplicable urge to pick up the kitchen chair and smash it against the table. Instead, I get up so quickly that I almost knock over the chair. I collect my briefcase and grab my coat from the foyer closet.

I'm about to head out when Sarah calls to me from the kitchen: 'She's beautiful.'

When I return, I find her standing at the table, sipping coffee and looking down at six folded and creased pieces of paper – colour printouts of the women I've researched.

'She's beautiful,' Sarah says again, and points to a picture of Tricia Lamont coming out of her parents' home. 'Is this Tricia?'

I don't answer: my mouth is as dry as bone. Bacon sizzles in the skillet and the weatherman on the radio is talking about an upcoming storm that could dump three to five feet of snow through central Colorado.

'But this one,' Sarah says, tapping a finger against the picture of 37-year-old Angela Blake, a tall woman with blonde hair and wide hips and fair skin. She wears perfume that smells like fresh citrus and when you get up close to her you can see the fine spray of freckles along her nose and shoulders. 'This one is . . . what's her name again?'

'Angela.'

'Angela,' Sarah repeats, almost dreamily. She sips her coffee while she studies the women, appraising each face as though it were a painting in a museum.

Then she places her mug on the table and picks up the sheet of paper holding Angela's picture. Sarah folds it as she shuffles towards me, her slippers scraping against the floor.

'This one,' she says, and tucks the paper in my coat pocket.

'Why?' My voice is thick and wet in my throat.

'Because she looks like a fighter. You like the ones who fight back.'

Then Sarah raises herself on her toes and, touching me lightly on the neck, kisses me goodbye.

19

'You think he might've recorded himself in the act?' Terry Hoder asked, his voice flat, almost dismissive.

Darby swallowed her coffee. 'Don't you?'

Hoder finished pouring coffee into a paper cup. It was 7.35 a.m., and they were the only ones inside Red Hill PD's break-room. Bright morning sunlight flooded through the small window, a welcomed presence in the grey surroundings.

He leaned the small of his back against the counter; the hand gripping his cane was white-knuckled. 'I know that type of software exists for home computers, but I don't know anything about iPads and tablets. Totally different operating system and different software, right?'

'Right. And, yes, the software exists for both iPads and iPhones. The iPads, phones and the laptops in the bed-room photos all had cameras and microphones. He could stream the video to his own phone or a laptop halfway around the world if he wanted to, and replay it at his leis-ure. All he'd need was the family's network name and password. They all had Wi-Fi in their homes, I've checked.'

'It's an interesting theory. Solid.'

Hoder seemed distracted. Lost in thought.

Then he stared out the window, at the snow-capped mountains in the distance. The sky was a ceramic blue and cloudless, the perimeter of the empty parking lot dotted with aspens and tall pines that creaked and swayed in the wind.

Darby had heard the stories about the man's two broken marriages; the grown son and daughter who barely spoke to their father, a relentless workaholic who had suffered a nervous breakdown and almost died from encephalitis. With a little over a year to go from the FBI's mandatory retirement age of fifty-seven, Hoder should have been at home resting, recovering from his knee surgery or coasting through his remaining time. He had certainly earned it.

Instead, he was here in Colorado. Why? Because he had nothing left in his life. As Darby drank her coffee, she felt a vague and uncertain horror about her future. She was at the halfway point in her life where the finish line was no longer hidden behind the fog of youth; it was real, it was approaching, and there was no turning back. Looking at Hoder, she felt as though she were being paid a visit from her own Ghost of Christmases Yet to Come.

'It can't be a coincidence that in all the crime scenes there was an electronic device with a camera pointed at bound family members,' Darby said.

'Agreed. I'm afraid I have a rather embarrassing confession.' When Hoder looked at her, his eyes were bright and full of mirth. 'Don't tell anyone this, but I'm somewhat of a technophobe. Computers and smartphones and now these tablets – frankly the whole thing gives me a headache. I can't keep up with it, nor do I want to keep up with it.'

'I feel the same way.'

Hoder chuckled. 'I doubt it. All these gizmos and programs, they make me feel . . . old. Obsolete.'

'Technology and software changes from day to day. You've got to be a full-time geek to keep up with this stuff. The rest of us are left in the dust.'

Darby refilled her cup. The coffee was bitter, but it would do the job. 'Let's start with Wi-Fi. You know what that is?'

'Wireless internet connection.'

'See, you're not as bad as you think.'

'My seven-year-old grandson had to tell me what it meant.'

'Then I take back what I just said.' Darby smiled over her cup.

'If what you're saying is true – that the Ripper recorded his interactions with the families – then can I assume he may have been watching or listening or both yesterday, when you, Cooper and Williams went inside the bedroom?'

'It wouldn't surprise me.'

'How could he do that? Do you need some sort of special software?'

'That I don't know. The RCFL guys –'

'Who?'

'Regional Computer Forensics Laboratory out of Denver. Forensics geeks who specialize in phones and computers. Coop is going to meet with them first thing this morning, at nine.'

'You spoke with him?'

'This morning, about five.' Coop had been up all night with four other agents on loan from the Denver office.

'Did he have anything to say about the evidence he brought to Denver?'

'No prints were recovered from the plastic bag, duct tape or plastic bindings. But there are a few potential bright spots.'

'The blood Coop recovered from the bedroom flooring.'

Darby nodded. 'There's also a chance our man left either sweat or skin cells on that piece of latex stuck to the duct tape – and we have that fingerprint pressed into the polyurethane while it was still in the process of drying.'

'Wouldn't it be nice if our man was in our databases?'

'It certainly would be,' Darby said, although she wasn't pinning her hopes on it.

While there was a fighting chance the fingerprint might find a match on IAFIS, the FBI's Integrated Automated Fingerprint Identification System, CODIS, the Bureau's Combined DNA Index System, was another matter. The majority of DNA samples stored on that database belonged to unsolved violent crime investigations. If the blood found on the floor, or skin or sweat from the duct tape, did, in fact, belong to the Ripper, and if he had left a matching DNA sample at another crime scene, a link would then have been established. *If, if, if,* Darby thought. She could count on one hand the number of cases where CODIS came back with a match linked to a known offender.

'DNA testing will take longer,' Darby said. 'Coop is thinking of sending the samples directly to your lab. He's also going to send the duct tape there.' Because duct tape was often used in murders, the federal lab kept its own library of tape samples.

Hoder shifted uncomfortably and then moved the cane to his opposite hand. 'Why do you think the Ripper contacted you?'

'Like I said on the way here, we don't know that the man I spoke to actually is the Red Hill Ripper.' Darby had told Hoder the details of last night's phone call as she drove him to the station, which was conveniently less than two miles from the hotel, located on the outskirts of the downtown area. She had also given him a rundown of her encounter with Deputy Sheriff Lancaster. 'For all we know it was just some local guy with a pair of binocs who gets off on watching an old lady undressing.'

'You don't really believe that, do you?'

'That I'm old? Yes, I do. Unfortunately.'

'I'm being serious. How many peeping toms do you know who call to alert their target – and use a voice-changer to boot?'

'I'm not putting too much stock in what happened last night. Williams told me the Ripper has never called anyone associated with the case.'

Ray Williams had helped her to search the wooded area near her window for footprints. They hadn't found any. She had also searched the area again, early this morning, before going to the station, and had come up empty – which wasn't all that surprising. As Williams had correctly pointed out last night, there was a part of the main side-walk that offered a direct view into her bedroom window. If the man who had been watching her had used some-thing more powerful than a pair of binoculars – a monocular or sniper scope – he could have counted the crow's feet around her eyes.

'If the man who called you last night is the Red Hill Ripper,' Hoder said, 'I guarantee he'll call you again.'

'Does the media know you're here?'

'A reporter came up from Denver the day we arrived. He was waiting outside the hotel.'

'You talk to him?'

'No. But that didn't prevent him from writing a story on that "monster hunter" bullshit. It ran in yesterday's paper.'

'Did my name appear in the story?' asked Darby.

'I don't know. I didn't read the article, but I know I didn't mention your name to the reporter.' His eyes nar-rowed in thought. 'If your name wasn't in the story and if the man who called you last night was the Ripper, how did he know you're here?'

'Good question. I'm wondering if he was watching the house yesterday. There sure as hell are plenty of places to hide.' Darby polished off the rest of her coffee and tossed the cup into the trash. 'Maybe he called Lancaster for some ideas.'

'You should've woken me last night.'

'I called Williams. Besides, I thought one of us should get a full night's sleep. You looked like you were in a lot of pain yesterday, when you came by the house.'

'Just some minor swelling. Next time something like that happens, please include me, no matter what time of night and no matter how you think I'm feeling.'

Darby caught the undercurrent in Hoder's tone. The man was frightened of being put out to pasture – of becoming obsolete.

'You're right,' Darby said. 'I'm sorry.'

Hoder flashed his bright and youthful smile. 'I bet saying that hurt.'

'More than you know.'

Hoder grinned as he reached for a thick folder on the counter. 'Our lab identified the knot,' he said, and removed the page and handed it to her.

The sheet of paper contained two colour photos. The top one showed two loose pieces of nylon rope loosely wrapped together, forming a knot that hadn't been tightened. There were two twists in the bottom part of the knot and one twist on the top.

'It's called a surgeon's knot, or ligature knot,' Hoder said. 'That bottom picture shows what the knot looks like after it's tightened. The way the rope's bound together, the knot doesn't have much give, which allowed him to control the tension. He could choke them slowly over hours, listening to them beg and plead for their lives; or, after one good, hard yank, he could step back and then watch them slowly choke to death.'

The break-room door opened and a patrolman with a large Adam's apple poked his head inside. 'They're ready for you,' he said. 'Agent Hoder, the chief would like to see you in his office first.'

20

The Ripper Task Force operated out of a squad room with white panelled walls and insanely bright overhead fluorescents that reflected off the grey linoleum floor. A dozen or so cops and patrolmen packed the small room, the warm air smelling of coffee and cigarette-baked clothes. Posters advertising the state's $100,000 reward and toll-free number for the hotline had been tacked to the walls in the front of the room.

Ray Williams stood in the back, hands stuffed deep in his pockets. As Darby made her way to him, the haggard faces seated behind the scuffed desks regarded her with suspicion. Some blatantly looked her over from head to toe, like they were inspecting a piece of meat. She was the only woman in here – the only living one, at least. Crime scene photographs of the dead women were held by magnets to the rolling whiteboards on the far side of the room. A map of the town was pinned to a standing corkboard: the murder sites were marked with pushpins and beside each one was a Post-It note indicating the victims' names and time and manner of death.

'Any luck with the phone number?' Darby asked when she reached him.

Williams leaned into her, a breath mint clinking against his teeth. 'It belongs to a payphone two blocks from your hotel,' he whispered. 'Not going to get any witnesses, I'm afraid. Payphone's set between two stores, both of 'em out of business. You get any sleep?'

'Couple of hours.'

Darby leaned her back against the wall. Williams's cheeks glowed from a morning shave, and his skin smelled of sandalwood and leather. Had he worn aftershave for her? She hadn't smelled any on him yesterday.

'How you holding up?' he asked.

'Never better.'

Williams leaned closer, grinning, his eyes filled with amusement. 'Does it ever get tired?'

'Does what get tired?'

'Wearing all that armour.'

Darby found herself grinning. 'Sometimes I take it off.'

'Really? And when would that be?'

'Depends on the person, and the circumstances.'

Williams cracked his breath mint on his molars and smiled with his eyes.

Hoder entered with Red Hill Police Chief Tom Robinson, a tall and reedy baby-faced man with marbled skin and ruddy cheeks. Williams had told her that Robinson, a widower and grandfather who suffered from Crohn's disease, recently had part of his colon removed and wore a colonoscopy bag. The chief refused to step down from his position until the Red Hill Ripper investigation was closed.

Robinson made a point of distancing himself from the man who had entered the room behind them – Brewster Deputy Sheriff Theodore Lancaster, who was quickly finishing up a conversation on his phone. Darby, veteran of squad rooms and police debriefings, recognized a pissing contest when she saw one.

She looked sideways at Williams, who had straightened, his eyes riveted on a neutral spot ten inches from his nose. Blood climbed into his neck and she saw the cartilage working behind his jaws. Apparently he hadn't been told about Lancaster's surprise visit.

Lancaster matched glares with Williams as Robinson took to the podium. Darby wondered how much information the police chief would reveal to his people with Lancaster in the room.

Robinson's raspy voice had a slight nasal twang, as though he were recovering from the tail end of a cold. 'Everyone got their cells muted? Okay, good. Listen up. Most of you have already met Special Agent Hoder. And y'all know the man standing to my left, Teddy Lancaster.' The chief's face and tone echoed the contempt he felt for the Brewster sheriff. 'I don't have to tell y'all why Teddy's here with us this morning.'

Dead silence. Hostile silence. Darby could hear the hum of the Coke machine in the lobby.

'Okay, let's get down to business,' Chief Robinson said. 'The mobile lab from the FBI's Denver office had some sort of mechanical problem yesterday, so the evidence recovered from the Downes home was taken to Denver last night. Now, about what was found in the Downes house. Same setup as the others – family tied to chairs, male suffocated to death, the women strangled. Same duct tape and same plastic bindings. You'll know the lab results when I do.'

Lancaster spoke up. 'I'd like copies as well.'

The chief didn't answer or acknowledge Lancaster. 'The Bureau's lab identified the type of knot the killer used,' Robinson said. 'I'll let Agent Hoder explain while I pass these out.' He started to hand out pictures from a file as Hoder folded his arms and rested them on the podium. It was easier and more comfortable to lean against it than to try to balance his weight on the cane.

'It's called a surgeon's knot,' Hoder said.

The seated men leaned forward to hear Hoder's soft voice.

'A surgeon's knot is a figure-eight knot that's generally used in sailing and rock climbing, which leads me to believe the Ripper may have experience in one or both of these areas. Maybe he took sailing lessons as a boy or spent part of his youth working on boats. Maybe his father or grandfather was a fisherman; you get the idea. The other possibility is he could simply be a knot fetishist. And, yes, such a thing exists.'

Timid laughter, but not from Lancaster. His gaze, Darby saw, kept jumping between her and Williams.

'There are the usual internet forums where people who are into bondage and S & M discuss various knots and binding techniques,' Hoder said. 'There are also people, generally men, who are simply fascinated by knots. They get together and teach each other how to tie these sorts of complicated knots. These clubs, get-togethers, whatever you want to call them, are a relatively new phenomenon. As you can imagine, they don't advertise in the Yellow Pages. They don't want to attract any unwanted attention for obvious reasons, but a few do openly advertise on the internet. We should see if such a club is operating in or around Red Hill.'

Smart, Darby thought. *Damn smart*. She had heard about clubs that catered to knot fetishists, but she hadn't stopped to consider that the Red Hill Ripper might be a member of one.

'My computer people haven't found a local club listed on the web,' Hoder said. 'They might have a website that can't be accessed conventionally, one that's in the Deep Web or the Darknet. Our tech guys are going to see what they can uncover. I won't bore you with the technical details.'

'Good,' someone said.

Snorts and chuckles all around.

'We're looking for a white male in his late forties to early fifties,' Hoder said. 'He's an introvert but not a loner. He'll have a steady job and be married or in a long-term relationship. He'll have a normal sexual relationship with his wife or partner, but he won't share his love of knots with her or his desire to tie her up and strangle her.

'Check prostitutes to see if they had a john who was into knots, possibly tied them to chairs with plastic ties and used duct tape. I wouldn't be surprised to find out that he had practised using the same knot and the same items.

'He won't have a history of anger issues. He'll be a regular guy-next-door type who is neat in appearance. The same holds true for his house. Everything will be neat and orderly, possibly to the point of an obsessive-compulsive disorder.

'That's all I have at the moment. Questions?'

There were none.

Chief Robinson took centre stage again. 'It's possible that we have an interesting development. I'll let Dr McCormick explain. That's the lady standing in the back – and she's had great experience in these types of cases. Come on up and meet the fellas.'

Darby hesitated.

'No need to be shy,' Robinson said. 'Crowley over there doesn't bite any more.'

Snorts and titters.

Darby didn't want to go up to the front. She didn't want to turn this into a Q & A session. She didn't have any concrete proof that the Ripper had, in fact, recorded what he had done to the Downes families and to the other families, or that the killer had been listening in on yesterday's conversations. She could smell the desperation in the room. She didn't want to give these men false hope.

She went, though, the heels of her harness boots clicking across the floor.

Darby turned and faced the room. Her deep green eyes stood out in her tanned face.

'I have reason to believe the killer may have watched and possibly recorded what he did to the families,' Darby said, and then launched into her theory of how the camera installed in a smartphone, iPad or laptop had been pointing at the murdered family at each crime scene.

'At the moment it's just a theory,' Darby said. 'We'll know more later today, after the devices have been looked at.'

A cop with a buzz cut said, 'So if he was recording himself, it's possible he could've been listening, maybe even watching, what you guys were doing inside the house yesterday.'

'I won't know anything for sure until the FBI's computer guys in Denver finish examining the devices.'

'In other words, he could've been spying on us this whole time.'

'Maybe.'

Darby saw the exhaustion and defeat in their faces. Some had taken out their phones and were studying the screens.

'No tip or thought or theory is insignificant,' Darby said. 'Bring them to us. It goes without saying that this is your case. I don't give a shit about turf or who gets credit. That holds true for Agents Hoder and Cooper. I'm leaving a stack of cards here on this desk.'

Darby had started to walk to the back of the room when Lancaster said, 'I have some questions, Dr McCormick.'

21

Lancaster shoved his hands into his pockets. 'This theory of yours,' he said, puffing out his chest a bit. 'Something of a stretch, don't you think?'

'I worked a case where the perp left behind hidden microphones at the crime scene, so he could listen in on the police and forensics,' Darby said.

'Just one case?'

'So far.'

'So this sort of thing is pretty rare.'

'If you have an alternate theory or idea, I'm sure everyone here would love to hear it.'

From the corner of her eye Darby caught more than one man trying to suppress a grin. She looked only at Lancaster.

'I meant no disrespect,' Lancaster said. 'You and Agent Hoder have stellar reputations, and I'm sure I speak for everyone when I say we're glad to have you here with us.'

The man's tone hit all the conciliatory notes. Darby wasn't surprised. The deputy sheriff's position was an elected office. As a seasoned politician, he knew how to serve up bullshit and call it filet mignon. But all his slick-speak and well-honed gestures couldn't hide the fact that the man was a first-class asshole.

'I understand you received a phone call last night,' Lancaster said. 'At your hotel.'

Darby had told only Williams and Hoder about the phone call, and neither would have told Lancaster. How did he find out? *Because there's at least one person here leaking information to Lancaster*, she answered. Someone, maybe several people, were looking to score points with the deputy sheriff.

'I was told this person threatened you,' Lancaster said. 'Something about wanting to get you in the rope.'

'That's right.'

'Could you please tell us the contents of your conversation? It might be beneficial to our case.'

Not only was Lancaster trying to embarrass her – payback for last night – he was making an active play to diminish her worth as an investigator. If she didn't answer – if she showed the slightest hint that she was embarrassed or uncomfortable – every man in this room would view her with a limp sympathy, similar to the way many viewed women who had been sexually assaulted. They'd isolate her like a leper and refuse to talk about the case in front of her.

When Darby spoke, her voice was calm. Clear. 'He said I had nice tits. His words, not mine.' She smiled. A couple of men returned it. A few avoided looking directly at her altogether. 'Then he said he liked my choice of underwear, which, for the record, was a pair of white boy shorts made by Hanes. I buy them in a three-pack at Target.'

She got a few chuckles. It immediately diffused most

of the tension in the room. But not Williams's: his heated gaze bored into the deputy sheriff, and Lancaster returned it.

'He said he couldn't wait to get me into his rope. He ended his call with a long, drawn-out goodbye, and hung up. He called from a nearby payphone, and he used some cheap piece of shit voice-changer. That's it.' Darby turned back to Lancaster and said, 'Any more questions about my boobs and underwear, Sheriff?'

Lancaster remained stone-faced and serious; her words had washed right over him. 'Anything you'd like to add to Agent Hoder's profile? Maybe another avenue we should explore?'

Darby felt her iPhone vibrate inside her jacket pocket; a text message had been delivered. She ignored it but wondered if Coop had just sent her an update from Denver.

'I agree with Agent Hoder's assessment,' she said. 'The only thing I would add is that the Ripper's sexual sadism and need to bind and torture women – that's something he probably experimented with as a teenager, meaning he practised tying himself up. I wouldn't be surprised to discover he dressed up as a woman when he did it. I would also take a serious look at any suspect who's familiar with autoerotic asphyxiation.'

'Could you explain that please?'

'Explain what?'

'Autoerotic asphyxiation. I don't want to assume everyone here is familiar with the term.'

Her phone vibrated again. Another text had come through. She ignored it and said, 'It's cutting off oxygen to the brain, usually by using a rope, while masturbating. Supposedly, it heightens the orgasm.'

'Have you had any experience in this area?'

'I haven't, but I'm sure you won't mind answering any questions these boys might have.'

Someone stifled a laugh. Then she heard footsteps coming her way, turned and saw Ray Williams waving his hand at Robinson.

'Excuse me, Chief,' Williams said, 'but I need to borrow Dr McCormick here for a minute.'

Robinson gave a short, curt nod. Lancaster tracked Williams as he walked all the way to the front of the room. As Williams held the door open for her, the chief started to explain how Red Hill and the deputy sheriff's people were going to start working in shifts at Pine Hill Cemetery. Almost all of the Red Hill Ripper's previous victims were buried there. It was Hoder's belief that the killer would visit the graves to relive the murders.

Not if he recorded them, Darby thought as she stepped out into the hall. It was surprisingly quiet for a police station: the only sound was that of a janitor wringing out his mop in a bucket.

Then she remembered the text message that had come through. She retrieved her iPhone as the door swung shut behind Williams.

'What is it with you and Lancaster?' Darby asked. 'He couldn't keep his eyes off you.'

'May I see your phone? I'm having problems getting a signal on mine.'

Darby caught the slight hitch in his voice, and his eyes

seemed wired. He looked like he was going to snatch the phone from her hand.

She stepped away and hit the button on her phone; the screen came to life.

'Give it to me,' he said. 'Please.'

Williams looked alarmed. Sick. But Darby didn't hand over the phone. She swiped her thumb across the screen and felt her stomach drop.

22

Darby had received two text messages. Neither contained any words: there was just a thumbnail picture in each. She tapped the first photo and when it enlarged she broke into a cold and greasy sweat.

The photo had been taken through her window. It showed her standing inside her hotel room, naked and facing the camera, her back arched and her hands frozen behind her head; she'd been in the process of tying back her damp hair when the camera's shutter had snapped shut.

The second photo showed her standing in the low-rise underwear that hugged her hips.

She looked up at Williams, saw the expression on his face and knew he had been sent the same photos. His face blurred and she felt like she'd been kicked in the stomach.

Inside the squad room she could hear Police Chief Robinson speaking in low, hushed tones. When Darby went to look through the door's glass partition, Williams darted in front of her and blocked her view.

It didn't matter. The glimpse she had caught was enough.

Darby walked away and, finding her legs unsteady, stopped and placed a palm flat against the side of the Coke machine.

Then Williams was standing next to her. 'Listen to me,' he said, his voice sounding far away, as though he were speaking to her from down the end of a long tunnel. 'I'm going to go back in there and make sure every one of those photos is deleted.'

But you can't delete what just happened, Darby thought. *You can't delete what they just saw.*

She pinched the bridge of her nose and closed her eyes and, inhaling deeply, replayed what she had seen inside the squad room before Williams had blocked her view, how the men were standing together, each one looking at his cell. One stared lasciviously at his screen while another puckered his lips and arched his eyebrows and whistled approvingly at her nakedness.

'I don't know how the bastard got our numbers,' Williams said. 'But I promise you we'll find out. I'll get a court order and within an hour we'll have traced the cell.'

'Burner.'

'What?'

'Burner. Disposable cell.' Her voice sounded foreign in her ears, as though someone else were speaking. 'You can buy 'em for next to nothing in practically any convenience store. That's why anyone looking to avoid a wiretap uses them. He's probably already chucked it.' It was a dead end and Williams knew it.

'Let's go to my office. It's right down the hall. You want some water? A Coke?'

Screw this. Darby brushed past him, her heels clicking across the floor.

Williams caught up with her. 'What are you doing?'

'Going to see who else got these pictures.'

'I'll do it.'

Darby stopped walking. 'What do you want me to do, Ray, go and hide in your office? Hang my head in shame because this asshole sent out some tit shots of me? Screw that.' She pushed open the door and entered the squad room.

I still own the first weapon I ever purchased: a Springfield bolt-action rifle. It had an M84 telegraphic sight and fired .30–06 shells from a clip-loaded, five-round magazine feed. The Springfield was one of America's finest firearms. It became the standard infantry rifle during World War II and, because of its accuracy and reliability, was used by snipers during the Korean and Vietnam wars.

There's a range I sometimes go to just outside of Denver, one that offers paper targets printed with human silhouettes. Mostly I practise near my home. Twice a month, usually on a Sunday afternoon, I pack a lunch and a thermos of black coffee and head deep into the woods behind my house to keep up my long-distance shooting skills. I've conducted this monthly ritual for as long as I can remember. The reason is both simple and practical: no matter how meticulous and prudent I am with my planning and execution, there's always the risk of my secret life being discovered.

Every decision we make involves managing consequences. I have thought long and hard about how I want to depart this world, the mark I want to leave, and it doesn't involve my being handcuffed and escorted to a waiting patrol car. History doesn't remember compliance and co-operation. It records blood. When the police come for me, I'll turn myself into Colorado's version of Charles Whitman, the former Marine and engineering student who, after stabbing his mother and wife to death in their sleep, entered the Tower of the University of Texas at Austin the following morning and, armed with bolt-action rifles and several other firearms, killed seventeen people and wounded thirty-two others in a mass-shooting rampage. I have boxes of rifle ammo stored in strategic locations all over the house. I need only remember to save one bullet for myself.

The police, the FBI or anyone else for that matter will never be able to search my house. Before I die, I'll set the timer for the bomb I've constructed.

The only solace I take in this scenario is that Sarah will join me in death. Together, we'll travel through the next world – and there is a next world. I'm not a religious man, but I do know that the love we share is something that survives death. Only a monster would believe otherwise.

I could drive back home and do it now. Head downstairs to the basement and then come back up and spare us both what's coming down the road.

No, that won't work. There's no way Sarah won't see the rifle. I don't want to scare her. Better to wait until she's asleep. It'll be more peaceful that way. Humane.

There's another option: set the bomb, then crawl into bed and make love to her one last time before the blast rips us apart and scatters our remains for miles. The bomb's construction is simple but crudely effective: a timer connected to five sticks of dynamite, with blasting caps stolen from a locked storage facility at a construction site.

Then my thoughts shift to the picture tucked into my coat pocket. All that work I put into researching Angela Blake and the others, and now I can't take her or Tricia Lamont or anyone else, all because of that red-headed bitch the FBI sent here.

In my mind's eye I see my father's steamer trunk. It sits in a corner of the basement, near my Springfield. The magazines are long gone – my whore of a mother saw to that, burning them in our backyard fire pit – but I still have my father's uniform and belt, which, while snug, do fit me. In addition to the dynamite and blasting caps, the trunk houses a few other treasures I've collected over the years. I pull over to the side of the road, complete a U-turn and drive home.

23

After the briefing, Darby and Hoder went to Police Chief Robinson's office, a cramped, windowless space with a pair of well-worn chairs placed in front of a well-worn desk that looked like it had been picked up at a garage sale. All the furniture had the same discarded feel. The only brightness in the room came from the scattered framed photographs hanging on the wall – pictures of the police chief hunting and fly-fishing with friends and his grandson, a small boy with a thick mop of brown hair that covered his ears.

Hoder took a chair in front of the police chief's desk. Robinson sat on the other side, the receiver for his office phone pressed against an ear, one hand massaging his forehead. Darby was too wired to sit, but she didn't want to pace around the room and have Hoder and Robinson think the texts had rattled her. Instead, she leaned against a filing cabinet, her arm propped on the top.

The man who had photographed her last night had sent copies of the pictures to every Red Hill cop. Ray Williams had signed out a squad car and gone to meet the four men who were out on patrol this morning, to make sure they deleted the pictures from their cell phones. Deputy Sheriff Lancaster had received copies as well.

Coop had tried to call her on her cell, but the signal had

dropped. She'd phoned back from a land-line but had been connected straight to voicemail. She'd left a message explaining what had happened.

Robinson was saying something to her.

'Sorry, could you repeat that?'

'I said I'd appreciate it if you didn't share anything with Teddy Lancaster until these cases are pulled from us.'

'Is Lancaster a part of the investigation now?'

'Right now, I'd say he's more like an overseer, you know, making sure our people do their jobs. But it's only a matter of time until the powers that be yank this from us. Thing is, and it pains me to admit this, Teddy's got the manpower. We don't.'

Robinson leaned back in his seat and folded his hands across his stomach. 'Ray told me about your little run-in with Teddy last night. Nelson's version is that Teddy bullied his way into the house. Told him to keep his yap shut. Nelson said he went along with it because he didn't want to be out of a job. When the incorporation goes through, Teddy's gonna have the power to hire and fire.'

'Shit always rises to the top.'

Robinson laughed softly. Then his face turned serious. 'Nelson's suspended for two weeks, without pay. After that, he goes in front of a conduct review board comprised of Brewster cops. Want to guess which way that's gonna turn out?'

There was no anger in the police chief's voice, just a matter-of-fact weariness. He turned to Hoder and said, 'We've got a website like everyone else on the planet. Our office emails and phone numbers are listed on it, but not our cells, so I have no idea how this guy got access to those. What about you? You advertise?'

'I'm not listed on the Bureau's website,' Hoder said.

'Miss McCormick?'

'I don't have a website and I'm not on Facebook, Twitter or any of those things,' she said. 'He got our phone numbers some other way.'

Robinson scratched his chin thoughtfully, his fingernails scraping across his whiskers. 'Here's what I don't get,' he said. 'The Ripper hasn't made contact with anyone associated with the case before. Then you arrive and he decides to come out of the woodwork. Why?'

'Calling me last night and sending out those pictures within the space of twelve hours – the whole thing smacks of desperation. He's afraid we'll find out something.'

'Not we. *You*. Why'd he call you and not Hoder? He's got the higher profile.'

'Hoder's not a woman,' Darby said. 'Our guy's thinking he can rattle my cage. That I'm going to, I dunno, break down and cry, pack my bags and skedaddle.

'I think he made a mistake at the Downes house – that clean-up job in the corner of the bedroom. Now he's trying to scare me off with the pictures. Were you told that I was coming here to assist Agents Hoder and Cooper?'

Robinson nodded. 'They both told me. And Williams.'

'What about the rest of your men? Was some sort of email sent out? Announcement made?'

'No and no. Why?'

'Agent Hoder told me this morning that a reporter tried to interview him for a piece that ran in yesterday's paper. After the meeting, I used the computer in Williams's office to read the story. My name wasn't mentioned anywhere in the article. I arrive yesterday to find that another family has been killed. Then it's like you just said – within the space of twelve hours I receive a phone call and then skin pics of me are sent out. What's that say to you?'

Robinson looked like he had swallowed a jar of thumbtacks. 'You're suggesting the Red Hill Ripper might be a *cop*?'

'I'm saying someone has access to restricted information – in this case, all the cell numbers of your people. Could be a cop or it could be a civilian who works for you or in another department. Your people's contact info is stored on a computer database, right?'

'Sure. All your details are in here. I added them myself.'

'What about the place where I'm staying? Is that listed?'

'Everyone in town knows where you're staying. It's the only hotel left in town.'

'But how did he know which room to watch?'

Robinson didn't answer. He wiped the corner of his mouth with the back of his hand. 'Miss McCormick, I'm not trying to cause you any further embarrassment, but I'd like to be frank, get my thoughts –'

'Ask your questions.'

'It's fair to say the Ripper gets his rocks off strangling women. We know for a fact that someone watched you undressing in your hotel room last night, called and threatened you, and then sent out the pictures.'

'You're wondering if he's targeted me as a potential victim?'

'I'm inclined to take this threat seriously. Aren't you?'

'Has he contacted any of his previous victims?'

'Nothing we've found indicates he did.'

'Then why would he suddenly break the pattern with me? Why bother putting himself on our radar screen? If he really views me as a potential victim, he wouldn't announce himself that way. He'd stay in the shadows and wait. The only reason for calling me and sending out those pictures was to embarrass me. To get me to leave.'

Robinson looked to Hoder either for confirmation of her words or for a second opinion.

'It's a valid point,' Hoder said.

'Still,' Robinson said, his gaze sliding back to Darby, 'I'd sleep a bit better knowing someone was keeping a close eye on you.'

'I'm staying in a hotel packed with federal agents. What safer place is there?'

'What I meant was I'd feel better if you didn't travel anywhere alone.'

'You want someone from the swinging-dicks club by my side.'

'I'm not sure I follow.'

'I'm a woman, so I can't handle myself. Because I don't have a swizzle stick and a big pair of peaches between my legs, I need a man by my side. If I did, you'd tell me to be careful out there and watch my back.'

'I genuinely meant no disrespect, Miss McCormick.'

Darby could see that this was true. She sucked in air

through her nose, pushed herself off the filing cabinet and let out a long breath. 'Sorry,' she said. 'I'm operating on only a couple of hours of sleep. It doesn't help my disposition.'

Her phone vibrated in her jacket pocket. Another text message had been delivered.

24

Darby took out her phone and read the message displayed on the screen.

'It's Coop,' she said. 'He wants me to call him from a land-line. May I borrow your phone, Chief?'

Darby stood while she dialled the number Coop had included in the message. The line on the other end rang once.

'Cooper.'

'It's me. I tried calling you earlier.'

'I had my phone turned off. The computer guys at RCFL make you turn it off when you go into this particular section of the building, something to do with the cell signals screwing up some of their equipment.'

'You got my message?'

'About the pictures? Yeah, I got it.'

'I take it you received copies as well.'

'Two of them, texted to my phone.'

Darby heard the sorrow in his voice – and some pity too. The latter cut more deeply.

'If it's any consolation, you've got nothing to be ashamed of,' he said.

'That's it? No smartass comment?'

'I always wondered if the carpet matched the drapes, and now I know.'

'That's better,' Darby said. As embarrassing as the situation was, she needed him to be normal. She didn't want him to be tiptoeing around her like every other man here. 'Have you been productive this morning, or have you squandered your time leering at my nude shots?'

'Since I'm a professional FBI agent first and foremost, I managed to put aside my horn-dog tendencies and get some actual work done. Is Hoder with you?'

'I'm standing next to him. We're in Chief Robinson's office.'

'Any way to put me on speakerphone?'

'Hold on.'

Darby relayed the request to the police chief. Robinson reached into his desk drawer and his liver-spotted hand came back with a small peach-coloured speakerphone unit that looked like it had been invented around the time of the rotary phone. It took him a couple of minutes of fumbling with the wires and appropriate knobs and buttons before Coop's tinny voice could be heard over the speaker.

'Can everyone hear me? Good. Okay, let's start with the iPad found on the nightstand in the Downes bedroom. Darby's theory about the killer recording what he did to the family is correct.'

Hoder's eyebrows arched in surprise and admiration. The police chief gaped openly at her from the other side of the desk. Darby wrote in her notebook.

'The Nerd Herd – that's what these guys call themselves – found an app called iSeeu installed on the iPad,' Coop said. 'Software's free, can be downloaded to iPads and iPods and iPhones, Android smartphones, Macs and PCs, you name it. It's designed so you can spy on your significant other to see if he or she is cheating on you. Or maybe you want to monitor your teenage son, make sure he isn't cruising around the internet looking for free porn. You can set up the software to send copies of texts, emails and your browsing history to your computer. Software runs invisibly in the background without the user knowing. Here's the best part: you can set it up to record without alerting the user.'

'Meaning?' Darby asked.

'Let's say I suspect you're cheating on me. I go off to work and because you're a MILF, which stands for a Mother I'd Like To –'

'We know what it stands for.'

'Just wanted to be sure, as we have some older gentlemen in the room. Now, this app, if I've got it installed on my iPad and if I have its camera pointed at the bed when you're going at it with your 22-year-old boy toy, enables me to watch you live and in stereo, or I can record you on my computer to enjoy at a later date. The iPad screen doesn't have to be on. You don't know you're being watched and recorded, but I suddenly find out the reason why you've been walking around bowlegged three mornings a week.'

'What about sound?'

'Included. So in our scenario, let's say the iPad's camera isn't pointed at your bed. I'll still have audio of you initiating this innocent young man into the ways of the Karma Sutra. Again, the screen doesn't need to be on.'

'And the user really doesn't have any idea that this software is running, turning the iPad, computer or phone into a spy device?'

'Not a clue. The software is invisible. Runs in the background after you install it. The software does, however, do a number on the battery, since the electrical device is constantly on even when it appears to be in sleep mode. I suspect the Red Hill Ripper knows that, as we found the iPad plugged into the charger.'

'Can you find out when this app was installed?'

'Already did,' Coop said. 'It was downloaded and installed this past Tuesday, at 12.38 a.m.'

'That would fit with the estimated time of death.'

'The Ripper enters the house, and after he gets the family tied up he downloads the software and starts the show.'

'Any technical expertise needed to install this software?'

'No. It pretty much self-installs. The only thing you need to know is where to find it when you want to change the settings. The instructions, the how-to guide, whatever you want to call it, are posted online. It's so simple a kid could do it.

'Guys here said the app started running – started streaming audio and video over the home's Wi-Fi – at 12.48 a.m. It was still streaming when we removed it from the Downes house last night.'

'Meaning there's a strong possibility he was watching us inside the bedroom yesterday.'

'Watching *and* listening,' Coop said. 'The software was set to do both. That's my guess on how he found out you were here, saw you moving around the bedroom yesterday.'

Maybe, Darby thought. *Maybe he did find out that way. If the Silver Moon Inn is the only hotel in town, maybe he assumed I was staying there. But how did he know which room to watch?*

Darby thought of the girl working the front counter last night. Laurie. *Did he talk to her earlier in the day and find out my room number?*

'As for where the streaming data packets were sent – the Nerd Herd don't know,' Coop said. 'The app uses something called the Advanced Encryption Standard, which is . . .' The sound of pages being flipped echoed over the speakerphone. 'Here it is. AES is a symmetric-key algorithm that runs on a substitution-permutation network, rather than the Feistel network, which is geek-speak for the kind of encryption that won't allow them to trace to where the data packets were sent.'

'And there's no way to hack it?' Darby asked.

'No. That's why governments, including our own, are so fond of it. The encryption takes place at both ends – when it's sent, and when it's delivered. At the point they started to talk about keys, they lost me. The bottom line is that, while we know the family was recorded, tracing the data packets through a bunch of networks is a dead end. That's all I've got right now. Questions?'

'The pictures we all received,' Darby said. 'Is there any way they can be traced back to their original source?'

'I gave my phone to the Nerd Herd, who are examining them right now – that's all I know.'

'Where do we stand on the court order to access the

medical records?' Darby wanted to know if anyone in the Downes family had been taking the antibiotic neomycin.

'Hayes is working on it,' Coop said. 'Any other questions?'

There weren't any.

'Okay, a couple of things before I go,' Coop said. 'First is the MoFo. The satellite part is going to be delivered no later than one. After that, it'll take a couple of hours to install. Moment it's done we'll be on our way. If, for whatever reason, there's a delay, we're going to hit the road no later than four or so. They're saying a major storm's working its way towards Colorado tonight, dumping anywhere from three to five feet before it's finished.'

Robinson nodded from across the desk.

'Second thing is the duct tape,' Coop said. 'Based upon what I've seen, I'm pretty sure it all came from the same roll. There's nothing more I can do with it here, so I Fed-Exed it out this morning. They'll get to our lab no later than 9 a.m. tomorrow. Since your cells aren't that reliable up there, if I need anything or have anything to report, I'll liaise with Chief Robinson. That work for you?'

Robinson nodded. Then he remembered he was on speakerphone. 'Yes,' he said. 'Absolutely. Anything you need.'

Coop clicked off. Darby flipped her notebook shut. It was too warm in here, and cobwebs had formed in her mind. She wanted to get moving. Get busy. She stood and picked up her jacket.

'Where you off to now?' Robinson asked.

'I'm going back to the hotel to investigate how the Red

Hill Ripper discovered my room number.' She checked her watch: plenty of time before the autopsies. 'If you see Williams, tell him to meet me there.'

'So you're on board with the idea that the man who called you last night is, in fact, our killer,' Robinson said.

'We'll see.' Darby placed the car keys on the desk, in front of Hoder. 'In case you need to go back to the hotel.'

'How are you going to get there?'

'Walk. It's only a couple miles. The fresh air will do me good, help me clear my head.'

Hoder gripped the cane with both hands and groaned as he struggled to his feet. 'I'll see you out.'

25

'Let me guess,' Darby said after Hoder shut the police chief's door. 'You want to chaperone me to the hotel.'

'If I walked with you, we wouldn't arrive until sometime after lunch. Besides, after that tongue lashing you gave Robinson, I wouldn't dream of suggesting such a thing.' Hoder smiled warily. 'How about we step outside for a moment and get us some fresh air?'

Darby slipped on her sunglasses and zipped up her jacket on her way out of the station. It was cold in the shade but the parking lot was bathed in sunlight. The air embraced her like a long-lost friend and kicked away the exhaustion and the station's stale, antiseptic odour from her nostrils.

Hoder shuffled to a nearby patrol car, which was covered in a film of rock salt. He leaned the small of his back against the truck and seemed unable to catch his breath. Were his lungs having problems adjusting to the higher altitude, or was he sick? His face had a deathly pallor, and she saw his hands tremble.

'There was this sexual sadist, guy by the name of Carlos Santos, who killed twenty-three people in and around southern New Mexico. Brought each one to a homemade torture chamber he'd constructed himself. Called it the "toy box". I don't need to spell out what happened there.'

'Was he caught?'

'Eventually.' Hoder's attention had drifted to the main road, where a solitary truck with mud tyres made its way towards Red Hill's barren downtown district, a place that resembled the kind of ghost town seen in a Clint Eastwood Western.

Darby shifted on her feet, impatient, wanting Hoder to get to the point behind this impromptu powwow so she could start moving. In deference to his status and obviously frail health, she decided to keep her mouth shut. She stuffed her hands into her jacket pockets and waited.

'I wasn't actively involved in the investigation; I was there just as a consultant,' Hoder said. 'I spent three or four days with people from the local police and sheriff's office. The phone calls to my home started a week later.'

'From Santos?'

'Maybe. Probably. Santos killed himself before anyone could speak to him. Later we found out the phone calls had been made within one or two hours after Santos had abducted his victims. My home number has a longstanding trap-and-trace, but it didn't matter, since all the calls originated from payphones.'

Hoder wiped spittle from his lips with the back of his hand. 'I tried to engage him in conversation but he never spoke. A couple of times, though, he cried. I was sure he was reaching out to me because he was trying to stop. You know what ricin is?'

'A poison derived from castor-oil seeds.'

Hoder nodded. 'When castor oil is made, ricin is what they call the "waste mash". It's a very stable poison.

Doesn't break down easily in extreme indoor or outdoor temperatures. It can be used as a powder or a mist, or as a pellet that dissolves in water. You don't need to use a lot – a pin-sized amount is enough to kill an adult. The ER doctor who treated me managed to keep my organs from shutting down, but there was no way to repair the damage. Now you know why I look like I'm standing at death's door.' He smiled grimly, as if the act defused the memory. 'I still don't know how Santos did it.'

'But you're sure it was him.'

'Yes. Absolutely. Santos was a chemist. The police found ricin in his torture chamber. Later, they found out he had booked a round-trip ticket to Virginia. We still don't know how he found out where I lived, my home number or how he poisoned me.'

'He refused to tell you?'

'He killed himself. The police showed up at his house: Santos went upstairs to his bedroom and ate his gun.'

A sudden blast of wind kicked a nearby Styrofoam cup and candy-bar wrapper across the pavement.

'The Bureau checked every square inch of my home – food and clothing, garbage, even my mail. My gut – what's left of it – tells me he did it at the restaurant, where I met a friend for drinks. It was the only time I went out that week. Three days later, I was sick.'

Darby glanced discreetly at her watch. 'Why are you telling me this?'

Hoder refocused his attention on her, squinting in the sunlight. 'Because I don't think you entirely understand or appreciate the predatory psychology of a sexual sadist.'

There was no admonishment or lecture-type quality to his tone. He spoke simply and frankly, one professional to another.

'A great white shark doesn't feel guilt when it attacks a seal or a surfer,' Hoder said. 'It doesn't feel empathy or remorse or anything else, because it doesn't have a conscience. When it's finished, it simply swims off in search of other prey. A sexual sadist functions in exactly the same manner but with one major distinction: when it sights its prey, it waits and plans the perfect moment to strike. The victim never sees it coming.'

Darby said nothing. She didn't disagree with Hoder's assessment; that had been her experience as well. She didn't say anything because her thoughts had drifted away from the conversation again. Something nagged at her and she couldn't put a finger on it. Not yet.

Hoder wasn't finished. 'The Red Hill Ripper is the worst kind of sadist – an anger-excitation rapist who is not only highly intelligent but also has a high level of control over his surroundings. Just look at how meticulously he moved in and out of the Downes home.'

'He didn't rape any of his victims. The phone call, the photos of me – he's trying to scare me off.'

'I wouldn't be so sure, Darby.'

'He went to great lengths to clean up that corner of the bedroom. He made a mistake, and he's shitting his pants that we're going to find it – find *him*.'

Hoder pushed himself off the trunk and placed all his weight on his cane. Then he shuffled a few steps towards her and turned his back to the sun, so he didn't have to squint. From behind the green tint of her sunglasses Darby could see the deep lines and grooves around his eyes and mouth. She could also see the irritation growing in his face.

'You know what you are?' Hoder said. 'You're a meddle-some whore.'

26

'That's how the Red Hill Ripper views you,' Hoder said in his soft Southern drawl. 'That's why he called you last night and that's why he sent out those naked pictures of you. Like all sexual sadists, he despises women. You're a bitch and a slut, and he seeks complete control over you because you're a woman and women are the enemy. Right now he's planning on how he's going to get to you and punish you. He's rehearsing every single detail.'

Darby didn't reply, her skin crawling with anxiety.

'You're an intelligent woman,' he said. 'You have a PhD from Harvard in criminal behaviour, and you've had first-hand experience with sadists. You know he's fixated on you now. At some point he's going to strike, and when he does he's going to take you someplace where he can degrade you and torture you until your heart gives out. Tell me I'm wrong.'

You're not, Darby told herself. She looked away, at the notches in the mountains, and that thing that nagged her reappeared along the edges of her mind. She tried to chase the thought or feeling or whatever it was, but it had vanished like vapour scattered in the wind.

'Why do I feel like I'm talking to a storm drain?'

'I hear you,' Darby said, and turned her attention back

to him. 'You want to be my chaperone for the day? You're hired. Give me the car keys.'

'What would make me feel better is for you to go back to Sarasota.'

'And what, exactly, is that going to accomplish?'

Hoder's irritation had vanished, replaced by what appeared to be an almost paternal concern. 'I never intended to put you in harm's way,' he said. 'Maybe I should have shown better judgement before asking you to come here, I don't know. What I do know is that I'm truly sorry for what happened to you this morning.'

Hoder wasn't paying her lip service; she heard genuine regret and sorrow in his voice, and for some reason it triggered the image of David Downes tied to the dining-room chair, suffocating inside the bag, trying to scream at the killer to stop and then at the end trying to scream to his daughter and wife that he loved them, his last words forever lost, sealed behind the tape wrapped around his mouth.

Then the image vanished, leaving with her the cold certainty that when she found the killer she would do something horrible to him. If given the opportunity, she'd feed him into a wood chipper, slowly, inch by inch. Without regret and without remorse.

'I'll take care of the arrangements,' Hoder said. 'Go home, Darby. Please.'

'Our guy already knows my name. If that Carlos Santos character found your unlisted home number and where you live, who's to say the Red Hill Ripper won't do the same with me?'

Hoder studied the scuffed tops of his loafers.

'Besides,' Darby said, 'running away isn't my style.'

Hoder swallowed, clearly pained. 'I'm sorry.'

Darby was about to speak when the thing that had been nagging at her rose like a bubble in her mind and popped: the Ripper had called *after* she had hung up with Coop.

She spoke in a clear, calm voice. 'I need to get to the hotel now.'

Hoder handed over the keys. She held the door open for him and, after a moment of deliberation, got in.

Hoder sat with the cane between his legs and stared out of the front window as they left the parking lot. She drove slowly, as if the thought she carried in her mind was a fragile, teetering thing that was about to crash into a million little pieces against the floor.

'I went to school nights to get my master's degree,' he said, the tyres crunching across the gravel. 'For my thesis, I interviewed soldiers who had survived combat. My plan was to write about the commonalities of post-traumatic stress disorder, but what I ended up writing about was something I called "second life syndrome".'

Darby concentrated on the road, on the thoughts bouncing around in her head.

'It refers to soldiers who, having survived combat, believed they'd been touched by God's hand or some other divine presence,' Hoder said. 'Because their life had been spared under the cruellest circumstances, they thought nothing bad would ever happen to them again. They lived their lives recklessly, marching headfirst into danger because the normal rules of life no longer applied to them.'

Darby knew where he was heading. 'I don't share that view, Terry, and I've never been a soldier.'

'But you've survived combat with Traveler and the others that followed him. And then there's that cult you and Cooper investigated, what, two years back, the one that abducted Jack Casey and his daughter and turned his wife into a vegetable.'

Images of what she had seen on that remote island off the coast of Maine flashed through her mind, and she unconsciously shifted in her seat.

'There's another psychological component at work here,' Hoder said.

'All due respect, how about giving the five-and-dime psychoanalysis a rest?'

'You're deliberately putting yourself in harm's way because you want the Ripper to come after you. You want to kill him.'

'Wrong.'

Hoder made no reply.

This morning's depression has mercifully lifted. As I near my house, I feel more in control than ever. More hopeful.

And why shouldn't I? I'm still safely hidden inside the shadows, and I still have the power to choose. I can take Angela Blake, Tricia Lamont, even the McCormick bitch, whenever I want.

Sarah gave me Angela's picture because she knows I like a fighter. In that regard, Darby McCormick would be the ultimate challenge. She wouldn't submit herself willingly to the rope, the way some of the others did. She wouldn't scream or beg or cry. She'd lash out. I did a Google search on her last night, surprised by the number of articles that came up. I only had to read a handful to know that she gets off on killing. Given the chance, she'd blow my head off or slit my throat and then sleep like a baby. The woman has no conscience.

Women are fragile, delicate things; they break easily. And, like all things that break, they don't look or function the same way after they're put back together. You always see the cracks. The weak and vulnerable spots.

And hers is fear. The photos and last night's phone call have put her into full red-alert mode. She'll be constantly looking over her shoulder and watching her rear-view mirror, terrified the Red Hill Ripper is coming for her. Every time the phone rings and every time she gets undressed her anxiety will go into overdrive. I have to stoke her fear, keep her simmering in it, so that she can't sleep. She'll become run down and, eventually, exhausted. She'll be jumpy and irritable and prone to mistakes and she won't see me coming.

The real challenge will be what to do with her. Training a woman to obey is really no different than training a dog. Some dogs take to their lessons easily. A few swift corrections and they're in line. The more stubborn ones, you have to systematically break their spirit. Sometimes you have to drive your point home with a hand or fist. You have to be patient and find the way to deliver the message so it lives in their bones.

I pull into the driveway, as excited as a child on Christmas morning, and park. Sarah's car isn't here; today is Thursday, her errand day. I hit the button on the garage-door remote clipped to my visor and leave the truck running. I only need a few minutes in the basement.

I open the steamer trunk, a blast of dust hitting my nose as my eyes pore over a dozen fragmentation grenades and a sawn-off Mossberg shotgun; a bulletproof vest designed to withstand armour-piercing rounds; night-vision binoculars and goggles. I find what I'm looking for in the corner: a box holding a vial of Etorphine and a half-dozen syringes, held together with an elastic band. A small injection of that opioid and a normal, healthy adult will black out in less than a minute.

I tuck the box and syringes into my pocket, wanting to

have them close by for when the time comes. I can hear the radio playing upstairs. Sarah puts it on every time she leaves the house, believing that the news and an assortment of talk-radio hosts will convince a potential burglar that someone is home.

A reporter is talking about the Downes family, the latest victims of the Red Hill Ripper. The piece ends with a mention of the FBI sending Terry Hoder to Red Hill to hunt the killer.

Has Sarah heard this? Does she know? At some point I'm going to have to tell her.

I start up the stairs but my thoughts turn back to the other items inside the trunk.

What if the police come for me when I'm not at home? The FBI? I move back to the trunk and stand over it for several minutes.

I decide against taking the Mossberg. While the shotgun has massive stopping power, it's useless against long-distance targets. If I'm bunkered down somewhere and locked in a firefight, I'll need the Springfield. I sling the rifle strap over my shoulder and stuff a box of ammo into an empty pocket.

At the last moment I decide to take three grenades with me. If I'm forced to leave this world, why not go out in a blaze of glory?

27

Darby entered the hotel lobby and went straight to the reception desk in search of Laurie, who had checked her in last night. Laurie wasn't there; nor was she inside the small office behind the counter.

Darby would deal with that later. First, she needed to go to her room.

She had drawn the blackout curtains after last night's phone call and left them that way when she locked up this morning. Now she found them still drawn, the room caged in a partial darkness.

Darby hit the wall's light switch and the matching lamps on the nightstands came to life. She left the door open behind her and the curtains as they were. She looked around the room for the TV remote, found it on the bureau and turned on the TV.

A commercial for a new medication used to treat erectile dysfunction started to play on the screen. She increased the volume slightly, then tossed the remote on her bed and slipped out of her boots. She went to the bathroom and turned on the shower. When she stepped back into the room, she left the bathroom door open behind her and moved to the nightstand with the phone.

The cordless handset didn't have any visible screws, but it did have a back cover. She fitted her thumb into the groove and, careful not to make any noise, gently wiggled it forward until the cover came off.

The rectangular-shaped area behind the cover housed a pair of rechargeable batteries; it was connected to the rest of the handset by a pair of Phillips-head screws. Using a fingernail, she carefully removed the batteries, not wanting to make a sound, and found two more screws underneath. She studied them underneath the nightstand lamp's bright light for a moment. Then from her back pocket she removed the zippered pouch she had taken from her kit.

Tucked inside the pouch's black mesh was a small adjustable screwdriver with a dozen different point heads. Fortunately it had the small head size she needed.

Darby sat on the edge of the bed and went to work removing the screws with the methodical care of a bomb technician tasked with defusing an improvised explosive device. If her suspicions were correct about what was inside the handset she needed to be as quiet as possible.

It took her two minutes to remove the screws and another five to dismantle the rest of the handset. She had to switch from the Phillips-head to a flathead in order to carefully prise apart the plastic shell.

She found what she was looking for in the nest of wires near the earpiece.

Darby put everything on the bed and in her stocking feet moved back into the hall of dim light and stone flooring. Hoder stood at the opposite end, waiting. She had told him to remain there to make sure no one came into the hall.

He leaned forward, both hands gripping his cane, and

looked at her questioningly. She nodded and surprise lit up his face. He raised his eyebrows until they almost met his hairline.

'Definitely an audio bug,' Darby said after she reached him. She had explained her theory about a listening device having been installed inside her phone as they were entering the hotel. 'Looks like an older model, battery operated, but I'm sure.'

'You think he heard you?' Hoder kept his voice low, as if the bug were hovering inches away from them.

'I turned on the TV and shower so I doubt he heard me taking the phone apart, and I took my boots off so he didn't hear me walking out of the room. I don't have the proper equipment to know if he is, in fact, listening right now. I doubt Red Hill does – we can ask – but if they don't I'm sure Coop can scrounge up what we need from the Denver office.'

'How did you know?' Hoder asked.

'The bug in my phone? Because he called almost immediately after I hung up with Coop.'

'That it?'

Darby nodded. Hoder visibly stiffened, as if she had betrayed him somehow. As if she had come across information and refused to share it with him.

'It was a hunch,' she said. 'A lucky guess.'

Hoder looked like he had come to some sort of private conclusion about her. Or maybe she was reading too much into it. Maybe Hoder was privately admonishing or punishing himself for not having figured it all out earlier.

His smile was forced, his voice flat when he said, 'What about the range of this thing?'

'No idea. I'll know more once I find out the serial number – provided I can find one.' Darby sighed and tucked her hair behind her ears. 'We have a bigger problem.'

'What?'

'The bug was placed directly behind the handset's earpiece, so it could pick up conversations, any noise, in fact, inside my room. That means he heard me talking to Williams and Coop last night. It also means he heard me discussing the crime scene photos with Coop and Williams, how I noticed an electronic device with a camera positioned on each of the families.'

'It's not like that was going to do us any good. Coop said tracing the signal is a dead end.'

'I'm more worried about our man's state of mind. If he knows we've found out how he recorded the families, watched the police at the crime scenes, it's going to ramp up his anxiety and –'

'He may lash out,' Hoder said, finishing her thought.

'I'll call Coop, have him bring some equipment that will allow us to find the bugs without having to take each phone apart. Until we know for sure, I wouldn't use the hotel phone to make any calls – or talk about the case inside your room.'

'Agreed.'

'I'll also see if the Denver office has the right equipment to allow us to lock into a bug's frequency and trace it – which is why I left it in the handset. I don't want him to know we've found it. Let me go shut down everything in the room and then we'll go to see if that woman who worked the reception desk last night is here.'

'She is,' Hoder said. 'She came into the hall while you were in your room. Her full name's Laurie Richards. She's waiting for us out front.'

'Take her outside. I'll meet you there in a couple of minutes.'

'Outside?'

'If the Red Hill Ripper managed to get his way into my room and bug my phone, who's to say he didn't place a listening device near the reception desk or somewhere else?'

28

Darby stepped outside the hotel's front door and found Laurie Richards standing a few feet away from the entrance, in a patch of sunlight. The woman's dark blue puffer jacket was zipped all the way to her throat. It was frayed along the cuffs and there was a dime-sized hole in the elbow that exposed the downy feathers to the wind.

Hoder was making polite chitchat about the approaching storm while the woman looked around the street, a caged anxiety visible in her face and posture. She refused to look at him, her attention fixed on something further down the street. A black Ford van with tinted windows, its sagging rear bumper held up by rope, was parked in front of the Wagon Wheel Saloon.

Had Hoder said something to scare her, or was the woman intimidated simply by the idea of talking to a federal agent? Was she afraid of men?

Hoder, a divining rod of buried human emotions, had tuned into the woman's mood. So Darby wasn't surprised when he turned to her and said, 'Ms Richards said there's a diner a few blocks from here. I need to eat something before my hypoglycaemia goes into overdrive. Would you like me to bring you back some coffee?'

'Black, please,' Darby replied.

'Ms Richards?'

'No, thank you.'

Darby handed him the car keys. Richards watched Hoder as he shuffled on his cane towards the corner. The woman looked exhausted, a wired energy flitting behind her eyes.

'We met briefly last night. My name is Darby McCormick. I'm assisting Agent Hoder with the Red Hill Ripper investigation.'

'Yes, I know. He told me.' She shifted on her feet and then seemed to stand absolutely still, as though the solid pavement had turned to a thin sheet of ice. 'Am I in some sort of trouble?'

'Why would you think that?'

'He wouldn't let me go to your room to change the sheets. He told me to go wait at the front desk and not to go anywhere. Did I do something wrong? And why are we standing outside?'

'I've become addicted to this fresh country air.' Darby smiled pleasantly. 'How many people work here?'

'Just me.'

Darby blinked in surprise. 'You run the entire hotel by yourself?'

'It's not as daunting as it sounds. We generally don't have guests. Nobody comes to stay in Red Hill any more, not since the ski slopes in Ridgewater closed, oh, must be six years ago now. Recession hit Ridgewater real bad. People used to stay here 'cause it was cheaper.'

'Where do you live now?'

'Here, at the hotel. At least until it's sold.'

Darby recalled the cot she'd seen in the back office.

'Charlie prefers to have me here around the clock, anyway,' Richards said.

'Charlie?'

'Charlie Baker. He owns the hotel, and he hired me to keep an eye on everything – make sure the pipes don't freeze and burst, keep the place nice and clean for when potential buyers come around, stuff like that. They don't always telephone ahead, you know.'

'Buyers?'

Richards nodded, her attention riveted on the notebook Darby had removed from her back pocket. 'Most of 'em just drop by unannounced. When they do, I've got to make sure everything's spic 'n' span.'

'You said "they". Do buyers always come in groups?'

'Usually.'

'When was the last time a buyer stopped by the hotel?'

'December. I can't recall the date off the top of my head, but it was early in the month. I'd have to consult the book.' She smiled brightly. Proudly. 'I keep very detailed notes for Mr Baker.'

'Does he work at the hotel too? Come in and do paperwork, stuff like that?'

'No, he lives in Arizona. With his son.'

'The buyer in December,' Darby began.

'*Buyers*. Three men and an older woman, from Weinstein and Glick, some building company based somewhere on the East Coast. New York, I think.'

'Has a single buyer come by recently to look at the hotel?'

'No. Never.'

'You sure? Maybe someone who was taking a look around the outside?'

'I'm positive. They always come in groups.'

Scratch that theory, Darby thought. 'Ms Richards, can you tell me who booked my hotel room?'

The woman seemed puzzled, nervous, as though she'd been asked a trick question designed to lead her into a trap. 'Agent Hoder,' she said tenuously.

'He called and told you to book me a room?'

'No, he told me the day he checked in.'

'That would be this past Wednesday, the fifteenth.'

'That's right. He came into the hotel around noon or so with another agent, a tall man with blond hair and differently coloured eyes.'

'Cooper.'

'He didn't introduce himself, and Agent Hoder didn't tell me his name. But he had a badge and everything. Agent Hoder checked in and told me he needed another room and gave me your name.'

'When did the FBI book the other rooms?'

'Right after the first of the year, I think. I'll have to check the ledger.'

'You don't use a computer?'

'Not any more. Mr Baker used one at one point, but when it broke he didn't want to replace it – there wasn't a need since the hotel wasn't busy. I've been working here almost a year, and all I've ever used is the ledger. We still have the credit card machine, though. You need that since everyone pays with plastic.'

'Where do you keep the ledger?'

'Next to the phone.'

'Is it always next to the phone?'

'There or behind the desk.' The woman's brow furrowed. 'Why?'

'Could you bring it to me, please?'

29

Laurie Richards clearly wanted to ask why she had to bring the ledger outside instead of taking Darby back into the hotel to read it.

She didn't, though. She opened the big, heavy glass door, and Darby watched as the woman moved to the corner of the front desk and picked up something next to the phone. Richards returned carrying a book bound in green imitation leather. A red ribbon acted as a bookmark.

'The entry's right here,' Richards said, and pointed to the kind of impeccable cursive handwriting instilled by Catholic school nuns. 'Mr Stephen Drake from the FBI's travel office in Washington called me on Friday, the third. That's his phone number right there, next to his name. He said four agents would be staying with us for a week starting on Wednesday, the fifteenth.'

Darby nodded, reading along. Richards had taken meticulous notes.

'Mr Drake specifically asked for two rooms, by the way,' Richards said. 'I told him we had plenty of availability but he told me the FBI have their agents bunk up.'

Darby nodded, familiar with the FBI's budget-saving protocol. 'This notation right here,' she said, and pointed to a line that read '+1R. 8.'

'That's shorthand for plus one extra room. I put you in

Room 8,' Richards said. 'I wrote that down after Agent Hoder told me you'd be staying here. I called Mr Drake to tell him, you know, just in case.'

'And you made this notation on Wednesday morning, when Agent Hoder checked in.'

'Yes.'

'You're sure? You didn't add it in later?'

'No. I make the notes right then and there. I don't wait because you can't always trust your brain to remember – at least mine, anyway.'

Darby had flown in yesterday. Thursday. She had arrived at the Downes home at roughly 11 a.m. and checked into her room last night at little after 9 p.m. Sometime during those ten hours the Red Hill Ripper had found out her room number and bugged her phone.

Darby closed the ledger and handed it back to her.

'Did you see anyone inside the hotel yesterday who didn't belong here? Someone who wasn't a guest?'

'No.'

'You're sure?'

Richards nodded vigorously.

'Were you working the front desk the entire time? Did you go anywhere?'

'Well, I can't be in two places at once,' Richards said. 'I've got to do cleaning and maintenance and other stuff. When Agent Hoder told me he needed an extra room, I had to go and get it ready.'

'How many times were you away from the front desk?'

The woman crossed her arms over her chest, holding the ledger like a shield.

'I'm not questioning your work ethic,' Darby began.

'Then why are you —' Laurie Richards cut herself off, blood draining from her face. 'Oh my God, are you saying the Red Hill Ripper was *inside* the hotel yesterday?'

'Why do you think that?'

'Why else would you be asking me these questions? Oh my *God* —'

'Ms Richards —'

'I can't believe this is *happening*.'

'The Ripper was not inside the hotel,' Darby lied. She needed to keep that information contained; it couldn't be allowed to leak all over town. 'These are routine security questions.'

'You think the Ripper is going to attack Agent Hoder? Is that it?'

'I'm concerned about reporters. They like to sneak into hotels.'

Richards puffed up her chest a little. 'Not on my watch.'

'Is there a service entrance?'

'There is. Or was. It's chained up.'

'Inside or outside?'

'The chain is inside. Padlock. I don't have the combination, if that's what you're wondering.'

'When you were off cleaning and what have you, was the ledger by the phone?'

Richards's anxiety increased, her expression changing into that of someone who had just been handed a live grenade.

'Ms Richards?'

'Yes. Yes, it was there.'

'Last night, after I checked in, did you receive a phone call that you forwarded to my room?'

Laurie Richards swallowed, her eyes glistening with tears. She blinked them back and inhaled deeply through her nostrils.

'Ms Richards?'

'I don't understand what I did wrong.'

Darby tried to hide her impatience. 'Please, just answer the question.'

'He asked to speak to you. I forwarded the call.'

'He,' Darby said. 'You're sure it was a male voice.'

'Yes.'

'Did you recognize it?'

Richards considered the question, her gaze sweeping across the cracked sidewalk.

'No. No, I didn't.'

'What did his voice sound like?'

'Like a . . . Like a man's voice. You know, older. Deeper.'

'Did he ask you anything else? My room number?'

She shook her head again, lips pursed, tears streaming down her cheeks. 'I didn't do anything wrong.'

'I haven't once suggested you did, Ms Richards. Yet you keep on asking me that question. Is there something you want to tell me?'

'I can't afford to lose this job. If I do, I'll be out on the street.'

'You're not going to lose your job. After you finished cleaning my room, did you leave the curtains open, or were they closed?'

'I won't have nowhere else to go.'

'Ms Richards, I'm simply asking whether –'

'I won't have nowhere else to go. If Charlie Baker thinks I did something wrong, he'll fire me. You don't understand. You don't understand.'

Darby tried to speak to the woman, but it was pointless. Laurie Richards was no longer listening; she had turned away, sobbing.

Darby put her arm around the woman's shoulder, about to escort her into the hotel, when a sheriff's car turned the corner, Lancaster behind the wheel.

30

Deputy Sheriff Lancaster worked a pack of Lucky Strikes out of his pocket as he moved around the front of the cruiser and stepped on to the sidewalk. He wore a Stetson and a pair of mirrored sunglasses that seemed too big for his small face.

He was about to put a cigarette into his mouth when he saw the sheets of tear shining on Laurie Richards's cheeks and froze. His gaze darted between her and Darby.

'Everything all right here?' he asked.

Laurie Richards straightened and almost stood at attention, like a weary foot soldier who suddenly found herself in the presence of a colonel. 'Everything's fine,' she said, and used the back of her hand to wipe the wetness from her face. Then, to Darby, 'If you don't have any more questions, I'd like to go back to work. I got a busy day ahead of me.'

Darby nodded. 'Thank you for your time, Ms Richards. Before you go, can you give me directions to Cindy's Diner?'

'Go straight up Main and take your second left on to Cranmore Avenue. From there, it's about three, maybe four blocks, right across from Gilly's Hardware.'

'Thanks.' Darby slipped on her sunglasses, wanting to leave. But she'd be damned if she was going to slink away.

Lancaster waved his hand at Richards, who had started towards the door. 'Hold up there a sec, Laurie, I actually came here to see you.'

Richards perked up.

'I need three, maybe four rooms,' he said with avuncular affection. 'Think you could accommodate me at such short notice?'

Richards brightened. 'Yes. Yes, of course, Sheriff. Absolutely. Anything you need. You want them right now? I only ask because I'd like to air them out, give everything a good and thorough cleaning.'

'Don't need 'em till later this evening, so you take your time. If there's a problem, just give me a call. Otherwise I'll be back here around five or so with the boys.' He placed a hand on her shoulder as he handed over his card. He winked. 'Thanks, hon.'

Laurie Richards was either the world's loneliest woman or she had completely bought into Lancaster's aw-shucks corn-pone sincerity. The woman blushed and, smiling, shuffled away, the ledger cradled against her chest. She glanced once over her shoulder.

Lancaster didn't notice; his attention was on Darby. With his head he nodded towards Richards, who had already disappeared inside the hotel. 'What was that about?'

'I had some questions about what happened last night. Why you staying here?'

'With gas prices the way they are, it'll be cheaper than me and my people driving back and forth every day from Brewster. Laurie see or hear anything?'

'No.' *And even if she did, I wouldn't tell you*, Darby added privately.

'So what did you say that made her burst into tears?'

'She was afraid she'd done something wrong. She thought she was going to lose her job.'

'You always conduct your interviews outside?'

'I like the fresh air.'

'Well, you'll get plenty of that here, although the view's for shit.'

Lancaster was telling the truth. Downtown Red Hill looked even more depressing in the daylight. Abandoned and forgotten. The movie theatre on the corner had the word CLOSED in crooked letters on the weathered marquee. The tallest building, made of brick, had a clock with a broken hand and OUT OF BUSINESS signs plastered on soaped windows. It was an old Sears building, the faded letters still visible on the rotted sign hanging on the roof.

'Laurie's got a right to be scared,' he said. 'Man who owns this place is one mean prick. Takes a certain delight, maybe even pride, in it.'

'Charlie Baker.'

Lancaster nodded and removed a cigarette from his pack.

'You know him?' Darby asked.

'Well enough to know he's the type of guy who wakes up with a haemorrhoid and looks for someone to blame. So he goes to the pool of people who work for him. Woman like Laurie, he knows he's got her painted into a corner and he takes full advantage of it – of her. She don't hop-to the right way he'll shitcan her and she'll be out on the street.'

'Like the way you shitcanned Nelson last night?'

Lancaster looked into her eyes as he lit his cigarette with a Zippo. He inhaled deeply.

'I know what you think happened last night, the version Nelson fed you,' he said, tendrils of smoke drifting from his nostrils. 'Truth is, the second you left he went into the house to take pictures with a disposable camera. Why would he do such a thing? Glad you asked. Mr Nelson, like every other cop in Red Hill, is looking for ways to supplement his income. There's a tabloid website and supermarket rag-mag with the oh so original name of *Crime & Punishment*. You familiar with it?'

Unfortunately, she was. The popular website for true-crime fans had posted a lot of articles about her over the years, the majority of which were filled with bullshit quotes from a 'close pal' of hers and 'a source close to the investigation'.

'Williams tell you they and a few other reporters were here sniffing around last month?'

Darby shook her head and glanced at her watch.

'What a surprise,' Lancaster said. 'These bottom feeders were all over town. A serial killer who targets families makes good copy, brings in a lot of traffic to their websites – especially if photos are involved. You know how much a couple of crime scene photos would be worth? Take a guess.'

'A few hundred bucks?'

'Try two gees. Autopsy photos are worth more. I know

this because the same reporter from *Crime & Punishment* who approached Nelson approached me. This guy gave me the whole song and dance, promised to pay in cash, no questions.'

'You take him up on it?'

Lancaster ignored the barb and steamrolled ahead. 'This reporter, I found his card tucked into Nelson's wallet. I'm willing to bet he neglected to tell you that little detail, didn't he?'

Darby said nothing. She slipped on her sunglasses as Lancaster took another deep draw from his cigarette.

'When I found out about the Downes family,' Lancaster said, 'I drove here in my truck, not a cruiser, and parked at the house and watched the action through a pair of binoculars. I did that because Red Hill PD's leaking info like a sieve. My boss and the people he reports to don't want that to happen any more, so guess who gets to be the bad guy? State's trying to attract some major players to Red Hill, get them to build a Walmart and some other big box stores – places that'll create jobs. We don't want to scare them away with stories of a serial killer and a police station that can't do *its* job correctly.'

'Anything else?'

'Why you in such a rush to leave? I got BO or something?'

'Agent Hoder's waiting on me.'

'Okay, I'll make it quick, then. You and I got off on the wrong foot. My fault entirely.' He took another drag from his cigarette and pushed his tongue against the inside of his cheek. Then he blew out a long stream of smoke.

'Both my ex-wives said they've met autistic kids who've got better social skills, and the woman I'm with now, I'm pretty sure she shares their view.'

'My apologies.'

'For what?'

'For the woman you're currently with. She has my deepest sympathy.'

'See, there you go again with the mouth. I'm trying to be sincere and you're treating me like I'm a walking case of syphilis.' He sighed heavily. 'Look, when I work a case, I've got all the subtlety and personality of a heat-seeking missile. All I see is the target. My manners go right out the window. I didn't mean to jump down your throat last night or make that Midol crack. That was wrong. Out of line. But you came on hard and strong, and I went into overdrive. You feds get my dander up.'

'I don't work for the feds. I'm just a consultant.'

'But you *have* worked on my side of the fence. You know what it's like when the feds come in and invade your turf. They piss on you and then expect you to clean it up with a smile and say thank you, Massa. I don't operate that way. I'm not built for bullshit. So the thing last night and what happened in the squad room – I was in attack mode. I was wrong, it was out of line, and I apologize.'

His tone had been conciliatory and humble, and his speech had hit all the right notes. It also smacked of delivery by rote.

Lancaster held out his hand. Darby stared at it a moment, thinking, about to shake it to make peace and get on with her day, when she saw his gaze, whether on purpose or unconsciously, fix on her chest and compare what he saw in the daylight to the pictures on his phone.

Darby tucked her hands in her jacket pockets.

'They said you weren't big on apologies,' he said.

'Who's "they"?'

'Your former colleagues in Boston. I talked to a couple of them this morning, wanted to see if I'd read you wrong. They had all sorts of interesting things to say about you. Guy who runs the Crime Lab, your former boss, Pratt? He called you Dick Cheney with tits. I now understand what he meant.'

'Does it ever bother you?'

'Does what bother me?'

'Being the product of a busted rubber.'

Lancaster took a long draw on his cigarette, his narrowly set eyes void of expression. 'Not that I expect it to change your mind or stop you from treating me and everyone else here like yesterday's dog shit, but you should ask Ray about the pictures *he* took inside the Connelly house.'

What's he talking about? Lancaster had accused the patrolman Nelson of taking pictures inside the Connelly house.

Lancaster saw her puzzlement and, grinning, added, 'That's right. Williams also took pictures inside the house. That man, I'm coming to learn, is full of all sorts of surprises.' Lancaster flicked his cigarette into the air. 'Have a nice life.'

Cindy's Diner operated out of a refurbished trolley car built against the side of a decrepit brick building. The red-and black-painted wood had a high-gloss lacquer, and a bright neon band of blue light glowed around the edges of a mansard roof. Smoke puffed from a roof vent and scattered in the breeze.

The inside was small and hummed with activity. A single waitress, a tall, slim woman with long black hair held behind her head with an elastic band and wearing blood-red lipstick, hustled around the room delivering steaming plates of food and refilling coffee cups. The long stainless-steel counter running the length of the diner held an assortment of scraggly men dressed in hunting jackets.

Darby found Hoder sitting to the far left, next to a window, in a booth made of red vinyl. He had a stack of blueberry pancakes in front of him and his hand shook when he picked up a mug and slurped his coffee.

She slid into the bench across from him. 'You really hypoglycaemic?'

Hoder nodded. 'My doctor thinks I'm fast approaching adult-onset diabetes,' he said. 'Plus I had the distinct feeling Ms Richards would be more comfortable talking to a woman, alone.'

Darby told him about her conversation with Laurie Richards. She was about to tell him about Lancaster when the waitress came over, coffee pot in hand.

Hoder said, 'She'll have coffee – and a full breakfast.' Then, to Darby, 'Eat something. That's an order. I can't have you passing out from hunger.'

Darby ordered steak and eggs, with a side of hash and pancakes. When the waitress left, Darby told Hoder about her interaction with the deputy sheriff.

'This Charlie Baker fellow sounds like a real mensch,' Hoder said wryly. 'That explains Laurie Richards's odd behaviour. She's been acting like a cat trapped in a room full of rocking chairs ever since we arrived.'

'What's your take on Lancaster?'

'You want to know if he's a psychopath.'

Darby chuckled, shook her head. 'Am I really that transparent?' she asked.

'No, not at all. I've been wondering that myself.' He slurped his coffee and then wiped his mouth with a balled-up napkin. 'I was told he started out his career at the sheriff's office writing speeding tickets. Then, three years later, he was promoted to deputy sheriff. What's that say to you?'

'That's he's a career climber and opportunistic son of a bitch with a grandiose sense of self-worth. Someone with superficial charm who's ruthless and lacks remorse.'

'All the traits of a psychopath.'

'Or a successful politician.'

Hoder tapped his palm against the table and pointed a

finger at her. 'Exactly the point I was going to make,' he said. 'These two Harvard psychiatrists, you may know them, Doctors Rand and Hein, they did a landmark study on how the personality aspects we generally associate with psychopaths – confidence, fearlessness, charisma, ruthlessness and a laser-like focus – are, in fact, the same character traits found in highly successful politicians, surgeons, CEOs and world leaders.'

'I read their paper. Lancaster hits all the right notes, minus the charisma.'

'Yes. Unfortunately for Mr Lancaster, he was cursed with a personality that makes you want to drive your fist through his skull. My guess is he compensates for it with sheer ruthlessness, manipulating people who are powerless and moving them around like chess pieces.'

'So explain to me why he's suddenly developed such a major hard-on for the Red Hill Ripper.'

'The killer represents an opportunity.'

'For career advancement.'

'And fame,' Hoder said. 'Look at your own career. You caught a serial killer who eluded capture for, what, almost three decades, and you became a minor celebrity in both the legitimate press and tabloids.'

'That wasn't my choice. I didn't seek it out.'

'I wasn't suggesting you did. And by fame I don't mean he simply yearns to see his face plastered in the papers and all over TV, although I'm sure that plays a part in his psychological drive. It's recognition he craves. By catching the Ripper, Lancaster proves he's not only smarter than the killer but also smarter than you, me, the FBI. He's angling to take over the case now because we represent a collective threat – you, especially.'

'Because he's a misogynist.'

'That's probably true,' Hoder said. 'He finds you particularly vexing.'

'Meaning?'

'You didn't flinch when he tried to embarrass you in front of a roomful of men, and you didn't run away and hide in shame or embarrassment when those pictures of you were exposed.'

'The way a normal woman should,' Darby added.

Hoder's smile was warm. Paternal. 'You're far from normal,' he said. 'In all my travels, I can honestly say I've never met a woman like you. It's your capacity for violence that threatens men like Teddy Lancaster. You can handle yourself physically, and you're a killer.'

'I'm not a killer.'

'You've killed before and you have the *capacity* to kill again. And you will, in the right circumstances, without hesitation.' There was no judgement in his voice, just a cold, clinical tone. 'You represent castration anxiety in the metaphorical sense – you have the power to emasculate men, make them feel powerless.'

'Do you feel that way?'

Hoder didn't have a chance to answer; the waitress had returned, but she wasn't carrying any plates, just a cordless phone. She pressed a finger to her lips, signalling for them to be quiet. She placed the phone on their table and then she reached inside her apron and came back with a receipt that had been folded once and handed it to Darby.

Darby unfolded the piece of paper and read the bold, black writing:

DON'T SPEAK

LEAVE YOUR CELL ON THE TABLE & STEP OUTSIDE W/CORDLESS

ALONE.

32

Darby handed the note to Hoder as she got to her feet. Phone in hand, she left the diner and moved down the short set of steps to the sidewalk. The afternoon sky was filled with bright sun. She put on her sunglasses.

Two vehicles, a compact car and a truck, were parked on the kerb across the street, in front of a hardware store called Gilly's. She could see shadows moving behind the glass as her gaze broke to her left, to another street dotted with maples and aspens, the mountains visible in the distance. To her right, on the route she'd used to come here, she saw a pawnshop. There had been cars parked in front of it moments earlier; now they were gone.

The cordless rang. A spike of fear shot its way up her arm as she pressed the TALK button and brought the receiver up to her ear.

'Hello.'

'You leave your phone on the table?'

The caged breath trapped in her throat dissolved. The caller on the other end of the line was Ray Williams.

'That was you who gave the waitress that message?'

'Yeah,' Williams said. 'She told you guys not to talk, right?'

'She did. How'd you know I was here?'

'Laurie Richards told me. I –'

'You there right now, at the hotel?' Darby was thinking about the possibility of another listening device having been placed somewhere on the front desk.

'No, I'm calling you from a payphone on Main,' Williams said. 'Coop called Robinson looking for you and Hoder, and then the chief got on the horn to me, on the police radio. Told me to call him on a land-line. Sorry for the cloak-and-dagger shit, but Coop's instructions were real specific. You got a pen?'

'Yeah.' Darby fished out a ballpoint from her breast pocket. 'What's going on?'

'I don't know the details yet, just the broad strokes. Coop wants you to call him, said it's urgent. I've got the number for you.'

Williams gave it to her. He agreed to meet her at the diner and then hung up.

Darby dialled Coop's number. The phone on the other end of the line had barely rung before Coop said, 'Darby?'

'I got your note and I'm standing outside a diner talking on a cordless.'

'It's about those pictures of you in your birthday suit. It's malware. We're talking two separate programs. The malware hidden in the first photo, it runs a program that turns your cell's speaker into a portable, walking microphone. You type in the number for the infected cell and you can listen in on any conversation.'

'And the second one?'

'Turns your cell into a GPS tracker. The son of a bitch knows where you are – where we all are – at all times, even if your phone is turned off. As long as the battery is connected, he can listen in on any conversation and check your GPS signal whenever he wants, using a laptop or a portable surveillance receiver.'

'What sort of range are we talking about?'

'Don't know yet,' Coop said. 'Cell signals are spotty, at best, in Red Hill. You may get a bar or two, but there's a good chance the signal will drop altogether. The geeks here who specialize in this stuff think he's using either a satellite phone or a laptop with a 4G connection, maybe even a satellite internet card. We don't know the frequency yet. For all we know he's simply using a portable receiver and is parked somewhere within a quarter of a mile of you. You seen anyone following you?'

'No, but I wasn't really paying much – oh shit.'

'What?'

Darby squeezed the phone and rubbed the back of her head. 'He knows, Coop.'

'Knows what?'

'Everything.' Darby pinched her temples between her fingers and then gave him a quick rundown about the bug she'd found inside her hotel phone. 'When I came back to tell Hoder, I had my iPhone on me. It was in my pocket. He heard me talking to the woman who works the reception desk, Laurie Richards. How is it this guy always seems to be two steps ahead of us?'

'Maybe not,' Coop said. 'I'm looking at a satellite map of your area. Street you want is called Lomas.'

'What's there?'

'The phone used to send out your nudie pics. I gave the number to the geeks, and they plugged it into their tracking system. They couldn't trace the signal earlier because there was no signal trace. Our guy must've disconnected the battery from his phone right after he sent them. Then, five, maybe ten minutes ago, the signal for that number came back on. It's coming from Lomas Street, near the Red Hill Public Library. You're 2.3 miles away from it. You drive there?'

'Hoder did. He's inside the diner. Has the signal moved at all?'

'No, it's remained stationary since it came back on.'

'Give me the directions – never mind, there's a police cruiser coming my way. It's probably Williams.'

'I'll be here for another hour,' Coop said. 'Mobile lab's almost done being fixed.'

Darby ran into the street, her heart bursting with adrenalin, and waved down the patrol car. She saw Hoder watching her from the diner window.

'Stay there,' she called to him as the patrol car accelerated towards her, its engine climbing.

Ray Williams stopped next to her, his window down, his face etched with concern and worry. He was about to speak when she motioned for him to be quiet.

Williams looked at her, puzzled. She leaned inside the car, feeling the rough grain of his whiskers against her cheek and inhaling the leathery scent of his cologne as she whispered into his ear: 'Give me your phone and pop the trunk. I'll explain later.'

His phone was a standard flip model. She opened the compartment in the back, removed the battery and tossed it inside the trunk.

'Public library on Lomas,' Darby said as she slid into the passenger's seat, shutting the door behind her. 'Take a right –'

'I know where it is.'

'Drive fast. No sirens. Here's what's going on.'

33

Ray Williams came to a three-way stop; Darby leaned forward in her seat and, looking to her left and up Lomas Street, saw two vehicles parked against the kerb in front of the library: a white Toyota Camry with a moon roof and, in front of it, a black Ford Econoline van with tinted windows the colour of smoked charcoal and a sagging rear bumper held up by rope.

'That van was parked across from the hotel this morning,' Darby said.

'You're sure?'

'Positive. Same rope, and it didn't have a back plate.'

Williams turned left, on to Lomas, and, as they approached the library, a small, ranch-like building shaded by trees, she saw a mother trying to cradle an overexcited toddler against her thin chest while she fed a stack of books and DVDs, one by one, into the returns bin set up near the front doors. The building's windows were dark.

'You see her?'

'I see her,' Williams said, his gaze locked on the mother who had placed her child, a boy with blond hair like fine thread, on his feet. 'Camry's got to be hers. There's no one in there.'

Darby found it difficult to sit still, and her mouth was dry. A hot wire had lit up inside her brain. She shifted in her seat and reached for the door handle as the mother gripped her son's pudgy hand. The boy wobbled, swaying, and then he began to march forward on his unsteady legs, bringing his sneakered feet up and down, up and down, slamming them against the pavement with purpose, like a drunk assigned the task of stomping grapes for wine.

Darby reached inside her jacket. 'I don't see any other vehicles here,' she said, and undid the strap for her shoulder holster. 'I don't want to wait for backup either.'

Williams was nodding. 'If our boy's in the van, he might panic, decide to come out shooting. We don't need a hostage situation here.'

'Agreed. Let me out and light it up.'

Williams slowed as Darby threw open the door. She got out, gun in hand, slammed the door shut and started running. Williams pulled ahead, tyres biting into the pavement and sirens blaring. The mother scooped her son into her arms, her eyes wide with terror and her face turning as white as chalk.

'Go,' Darby said to the woman, waving her hand. 'Get out of here.'

The mother ran with her son clutched to her chest, the boy shrieking not from fear but from agitation at having been denied his walk to their car. Williams came to a stop directly in front of the van, parking diagonally so the van couldn't move, boxing it in between the Camry and the cruiser. Then Williams emerged from the car gripping a Mossberg 12-gauge shotgun with a tactical light and a heat shield. Darby approached the van from her right. It didn't have a back licence plate.

Williams placed the shotgun on the top of the car roof. He looked down the target sight and yelled over the siren: '*Get out of the van with your hands locked behind your head.*'

Darby had reached the van's passenger door. The glass was tinted; she couldn't see who was in there. She gripped the door handle and pulled, hearing the lock click back as Williams called out, '*Come out of the van with your hands locked behind your head.*'

The van's front cab was empty. Darby left the door hanging open as she darted in a crouch around the front. She looked at Williams, gave him the clear signal and then crab-walked to the van's sliding side door. She reached it, stopped. Another glance at Williams. He nodded and she put her hand on the handle.

'*Come out of the van,*' Williams called out again, and Darby turned the handle. The door was unlocked and she slid it open, her stomach clenching.

'*Down,*' Williams screamed over the sirens. '*Down on your stomach, right now.*'

A high-pitched scream came from somewhere inside the van. Darby heard movement and, still crouching, she swung around the corner, looked down the target sight of her SIG and saw a heavy-set woman dressed in black sweatpants and a matching sweatshirt, her stomach swelling like a balloon behind the thin fabric. She sat on a bare mattress and the feet of her wool socks had holes in them and her dirty blonde hair looked damp. The woman's hands were held up, her arms trembling. She didn't have a weapon.

'It was an oversight,' the woman said. She had a reedy and nasal voice. 'I meant to –'

'Shut it,' Darby said, her eyes roving through the van and knowing something was wrong. The interior was stacked with milk crates full of clothes. A handful of business suits hung from a ceiling rail. The cardboard boxes scattered along the floor held canned food, meal-replacement bars and bottled water. Darby saw rolls of toilet paper and paper towels and a laptop sitting on a desk made of plywood.

The woman was the only one there, and, while she wasn't armed, Darby still had to play it safe. 'Face down on the mattress. Do it.'

The frightened woman complied.

'Now put your hands behind your back,' Darby said, the adrenalin shifting into low gear.

After the woman complied, Darby moved inside the van and cuffed her wrists. Darby looked to Williams, who was still peering down the shotgun propped up on the car roof.

'*Clear*,' Darby yelled to him.

Williams pushed himself off the roof with a dejected expression on his face. He moved back inside the cruiser and killed the sirens.

34

Darby found the woman's Coach wallet lying on the floor. She pulled it open and read the name: 'Elisa Pike'.

The woman turned her head to the side. She had a fine web of lines around her eyes and mouth, and she had put on mascara. Her damp hair smelled of shampoo, and her skin and clothes smelled clean. There was also a faint whiff of perfume, a sickeningly sweet scent that reminded Darby of Love's Baby Soft.

Darby looked at the date of birth printed on the licence. Elisa A. Pike was fifty-seven years old.

'It says here you live at 123 Alabaster Lane,' Darby said. 'In Red Hill.'

'I used to, until the bank took away my house.' The woman's face darkened.

'And now you live in this van.'

'It's perfectly legal,' she said coldly. 'As long as I don't have any kids or animals, which I *don't*, and as long as I'm not bothering anyone, which I'm *not*, I can live here. I checked. You can't arrest –'

'Your cell phone, where is it?'

'I don't own one.'

'Don't lie to me.'

'*I'm not!*' she shrieked, indignant. Her sweatshirt had

ridden up from her waist and Darby saw skin as white as a fish's belly. 'I had to cancel my cell three months ago because I couldn't afford it any more. I haven't owned –'

The Pike woman cut herself off. Her eyes widened and her small lips formed an **O**. Williams had stepped up to the van's doorway. She looked at him as she said, 'It's not mine.'

'What's not yours?' Darby asked, handing the woman's licence to Williams.

'The phone I found this morning,' Pike said. Williams had moved away, back to the cruiser, to use the radio to call in the licence. 'I woke up and found it sitting on my windshield. It was tucked underneath the windshield wiper so it wouldn't blow away or fall when I drove off. I didn't know why it –'

'Stop. Let's start at the beginning. What time did you wake up this morning?'

'Early. Around eight.'

'Where did you sleep last night? What street?'

'This one. I slept right here. I sleep here because I use the library computers. They have free internet. I use them for job hunting. Go ahead and check if you don't believe me. They open in another hour.'

'Then why did I see this exact same van parked this morning in front of the Wagon Wheel Saloon? Can you explain that to me?'

The woman visibly stiffened, the rolls of fat jiggling underneath her clothes. She didn't answer.

'And you showered this morning,' Darby said.

'Being clean and looking presentable, that's a crime now?' No attitude, just a mild bewilderment.

Then Darby remembered the anxious way Laurie Richards had stared at the van, and she said, 'I think you parked outside the bar because you and Laurie Richards have some sort of arrangement whereby she lets you use the hotel shower. Only you didn't go there right away because you saw cops standing out front and didn't want her to get into any trouble. Am I right?'

Elisa Pike's gaze had retreated inwards. Her mouth was a tight seam, her lips quivering, as if to cage the riot of words that were trying to escape.

'Here's the thing I want you to understand, Ms Pike. I don't care about whatever . . . arrangement you've got with Laurie Richards. The only thing I care about is this phone you supposedly found magically sitting on your front window.'

'I *did* find it. It *was* sitting on my front window, right under the windshield wiper. I swear on the Holy Father and our Lord and Saviour Jesus Christ.'

'What time was this?'

'Is Laurie gonna get in trouble, because I promised her I wouldn't tell anyone about –'

'Tell me what time you found the phone.'

'Noon, I think. Maybe a few minutes after. After the sheriff left, I went into the hotel and used the shower. When I came back, the phone was sitting on my windshield, just like I said.'

Darby pulled a pair of latex gloves from her back pocket. 'Where is it?'

'In the box with my résumés and Bible. Look up to your left, the box next to my socks.' The woman nodded with her chin. 'Can you please take these handcuffs off me? They hurt like the dickens.'

'I will when Detective Williams comes back.'

'Why? I didn't do anything wrong.'

That's probably true, Darby thought as she snapped on the latex. Elisa Pike seemed harmless enough: a woman in unfortunate circumstances struggling to get by with grace and dignity. But that didn't mean Darby could afford to be careless.

'May I at least sit up?' Pike asked.

'No, please stay right where you are. This will only take a minute.' Darby pinched the small antenna between her fingers and lifted it out of the box.

'I thought a Good Samaritan had left it there for me,' Pike said. 'They sometimes do that, you know. Leave a box of things on my car, right near the windshield, things like baby wipes and toothpaste, cans of soup. They're not looking for anything in return, they're just kind, good Christian people.'

The phone was a disposable model, a high-end burner that allowed you to send text messages and pictures. It also came equipped with a camera.

'I thought someone had left it there to help me with my job search, or so I could call my ex and say hello to my kids.' The woman swallowed, pained, and blinked back tears. 'I can't always use the phone at the hotel or the library.'

Darby worked an evidence bag from her back pocket. 'Laurie Richards takes your messages?'

'Yes. It wasn't charged. The phone.'

'Meaning?'

'Meaning when I turned it on it didn't work. I didn't think someone would deliberately leave a broken phone on my windshield, so I opened the compartment there in the back, the one where you put the battery, and found that it wasn't plugged in. So I plugged it in and it worked fine. It's got fifty-six minutes of talk-time left.'

Williams's head popped up over the cruiser's roof. Darby signalled for him to wait.

'Ms Pike, did you see who left the phone?'

'No.'

'Did you see anyone on the street, someone you recognized maybe, loitering near your van?'

'No. The only thing on my mind at that moment was . . . getting out of the hotel without being spotted. Laurie has done me a huge favour, allowing me to clean up there and sometimes sleep, and I don't need anyone spreading gossip and having it get back to that awful excuse for a human being, Mr Charles Baker!'

Darby stepped outside with the phone wrapped up in the evidence bag.

'She's one of our town vagrants,' Williams said. 'She's got a sheet of complaints —'

'*What did you call me?*' Pike shrieked.

Darby turned around and saw that the woman had rolled herself on to her side. Then Elisa A. Pike suddenly hoisted her enormous bulk into a sitting position, a deep level of injustice burning in her damp, bright eyes.

'I'm not some panhandler! I haven't taken one gosh-darn nickel from the state or the federal government or from anyone else after I lost my job or after the greedy banks took my home away!'

Darby said, 'Miss Pike, we're going to need to take you to the station and get you fingerprinted. We need your prints for comparison purposes. It's just a formality.'

But the woman was no longer listening. Her eyes were fixed on Williams, who now stood in the van's doorway, his hands held in the air, by his shoulders. 'I meant no disrespect, ma'am,' he said. 'I apologize if –'

'I don't want one of your rinky-dink apologies. I bought this van legally, with my own hard-earned money – go ahead and check the registration if you want to!'

'Yes, Ms Pike, I understand, but –'

'YOUR DAY IS COMING, SIR!' The woman's face had turned scarlet, and when she trembled it made Darby think of a volcano seconds away from erupting, its flames and lava about to burn everyone and reduce them to ash. 'THE WHOLE GOSH-DARN BUNCH OF YOU ARE GONNA SEE WHAT IT'S LIKE TO SCRAPE BY LIKE THE REST OF US HARD-WORKING AND GOD-FEARING FOLKS! NO MORE SUCKING OFF THE GOVERNMENT TIT, YOU'RE GONNA BE FORCED TO SEE HOW REAL PEOPLE LIVE, HOW WE –'

The woman cut herself off. Beads of sweat ran down

her forehead and her lips trembled and then her eyes widened in fear at an image only she could see.

'My heart,' she said. 'Oh God, no.'

Then Elisa A. Pike, formerly of 123 Alabaster Lane in Red Hill, Colorado, fell back against the van's wall, clawing at her chest.

35

Darby darted inside the van. The second she removed the handcuffs from the woman's wrists, Elisa Pike flopped down on the mattress, her enormous bulk momentarily shaking the vehicle. Darby tried to perform CPR – chest compressions following by mouth-to-mouth – but the woman wasn't interested. Pike pushed Darby's hands away; she kicked and thrashed. At one point Pike slapped her face.

When the ambulance arrived three minutes later, along with three patrol cars, Elisa Pike had a sudden change of heart, so to speak. The moment she sighted the male EMT with the sandy blond hair and button-shaped nose, she stopped fighting. Her eyes rolled back into her skull and once more she started to thrash against the mattress, as if she were experiencing an epileptic seizure, maybe even a stroke. She clawed at her chest again, bellowing, 'My heart, oh dear Lord, my heart.'

Darby stood outside the van, the sun warm against her scalp, as the EMTs worked on the woman. Williams had watched the whole thing as though it were an impromptu circus performance.

'Don't feel bad,' he said. 'She's does this every time.'

'She's done this *before*?'

'That's what they told me over the radio.' He scratched

the corner of his mouth. 'Seems every time she's caught loitering, she fakes a heart attack or some other major trauma and wins a free trip to the ER. She gets a soft bed and three squares and free cable TV for forty-eight hours. And she's not the only one doing it either.' Then, with a long sigh, he added, 'She'll probably turn around and try to sue the town for harassment or negligence, probably both, whatever the phonebook lawyer recommends. Not that it'll amount to anything. What's that saying, you can't get blood from a stone?'

Darby touched the cheek where Pike had scratched her, pulled away her finger and saw blood. 'I need to go back to the diner.'

Williams checked his watch. 'We should hit the road and get going to Brewster. We'll need some time to go over the bodies.'

'Hoder's waiting for me in the diner.'

Williams drove her back to Cindy's and dropped her out front.

Darby found Hoder sitting in the booth where she'd left him. The foot traffic had thinned out, and his plates had been cleared away. He had a glass of water in front of him, his expression that of a man who was suffering from a sudden bowel obstruction. Darby thought it might have to do with the man sitting across the table from him: Teddy Lancaster.

Darby returned the cordless to the front counter, thanked the waitress and approached the table. The breakfast she'd ordered was packed up in a Styrofoam container, a plastic set of utensils wrapped in a paper napkin resting on its top.

Hoder didn't speak as he held out her iPhone. His expression was grave now, loaded with an I-told-you-so wisdom she didn't want to face or acknowledge.

She had received a new text message. The incoming phone number was different, and there were no pictures this time, just words:

NICE TRY, BITCH

I CAN'T WAIT TO HEAR YOU BEG

I change my mind about the grenades within five minutes of leaving my house. There are two reasons. First, a grenade is not a precise explosive. You pull the pin, throw it and hope for maximum collateral damage – and pray that you aren't one of the casualties. But the second and more pressing reason makes me return home. The grenades I own – while military-issue and used effectively in combat situations in Third World desert countries like Iraq – were purchased through black market channels in Montana, and I don't want to be driving across bumpy roads with them rattling underneath my car seat.

Besides, I have come up with a simpler and more effective plan: create a bomb that I can detonate remotely, using the prepaid disposable cell in my glove compartment. It would be easy to do, no more than half an hour's work. A single stick of dynamite can not only create a bone-crushing blast radius and pressure wave, it can also turn any vehicle into a massive high-velocity fragmentation grenade. A single stick strategically placed inside the Silver Moon Inn won't leave a sole survivor. Wait until night, when they're all asleep.

Then my thoughts shift back to the mistake I made at the Downes house, and the ground suddenly seems unsteady beneath my feet. I feel like a nauseous drunk standing on the bow of a ship that's cresting a wave. Sweating, I take out my cell phone.

I have only a single bar. I start to walk quickly, watching for the signal to jump. The second it does, I dial the number for the burner I gave Sarah, the one she carries with her at all times in case of an emergency, and duck into the alley between the old Army & Navy store and the building that once housed a Mexican restaurant.

Sarah answers immediately. 'What's wrong?'

I try to remove the fear from my voice. 'Nothing's wrong,' I say. 'I'm calling because I need you to do me a favour.'

'Okay.' Sarah is understandably nervous. Wary. I can count on one hand the times I've called her burner.

'I want you to hide,' I say. 'You know where to go.'

'Are you in trouble?'

I am, Sarah. I'm in deep trouble. I made a mistake at the Downes house, a huge, critical mistake, and I tried to fix it – I *thought* I'd fixed it. For the first time in my life, Sarah, I'm truly frightened.

'Baby?'

I'm thinking about the old furniture warehouse on the other side of town, where I've hidden a locked briefcase packed with $30,000 in cash and two fake Wyoming state licences with matching Social Security cards and passports. The passports won't stand up to scrutiny in this post 9/11 world, but the licences and cash will allow us to set up somewhere else – provided we can get out of town cleanly. I need to think about how to do that, and there's too much to think about, it's all going to come crashing down, I know it –

'Everything's fine,' I lie. 'This is just a precaution.'

'You want me to grab the suitcases?'

Yes, I want to say. Grab the suitcases and meet me at McClaren's Furniture, and we'll hit the road together. We'll have to ditch your car for another one, and then it's going to be just as I told you, we'll have to be real careful the first year or so because our faces and everything I did here in Red Hill will be plastered all over the internet, it's not like it was years ago when you could just pack up and hide, no, you're a fugitive every second of the day for the rest of your life and –

'No,' I say. 'There's no need for the suitcases. Just go and hide for me – and keep the burner with you.'

'Are you coming home?'

'Soon.'

'I love you.'

I hang up, thinking about the money, how much easier and simpler my life would be if I only had to worry about myself.

36

After Darby whispered in Hoder's ear that his phone was bugged, she asked him leave it on the table. Then she moved to the other side of the small diner, to a short hall leading to the restrooms, and waited for him to join her.

He did so a moment later. Lancaster remained at the booth, sipping coffee and staring idly out the window at Ray Williams.

'What does shithead want?' Darby asked, nodding at Lancaster with her chin.

'Trying to pry information out of me. What's going on?'

Darby gave Hoder a quick summary of her conversation with Coop and of the burner Elisa Pike had found on the front windshield of her van. Hoder kept shifting on his feet, nervous, like the floor beneath had turned to a thin sheet of ice that had cracked and split and was now possibly moments away from breaking.

'Right now our guy's hidden and safe and planning his next move,' Darby said. 'Maybe's he's already got another family picked out.'

'God forbid.'

'I think we can use his hatred of women against him, even flush him out of his hiding place.'

'How?'

'By focusing his rage on a particular target.'

'You.'

'He's already fixated on me, Terry. I say we keep it there.'

Hoder didn't balk, and he hadn't shown any surprise, and right then she knew he had already mulled over the idea of how he could use her as bait.

'What do you have in mind?' he asked.

Darby told him her plan. Hoder asked a few questions, and they went back and forth for a couple of minutes, hashing out minor details.

'Let me see what I can do,' he said.

Darby agreed to meet him at the station later that evening. Then she left the diner with her box of food and climbed back inside Williams's waiting cruiser, feeling exhausted and pissed off, her stomach grumbling with hunger. As an added bonus, she had a migraine-level headache.

Her iPhone and Williams's flip cell were still in the trunk; it was safe to talk. In a voice that seemed other than her own, Darby gave him the same rundown that she had just given Hoder. She didn't have to tell him about the software installed on the iPad in the Downes bedroom; Police Chief Robinson had already done that.

Williams got on the radio and sent out word about how the malware-infected pictures turned everyone's cell phone into a walking microphone and GPS device, and that the only way to shut it down was to disconnect the battery from the phone. For those people who, like Darby, owned an iPhone, there was no way to disconnect the battery. They were told to isolate their phones someplace safe, preferably at home. Chief Robinson was going to follow up with a departmental email.

Then Darby summarized her conversations with Laurie Richards and Teddy Lancaster. She left out the part where Lancaster had also accused *Williams* of taking pictures inside the Connelly home – not because she didn't want to broach the topic but because they had arrived at the Silver Moon Inn so that she could pick up her kit.

While inside the hotel, they ran into Laurie Richards, who, without much pressing, willingly admitted to allowing Elisa Pike to use a hotel room for the occasional shower, provided the woman coughed up the necessary five bucks.

Pike wasn't the only one. Richards also admitted to accommodating a certain number of discreet Red Hill townsfolk who had fallen on hard times. Showers were five dollars per family member, rooms twenty bucks a night, everything paid in cash, no food stamps accepted. Charlie Baker, the man who owned the hotel, knew nothing about any of this. The thought that he might find out reduced the woman to soul-tearing wails.

'Now I know why she was acting like someone with a hot coal pinched between her cheeks,' Darby said from the passenger's seat. She had her window half open and was balancing the Styrofoam box of food on her knees. 'She's terrified Baker's going to find out about her little sideline.'

'I'm sure as hell not going to tell him.'

They were driving on yet another long and seemingly endless road bordered by trees on both sides. Apart from the clean, fresh air, she couldn't fathom why anyone would willingly submit to living in such a barren and lonely place. As she ate, shovelling food into her mouth as though the container might be ripped from her hands at any moment, she kept glancing in the side-view mirror to see if they were being followed.

'Lancaster probably won't tell him either,' Williams said.

'Why's that?'

'Because Laurie's more valuable to him under his thumb. He'll use her to keep an eye on you guys. She'll do it too. What you told me about how Laurie bounced to attention when he came by? It's because she knows Lancaster's a power player in this whole incorporation thing. If she plays her cards right, he might throw a job her way, one with benefits. God knows she needs it.'

'You know her? Laurie?'

'Not personally. Her husband died in his sleep, and I had to go over and investigate, you know, rule out foul play.'

Williams had one hand draped over the steering wheel and was staring out the window, clearly distracted. Darby was sure he was processing the boatload of information she had just given him; she was having a hard time processing it herself. Her thoughts felt scattered, like a glass vase that had fallen and exploded into a hundred shards.

'I don't even know where to start,' he said.

Darby swallowed her food. 'Maybe that's the point.'

'What do you mean?'

'Chances are he was watching us yesterday inside the

bedroom,' she said. 'He knows I found the area he cleaned up. Maybe he's scared we found something. Or maybe he's scared we're going to find something.'

Williams shifted uneasily in his chair.

'What, you disagree?'

'No,' he said. 'Not at all.'

'So what does our guy do? He decides to crawl out from whatever rock he's been hiding under all this time and makes contact with me. Threatens me. But he knows I'm not going to blow Dodge because of a single phone call. So what does he do next?'

'He sends out those pictures of you and your . . . lady parts.'

Darby spoke with her mouth half full. '*Lady parts*? What're you, a nun?'

Williams chuckled. 'I was trying to be respectful,' he said, and glanced at her. 'You know, there's a stable right up the road. I can stop by and get you a feedbag.'

'Sorry, I'm starving.'

'Really? I hadn't noticed.'

Darby chewed, glad that Williams was joking around with her. She didn't want him feeling stiff and embarrassed over what had happened with the pictures.

Then, as if reading her mind, he said, 'This morning, everyone getting those photos –'

'It's over with. Done.'

'You always this cut and dry?'

'Once a psycho tries to split your head open like a cantaloup,' Darby said, forking a piece of steak, 'it puts everything else into perspective.'

When he didn't ask any questions, Darby knew he had Googled her and read all the articles about what she'd seen and endured inside Traveler's basement of horrors.

'I admired the way you handled it. And I'm sorry you had to go through that.'

'Thanks. Now back to our guy,' Darby said. 'He sends out these full-frontal shots showing my lady parts, as you described them, to everyone in Red Hill PD. On the surface it looks like he's trying to embarrass and frighten me. He hates women; it's a part of his MO. Maybe a part of him is hoping I'll pack my bags and leave. At the very least, he knows that sending out those pictures will throw me off my game, direct my attention elsewhere.

'But our guy's devised a more insidious plan. He places malware into the pictures and turns our phones into walking listening devices and GPS trackers. It's brilliant when you actually stop to think about it.'

'You *admire* this guy?'

'You don't?'

Williams glanced over to see if she was joking. She wasn't.

'The Red Hill Ripper isn't your average garden-variety sadist,' Darby said, and dug her fork back inside the container. 'He's completely unique, and extremely intelligent. And cunning. Don't ever forget that part. The pictures he sent of me, leaving that burner on Pike's van window – he's creating these multiple distractions to keep our focus away from what happened inside the Downes home, from whatever mistake he made there. And he's doing a great job of it. He's pulling the strings and making us dance. He's got us all involved in the world's biggest circle jerk.'

'Circle jerk,' Williams repeated flatly.

'They taught us to speak that way at Harvard. Part of the curriculum.'

Williams cracked a smile and then it suddenly died on his lips. He had withdrawn his attention again.

He inhaled deeply and visibly stiffened.

'There's something I need to tell you,' he said.

37

Darby speared the last piece of steak on her fork, wondering if Ray Williams was going to tell her about the pictures he'd been accused of taking inside the Connelly house.

'Teddy and his people are going to be a permanent fixture in our lives from now on,' Williams said.

'I kind of got that impression when Lancaster asked Laurie Richards to book him a few rooms. What's going on?'

Williams scratched the corner of his mouth. The air blowing inside the cruiser was cool and smelled of pine and wood smoke from a nearby fire.

'Robinson tell you that those pictures of you were also sent to four uniforms who were out on patrol this morning?'

Darby nodded. 'He said you went out to meet them, to make sure they deleted the photos from their phones,' she said. 'Thank you for that, by the way.'

'You're welcome. One of the guys I met after the debrief, Ricky Samuels, told me he saw a Brewster crime scene van parked in the driveway of the Downes house at about nine or so. I drove over to the house but the van wasn't there. No one was.

'I went back to the station and told the chief. Robinson

got on the horn and called the Brewster sheriff, guy by the name of Patterson. He told Robinson he thought it might be a good idea to have a second set of eyes go through the house. Form a joint task force that will take a good, hard look at –'

'The feds are already handling the evidence,' Darby said. 'Robinson mentioned that.'

'Their Denver office is sending back the two agents with forensics experience, along with the mobile lab.'

'This isn't Boston. Here, the sheriff's office has more power than a local police precinct.'

'You telling me this bozo sheriff believes he's got people who are better equipped and more experienced than those employed at the federal lab?'

'I'm saying there's a movement afoot to hand over the reins of the Red Hill Ripper investigation to Teddy after what happened last night at the Downes house.'

'That bullshit story about the patrolman, what's-his-name, Nelson, taking pictures inside the house?'

Williams sighed, like he was about to relieve himself of a great burden.

'There might be some truth to it,' he said.

Darby tossed her fork inside the container, closed the lid and gave him her full attention.

'The previous victims, the Connelly family,' Williams said. 'The state handled the crime scene like all the others. Only the photographer they had on call that night, a guy who has since been fired – he was doing a rather shoddy job, in my opinion. I think he might've been shitfaced – the guy reeked of booze. It was out of my control, but that didn't mean I had to take a back seat and let him do a shit job either. So I decided to take my own pictures. Only I made a mistake.'

Then his face contorted in shame and embarrassment. 'It was late and I was exhausted. Instead of heading back to the station and getting the digital camera, or going out and buying a disposable one, I used my cell phone.' He gripped the steering wheel so hard his knuckles looked like white moons. 'Some of the pictures I took? They wound up on *Crime & Punishment*. It's a website and –'

'I know what it is,' Darby said. 'How does this connect back to Nelson?'

'He was the first responding officer at the crime scene, and he saw me using my cell to take pictures. The following morning, I'd gone off to a budget meeting. I left my cell on my desk, maybe in my coat pocket. I can't remember. But I knew I had it when I went into the office that morning.

'When I came back from the meeting, I couldn't find my phone. A couple of people said they saw Nelson in my office right after I'd left. He didn't deny it – he'd gone in there to drop off a report – but he said he didn't know anything about my cell. The pictures were on the website the next day. Guess who got caught holding the shit-end of the stick?'

'You have any proof he took your phone?' Darby asked.

'Who else could it have been? He was the only one who knew I'd taken those pictures on my cell, and I sure as hell didn't do it.'

'Okay.'

'IAD cleared me. I agreed to take a poly. Passed it with flying colours.'

Darby was surprised a station as small as Red Hill had their own Internal Affairs Department. 'And Nelson?'

'He refused.' Williams smiled in sour triumph. 'The reporter who posted the pictures wouldn't give up his source, naturally, and when IAD couldn't link the pictures back to either of us, the case hit a dead end. Nelson and I both got a five-day suspension without pay and a letter of reprimand in our jackets.'

Darby stared out the window, the hum of the car tyres against the road and the wind blasting through her window vibrating against her ears. The sky was blue and cloudless, the air comfortably cool, like early autumn; it was hard to believe that a major snowstorm would roll in later today. She wondered what progress Hoder was making on their plan.

'I'm telling you the truth,' Williams said.

Darby heard a lot of heat in his voice. She rolled her head to him and saw his anger rising and falling, searching for an appropriate target.

'I believe you,' she said.

'Really? 'Cause your expression says otherwise.'

'If you're looking for absolution for something, Ray, I'm not wearing the right collar.'

'What's that supposed to mean?'

'Find someone else to be your whipping post.'

Williams's face burned, the skin as thin as paper, as if he'd been slapped. Then he sighed deeply, and the heat left his face and eyes.

'I'm sorry,' he said. 'I don't mean to take this out on you. When the subject of Teddy comes up, when he comes around here . . . Red Hill's too small to have its own IAD, so any conduct and personnel problems get kicked to Brewster. Teddy personally spearheaded my investigation. He acted like a kid who had just got his favourite toy for Christmas. When I passed the poly, the son of a bitch wouldn't let it go. He got off on ramming a two-by-four up my ass on a daily basis. The guy missed his calling as a plantation overseer.'

'Forget Lancaster,' Darby said. 'Don't let him bait you, he's not worth it.'

Little did she know she was about to eat her own words.

38

The Brewster County Coroner's Office serviced Red Hill and three other surrounding towns. Built during the Hoover administration, the old building contained a single autopsy suite that was nearly identical to just about every one Darby had visited over the course of her career: brick-red tile floors and grim white-painted walls; damp rubber mats arranged around an elevated steel surgical table, stainless-steel everywhere.

At 400 square feet, the autopsy room felt too small to accommodate her, Ray Williams and the coroner, Dr Felicia Gonzalez, a tiny woman with black hair and small, almost childlike fingers. She was slipping into a pair of fresh scrubs when they entered.

'Where should I set up?' Darby asked after the introductions were over.

Gonzalez opened her mouth to speak but no sound came out. She eyed Darby's rolling forensics kit, then looked at Williams like he was a Martian who had suddenly materialized out of thin air.

'We're here for the Downes autopsies,' he said.

'We did those first thing this morning,' Gonzalez replied.

Darby felt the air rush out of her lungs. The room went out of focus for a moment and the only sounds she heard were the insect-like hum of the fluorescent tube lights and water dripping from a nearby faucet.

'Harry came to see me personally,' Gonzalez said, perplexed. 'He moved the whole schedule around for you, Ray.'

'For *me*?' Williams blinked like a bright light had suddenly and without warning exploded in his face.

'Didn't he tell you?'

Williams spoke slowly, as if each word were a red-hot coal he had to pick up with his bare hands. '*If* he had told me, Felicia, do you think I'd be standing here right now with my dick in my hand?'

The woman stiffened at the word 'dick', hit with a sudden prudish streak. 'You don't have to use that type of lang–'

'Who collected the evidence?'

'Who do you think? Brewster forensics, the same people who did the other victims.'

Williams scratched the corner of his eye, his face crimson. He kept swallowing, his jaw muscles bunching like walnuts.

Gonzalez waved her hands in defiant surrender. 'Don't take this out on me, Ray. You have an issue with Harry, take it up with him.'

'I plan on it.'

Then Williams pushed open the swinging door and bolted into the hallway.

Darby stared at the autopsy table and thought about the nameless and faceless forensics people from Brewster who had collected the victims' clothing and examined their bodies prior to the autopsy. She had no idea of their collective experience, or their level of commitment, or the type of equipment and chemicals they had used. And she had been denied the chance to look over everything herself; all she could think about was the possibility of some missed or overlooked piece of evidence, some key piece that had been washed down the drain at the base of the stainless-steel table.

Gonzalez got busy, dressing. When she spoke, her voice suddenly seemed loud in the cold room. 'I thought he'd been told. Ray.'

'Who's Harry?'

'The chief medical examiner, Harry Stein. The man responsible for this lovely establishment.' Then: 'I'm sorry your time was wasted.'

A rumbling, grinding sound filled the room. Then it stopped and the door to an outdated freight elevator opened, revealing a morgue attendant and a rolling cart with a body bag on top. They were barely able to fit inside the tight space.

'Where are the bodies now?' Darby asked.

'Dunnigan & Sweet Funeral Home in Red Hill,' Gonzalez replied.

'I'd like to read your report and see the pictures.'

'I'll let Ray know when I've finished my report.'

'And when do you think that might be?'

Gonzalez made no effort to hide her displeasure. 'When I get a moment to breathe,' she said curtly. 'We're backed up, in case you haven't noticed. Now, if you'll excuse me.'

The door swung open and Theodore Lancaster stepped into the room.

'Sorry I'm late,' he said, and moved to the corner of the room where the disposable scrubs, masks and gloves were kept. 'Who do we have up first?'

'The Downes autopsies were done this morning,' Darby said. 'But you already knew that, didn't you?'

Lancaster put on a decent show of appearing shocked. But he couldn't hide the confidence and self-satisfaction exuding from his pores and posture.

'This is the first time I'm hearing about it, swear to God.' He looked at the body being lifted on to the table, an older woman with saggy breasts and thick hips and legs dimpled with cellulite, and Darby heard a ripping sound in her head, like cloth tearing, and in her mind's eye she pictured a sutured wound, the incision disturbed and bleeding, infected.

He isn't worth it, Darby thought.

Lancaster turned to her and said, 'You mean to tell me I drove all the way here for nothing?'

Darby moved to her rolling kit. As she leaned forward to grab the handle, she saw Lancaster's reflection in the glass cabinet directly in front of her. He stood a couple of feet away, looking at her backside and her legs, comparing what he saw now to the photographs of her stored in his mind. His mouth parted slightly and his eyes lit up with pleasure as his imagination conjured up all sorts of lascivious images.

Then he blinked and pushed them back into hiding. He stepped behind her and put a hand on her shoulder when she straightened. He moved his head closer to hers, and she heard a wet click in his throat.

'Those hotel shots of you,' he whispered against her ear, his breath hot and rank with cigarettes and coffee. 'Body like yours, you've got nothing to be ashamed of. You shouldn't let it go to waste either.'

Lancaster winked at her. When he wet his lips, Darby spun around and raked him with her elbow so hard blood and spittle flew from his mouth and stained the wall and shelves holding the morgue clothing. He staggered against the autopsy table and gripped its edge with both hands to keep from falling. She drove a fist into his kidney, and his back arched like he'd been jolted with electricity, and when he turned she jabbed him with her left and broke his nose, and then she followed it with a right cross that slammed into his left eye and knocked him against the naked corpse lying on the stainless-steel table.

'*Stop*,' Dr Gonzalez shrieked. The male morgue attendant stood frozen, his face white with shock. '*Stop it right now!*'

Darby hit Lancaster again, a solid blow to the kidneys. A girlish scream roared past his lips, and as she cocked back her fist to hit him again the male morgue attendant grabbed her in a bear hug. She didn't try to break free, and she didn't fight him when he started dragging her towards the door.

Lancaster gripped the edge of the autopsy table and staggered to his feet. Blood as bright as paint had pooled on the floor. As she was ushered into the hallway, Darby saw Lancaster turn to her, blood roaring from his broken nose, and just before the door shut he smiled, his teeth pink and his eyes burning with pleasure and satisfaction.

39

Jackson Cooper stood with Terry Hoder in the squad room. The front desks and chairs had been moved in order to make room for the TV camera and lighting equipment.

A reporter from the local paper, the *Red Hill Evening Item*, and a TV cameraman were inside the police chief's office, waiting for Darby to arrive. After Hoder had explained the plan he and Darby had cooked up to trap the Red Hill Ripper, Coop pulled Hoder into the squad room to talk privately.

'This is stupid and dangerous and you know it,' Coop said.

Hoder sat on top of a desk, gripping it with both hands. His face was haggard and his colouring was off. He had spent the last three hours working and fine-tuning the list of questions the reporter would ask Darby. Hoder had also scripted her answers. The reporter had agreed to let Hoder script the video interview and edit the article in exchange for exclusives with Darby, Hoder and Ray Williams after the Red Hill Ripper was in custody.

Before the video was posted on the home page of the newspaper's website, it would be emailed to Hoder's point man at the Denver Regional Computer Forensics Laboratory. There, the Nerd Herd, as they called themselves, would insert a hidden program into the video, which would allow them to trace anyone who clicked on it. Both Darby and Hoder believed the Red Hill Ripper was an extreme narcissist who religiously followed – and possibly collected – his own press clippings. The killer, they believed, wouldn't be able to resist watching the video. In order for the trace to work, the person had to watch the video for at least a couple of minutes.

'Let Williams do the interview,' Coop said. 'He's head of the task force.'

'The Red Hill Ripper isn't interested in or threatened by Ray Williams.' Then Hoder's eyes narrowed, like something of interest had come into his vision. 'Or me, for that matter.'

Coop hated the way the guy seemed to read minds.

'Right now this creep is looking for a way to get to her. He wants things to be all close and personal, remember?'

'The interview was her idea,' Hoder said. 'I voiced my reservations.'

'But you didn't say no, did you? You could've put a stop to this, and you didn't.'

'I understand your objections. It's difficult to put someone you're deeply in love with in harm's way.'

Coop looked at him sharply. Hoder craned his head and stared at the acoustic ceiling tiles.

Coop moved closer. 'You voiced your reservations, as you so eloquently put it, so if something happens to Darby you can soothe your conscience by saying, "Hey, everyone, I told her not to do this." And since she's not a federal agent, if something happens to her, there won't be any blowback on you or on the Bureau. Am I getting warm, Terry? No, don't answer. It's written all over your face.'

Hoder sighed. He looked and sounded incredibly tired and bored, as if he'd been asked to explain the meaning of life to a kitten.

'What would you suggest I do?'

'Put a stop to this,' Coop said, irritated by the man's soft drawl and laconic replies.

'Again, this was her idea. She insisted on doing it and –'

'*And* you're going along with it because, like her, you've developed a major hard-on for this nut-job. Only your reasons are about your legacy. You're set to retire next year, and this little experiment you dreamed up – a rolling forensics unit full of specialists with direct access to our lab – will prove your point to the director if you find the Red Hill Ripper. That's what this entire thing is about, Terry. Preserving your legacy.'

'All due respect, you're out of line.'

'Cut the bullshit. We both know why you're scripting this video.'

'Darby will be well insulated. He won't get to her.'

'You're deliberately lighting a fire under this guy's ass. Why not let him go on thinking he's intellectually superior to us while we work the evidence?'

'Is there some new piece of evidence I don't know about?'

'We're still examining the blood we found. And don't forget about the plastic fingerprint. We're waiting on that.'

'Otto told me the blood samples were destroyed by the bleach.'

'He's still got other samples to go through,' Coop said confidently, even though the truth was that it wasn't looking good.

'And then what? Who's going to do the DNA?'

'We are. The rolling lab has PCR kits. We can get a DNA sample in two to three hours.'

'And then we'll have to mail the kits back to our lab. More waiting. What about that residue Darby found on the sliding glass door? Was it cutting oil?'

Coop shook his head. 'Mineral spirits,' he said. 'There's no way to identify the brand. But the duct tape? The samples will arrive tomorrow morning no later than 9.30 a.m. Second the package arrives our guys are going to get to work comparing them to those in our duct tape library. They'll be able to identify the brand. We might get lucky.' Coop instantly regretted his last words.

'The Red Hill Ripper is already focused on Darby,' Hoder said. 'That's not going to change. *I* didn't make that happen, by the way. He did that all by himself. If we can get him to watch the interview, we may be able to locate him and save the next family.'

'Or maybe he'll decide to stay in the shadows. He knows we're not going to be here forever, so he can afford to wait us out. After we leave, maybe he'll decide to visit Darby next month, a year later, break into her home in the middle of the night and do that.' Coop jerked his thumb at the whiteboards holding the crime scene photographs of the strangled women.

Hoder studied his hands. 'Your anger is misdirected,'

he said. 'You should be having this conversation with Darby.'

'Don't worry, I'm planning to.'

'Good. Because if she doesn't want to do this, she doesn't have to.' Hoder seemed disappointed, almost sad, when he said it.

40

Darby insisted on doing the interview. She stood in the hall outside the squad room and listened to Coop rattle off his objections for about half a minute before she broke in and politely but firmly told him she was going through with it.

'This isn't just about your safety,' Coop said. 'What happens if this plan of yours backfires and you rile this guy and he decides to go after another family?'

'He's going to do that anyway.'

'And what if this interview makes him decide to move up his timetable? Have you stopped to consider that?'

'I have, which is why I'm doing the interview. I want him to focus his attention on me – and he will. *The Red Hill Evening Item* has been promoting my name all day, this exclusive interview with me. They've sent out Twitter and Facebook messages announcing it. He's going to watch it, Coop, and we're going to find him.'

'You're taking a baseball bat to a hornet's nest.'

Darby made fists by her sides, wincing slightly. Her right hand was swollen, covered by a glove; the abrasions along the knuckles rubbed against the stiff leather. She turned slightly, looked down the hall and saw Ray Williams standing in front of the police chief's desk through the office-door glass. Hoder sat in the chair, his face solemn and downcast as he listened. She couldn't hear what Williams was saying. She didn't need to.

Williams had torn a strip out of her when he discovered that she had sucker-punched Deputy Sheriff Lancaster – in an autopsy room, no less. His rage momentarily extinguished, he stopped speaking, and the silence inside the cruiser had felt like a dirge for the remainder of the ride. She didn't blame him. She'd let her anger get away from her. Not only had she given Lancaster sufficient ammo to take the investigation away from Red Hill, but her actions had most likely killed Williams's employment chances in the new law enforcement regime.

'I saw the list of questions and answers the two of you came up with,' Coop said, struggling to remain calm. 'You go on the record saying those things, you might as well be jamming a stick of dynamite up this guy's ass. Once you light the fuse, who the hell knows how he's going to react? Maybe he'll decide to take his aggression out on someone else instead of you.'

Darby couldn't hide her irritation. 'So what do you suggest we do, then? Cross our fingers and hope for a stroke of luck?'

'We keep working the evidence. That's what you and I do best. The lab's running with the things we took from the Downes –'

'This guy is too goddamn careful, Coop. It's not like he's left us a lot to work with.'

'You haven't had time to fully study the other case

235

files. Let's go over each one together, now, and maybe we'll find something that was overlooked, a piece of evidence that –'

'We need to be proactive here. We can't stay on this investigation forever. At some point we're going to have to pack up and leave, and if we haven't found him by then, guess what happens next? Right now we have a tremendous opportunity to trap him, and you're asking me to ignore it?'

'You can't orchestrate the behaviour of a psychopath. You told me that, remember?'

Darby said nothing.

Coop put a hand on the wall and leaned in closer. 'This is about you wanting this guy to come after you,' he said in a low voice. 'That way you'll have an excuse to blow him out of his socks.'

Darby brushed past him and entered the squad room. She was glad to see someone had hung sheets over the whiteboards to hide the grisly crime scene photos from the reporter and cameraman.

Hoder excused himself from the group and motioned for Darby to join him in the corner. He handed her two sheets of paper: they held the questions and her scripted answers.

'A sexual sadist like the Red Hill Ripper thinks he's intellectually superior to you, me, the Bureau, everyone,' Hoder said. 'The questions I wrote down are going to highlight *your* intellectual superiority. The answers are designed to make you come across as some sort of super-cop, make him feel that he has a self-inflated sense of his own importance and prowess. Leave the leather jacket on, by the way. It'll help sell the image. And unzip it so he can see your shoulder holster.'

And my chest, Darby added privately.

Again, Hoder seemed to sense her thoughts. 'He despises women. All sadists do,' he said. 'His hatred is already locked on you, and you're going to channel it by driving home the point that you've solved all the serial cases you've worked on, that the Red Hill Ripper isn't going to be an exception because he's nowhere near as smart or as cunning as the others. You'll go to the ends of the earth to find him, crawl under every rock – that sort of thing. I wrote some things down right there on the first page, the part marked "statement". We want to trigger the guy's deep-seated feelings of self-hatred and inferiority and, hopefully, keep him logged on to his computer.

'Look relaxed and speak confidently, maybe even with contempt. I wrote everything down for you, but the important thing here is for you to say it in your own voice. Do whatever feels natural. Go with your gut.'

Then Hoder put a fatherly hand on her shoulder. 'I can't stress this next point enough,' he said. 'If at any time you feel uncomfortable or uncertain about this, if you change your mind about wanting to go through with the interview, you end it. You're the one in charge.'

'Let's do this.'

The reporter, Chad Levine, was an affable, pudgy man with a handlebar moustache and a bad comb-over. He wore a corduroy sports coat with a pair of pressed Dockers khakis and suede chukka boots, and he radiated the excitement of a child whose long-held secret wish had suddenly been granted.

'Do you need to read these?' he asked, holding up the pages containing Hoder's scripted questions and answers.

Darby shook her head and took the seat across from the reporter. She couldn't see the cameraman behind the hot, white lights aimed on her. She took off her gloves and covered her right hand with her left so the camera wouldn't see the split skin and the swelling.

'We can do as many takes as you like,' Levine said, pinning the microphone to her leather jacket.

Darby pointed behind her, to the poster advertising the reward and hotline. 'Make sure that's in every shot.'

'It will be. We'll also have the number posted on the bottom of the interview. Agent Hoder said you have a statement you'd like to make. Do you want to read it now or at the end of the interview?'

'Now. And make sure it runs at the beginning of the interview.'

Levine nodded encouragingly. 'Agent Hoder told me,' he said. 'Let me know when you're ready.'

'I'm ready.'

The cameraman spoke from behind the lights. 'In five, four, three, two, one.'

Darby looked directly into the camera, knowing this was going to be her final stab at the case, a Hail Mary pass to catch the Ripper. She spoke slowly and deliberately, in order to hold the killer's attention and, hopefully, add some much needed time for the computer trace. She made false statements and the sort of claims no reasonable investigator would ever say in public, and she deliberately baited him.

'My name is Dr Darby McCormick. I want the people of Red Hill to know I will turn over every rock and exhaust every single lead and work every piece of evidence until I find the individual responsible for these murders. I am a forensic specialist, and I have dedicated my life to studying and apprehending this type of deviant criminal. A sexual pervert like the Red Hill Ripper will not be an exception. He is a lonely and impotent man who, like every other sadist, is a moral coward. He is hiding in plain sight somewhere in your neighbourhood. You have seen him at church and at social gatherings, in stores and in restaurants. When I find him, justice will be served, either in handcuffs or in a body bag.'

I'm about to call Sarah when I notice my burner only has a couple of minutes left on it. I pull over to the side of the road, my hazards flashing, and after I remove the battery from the phone and wipe everything down with a handkerchief, I step out of my car and toss the pieces deep into the woods.

The roads have been pretty quiet on account of the storm, which, at the moment, seems to have paused to catch its breath. The wind is no longer howling but the snow is still coming down hard and fast, my windshield wipers working double-time to clear it away. Five or so inches cover the lot belonging to the Happy Valley Auto Garage. Its windows and the lights for the gas pumps are dark. I'm alone and, having had my cars serviced here many, many times in the past, I know I don't have to worry about a security camera recording me.

The payphone is to my far left, next to the coin-fed air hose and vacuum. I leave the car running and the headlights on so I can see. I thread a couple of quarters into the slot and dial Sarah's number.

'Thank God,' Sarah says when she answers. Her sigh reminds me of pressure being released from a hot-water tank on the verge of exploding. 'Oh, thank God, I've been worried sick about you.'

'I'm fine. I –'

'It's been *hours*. Are you okay?'

'I just said I'm fine. Everything's fine.'

'When I didn't hear from you I thought –'

'WILL YOU SHUT UP AND LISTEN.'

'I'm sorry,' she says, and her voice sounds so small, so hurt and lonely, it triggers a memory of the first time I held her hand in mine. The moment her skin touched mine I knew I had found my home.

My anger dissolves in my throat, but my heart is still beating furiously.

'I'm sorry,' I say. 'I'm tired and it's been a long day.'

'Please tell me you're coming home.'

'Not yet. Not for a while. That's why I'm calling. I've got some things to take care of and didn't want you waiting up for me.'

'I heard about the FBI. On the news.'

'TV?'

'No, the radio. I have the portable with me.'

'What are they saying? On the news?'

She doesn't answer, and for some reason it makes me want to run back to my car. The briefcase with money and passports and everything else is sitting on the passenger's seat.

Leave now, an inner voice urges me. *Save yourself.*

'If everything goes right tonight,' I say, 'we'll be fine.'

'Did you make a mistake? Is that what you're trying to tell me?'

For some reason I'm thinking about my mother, how she collected quotes from famous historical figures and philosophers. She could recite them from memory, thought it made her sound like an intelligent and educated woman of substance and sophistication instead of the person she was, that corn-pone little girl who'd grown up on a farm and wore her older sister's hand-me-downs and ran away from home at fifteen and never finished high school.

'Tell me,' Sarah says, her voice so soft and gentle and understanding it makes my heart ache. 'You know you can tell me anything.'

'I know.'

'Did you make a mistake? Is that what you want to tell me?'

And then I'm thinking of St Augustine, of how much my mother liked to quote him, especially that line about truth being like a lion you could let loose because a lion could defend itself. But St Augustine left out the part about how the truth, like a lion, is capable of mauling and maiming, leaving its victim for dead. The truth is a hunter. The truth doesn't care.

And yet I still want to unburden myself. But, once I set my lion free, I'll no longer have control. I can't call it back, make it return to its cage.

'Baby?'

'I'm still here,' I say.

'I'll love you no matter what. You know that, right?'

And then I tell her. Everything.

41

Darby finished the interview in less than an hour. The cameraman had stopped recording after each question to give her time to confer with Hoder. They did multiple takes and the cameraman shot from multiple angles, pausing each time to fiddle with the lighting. Coop watched from a corner.

The video footage would be compressed into ten minutes. The statement she'd made at the start of the interview; the reporter's questions about her background and experience hunting serial killers like Traveler, who had successfully evaded law enforcement; and her summary of the Red Hill Ripper case – those items would run at the start of the interview and hopefully catch the killer's interest.

In order for the trace to work, the Ripper needed to watch the video for at least two minutes. During that time, the program embedded in the video would determine the operating system – Windows, Mac, Android or iOS – install the appropriate software and then broadcast its location back to the RCFL guys in Denver. They assured Hoder the program wouldn't be detected by antivirus or malware-prevention software.

To entice the Ripper to keep watching, Hoder had provided 'exclusive' and 'never before revealed crime scene photos' – close-up pictures of the plastic cuffs and ligature marks. Hoder believed the Ripper wouldn't be able to resist wanting to see his handiwork on display. The photos would be spliced into the video somewhere after the two-minute mark – more than enough time for the tracking program to install itself. Anyone watching the video from Red Hill, Brewster and the surrounding towns would be moved to the top of the search list. All information would then be forwarded to Hoder, who would analyse it, along with Otto and Hayes, inside the MoFo.

While the cameraman edited the video footage under Hoder's watchful eye, Darby left the squad room to speak to the police chief. Neither Robinson nor Williams had entered the room at any point during the interview.

Robinson's office was dark, the door locked. She moved around the corner and saw the light on in Williams's office, but he wasn't there. She searched the station for him, and when she didn't find him she used his office phone to call his cell. It went straight to voicemail. Then she remembered he'd left his cell in his trunk.

Darby left the office, a nagging feeling worming its way through her stomach. If the Red Hill Ripper were skilful enough with computers to use malware that automatically installed itself on their cell phones, would he also have installed safeguards while using the internet?

A patrolman she recognized from this morning's debrief stepped into the lobby with a tall and slender woman dressed in tight-fitting designer jeans, over-the-knee black leather high-heel boots and a dark fur coat that ended at her waist. It had an oversized shawl collar and an open front; she wore a cream-coloured and Henley-inspired blouse with a split-neck and a deep V that proudly displayed an ample amount of surgically enhanced cleavage.

'Ray in his office?' the patrolman asked Darby. He had broad shoulders and the thick and callused hands of a bricklayer. His nametag read L. GRIFFIN.

'No, he's not there,' Darby said, and shifted her attention back to the woman. She was Saks Fifth Avenue pretty, and had the air and appearance of a successful young cosmopolitan woman or trophy wife who whiled away her days at luxury spas and shopping at Nordstrom. 'I don't know where he is.'

'Maybe you can help me, then. This lovely young lady is Ms Rita Tuttle. Rita, meet Dr McCormick. Rita lives in Brewster, works in the . . . what did you call it again, Rita? The gentlemen's services industry?' Patrolman Griffin's eyes crinkled in humour.

Rita Tuttle pulled back her coat sleeve and glanced at her watch, a rose-gold EBEL with a sapphire-crystal face encrusted with diamonds. 'I've got to catch a flight at nine in Denver,' she said. 'How about we get to it?'

'She's going to Barbados,' Griffin said. 'With a friend.' He smiled coyly. 'I'll take you to our luxury interview suite. This way, ladies.'

The small interrogation room had white-painted walls and overhead fluorescent lights. A pair of folding chairs were placed on either side of an office-furniture store-bought desk made of particleboard.

Rita declined Griffin's offer of coffee. She took a seat and crossed her legs.

'I'll let you two get acquainted,' Griffin said. 'Be a good girl, Rita, and tell the good doctor here everything you told me.' Griffin winked at her and shut the door.

Rita stared after him. She didn't take off her jacket or her thin black leather gloves. Her dirty blonde hair had been cut into a stylish bob, and she wore a trace amount of makeup. Given the smoothness of her skin, and the lack of crow's feet around the eyes and mouth, Darby had the woman's age pegged somewhere north of twenty-five but no older than thirty.

Darby took the opposite chair. Rita wet the pad of her thumb and rubbed it across a smudge on her leather boots.

'Nice boots,' Darby said.

'They're Jimmy Choos.' Then Rita Tuttle sighed like a child who had been confined to the principal's office. 'Go ahead, ask your questions.'

'How about we start with what you're doing here?'

'That walking dildo who brought me here thinks I might know something about this guy you're looking for. You know what edge play is?'

Darby nodded. 'Sexual play involving the serious risk of harm or death.'

Rita smiled brightly, as if she had encountered a kindred spirit. She had capped teeth, the veneers so startlingly white they reminded Darby of a porcelain toilet.

'What sort of flavour are we talking about?' Darby asked.

'Erotic asphyxiation. What we call breath play. The gentleman in question would tie me up to a chair and –'

'Sorry to interrupt, but tied you up to a chair using what?'

'Plastic ties. He'd put them on my wrists and ankles. After I was trussed up, he'd take out the rope. This guy was really into knots.'

42

'What kind of knots?' Darby asked, reaching for her notebook.

Rita stared at her from across the table. 'I look like a sailor to you? They were, you know, *knots*. Complicated ones. Intricate. He tried all different kinds on me.'

'Name?'

'Timmy. At least that's what he called himself. Never gave me a last name. Most of 'em don't.'

'The rope this guy used,' Darby began.

'Not rope. *Ropes*. He used the same two pieces every time we got together.'

'We talking about the kind of rope you find on a clothesline?'

'No. This was thicker. Blue, I think.'

Darby opened her folder and rooted through the pages, stopping when she found the sheet depicting a surgeon's knot. She showed it to Rita.

'That one was his favourite,' Rita said.

'Why?'

'Because that was the one he used to make me pass out.' Rita stifled a yawn. 'The nooses he made with some of the other knots – they required him to stand behind me and, you know, apply constant pressure until I passed out. This one, though,' she said, tapping a fingernail against the sheet of paper. 'With this one, when he pulled the rope the knot stayed right where it was. It didn't, you know, come undone or anything. The knot did all the work, maintained constant pressure around my neck. He could control the tension, which is what gets these kinds of guys off. He'd give the rope a good, hard yank, then move round the chair to watch me choke and pass out.'

Rita spoke dispassionately, as though being tied down and nearly strangled to death not once but over and over again was a normal, everyday occurrence, like brushing one's teeth.

'I kind of liked passing out,' Rita said. 'Gave me a break from the stench.'

Darby felt her scalp prickle. 'What stench?'

'Guy was a BO factory. He had some sort of skin condition that made him smell like he'd spent his nights rolling around in a bed of rotting fish. I don't know what it was, and I never asked. I got round it by dabbing some of that Vicks VapoRub under my nostrils. My clothes? Had to put them in the wash the second I got home. Had to scrub my hair too. This guy had an Olympic-grade stink.'

'When was the last time you saw him?'

'Over a year ago? Maybe longer. We got together four, maybe five times.'

'Why did you break off it off?'

'I didn't. He just stopped calling. Which is too bad, because this guy paid *really* well. He told me he lived here in Red Hill, but I never went to his house or anything. We always met at the Beacon. That's a hotel in Brewster.'

'How did he contact you? Phone? Email?'

'Phone,' Rita said. 'I don't do email or Facebook or any of that stuff. My line of work demands discretion. I can't have you police types sticking your noses where they don't belong, harassing my customers.' The woman grinned broadly. 'He always called me from different numbers – payphones, a burner. All my clients usually do. Don't like their wives or girlfriends finding out about their particular needs.'

'You remember anything flashing up on your caller-ID?'

'Nothing came up on my caller-ID except a number.'

'You didn't put his name and number into your contacts?'

'I don't record any of my clients' details in my phone.'

Darby leaned back in her seat and tapped her pen against the notepad. 'Timmy was into some rough stuff. Guy like that, I'm assuming you'd ask around, look into his background.'

'Jeannie vouched for him. Jean Derry. She's a dominatrix. Or was. She did some BDSM work with him until she had to move back to Arizona. Her mother was sick, lung cancer or some shit, so she referred him on to me.'

'Where in Arizona?'

'No idea. She used to live in Brewster. That's how we know each other. My mother lived there. When she croaked, I inherited her shitty two-bedroom ranch. But it was paid off, no mortgage, and the property taxes here are chump change. I'm rarely home – I'm always travelling – so I decided to sublet my two-bedroom in Manhattan to a yuppie couple for five gees a month. Sixty grand a year for doing absolutely nothing.' Again, she pulled back her coat sleeve and checked her watch.

'There a local BDSM scene here?'

'I'm sure there is; every place has one. But I'm not tied into the local scenes. They don't pay as well and can't meet my price.'

'Why'd you make an exception with Timmy?'

'Because Jeannie vouched for him, and because he parted with a grand for an hourly session.'

'What'd Timmy do for a living? Was he married? Single?'

'No idea, and no, I didn't ask. I was there to get paid, not help him on his Facebook or match.com profile. I got the feeling his junk didn't work.'

'He was impotent?'

'No clue. He never pulled it out. Most guys who are into this stuff, the second you start choking they start beating their meat like it owes them money. Don't get me wrong; Timmy got all hot and bothered, but he always kept his clothes on. He was pretty normal for a guy who was into this stuff. He never pranced around in women's clothes or anything weird like that, and he never tried to film me.'

'You have any pictures of him? Anything he might have given to you as a gift?' Darby was hoping for a fingerprint.

'No and no,' Rita said. 'He was six feet, maybe five eleven. Looked like a guy who spent his whole day in front of a computer – flabby, bald, weak chin, all that.'

Darby's gaze dropped to her notebook. She doubted

Red Hill PD had a sketch artist on staff. Brewster probably did, but he or she wouldn't be as talented as the federal agents who worked in the forensics facial imaging lab. Hoder could rustle one up with a single phone call. *Put the guy on Skype and have the Tuttle woman talk to him over the MoFo's secure satellite feed.*

'We about done here?' Rita asked.

'I'd like you to talk to a sketch artist.'

'How long will it take?'

'Five families are dead, Rita – it'll take as long as it takes.'

'See, this is why people like me don't like helping people like you.' Rita's eyes were smiling again. 'You guys are always taking advantage of someone's generosity.'

'So why *did* you come forward?'

'Because I happened to be talking to a friend who shall remain nameless, and this friend, this person, was telling me about how you guys have been running all over Red Hill and Brewster, some of you even making calls to Denver where a lot of us work, asking questions about BDSM guys who are heavily into knots and tie up women to chairs and shit. I thought of Timmy and placed a call. When Officer Dipshit showed up on my doorstep, I told him everything and yet he insisted on dragging me here.'

'Did Timmy scare you? Hurt you?'

'No, he was very considerate. Even gave me a special collar for my neck so he wouldn't leave any rope burns.'

A true gentleman, Darby thought. 'If he was so considerate, why you here ratting him out? That can't be good for business.'

'The reward money. Duh. If Timmy ends up being the perv you guys are looking for, then I get the hundred grand, right?'

'That why you waited all this time to tell us about your client? Original reward money not good enough?'

'Number one, I already told you Timmy was a *former* client. Number two, I just found out about the reward money today.'

Bullshit, Darby thought. *You're lying. I can see it in your eyes*.

'Anything else you can tell me about Timmy?' She asked. 'Any distinguishing features or characteristics?'

'He wore a brown suit from J. C. Penney's and Hush Puppies. Look, you want me to do this sketch artist thing, let's get the show on the road. And I want to use a phone right now so I can talk to my pilot, see the latest time we can fly out. There's a big storm rolling in tonight and I don't wanna get stuck in this shithole.'

43

Darby spoke with Rita Tuttle for another fifteen minutes, trying to get specifics on her former client's skin condition. Rita said she didn't know. The man named Timmy refused to discuss it with her, and he never took off his clothes.

When Darby flipped shut her notebook and left the interrogation room, she locked the door behind her in case Rita Tuttle had a sudden change of heart and decided to make a break for the private plane waiting to take her to Barbados. She headed to Williams's office to use his computer. It took only a few minutes to find what she was looking for.

Then she sorted through the case files tucked into her backpack. After she finished, she went to find Officer L. Griffin.

She found him standing outside the station's front doors, pacing and chain-smoking under the porte-cochère. The sky was pitch-black, and it had already started to snow. A fine white dust covered the parking lot and cars.

'So,' he said. 'Whaddya think of Rita?'

'She's got some solid info. What's her story?'

'Local, born and bred. No record, not even a parking ticket. We went to high school together. She was a couple of years ahead of me and had a reputation for being wild and uninhibited. Supposedly she arranged a private gang-bang for our football team and made five hundred bucks.' Griffin raised his hands. 'Hey, I'm not judging.'

'How old is she?'

'Twenty-six. She's been entrepreneurial since day one. Left here when she was eighteen, and from what I've heard she makes a pretty good living servicing rich old guys who live out on the coasts.'

'She mentioned a woman named Jean Derry.'

'Yeah, Rita told me about her. Her last-known address is in Brewster. Rented an apartment there. Heard she had a thing for nose candy, did a couple of rehab stints.'

'I'd like to talk to her.'

'I figured as much – I'll run her down for you.' Griffin dropped his cigarette and stubbed the butt out underneath his thick, black-soled boot. 'Anything else I can help you with?'

'You mind taking Rita's statement for me?' Darby needed to talk to Hoder about getting a sketch artist.

'Sure thing,' Griffin replied. 'Just do me a favour: if anything comes of this lead, I'd appreciate it if you put my name out there. It'll go a long way with all this transition shit.'

'You got it.'

'Wait, before you go, I spoke to Ray. He wanted me to tell you about Nelson.'

'What about him?'

'The disposable camera Lancaster said he found on

him? Nelson's prints were all over it. Chief pressed him on it, and Nelson finally copped to taking pictures inside the Downes house last night.'

So Lancaster had been telling the truth.

'He also admitted to taking Ray's cell phone,' Griffin said. 'There was an incident last month, in December, with the Connelly family.'

'Ray told me about it.'

'There won't be any charges. Chief wants this to go away quietly, so Nelson agreed to submit his resignation. It was coming anyway. He and his wife have been thinking about moving to the north-east – New Hampshire, I think. His father-in-law is some big-time builder, offered Nelson a construction job.'

'Where's Ray now?'

'In Brewster with the chief. Some meeting, I don't know what it's about.'

'Ray say anything else?'

'You mean beyond you having a mean left hook?' Griffin grinned broadly.

Darby found Hoder inside the squad room, talking to the reporter, Levine, who seemed to be on his way out. The cameraman was already gone.

Hoder caught Darby's urgent expression, then shook the man's hand and joined her. He looked especially haggard, his thoughts and emotions veiled. She wondered if he knew about what had happened with Lancaster.

Darby told him about her conversation with Rita Tuttle.

'She identified the knot?' Hoder asked after she finished.

Darby nodded. 'There's something else,' she said. 'Downes's secretary, Sally Kelly, told me she overheard Samantha talking to her father about a guy in her class who smelled like garbage. This guy was only there for one class, though. Remember that antibiotic I found on the bedroom floor?'

'The neomycin. That reminds me: Hayes spoke to the family's physician. He never prescribed it.'

'It's used to treat severe cases of liver disease, hepatic coma, intestinal infections, by targeting certain types of bacteria in the gut, prevents them from producing ammonia and some protein they need to survive. Turns out it has other uses.' Darby flipped her notebook open. 'Type "neomycin" and "fish odour" into Google and it comes back with this rare genetic metabolic disorder called –' She looked at her notes. 'It's called trimethylaminuria, or TMAU, otherwise known as "Fish Odour Syndrome" or "Fish Malodour Syndrome".'

Hoder's eyes narrowed in thought.

Darby continued. 'People who inherit this condition have a defect in the production of some enzyme called FMO_3,' she said. 'What happens is trimethylamine builds up in the person's system, then it's released through sweat, breath and urine, giving off a strong fishy or garbage-like body odour. There's no cure for this thing. If you're born with it, you're stuck with it.'

'How does the neomycin fit into this?'

'It helps to minimize the fish odour with some people. In order for the antibiotic to work effectively, you've got to modify your diet. People who suffer from TMAU, though – no matter what meds they're taking, no matter how much they've modified their diet, you put them into a stressful situation, they start to sweat even more, and the fish odour goes into overdrive.'

'The bedroom window at the Downes house,' Hoder said. 'It was open.'

'And the windows in the other house were open, too. I looked through the photos taken of the bedrooms. At each crime scene the Red Hill Ripper opened all the bedroom windows. If our guy has this TMAU disorder, I bet he opens all the windows to clear out that fishy odour.'

Hoder made a fist and rubbed it across his bottom lip, thinking.

'Look, this was just a quick Google search,' Darby said. 'It could be some sort of other metabolic disorder, maybe a skin condition, like Rita Tuttle said, maybe something else entirely. But two separate people who said something about a guy with a particular fishy and garbage-like body odour? That's something we can't ignore.'

'Agreed. Where's the Tuttle woman now?'

'Interview room. Griffin's going to take her statement. I think we should get a sketch artist, preferably one of yours. We can take Tuttle to the MoFo and have her talk to this guy over Skype.'

Hoder nodded and removed a satellite phone from his jacket pocket.

'Where'd you get that?'

'Coop,' he said. 'He brought them from Denver, one for each of us.'

'Where is he?'

'At the hotel with Hayes, sweeping our rooms for bugs. Otto's inside our rolling lab, working his way through the blood samples.' Hoder sighed. 'It's not looking good. In addition to using bleach, our guy used hydrogen peroxide on the floor. He knows forensics.'

'If this Timmy guy signed up for a class and dropped it, the college will have his name and address on file.'

'We'll need a court order before we go fishing.'

'I know. I say we skip the local route and go federal. People get real co-operative when they see a federal warrant. We can also use it to target local pharmacies, see who's getting neomycin prescriptions filled. We should also start asking around, see if anyone knows anything about a guy named Timmy who has a permanent BO problem. What's the status of the video interview?'

'The RCFL guys have it,' said Hoder. 'They're installing that hidden tracking program. It'll go live in about twenty minutes or so.'

'What do you think about putting out the information on the knots?'

'I think it's too early. If we go out with the knots and the sketch tonight or tomorrow, he might get spooked and decide to leave town for a while. Let him keep thinking he's got the upper hand. We'll give it a day or two to see what the trace comes up with.'

'You look like you could use some sleep,' said Darby.

'Couldn't we all. I'll meet you in the interview room.'

Darby returned to Williams's office and used his computer to get a list of local pharmacies.

There were two in Red Hill; Brewster had four. She

could sit around and wait for a court order that, most likely, wouldn't come through until sometime tomorrow, or she could try to do something now.

Five minutes later, she was behind the wheel of her rental, with the case file and the pharmacies' addresses lying on the passenger's seat.

44

Baylor Apothecary was the closest, located inside the ground floor of a small brick-faced building right around the corner from Cindy's Diner. The windows were dark, but the pharmacy was still in business. Darby pressed her face against the glass and in the gloom she could make out fully stocked aisles. Baylor's opened every morning at eight. She'd have to wait until tomorrow.

She had better luck at the Rite Aid on the other side of town, off the main highway, Route 6. It was in a strip mall that at one point in time had included a Blockbuster video store and a discount lumber liquidator. The snow had picked up, growing in intensity. A white blanket covered the two cars in the lot.

The inside of the pharmacy was brightly lit and eerily quiet, as though it had suddenly been abandoned. It was also uncomfortably warm. Darby unzipped her jacket as she made her way to the back with the case file for the Connelly family pinched between the fingers of her left hand.

The pharmacist was a thickset middle-aged woman with a button nose and brittle black hair that had thinned to the point that her scalp was visible. Her nametag read BARBARA.

'Evening,' Darby said pleasantly. 'I need your help with

a medication called neomycin – the oral antibiotic and not the topical treatment.'

Barbara smiled as she turned to the computer. 'Your name?'

'Not me. One of your male customers.' Darby showed her federal ID, and the woman's smile collapsed. 'His first name is Tim or Timothy.'

'Do you have a court order?' The woman's attention was glued to the butt-end of the 9-millimetre tucked inside Darby's shoulder holster. 'I can't help you without a court order.'

'The FBI are getting it together. All I need to know is whether or not you have a man named Tim or Timothy in your system who gets his neomycin prescription filled here. If he is, great, I'll come back with the court order. If he isn't, then I'll get out of your hair.'

Barbara was shaking her head the entire time. 'I can't tell you anything unless you have a court order,' she said. 'HIPAA and the state's Medical Information Act prevent me from sharing any information regarding a person's –'

'I understand.' Darby had expected to encounter this reaction. During the drive, she had come up with a way around it – provided she could get Barbara the Pharmacist to agree to play along. 'I'm sorry, I didn't explain myself correctly. My fault. You live here in Red Hill?'

'Why?'

'Are you familiar with the Red Hill Ripper?'

Barbara didn't answer. Didn't have to. The skin of the woman's face flexed and tightened against the bone.

'You can see why I'm anxious to see if this man is in

your system,' Darby said patiently. 'I'm not asking you to do anything illegal. I just need to know whether or not this man is one of your customers.'

'I'm just . . . I should really talk to my supervisor.'

'I understand. But while you're on the phone – while you and I are standing here, talking about rules and procedures, the Red Hill Ripper is planning on doing this to another family.'

Darby brought out her folder, her finger marking the spot she needed. She opened it and showed the woman a close-up of the noose wrapped around Linda Connelly's neck, the skin swollen, bloated and purple.

The photo had the desired effect. Barbara the Pharmacist's breath caught in her throat and she backed up slightly, wincing. Her attention swung to the pharmacy computer.

'Just tell me if he's in there,' Darby said. 'There's no law against that, right?'

'I . . . Well, no, I don't think so.' Barbara looked around uneasily, to see if anyone was nearby.

'I really appreciate you helping the Bureau out on this,' Darby said. 'Thank you.'

The phone behind the counter rang.

Barbara looked relieved. 'Excuse me for a moment,' she said.

As the woman hustled away, Darby stared at the computer on the counter. The Red Hill Ripper's name and address could be just a few mouse clicks away. She wanted to jump over the counter.

Then the pharmacist's head snapped to Darby. The

woman's features had gone slack, and the blood drained from her face. The person on the other end of the line said something that made her flinch. A low, guttural moan escaped her lips and she yanked the phone away from her ear.

'He knows where I live,' the pharmacist said, her voice stripped of colour.

'Who?'

'The man on the phone. At least I think it's a man. His voice sounds . . . He sounds like he's speaking through a computer.'

Barbara charged forward, her heavy footsteps pounding against the floor. 'He said he was going to use a special knot on me.' She held the cordless away from her as though she were carrying a snake. 'He wants to talk to you.'

Darby dropped the file on the counter and took the phone. *He must've followed me here*, she thought as she moved across an aisle stocked with diapers and baby formula and jars of food. But how? She hadn't seen anyone following her.

The front door came into view and Darby saw a young, pony-tailed guy minding a cash register, reading a weight-lifting magazine. He lowered it and watched her with curiosity and a growing alarm.

She brought the phone up to her ear. 'McCormick.'

The disguised voice on the other end of the line spoke through a burst of static. 'My girl,' he said, and then let out a long moan, like someone riding the swell of an orgasm.

Darby couldn't see the main road or much of the

parking lot behind the curtains of snow, but she could make out her car, the driver's side door hanging open.

'I can't wait until we get together. I'm gonna split you in half.'

Click.

Darby placed the cordless on a shelf stocked with discount boxes of Christmas cards. She took out her nine and from the corner of her eye saw the cashier drop his magazine, his face pale with shock.

She doubted the Red Hill Ripper was somewhere outside waiting for her to come out. He wanted to take her, and he would do it when she didn't expect it, when she wouldn't be able to see him coming. He wouldn't call to alert her of his presence, and he wouldn't make a move on her here, in a public place, with two potential witnesses. He had called because he wanted to remind her of his superiority. He wanted her to feel dread. She pushed open the doors and went outside.

Footsteps led away from her car. They were covered by snow; there wouldn't be any way to get a mould of the impressions. Gun in hand, Darby slowly advanced to her car, snow flying into her face and the wind blowing her hair. The interior light was on; she moved around the open door, looked inside at her seat and saw two pieces of blue nylon rope speckled with white and red wrapped together to form a surgeon's knot.

When I turn left on to Sidewinder Road, I'm relieved to find it freshly ploughed. I had my doubts: the town's four snowploughs, which have been out working since eight or so, might've skipped this street, since no one lives here any more.

There is the long trailer, still attached to the semi; both are parked near the kerb outside the Downes home, looking as small as toys from my driver's seat. I kill my headlights and then creep forward slowly. Light glows from the trailer's tiny side windows.

I pull against a ridge of freshly ploughed snow, put the car in park and leave the engine running. If everything goes right, I'll be back here in only a few minutes.

I step out of the car with the backpack gripped in my hand. I'm wearing a fleece hat underneath the hood of my coat, but even under all those layers I can still hear the deep, rumbling throb of the semi's big diesel engine, which is providing power for the lights and whatever other equipment is being used in there.

I cross the street and start running towards the trailer with the backpack hugged against my chest to keep its contents from accidentally breaking. By the time I reach the trailer's back doors, the sound of the diesel has become near-deafening, and I can feel the ground vibrating beneath the soles of my boots.

I know the trailer belongs to the FBI: the FBI insignia, lettering and words MOBILE FORENSICS UNIT were prominently displayed in big, bold lettering on its side. It was parked here late yesterday afternoon. Yesterday a ramp descended from the back to allow the agents to come and go as they pleased.

Tonight the ramp is gone, rolled back underneath the trailer. But the side door has a short set of metal steps, all of which are covered in snow. After I lay the backpack on the ground, near one of the rear tyres, I unzip my coat, remove the .44 Magnum tucked in the front waistband of my jeans and make my way across the length of the trailer to the side door, ducking underneath the small windows. My hands, protected by only a thin layer of latex, are already cold, and my knuckles and joints ache.

I want to take them by surprise, if possible, so I mount the steps slowly and carefully. The handle feels ice-cold as I slowly turn it. I don't encounter any resistance, and when I hear the lock click back I throw open the door; as it swings to my right I raise my Magnum and dart inside the trailer.

For the next few seconds time seems to slow, as if what I'm seeing has been captured inside a tableau: a big man with a shaved head sitting with his back to me and hunched over a counter; a second man who is much smaller and wearing ear-bud headphones attached to the iPod clipped to his belt. I immediately aim at the short man. He sees me and is reaching for the side-arm clipped to his belt when I pull the trigger.

The Magnum kicks; the roar of the gunshot explodes inside my head as the round hits the man square in the chest, spraying the doors behind him with a bright red mist. The bald guy is stumbling to his feet when I turn the gun on him and fire.

The wind slams the door shut behind me and my eardrums are ringing as I move to the bald guy. He's writhing on the floor, blood pouring out of his mouth and nose. He looks up at me questioningly, about to speak, when I shoot him in the head. I'm ducking around the counter and forensics equipment, when I notice a can of liquid nitrogen, which may prove very useful. I walk over to the small guy and examine the exit wound in his back: it's the size of a basketball but he's still moving, trembling, his arm reaching out for the Glock lying on the floor. I fire another round into his back and then I use the remaining rounds to shoot out the windows.

The refrigerator in the corner isn't locked. I open it and find all the blood samples collected from the hardwood floor sitting on the shelves. I remove everything, throwing it against the floor and then smashing the glass vials with my boots. I head to the back doors, open them and jump out.

Backpack in my hand, I jog next to the side of the trailer and mount the stairs again. My hands are shaking when I place the backpack on the counter and work the zipper – not out of fear but from the cold. I'm no longer afraid. The tables have turned. I have a way out of this.

Gasoline fumes rise from the backpack as I remove the BIC lighter from my jacket pocket. I remove the first Molotov cocktail, ignite the gasoline-soaked wick and toss it against the crushed glass and blood smeared across the floor. The glass bottle explodes in flames, and I can feel heat as strong as a fist punching me. I remove the second Molotov, ignite it and throw it against the counter where the bald man had been sitting, doing DNA testing. I throw the third towards the back and the fourth and last one against the floor in the middle of the trailer. The heat is stifling as I grab the backpack and exit through the side door.

The trailer is burning nicely. I could wait for the flames to ignite the liquid nitrogen and all the other chemicals stored in there, which would blow everything to kingdom come; or I could use the last item stored inside my backpack, a long piece of gasoline-soaked cloth and make quick work of it.

It takes me a moment to find the cap for the gas tank. I remove it and then stuff the wet cloth into the hole. I can feel the heat from the flames rocketing out of the windows when I light the last wick and run across the street, heading for my car and thinking about my next and, God willing, last stop.

45

Darby entered the Wagon Wheel Saloon at quarter past ten. Last night's Bible Belt crowd had been replaced with the kind of people she'd grown up with in Boston, blue-collar types and roughnecks who passed around bottles and pitchers of beer, everyone drinking, eating and laughing in an atmosphere that reminded her of a Roman banquet. The dining-room was at full capacity and the pool-room was packed with young guys in their twenties, the juke playing The Who's 'Pinball Wizard'.

For the next half hour, in the uncomfortably close atmosphere reeking of spilled beer, testosterone and sweat, deodorant and cologne, she interviewed the bartender and waitresses about any customer or local who may have smelled like fish or garbage. Coming up empty-handed, she moved to the pool-room and put the same question to a group of college-aged guys who had the collective IQ of a balloon. Most didn't listen to her, their gazes listless and their attention elsewhere, as they wondered what she looked like naked, she supposed, or how she'd be in the sack.

When she struck out with them, she went to tackle the dining crowd and found Coop standing by the corner of the bar, his chest rising and falling as he sucked in air. His nostrils were wide and white around the edges, and as she drew closer she could see his eyes glowing with the atavistic intensity of a boxer who was about to step into the ring and unload all of his dark energies.

Darby cleared her throat several times. She felt like a rock was lodged there.

'I was going to tell you, Coop.'

Coop said nothing. Darby couldn't meet his eyes. She turned her head, folded her arms on the bar and pretended to read the labels on a row of vodka bottles.

'*Well?*'

'Lancaster knew the autopsies had been rescheduled for this morning,' Darby said. 'He –'

'You had no proof of that when you cold-cocked him – *in an autopsy room.*'

'Guys like Lancaster lose a piece of their brain every time they sit on a toilet. You want a guy like that spearheading an investigation like this?'

'That's not the point.'

'Sometimes you've got to stick their dicks into a socket to rewire their thinking.'

Coop's head looked like it was about to explode.

'He's been screwing with us ever since we got here,' Darby said. 'The autopsies were the cherry on the sundae.'

Coop leaned sideways against the bar. 'The guy's an asshole. Everyone *knows* he's an asshole; it's an established fact. You've dealt with your fair share of career-climbing dicks who use cases as political leverage, pencil-pushers and bureaucratic cocksuckers who get off on napalming your work. But not once have you ever clocked one in public – at least not that I'm aware of. Then again, I'm learning all sorts of new and interesting things about your behaviour.'

'Like Williams says, Teddy Lancaster brings out the best in people.'

Coop dug his tongue hard into one of his back molars and took a deep breath through his nose. 'Lancaster decided not to press criminal charges, obviously, or we'd be having this conversation inside a holding cell,' he said. 'A civil case, well, that's another matter. He'll go after you first. He'll go after the Bureau, because we hired you and because we've got the deeper pockets. Lancaster will get a nice little payout to keep his mouth shut, and then the Bureau will need to make an example of someone, and it sure as hell isn't going to be Terry Hoder. Before you went all Mike Tyson on him, did you once stop to consider how poorly this would reflect on *me*?'

'I lost my cool.'

'No shit. Why? What happened?'

'He said something to me privately.'

'What? What did he say?'

'Does it matter?'

'You just tossed a Molotov on to my career, and you're not going to tell me *why*?'

Darby swallowed. Cleared her throat.

'It's done, Coop.' *And I don't regret it either*, she added to herself.

Darby could feel his eyes burrowing into the side of her face. When he spoke again, his voice vacillated between rage and disbelief.

'I went to the station looking for you. To give you this.' Coop placed a satellite phone on the bar. 'Hoder said you were at the station. After he filled me in on what was going on, knowing you, I figured you'd come here to ask around about this Timmy character. Little did we know you were at a Rite Aid. So you can imagine my surprise when that 911 call came through. The kid working the cash register called it in, in case you're wondering.'

'I showed him and the pharmacist my ID,' Darby said. 'After it was all over, I told them they had nothing to worry about.'

'That's not the point. You sneaked out of the station and tried to put the screws on the pharmacist.'

'I was following up on our lead.'

'You went alone. You're not supposed to go anywhere alone and, worse, after what went down you didn't call it in. The guy you spoke to, was he the same one who called you last night at the hotel?'

'I'm pretty sure. Voice was altered.'

'So why didn't you call it in?'

'Do you think he was standing around waiting after he left the rope in my car?'

'What rope?' Coop asked.

Darby realized that, in her exhausted state, she hadn't told anyone about it. She had gone straight to the Wagon Wheel after leaving the Rite Aid.

'While I was inside the pharmacy, he was inside my car. He left the door hanging open, and when I went outside I found two pieces of rope tied into a surgeon's knot lying on my car seat.'

Coop looked away, blinking. 'I can't believe I'm hearing this.'

'It's in an evidence bag in the trunk of my car – not that we're going to find anything on it.'

'There's a thing called procedure, remember? You *follow* procedure in order to build a *case*, and you have to *build* a case in order to –'

'IT'S A WASTE OF TIME.'

Darby had drawn the attention of nearby people. She scooped up her new satphone, stuffed it inside her jacket pocket, inched closer to him and, leaning forward, crossed her arms against the bar, their shoulders touching.

'Don't you see what he's doing, Coop? The bullshit with the photos, tracing the cell signal, calling the pharmacy, leaving the rope – the *second* this guy does something, we all jump. He wants us to keep spinning our wheels until we fall over exhausted or until we're forced to leave, whichever happens first. Finally we've got a lead on this guy, and you want to waste time turning my rental into a crime scene?'

Coop saw her point. His face softened a bit, but the anger was still in his eyes.

'Look, I'm sorry for what happened with Lancaster,' she said. 'And maybe I should have called after what went down at the pharmacy.'

'*Maybe*? Are you serious?'

'While I was driving, I kept checking my mirrors to see if I was being followed. There's no way he tailed me.'

'Maybe you couldn't see him through the snow.'

Darby shook her head. 'That's what I thought at first,'

she said. 'But I didn't see a single car light behind me during the entire ride – and he had to have had his lights on because almost every road I took was pitch-black, not a single street light on anywhere. And I passed hardly any cars.'

'So how did he know you were at the pharmacy?'

'I asked myself the same question,' Darby said. 'What's the best way to follow someone in today's high-tech world without being seen?'

'He put a GPS tracker on your car?' Coop asked.

Darby nodded. 'I immediately checked my car after I left the pharmacy. Found it wired in right near the engine block. It's one of those hundred-dollar units that send out their location every couple of minutes to a smartphone or laptop. He didn't have to tail me because he knew where I was going.'

'I love it when the pervs go high-tech.' Coop sighed. 'This tracker, where is it?'

'Still there. I don't want him to know I found it. If we can get its frequency, we might be able to lock on to it and track him down. Hoder told me you brought the equipment from Denver.'

Coop nodded. 'He swept our rooms for bugs and didn't find any, by the way. Yours was the only one.'

'Where's Hayes now?'

'Back at the MoFo working on the computer traces for Hoder. Nothing yet.'

'We should check all of our other vehicles, see if anyone else has been tagged with a tracker.'

'Sure.' Coop pinched his temples and then rubbed the

corners of his eyes. He stared down at the bar top for a moment, his anger seemingly abated. He looked hollow-eyed and sullen. 'Anyone here know anything about this Timmy guy?'

'No. If he doesn't live in Red Hill, he's got to be living somewhere nearby. Someone knows him. A person with a metabolic disorder or skin condition or whatever it is that makes him smell like a walking dumpster – a guy like that is going to stand out like a turd in a punch bowl.'

'You always knew how to turn a phrase.'

'There's something else, Coop.'

'What?'

'Nobody in this town wants to talk about the Red Hill Ripper.'

'And that surprises you? It's a small town. They're wary of outsiders.'

Maybe, Darby thought, picking up a plastic drinking straw and twirling it between her fingers.

'Look at where I grew up,' Coop said. 'In Charlestown, when you saw someone doing something illegal, stealing, mugging, shooting – whatever was going down, you never called the cops, and you kept your mouth shut when they came round asking questions.'

'The whole "code of silence" bullshit.'

'I'm not saying it's right; I'm saying how it was. Charlestown, East Boston, Southie – they all had that small town, tribal mentality. That's why a gangster and serial killer like Whitey Bulger was able to get away with all that shit for so long.'

And it certainly didn't hurt that the FBI *had been watching his back the entire time*, Darby thought. For two decades – while Whitey and his gang flooded cocaine into Boston's neighbourhoods, murdered their competition and smuggled guns across the sea to the IRA – he and his long-time business partner, Stephen 'The Rifleman' Flemmi, also worked as federal informants for the FBI's Boston field office. In exchange for information about the Italian Mafia operating in Boston and Rhode Island, their federal handlers gave them tips about wiretaps – and about criminal rivals, who were later killed by Whitey's gang. A witness who had come forward with information on Whitey's illegal activities was brutally murdered. Others mysteriously vanished, never to be heard from again. The corruption grew, the bodies piled up; yet, when sealed indictments were about to come down, Bulger's handlers ensured that he had plenty of time in which to leave town. For the next sixteen years, twelve of which were spent on the FBI's Ten Most Wanted List, he and his common-law wife lived as fugitives, until a call on a tip line revealed that the octogenarian couple were in an apartment complex in Santa Monica, California. The whole sordid affair read like a thriller – except that it was true.

She didn't need to tell any of this to Coop. Not only had he grown up during the Bulger era, he had barely survived it.

'Your people,' Darby said, catching how Coop bristled at the words, 'the people living in Southie and East Boston – they didn't protect Whitey because he was keeping the streets safe and free of drugs.'

'What are you getting at?'

'Evil doesn't operate in a vacuum.'

'Meaning?'

'Meaning nobody in this town is afraid of the Red Hill Ripper.' Darby tossed the straw back down on the bar top, then turned her head to him. He looked as exhausted as she felt. 'What if we're approaching this the wrong way? What if there's another component at work here? Something that isn't sexual?'

'You saying this guy isn't a sexual sadist? Because what we saw inside the bedroom yesterday says otherwise.'

'No. This guy's a textbook sadist. But not one of the female vics was raped. If we take away sex, what are we left with for motives?'

'Money and power. Revenge.'

Darby nodded. 'Here's another question: why is the killer only targeting families living in Red Hill?'

A cell phone trilled. 'That's me,' he said, and straightened. He reached inside his jacket pocket, came back with the sat-phone and flatted a palm against his other ear. 'Cooper.'

She saw him swallow, saw the alarmed expression on his face when his gaze cut sideways to her; then, with his head, he motioned to the front door and quickly headed towards it. Darby followed behind him, walking through the space Coop left in his wake, the pulse racing in her neck. *Another family is dead*, she thought as she stepped outside, on to the enclosed porch. *The son of a bitch watched that interview I did and he decided to kill another family*.

'Right around the corner,' he said into the phone as he moved down the steps. A blast of wind howled past them, temporarily blinding her.

Coop hung up. 'He called looking for you,' he said, fishing the car key out of his jacket pocket. 'Said he'll call back in ten. We'll take my car.'

'What does he want?'

'Don't know yet. He told the dispatcher – this is a direct quote – he said, "Tell her fifteen minutes or I'll kill them all."'

She buckled herself into the passenger's seat and set the stopwatch function on her digital watch.

46

Darby entered the lobby of the police station expecting to find cops gathered in anxious crowds, pacing and drinking coffee and talking among themselves, wondering aloud and privately if the Red Hill Ripper was just minutes away from butchering another family. That had been her experience back in Boston. Instead, she found the lobby peacefully quiet and most of the nearby offices dark. A phone rang from somewhere down the hall.

She glanced at her wrist as she followed Coop into the squad room and saw that she had a little over twelve minutes until the Red Hill Ripper called back.

Hoder sat on the edge of his desk, rubbing the sleep from his face. His tie was gone, but he was wearing the same clothes she had seen earlier. Police Chief Robinson was with him, dressed in a pair of badly wrinkled khakis and a grey sweatshirt with frayed cuffs. His boots were damp, flecked with melting snow.

The chief eyed her coldly. Hoder too seemed to be looking at her differently now, not with contempt but with disappointment and, she thought, sadness.

'He called 911 from a payphone in downtown Red Hill,' Hoder said. 'Chief Robinson sent a couple of cruisers. They're still there, dusting it for prints. When this guy calls back – if he calls back – the chief's got all his people standing by. Most of 'em got vehicles with four-wheel drive, so hopefully that will help their response time.

'The woman who spoke to him, Betty, said his voice seemed altered. He identified himself as the Red Hill Ripper and asked to speak to you. When she said she'd have to put him on hold, he replied, "Tell her or I'll kill them all." Then he hung up.'

'Where's the call centre?' Darby asked.

'Right down the hall. We may have a lead on this Timmy person.' Hoder turned his attention to the police chief.

Robinson said, 'Like every other station, we hire a cleaning crew to come in during the night and empty the trash and clean up our holding cells. Outfit called RBG Cleaning, operates out of Brewster. Services them, us and a good number of the surrounding towns. Until about two years ago, they used to come in every night. Now we've only got 'em twice a week.'

Darby glanced at her watch again. Just under ten minutes left. The snow on her head had melted, making her scalp itch, and she felt sweat gathering along the small of her back.

'Reason I bring it up,' Robinson said, 'is because a year ago, maybe a year and a half, the people working the night shifts complained about the halls stinking like rotten food. Couple of 'em said it smelled like fish. This was during the summer, so we thought that maybe someone dropped food somewhere or left it in a trashcan and it spoiled. We were bleaching all of our buckets. This went on for about a month or so and then it stopped.

'Terry told me about the interview you two had with

the hooker, escort, whatever she is, how this Timmy guy smelled, and it got me thinking, so I talked to Ray about it. He's on his way to Brewster to talk to Ron Gondek, the guy who owns the cleaning company, to see if he employed someone matching Timmy's description.'

'If he did, it means Timmy was in here before the killings started. Do the janitors have access to the offices?'

Robinson nodded, knowing where she was heading. 'All the cabinets and desks are locked up every night – at least mine are,' he said.

'Computers?'

'Password protected, every last one of them – and not with those rinky-dink passwords you can guess, shit like your birthday or your pet's name.'

Darby's attention had drifted to the pictures of the dead women on the whiteboards. For a moment the only sound she heard was Robinson jingling his change and car keys in his pockets.

Hoder said, 'The guy from our facial-imaging lab finished up with the Tuttle woman about half an hour ago. He should be emailing the sketch to us any minute now.'

She nodded absently, still looking at the pictures. 'You said he called the call centre's emergency number?'

'That's right.'

'That number in the phone book? On the internet?'

'No, it's a private line used only by cops.'

'So somehow he got that number. And we know he got all of our cell phone numbers, because he sent out those pictures of me earlier today.'

Darby glanced at her watch. Six and a half minutes left. *Plenty of time*, she thought, and moved to the door.

'Where are you going?' Coop asked.

'To check Williams's office. Be right back.'

His light was still on. The computer was a tower unit; it stood on the floor, underneath the desk. She took out her penlight, got down on the linoleum and examined its back. It took her a only moment to find what she was looking for.

When she returned to her feet, she found Coop standing in the doorway, looking at her expectantly. She moved into the hall, motioning for him to follow, and checked her watch again. Three minutes and forty seconds left.

'There's a small USB key installed in the back of the tower,' Darby said as they walked. 'Those things have PC-monitoring software on them. You plug them into someone's computer and bingo, you have access to emails, contacts, every single thing on their computer – and you can do it all remotely.'

'You got all of that from looking at a USB stick?'

'The words "Spy Cobra Delux" are printed along the side.'

'Well, that's a clue, sure.'

'How he got his hands on everyone's cell phone numbers has been nagging at me all day. Using a device like that makes sense since our man likes computers.'

'And bugged your phone,' Coop added. 'That USB spy device, I wonder why he left it there.'

'Maybe it does double-duty as an audio bug. We'll run the name through Google and find out what it does.'

Coop took her to the call centre, a warm, boxy room with long counters along the walls that served as desks. The dispatcher, Betty, a mountain of a woman poured into a tight-fitting black fleece sweatshirt, sat in front of a bank of three computer monitors. She kept shifting in her seat and swallowing nervously, like someone waiting for a bomb to go off.

The woman gave Darby a headset; everyone else had headphones so they could listen in when the Ripper called.

While they waited, Darby explained what she had found to Hoder and Chief Robinson.

Darby was checking her watch when a 911 call came through.

47

Betty spoke into her headset. '911, what is your emergency?'

On the end of the line Darby heard rapid breathing.

Crying.

Her attention was fixed on the monitor with the ANI/ALI screen. The software had caught the incoming number but there was no address.

Land-line calls were traced in a matter of seconds. Call from cell phones took longer; the software had to triangulate the signal as it bounced between towers. Betty moved her computer mouse with one hand and punched her keyboard with the other.

Now a frightened woman's voice: 'He's got us tied up in the bedroom. Me and my family.'

Darby felt cold all over. She leaned forward in her chair, elbows on her knees, and stared down at the scuffmarks on the floor. The voice had a slight echo to it. *She's on a speakerphone*, Darby thought.

'There's a rope tied around my neck,' the woman sputtered.

From the corner of her eye Darby could see Coop looking at her, and she recalled what he had said to her before she went into the squad room to do the interview: *I saw the list of questions and answers the two of you came up with.*

You go on the record saying those things, you might as well be jamming a stick of dynamite up this guy's ass. Once you light the fuse, who the hell knows how he's going to react? Maybe he'll decide to take his aggression out on someone else instead of you. 'Is the intruder inside the room with you?' Betty asked. While she had been taught to keep her emotions in check, to speak clearly and calmly, Darby caught a slight hitch in the woman's reedy voice.

The woman on the phone didn't answer. *He's listening in on the conversation,* Darby thought. *He's telling her what to say.*

'Ma'am, are you still there?' Betty asked.

'Yes,' the woman sputtered. 'Yes, he's here with me. With us.'

'Where do you live, ma'am?'

Another pause. Darby pictured the killer whispering the answer into the woman's ear. She looked again at the ANI/ALI screen. Still no address.

'He said to put her on the line. Darby McCormick.'

'I'm right here,' Darby said.

Then the woman broke down, sobbing hysterically. '*He just put a bag over my husband's head, please, you've got to help us. Twenty-two —*'

The woman started choking.

He's strangling her. Darby hit the mute button on her headset and whipped round to Betty. 'Why's the address taking so goddamn long to trace?'

Betty's eyes didn't move from the screen. Police Chief Robinson answered the question. 'We don't have the software to trace cell signals,' he said. 'Only the state police can do that, system called One-Click.'

The woman's choking filled their headsets.

Robinson continued. 'Betty already bumped up the call to them. They can't pinpoint a cell signal's exact location, but they can give us co-ordinates, longitude and latitude. We'll be able to get an address with that.'

'How long is this gonna take?'

Robinson didn't have an answer. Over her headphones Darby thought she heard the crinkling sound of a plastic bag and her heart leapt high in her chest. She got back on the line, reminding herself not to beg: begging was the lifeblood of a sadist, what fed their need to torture. Beg and he'd start to kill everyone.

'You wanted to talk to me,' she said into the microphone. 'I'm here. Tell me what you want.'

Silence. Still no address listed on the screen.

'Tell me what you want,' Darby said again.

Then a gulping and gasping sound roared over their headphones, like the noise of someone breaking to the surface of the water after having been submerged.

'Alone,' the woman managed to say. Her wretched coughs exploded over the line for what seemed like minutes. 'Come alone and he'll won't kill us.'

'I'll come alone; you have my word,' Darby said. 'Tell me where you live.'

Hysterical sobbing. 'Please help us.'

'I'm coming. Alone. Give me your address –'

'*Please.*'

Click and the call ended.

48

Palms damp and her throat dry, Darby glanced at Coop and saw the thinly disguised blame in his eyes. She looked away from him, at Hoder, who was standing near the doorway. The colour had drained from his face. Betty hit the redial button for the phone number.

Darby felt sick and clammy, and she had trouble swallowing. A voice that wasn't her own, cold and flat and without mercy, broke in and said: *He's using the family as bait. He's setting a trap for you so he can kill you.*

'No matter how we cut it, someone is going to have to go into that house,' Darby said. 'It may as well be me.'

Coop, not surprisingly, was the first to speak. 'The family's dead and you know it.'

Hoder nodded in agreement. 'Coop's right,' he said. 'He wants you to come alone so he can lure you into a trap.'

'And if I don't do as he instructed – if you send in the first responders, then the EMTs – who the hell knows how he's going to act?' Darby asked. 'If he wants me to come alone, chances are he's somewhere close by, watching the house. Once we get the address, I say we set up a perimeter and block him in.'

Then Darby looked at Robinson and said, 'You let the emergency people in there first, they'll be going in blind.

If our guy has set some sort of trap, they won't know what to look for. I will. I'm the best candidate, and besides, it's me he wants anyway.'

Coop threw up his hands. 'This is insane.'

'And what if the family's still alive?' Darby asked.

'There's no way you honestly believe that – I *know* you don't believe that. He wants you to go there so he can kill you – that's why he had that woman feed you that bullshit line about how he won't kill everyone if you come. He's playing off your sense of decency. You're letting a psychopath manipulate you.'

'I'll need a car. I left mine at the bar.'

'You can't save that family. They're gone. What this is about is your guilt.'

Then Coop's expression transformed itself into an odd mix of grief and sympathy – the look of a man about to suffer an irrecoverable loss. 'And it's going to kill you,' he said.

Betty spoke up. 'Staties traced the cell signal,' she said, and handed Darby a slip of paper. '22 Exeter Road, in Red Hill.'

'How far away is it?'

'In normal conditions, I'd say about six, ten minutes max.'

Darby got to her feet. She felt a cold and hollow spot in the pit of her stomach.

Robinson held out his car keys to her. 'Take my truck,' he said. 'White Ford parked out front. It's got four-wheel drive so you won't get stuck out there.'

'Your truck got GPS?'

'No.'

'Then I'll need you to give me directions. You can relay them to me over the phone. Tell me what number to call.' Darby gave the slip of paper in her hand to the police chief.

Coop looked at her longingly. *Don't do it*, his eyes said. *Please.*

Robinson handed the paper back to her. 'I'll coordinate everything from here,' he said. 'I have everybody's numbers.'

Darby left the room. When she reached the end of the corridor, she turned and, glancing back to the call centre, saw Coop setting down his headphones on the counter. He had the look of a man placing a rose on top of a coffin about to be lowered into the ground.

49

The snow was still coming down at a furious clip, thick and wet, but the roads Darby took had been ploughed. She parked the police chief's truck at the top of the drive-way belonging to the house at 22 Exeter Road. Coop was riding with Hoder, and their car was parked near the perimeters that had been set up in a quarter-of-a-mile radius around the house. It belonged to the French family, Robinson had told her. Luther and Carla French had a 23-year-old son named Sebastian and an older daughter, Rita, who was twenty-six.

In her headlights she caught glimpses of the pleasant brown Colonial with its attached two-car garage. There didn't appear to be a single light turned on. She could also make out a series of depressions, holes caused by the Red Hill Ripper's footsteps, in the driveway leading up to the front of the house.

'I'm here,' she said into the phone. She killed the engine and pocketed the keys. 'Don't have any of your people move in until I've cleared the house.'

'Understood,' Robinson replied. 'Good luck.'

Darby opened the door to a blast of cold air. She got out and clipped the satphone to her belt near the front of her jeans, so Robinson could hear her back at the call centre. Then she removed the nine from her shoulder holster and attached a tactical light underneath the muzzle. She clicked off the safety, pulled back the receiver and eased a round into the chamber. Then she shut the truck's door and trudged through the white, knee-high blanket covering the driveway.

Snow as sharp as needles blew against her face, and it was bitterly cold. As she got closer, she saw that the front door was wide open, like an invitation, and again she wondered what was waiting for her inside.

Was Coop right when he said she was allowing a psychopath to manipulate her? Probably. And maybe her need to go in there alone, as instructed, had something to do with her guilt about having gone ahead with the video interview. She had no way of knowing whether the Red Hill Ripper had watched it, and, if he had, if it had prompted him to vent his rage on another family. What if the Ripper had been planning this moment, this endgame, or whatever it was, from the moment she'd arrived?

During the journey, her imagination had gone into overdrive, conjuring up all sorts of grisly scenarios and possibilities. There had been a case just outside Boston where a serial killer murdered families and then planted bombs for when the police arrived. Her first major serial case had involved Traveler: he had blown up a SWAT van and later bombed a major Boston hospital. Had the Ripper taken a page from their book? What if he had come up with another way of killing her? In Boston a killer had booby-trapped a closed door with a shotgun. The first responding officer had opened the door and nearly had his head blown off.

Conjuring up different scenarios was both useless and unproductive. She wouldn't know anything until she got into the house. Right now she needed to keep her attention sharp and focused. She clicked on the tactical light beneath the gun's muzzle and brought up the nine as she mounted the steps to a small, enclosed front porch. The snow had stopped blowing against her face, but not the wind; it hit her like a fist and roared inside the dark house. She cleared everything in her immediate line of vision; and then she darted to the right side of the door and pressed her back against the vinyl siding, blinking the melting snow out of her eyes.

Darby took off her jacket – the thick leather would only encumber her – and dropped it on the porch floor. Her face and hair, which she had tied behind her head with an elastic band before she left the station's parking lot, were soaked. She used the sleeve of her shirt to wipe away the wetness from her face.

Was the killer lurking inside the darkness of the house? If so, where was he hiding?

50

Her chest tight, Darby swung around the doorway and swept the torch's bright and narrow beam of light on the areas on either side of the stairs, her blind spots. A formal living-room was to her right, a dining-room to her left. Both were clear, everything in order, no signs of a struggle.

She turned away and again pressed her back against the vinyl siding. The downstairs windows had been opened: the air inside the house was frigid, and she'd seen curtains billowing in the wind. She also saw that three of the dining-room chairs were missing.

Now she played her light over the doorway and threshold and foyer floor. She didn't detect anything remotely suspicious or out of the ordinary.

Gingerly, she placed one foot on the foyer's hardwood floor, as though testing her weight on a pond of ice. She entered the house.

A gust of wind blew past her and she started when the front door slammed. Heart racing, she searched the wall for a light switch. Finding a brass switch plate with four click buttons, she hit one at random. No lights went on. She pressed the other buttons, but the house remained dark. Moving to the base of the stairs, she pointed her light up to the next floor.

'It's me, Darby McCormick,' she called up into the darkness. Her light reflected off the upstairs banister and, beyond it, off an opened door leading to what looked like a bathroom. 'I'm alone.'

Her voice echoed and died.

Darby strained to listen. Heard nothing but the wind howling and shaking the nearby trees, the branches creaking and splitting. She examined the hardwood staircase in front of her. There were seven steps leading to a small landing, where she spotted a puddle. Melted snow from boots – the Red Hill Ripper's boots. There was a second set of steps hidden from view behind a wall.

First, she had to clear the downstairs. For the next forty minutes she worked systematically clearing each of the rooms, including the attached garage. She watched where she stepped and moved slowly and checked everything and found nothing suspicious or out of the ordinary.

At least not yet, she thought, returning to the base of the stairs. If the Red Hill Ripper had laid a trap, chances are it would be somewhere on the next floor.

Again, Darby called up into the darkness. 'I'm alone, just as you asked.'

Again, there was no answer.

Because they're all dead, Coop had said. *You know that.*

Her skin was soaked with sweat, and her shirt and jeans felt glued to her skin as she moved up the staircase quietly, taking one step at a time. The scrape of her thick-soled boots on the hardwood echoed throughout the house. She reached the landing. The door opposite the top of the stairs was the only one that was closed.

Darby climbed the remaining steps, shivering. The air was cold because all the windows upstairs had been opened. She could hear the wind blowing through the screens and she could see plumes of breath in the torch's halo of light. She thought of the metabolic disorder she'd read about on the web, TMAU or whatever it was called; then she thought about what the Tuttle woman had said about her client, the man named Timmy who reeked of garbage, and Darby surmised that the killer had opened all the windows to remove the stench of fish that seeped from his pores.

Darby systematically started to clear every room on the floor: the upstairs bathroom; a boy teenager's bedroom, judging by the posters of Pearl Jam and Bob Marley; and a smaller room that was used as a home office, the two opened windows blowing papers across the floor. By the time she returned to the closed door opposite the top of the steps, she had sweated through her shirt, and her mouth was as dry as paper.

She got down on her knees and ran the beam of light underneath the quarter-inch gap at the bottom of the door. The only thing she could see was a carpet. She got back to her feet and then she turned the doorknob slowly, checking for resistance of any kind. She encountered none. Body tense and sweat dripping down the small of her back, she gently placed her hand on the door, wondering if it had been booby-trapped in some way. *Assume it is*, she thought. *Assume the absolute worst until you can rule it out.* She opened the door a crack, checking for wires or rope, and didn't see any – but something was behind the door, something *had* happened inside this bedroom.

Slowly she released her grip on the doorknob and backed against the wall. She reached out with one hand, placed it on the door and inched it open further. She couldn't see the bedroom windows but knew they were open; wind blew past her hand and punched the door, almost forcing it shut. Now she could see part of the bedroom: a beige carpet and an opened door leading to a walk-in closet where women's clothing hung neatly above shoes displayed on racks.

She inched open the door further, then stopped to check. Now a floor-to-ceiling bookcase came into view. Tensing, she pushed open the door a few more inches and kept looking. Finally, she had the door all the way open. Nothing happened. It was time to go inside.

Darby raised her nine. *Don't mash the trigger, breathe and squeeze* – and, looking down the target site, she swung around the doorway.

51

In the tactical light's bright white halo Darby saw a pair of chairs at the foot of the bed. A man dressed in boxers and a dingy white T-shirt with coils of grey and white hairs sprouting out of the V-neck was bound to one, his head covered by a black plastic bag. The man's son, also dressed in boxers and a long-sleeve T, had been tied to a chair on the far right, and, like his father, he had a plastic bag wrapped around his head.

The mother, Clara, dressed in a dark flannel nightgown, sat between husband and son, her face the colour of an eggplant. She had been strangled to death, and this time the killer had left the rope tied around her neck. A cell phone sat on the woman's lap. The screen was glowing and a tiny green LED pulsed.

The killer had never before left behind a phone, and he had changed the chair arrangement. All three chairs had been positioned against the far wall and they faced the bedroom door – faced her – like a small, private jury.

Darby closed the door behind her. She crept forward, searching the neatly made bed, the carpeted floor and the tops of the bureaus and nightstands for anything odd. There was no computer or iPad in here, the sole electronic device belonging to the phone resting on the woman's lap.

Did it have a camera? Was the killer listening or watching or both right now?

There was an opened door to her left, for the bathroom, and she had to clear it. She spun around the doorway, the beam of light revealing a tiled floor and marble vanity.

It was clear.

Darby searched under the bed, looking for anything unusual, found nothing. Then she moved to the chairs and placed a finger on the man's neck, her attention fixed on the phone. She didn't see any wires.

The man didn't have a pulse. Darby knew the woman was dead but she checked for a pulse anyway and then she did the same for their son. All three were dead and the killer was nowhere to be seen.

Darby's attention shifted back to the dead woman. She was looking at the cell, at its pulsing green light, when the bedroom lights turned on.

She started, her heart leaping in her throat, moved back to the bedroom door and opened it. The hallway lights were on, and she could see that some of the downstairs lights were on too.

The house must have lost power because of the storm, Darby thought. *Now it's back on.*

Darby placed a wicker hamper against the door to keep the wind from blowing it shut. She stepped into the hall, shivering, and unclipped her satphone.

'He's not here,' Darby said.

'The family?' Robinson asked.

'Dead. The husband and wife and their son. I haven't

found the daughter. He opened almost every window inside the house, and he left a cell on the woman's lap.'

'Why?'

'To listen in and watch me? Us? Who knows? Does Brewster have a bomb squad?'

Darby heard the man's breath catch in his throat. She could also hear phones ringing in the background.

'What makes you think the phone is a bomb?' the chief asked.

'I don't know what to think. He left the phone here for a reason, but I'm afraid to touch it.' Darby rubbed the sleeve of her shirt against her forehead. She couldn't stop shivering. 'All the lights just came back on.'

'Power's going on and off all over town, on account of the storm. You find anything else beside the phone?'

'No, just the phone.' Darby was looking at it from the hall.

'So there's nothing in there.'

'At least nothing I can see. Maybe he just summoned me here to screw with my head – to screw with all of us.'

'But?'

'It doesn't feel right. I can't put a finger on it.'

The dead woman's eyes stared accusingly at Darby. *You did this*, her gaze said. *I'm dead and my husband and son are dead because of you. You did this.*

'Is it safe to send my people in there?' Robinson asked her.

'I don't know. Contact Coop and Hoder,' she said as she moved down the stairs to retrieve her jacket. 'Tell them what I found and ask them what they think.'

52

Coop and Hoder had decided to join her. Darby, watching from the dining-room window, her jacket zipped all the way up to her neck and her hands stuffed inside her jeans pockets, saw their car pull up behind the chief's truck.

The power for the house was still on, but it had flickered once or twice. The porch lights and the pair of floodlights mounted on the garage must have been turned on before her arrival, because they were turned on now.

It seemed Hoder was having trouble breathing, and his legs were shaky. Coop had gripped the man's arm tightly to keep him from falling, but Hoder was still doubled over, inhaling great gulps of air. Darby left the house to assist.

'It's the altitude,' Hoder said when she reached him. Snow whipped around their heads, obscuring his face. 'My lungs are still having a hard time adjusting, and I think my knee has finally given out.'

'Let's get you back in the car,' Darby yelled over the wind.

'No, I'll be fine, honest. Just help me inside the house.'

As Darby grabbed the man's other arm, she heard Robinson's tinny voice yelling over the satphone's small speaker. Although she had clipped the phone back on to her belt, she had kept the line open. She brought the phone up to her ear.

'They're here,' Darby told Robinson.

'A woman called 911 just a few minutes ago to report what she described as "a thundering boom". We've had a few more calls saying the same thing. I've got –'

A rifle report echoed somewhere in front of her, behind the wind. A split second later she thought she caught a glimpse of a burning white projectile heading straight for Hoder. She heard a dull thud and the sickening crunch of bone; then she heard the breath jump from his throat as he was knocked off his feet. The phone slipped from her hands, and she lost her balance.

The second shot came just as fast, and, as she staggered and fell into the snow, she heard the round split a tree directly behind her. She had let go of Hoder and was scrambling to her feet when the rifle fired again and there was a *whang* sound, metal hitting metal. She saw Coop lying face down in the snow, his hands covering the back of his head.

Grab him or Hoder: you can choose only one, she thought.

She went for Coop. The rifle fired again, and then suddenly there was an ear-splitting boom. House and car windows shattered, shards flying everywhere. A great pressure wave slammed into her and sent her spinning. The side of her head struck the driveway, and before she passed out she saw a huge ball of flame, like an eruption from the bowels of hell, light up the night sky.

Day Three

53

Darby awoke to the sight of a dozen eyes watching her.

Body slick with sweat and her heart banging like a snare drum, she blinked furiously until the dimly lit room came into a sharper focus.

Not human eyes – doll eyes. Glassy and lifeless, with long, unnaturally thick eyelashes set in tiny oval faces painted beauty-pageant pretty. All little girls, each one dressed in a different outfit: wedding gowns and farmer's overalls and period costumes that went as far back as the Civil War. They crowded the six white laminate shelves on the wall opposite the foot of her bed, a row of soft square track lighting shining down on their bright smiles and plump, outstretched arms.

Darby swallowed. Her throat was bone-dry, and the entire left side of her face was numb. Pain there, a faraway throbbing hidden behind some sort of narcotic.

It was then she realized she could see only out of her right eye.

The left eye was completely covered. Gently prodding it with her fingertips, she felt the fabric of a compression bandage. It was wrapped around her head to keep the thick, gauzy dressing from moving.

Darby had been placed in a sitting-up position to reduce the swelling in her head. She was in a hospital room, that much was clear. But this one had been designed for little girls. In addition to the dolls, the walls were decorated with pink-and-lavender wallpaper featuring Barbie the Ballerina, Barbie the Skater – Barbie everywhere, along with Tinker Bell and Disney princesses of every ethnic variety.

The door to her room was shut. A steam radiator hissed and clanked underneath a pair of snow-caked windows glowing with a silver light. Morning light. The wall clock read 8.45.

Then she remembered the rifle shots and Hoder being hit, followed by more shots and then an explosion. It had come from outside the house, she thought. In a panic she wondered if she had glass or debris in her eyes and had been blinded. She swung her legs over the side of the bed. The throbbing in her head increased as she slowly got to her feet.

Darby staggered towards the bathroom, the floor slippery beneath her socks. Her stomach lurched in protest, and the throbbing had transformed into what felt like hot nails being hammered into her skull.

Darby turned on the bathroom light. A bandaged, Frankenstein mess of cuts and swollen skin stared back at her in the mirror. After unwrapping the compression bandage, she slowly peeled away the gauze and found a snake of surgical staples stretching from her hairline to the middle of her cheek, the raw wound covered in a greasy ointment. She was staring at it when the door to her room clicked open.

A sprite of a woman dressed in jeans and a charcoal-grey turtleneck sweater stood in the doorway. The doctor. The stethoscope was always a dead giveaway.

'Coop,' Darby said in a thick voice.

'I'm sorry?'

'Jackson Cooper. He's with the FBI.'

'I don't know him.'

'Is he here?'

'No. The gunshot victim was transported to Brewster General and is in critical condition. The others are dead. I'm sorry.'

Darby's legs felt shaky. She gripped the edge of the sink.

The doctor grabbed Darby firmly by the arm. 'You're at the Rockland Family Medical Centre in Red Hill. I'm Dr Mathis. We need to get you back to bed.' A long sigh of irritation, and then the woman added, 'I need to redress that wound.'

Darby allowed herself to be led back to bed. She felt numb all over.

'Your CT scan came back normal,' Dr Mathis said, and went to work cleaning and redressing the wound. 'No inter-cranial bleeding or fractures. You have an unusually thick skull for a woman.'

Darby barely heard her, thinking about Coop. He had been lying in the snow not far from Hoder, and he hadn't been moving.

'Your eye is fine, by the way,' the woman said. 'Now, about your temple and cheekbone . . . I saw you looking in the mirror, and I know it looks like a God-awful mess, but there's no need to worry. The swelling will go down in a few days. The bruising should subside in about fourteen days, which will be right around the time the staples should be removed. The wound itself will take some time to heal, but you should consult a plastic surgeon – the same one who did that work on your other cheek. You can barely see that scar.

'I noticed your left cheekbone was replaced with an implant. What happened there?'

'Someone tried to split my head open with an axe,' Darby said, her voice sounding far away, as though someone else were speaking.

Dr Mathis looked uneasy. Nervous. *Nice ladies don't discuss such nasty things*, her prim expression said. *Nice ladies certainly aren't involved in such things.*

'How did I get here?'

The doctor stopped working. She tilted her head to the side and eyed Darby quizzically. 'You don't remember?'

'Remember what?'

'Speaking to Detective Williams. He was here twenty, maybe thirty minutes ago. You were awake.'

Darby had no memory of it.

'Don't be alarmed,' the doctor said. 'Short-term memory loss is common with brain trauma, even in cases of a mild concussion. I've also seen it in cases of post-traumatic stress disorder. It's a condition where –'

'I'm familiar with the term.' Darby rolled on to her side, picked up the phone from the nightstand and placed it on the side of her mattress.

'You can make your call after I finish up here.' Dr Mathis reached for the phone.

Darby gently grabbed the woman's wrist. 'Go tend to your other patients.'

54

Darby was about to dial information for the number of Brewster General when she felt a sick fluttering inside her chest.

The gunshot victim was transported to Brewster General and is in critical condition, the doctor had told her. *The others are dead.*

She had been speaking to Coop when the first gunshot went off.

Please, God, don't let him be dead.

That inner voice spoke up: *You need to prepare yourself.*

But you couldn't prepare yourself for something like this, even when you had time *to* prepare. She had been thirteen years old when her father had been shot. She'd insisted on going with her mother to the hospital. When the surgeon came into the ICU's waiting room, she saw the expression on the man's face and knew right then her father was going to die.

And then there was her mother who, at fifty-eight, had developed a stage four melanoma. A mole the size of a pinprick on Sheila McCormick's back had quietly turned malignant. The surgeon had excised the mole but the cancer had already spread past the lymph nodes and into her bloodstream; it had been greedily feasting on her healthy organs for months. *You need to prepare yourself*, the doctor had told Darby. She'd been thirty-three.

And Darby had tried to prepare herself. Every day she reminded herself that, in an odd way, she had been handed a gift: her mother was going to die – it wasn't a matter of *if* so much as *when* – but at least this time there was time to come to grips with what was happening. She'd spent every available moment in her mother's company.

But another part of her had, with a childish stubbornness, refused to give up hope. Her mother's immune system was incredibly robust, the doctors said, so the special chemotherapy cocktail *might* work. That new, experimental skin cancer vaccine being tested in Baltimore *might* save her mother – and there was a chance Sheila McCormick *might* survive long enough to be a part of the clinical trials. Darby still remembered those long days, scouring the internet for doctors who specialized in melanoma, phoning offices all over the country and believing some sort of magic bullet existed, that all she had to do was to find it.

That was the danger of hope. It made you believe endless possibilities existed.

In its own way, hope was a form of cancer. A disease that could be eradicated only when presented with an immutable truth: death. Until that moment, hope would remain alive, even flourish, because there was always a chance, no matter how slim or remote, that the overwhelming truth you were facing was, in fact, wrong. Darby had learned that hard lesson first-hand.

She summoned the courage to dial directory assistance and ask for the number for Brewster General. The operator connected her and, after wading through the automated options, Darby finally got a live voice on the line. She explained who she was and what she wanted, and she was transferred to patient care.

Darby was on hold, waiting for someone to pick up, when Coop walked into her room.

She blinked as though he were a mirage produced by her fear. But he was there, looking real in the sunlight. His overcoat was torn in several places and spotted with dried blood along the lapels – Hoder's blood – but he had changed into a new suit.

Darby hung up and stared at him, her eyes wet.

When Coop sat on the side of her bed, his eyes bloodshot, the skin under them bruised from exhaustion, she leaned forward, wrapped her arms around him and, clutching him close to her, sobbed into his chest.

55

When Darby's tears subsided, Coop gently pried himself away from her. She tried to grab him again, not wanting to let him go, but he was already shuffling towards the bathroom.

Darby heard running water. A moment later he came back and handed her a cold, damp facecloth. She wiped her eyes, careful of the wound and staples.

Coop slid out of his coat and draped it over the back of a chair. Then he returned to the warm spot he'd left on her bed. Darby stared down at the blood-stained facecloth in her hands, afraid to ask any questions.

Coop provided answers without her having to say a word. 'Hoder is in critical condition at Brewster General,' he said in quiet, weary voice. 'Fortunately Robinson had ambulances standing by. I stemmed the bleeding in his shoulder as much as I could before they arrived. Otto and Hayes are dead. As best we can tell right now, it looks like someone set fire to the trailer before it exploded.'

'The shooter?'

'Still in the wind. The explosion at the French home came from a propane tank that was sitting on the side of the house.'

'Tracer rounds,' she said.

'How do you know he was using tracer ammo?'

'I thought I saw a bright, burning white round just before it hit Hoder.' Because tracers had small pyrotechnic charges built into their base, they burned brightly when fired, which allowed the shooter to follow the projectile's trajectory and make aiming corrections. 'I heard one of the rounds strike metal, but I thought it was one of the cars.'

Coop sighed. Nodded. 'It makes sense,' he said. 'An ordinary round could pierce the tank without making it explode. A tracer, though, would.'

The room took on the sober silence of a funeral home.

'The owners of the house, the parents, Luther and Carla French, were pronounced dead at the scene along with Sebastian, their 23-year-old son. The couple also have a 26-year-old daughter, Rita. She's a ski instructor living in Aspen. Williams talked with her. She's on her way down to Red Hill to identify the bodies.'

Darby didn't want to say the next part, but she had to. Her throat burned and her eyes filled with fresh tears.

'You were right. About the interview stirring him up.'

Coop got back to his feet.

'It was my idea,' she said. 'I'm the one who pressed Hoder to –'

'It's done.'

His words echoed inside the room. Darby remained quiet.

'There's no rewind button,' Coop said. He stood by the chair and, leaning forward, picked up his jacket. 'There's no way we can fix it. Hoder is as much to blame for this as –'

Then he cut himself off, the unsaid *you* hanging in the air between them.

'Hoder could have put a stop to it and he didn't,' Coop said. 'I gave him ample opportunity.'

Me too, Darby thought.

Coop removed a thick stack of paper that had been folded so it could fit inside his inner jacket pocket. He came back to the bed and handed the pages to her.

The first page contained a laser-printed copy of a photograph from another time – an ancient Polaroid of almost blurred colours showing a Caucasian girl of around seven or eight. She wore a white tank top stained with what looked like spaghetti sauce, her stringy blonde hair spilling across her tanned shoulders. The camera had captured her big blue eyes and her broad, gap-toothed smile.

Darby's scalp tightened. The skin on her face flexed and her muscles constricted, and, as her stomach went into free fall, the photograph went out of focus and her mind snapped back to her own childhood, a time when children rode their bikes after dark and wandered through neighbourhoods, malls and stores freely, without adult supervision, secure in the knowledge that the world was a good place and that monsters were nothing more than creatures relegated to bad dreams and not kindly seeming men who hunted with smiles in broad daylight.

56

It happened on the morning of 15 August 1983. A Monday. At half past eight, Joan Hubbard loaded her seven-year-old daughter into the family's station wagon and made the 22-mile drive from her small but pleasant ranch home in El Dorado, Kansas, to the North Colony Shopping Mall in Wichita. The Carter & Sullivan circular in Sunday's paper had advertised its annual overstock sale of bed linen. Joan wanted new sheets and a comforter, maybe even a couple of decorative throw pillows, to replace the hand-me-downs given to her by her older sister.

Finances had been tight ever since Joan O'Donnell married Peter Hubbard. The first three years Peter worked as a shop sweeper at General Electric and went to school nights. It had been one hell of a long slog, but the hard work had paid off. When Peter graduated with his engineering degree – the same day Nicola turned five – he was promoted to GE's jet-engine shop. The bump in pay wasn't life changing by any means, but the extra money had given them some well-deserved breathing room. No more penny-pinching on the groceries. No more Ramen Noodles and Hamburger Helper or buying second-hand clothing and used toys at the Salvation Army. Joan felt as though she'd been liberated from prison.

Then the workers went on strike. To make ends meet,

Peter took a job at a local auto-parts store and drove a cab three nights a week and every other weekend.

But that was all in the past. The strike was months behind them, and Peter was back at work with GE. They could afford to celebrate a little. Instead of a night out on the town, they decided to redo their bedroom.

Joan arrived just as Carter & Sullivan was opening its doors. She parked her Buick station wagon with its wood-panel trim near the mall's south-east entrance. For the next three decades, whenever Joan was interviewed about what happened, she'd tell reporters she wished she'd parked near the store's north entrance. That way they wouldn't have passed the toy aisle.

Nicky stopped dead in her tracks when she spotted what would become that year's popular Christmas toy: the Cabbage Patch doll. Nicky wanted to stop and look. Joan wanted to get the bedding and go home. Unlike her mother and sister, she didn't care for shopping.

'Please,' Nicky begged, tugging her mother's hand. 'Please, Mommy, *pleeeeease*.'

'You promise you'll stay here? Right here, in this aisle?'

'I promise.'

'You promise what?'

'To stay with the dolls.' Nicky smiled her gap-toothed smile. 'I won't walk away.'

Joan left her daughter alone without giving it a second thought. Another girl was standing in the aisle, a cute tomboy with curly black hair. It was 1983; parents left their kids alone all the time.

Joan found the comforter she wanted easily enough,

but the advertised sheets were another matter. When she failed to locate them, she hunted around for a store employee. The pleasant older man she spoke with didn't know anything about the advertised linens but said they might be out back in the storeroom and went to investigate. It was 9.13 a.m.

During this time, recent high school graduate and newly minted Carter & Sullivan employee Brad Fisher was running late. He was supposed to arrive at work at 8.45, but he had somehow slept through his alarm – again. He headed for the toy department, which was next to the door for the stockroom. When he cut through the aisle displaying those creepy Cabbage Patch dolls, he saw a teenager or a boy of at least twelve kneeling next to a young girl matching Nicky Hubbard's description. Brad would later tell the police he remembered the little girl clearly, because her long blonde hair was pulled back from her face and tied with a white marble elastic band. They were all the rage that summer; his younger sister wore the same sort of stupid things in her hair. The stores could barely keep them in stock.

Brad would also tell police about the teenager, who he had assumed was the girl's brother. How when the boy got to his feet he was short, barely a few inches over five feet. How he wore dirty jeans, scuffed work boots and a stained black T-shirt.

The boy grabbed his sister's wrist. When she tried to take her hand back, he yanked her arm, hard. When she let out a small yelp, he smiled.

A brother wouldn't act that way, an inner voice whispered.

Then another voice countered: *Remember when you got so pissed at Maggie for ratting on you when you sneaked out to meet George and Tony? What did you do?*

Brad smiled at the memory. *I cut the hair on all her Barbie dolls and flushed the evidence down the toilet.* Maggie, with her big fat mouth, was a tattletale bitch. So he breezed right past the brother and sister and entered the storeroom. When he punched in, it was 9.19 a.m.

At 9.24 a.m. Joan Hubbard had her new sheets in hand. She went to collect Nicky, only to find that her daughter was no longer looking at the Cabbage Patch dolls.

She's probably wandered off to look at some other toy, Joan thought. With a frustrated sigh, she went to find Nicky, who would be spending the rest of the day inside the house, grounded, for breaking her promise not to wander off.

The frustration turned to a slow but growing fear when she failed to find the child anywhere in the toy department.

The kids' clothing section was nearby. But Joan couldn't see her daughter anywhere among the racks.

Had Nicky gone to look for her? Had she hurt herself? Joan dropped her bedding items on a nearby display table and hurried off to the customer service department at the front of the store. She bypassed the people standing in line to return items and with her voice rising in panic told the young girl working the counter that she couldn't find her daughter.

The counter girl called the manager over the loudspeaker. Joan, hysterical with nightmarish thoughts about

319

her daughter, about her being lost or hurt or – *Don't say it, don't say it or it will come true* – darted behind the counter and pressed the microphone button.

'Nicky. Nicky, it's Mom. Come to the front of the store, Nicky. Mom is at the front of the store. My daughter's name is Nicky Hubbard. She's wearing a yellow sundress and sandals. She has blonde hair. Her name is Nicky Hubbard.'

The Carter & Sullivan store manager acted quickly and promptly. He announced Nicky's name and physical description over the loudspeaker, and told his employees to stand by all the store exits and stop any little blonde girl from leaving. It was now 9.56 a.m.

Brad Fisher hadn't heard any of the announcements. He was outside, standing in the unbearably hot Kansas sun, doing the same thing he did every morning: using a utility razor to break down the mountain of empty cardboard boxes stacked next to the dumpster. He returned to the storeroom a few minutes after ten, surprised to find it empty. Usually there were employees going in and out to stock the shelves or to take one of their allotted ten-minute breaks. He ducked into the staff bathroom and splashed cold water on his face.

The moment Brad stepped back into the store he knew something was wrong. Customers were huddled together and speaking in hushed tones. Others were moving swiftly through the aisles, searching the clothing racks and looking underneath the display tables, concern and dread etched in their faces. Carter & Sullivan employees were posted near the store exits.

When Brad found out what happened, his stomach turned to ice. He would never forget that feeling or the way the polished white linoleum floor seemed to dip and sway in his vision, or how he wanted to slip inside a black hole and disappear. Brad was eighteen years old and felt like crying.

What would always come back to him – what would continually haunt him – was that moment in the toy aisle when the boy had grabbed the little girl's wrist. How the brother's smile hadn't been, in fact, brotherly at all but something more sinister, something more in line with the way Brad's father smiled when he discovered a raccoon caught inside a steel trap.

I should've done something, Brad Fisher would later tell himself, as he took another slug of beer stolen from his father's workshop refrigerator.

If only I had said or done something, he would later tell himself as he took another hit off the bong.

If I hadn't been so spineless, so selfish, maybe she wouldn't have been taken, he would later tell himself as he rode the needle; heroin was the only thing that banished the images from that day, the only thing that offered him comfort.

Over the ensuing years, Brad discovered that no amount or combination of heroin, booze or pills could stop him from wondering what had happened to Nicky Hubbard. Only God knew.

Sometimes he would ask God: *Why didn't you help her?*

Sometimes God replied, but His answer was always the same:

Why didn't you help her? You were there, not me. You could have stopped it from happening, and you didn't.

Darby stopped reading and skimmed the rest of the file, glancing at its meagre offerings – the pithy investigative notes and false leads, the lack of evidence. When she reached the last page, she looked up at Coop.

'Aren't you going to read the rest of it?' he asked.

'I don't need to.'

'I didn't realize you were already familiar with the case.'

'Nicky Hubbard is the nation's poster girl for missing children. She's the reason why Congress created the National Center for Missing and Exploited Children in '85. People wrote books about what they think happened to her, they made a TV movie of the week.

'Why did you give me this?'

'The plastic print I found in the polyurethane along the Downes bedroom skirting board – the database came back with a match,' Coop said. 'That fingerprint belongs to Nicky Hubbard.'

57

Darby's mouth and throat went dry.

No one knew what had happened to Nicky Hubbard – no one except her killer, who had never been caught. And now Coop was telling her he'd found Hubbard's finger-prints more than three decades later at the scene of a recent triple homicide in another state.

'I examined the print myself,' he said, and reached inside his rumpled, blood-stained overcoat. 'There's no question: it belongs to her. But don't take my word for it.'

He came back with another folded set of papers and handed them to her. It was the forensics report on the plastic fingerprint he had recovered from the skirting board.

The FBI's Integrated Automated Fingerprint Identifi-cation System had found four possible matches. The one with the highest probability belonged to Nicky Hubbard. Wichita PD had collected the girl's fingerprints from items inside her bedroom and they had been loaded into IAFIS when it was officially launched on 28 July 1990.

Someone at the federal lab had pulled Hubbard's ori-ginal prints and emailed them to Coop, who performed a visual side-by-side comparison with the plastic print recovered from the Downes home. The evidence was conclusive. Nicky Hubbard, the seven-year-old missing girl who had been adopted by the nation had, at some point in time, been inside the bedroom where David and Laura Downes and their daughter had died. It was impossible to tell *when* Hubbard had been in there; fingerprints couldn't be dated. There was no known method to determine how long a print had been on a surface.

'This came through about five minutes ago,' Coop said, pointing to the forensics report in her hand. 'The IAFIS office called to tell me. No one else knows yet.'

'Where d'you print these out?'

'Robinson's office. Williams is letting me use it.' Then Coop's face clouded, and he added, 'Robinson is at Brewster General too. Heart attack. At the moment he's in a stable condition.'

Darby placed the pages on her lap. She leaned back against her pillow and stared out the door, at the brightly lit hallway. Her mind felt empty, her body devoid of any feeling, as though she had been disconnected from everything that had happened since her arrival in Red Hill. It was as if her blood had been replaced with Novocain.

'How old were you when it happened?' Coop asked.

'Eleven. You?'

'Thirteen. You remember what that time was like?'

Darby nodded. 'You couldn't turn on the TV without seeing Nicky Hubbard. She was on the front page of every major newspaper, magazine and supermarket tabloid. Parents were suddenly terrified their kids were going to get snatched in broad daylight. After she disappeared, my parents never let me out of their sight.'

'My mother was the same way with me and my sisters,' Coop said. 'Forget about leaving the house after sundown. Suddenly I couldn't walk or ride my bike anywhere or play hoops without her chaperoning me.'

Darby's gaze dropped back to her lap. Nicky Hubbard smiled up at her. The now-famous photograph, Darby had remembered reading, was the last picture Joan Hubbard had taken of her daughter.

'The Hubbard case was really the first of its kind,' he said. 'A real watershed moment for the nation and for law enforcement.'

Coop wasn't exaggerating. The National Center for Missing and Exploited Children hadn't existed in 1983, and the FBI's Violent Criminal Apprehension Program was still years away. In 1983 there was no Megan's Law requiring law enforcement agencies to inform the public about registered sexual offenders living in or around their neighbourhoods. No internet or email, just Teletype and fax machines. In 1983 it was easier to find a missing horse than an abducted or missing child.

'Now we know why he cleaned up that area in the bedroom,' Coop said. 'That blood we found wedged between the hardwood floorboards must've belonged to her.'

'I wonder why he didn't try to remove the fingerprint.'

'He probably didn't see it. Christ, we could barely see it with the ALS machine.'

'How many blood samples were in the trailer?'

'All of them. They're gone.'

Darby smoothed out the wrinkles on her sheets, thinking.

'I think you were right about what you said to me at the bar,' Coop said.

'I said a lot of things last night.'

'I'm talking specifically about what you said about him running us around to exhaust us. I'm on Day Three with a total of maybe five hours of sleep and my head feels like it's stuffed full of cobwebs. I can't think straight. I want to shut my eyes and not wake up for a week.

'But the truth is, we haven't been able to conduct a full investigation,' Coop continued. 'We haven't been able to examine the other homes – all of which, by the way, are vacant. Including you and me, we had a total of five federal investigators here. Ray Williams is the only detective. Ever since we arrived, the perp has been taxing our resources. Why? Because of the blood he left behind. Can you imagine what would happen if it got out that Hubbard's blood was found thirty years later at the scene of a triple homicide? This place would turn into a geek show. Every reporter, retired cop and private investigator would be crawling through town. We wouldn't be able to get work done, and this guy would bolt – has probably already bolted. What, you disagree?'

'No. No, I'm with you.'

'But?'

'Why not just lay low or, even better, pack up and get out of town? Why stick around?'

'I had the same question.'

'And if the Red Hill Ripper brought Nicky Hubbard to

the Downes house three decades ago, why would he go back there and kill the Downes family?'

'Another excellent question. We'll have to ask Eli Savran.'

'Who's Eli Savran?' Darby asked.

'Our man Timmy,' Coop replied.

58

'His full name is Eli Timothy Savran,' Coop said. 'Remember the cleaning crew Robinson told us about last night, the one from Brewster that services the police stations and the sheriff's office?'

Darby nodded. 'Robinson said Williams was going to talk to the guy who owned it, Ron something.'

'Ron Gondek. Williams did, last night. Turns out Gondek hired Timmy – and that's what he prefers to be called, Tim or Timmy, not Eli. Timmy's forty-seven, and he worked for the cleaning company for about two months and then he quit.'

'Why?'

'He told Gondek his mother had died and left him a good sum of money and a mortgage-free house. He was going to go back to school to get a degree in business or computer science, Gondek couldn't remember which. But he did remember that Timmy cleaned the Red Hill station and that Timmy suffered from a rare metabolic condition known as TMAU, also known as Fish Odour Syndrome.'

'Williams get an address?'

Coop nodded. 'Timmy lives right here in Red Hill. Williams is petitioning a judge for a warrant to search Timmy's house as we speak. I sent that sketch of Timmy to Williams, by the way. Williams pulled up Timmy's licence photo and compared it with the sketch. It's a near-match.'

'Did you talk to RCFL to see if Timmy watched the interview?'

'I did, and he didn't. Which tells me he was already planning to go after the French family.'

'You said Timmy Savran lives in Red Hill.'

'That's what Williams told me,' Coop said. Williams said Timmy told Gondek that he came back to Red Hill to take care of his mother – she had cancer, needed radiation and chemo. Her son helped her out, and when it became a terminal situation – hospice and all that – Timmy started to look for work. He's been in town for about three years.'

'So he's been here for three years and no one in town knows this guy?'

'From what I was told, Timmy –'

'And let's stop with the Timmy shit. It sounds like we're talking about a five-year-old kid.'

'Okay, *Eli* was very sensitive about his condition. He dropped out of high school and started working odd jobs – nightshifts at factories and after-hours janitorial work where he wouldn't have to interact with a lot of people. Guys like that live like vampires, they're not around in the daylight.'

Maybe, Darby thought. Everything Coop had said sounded completely logical. So why was it eating at her?

'There's something else I need to tell you,' Coop said. 'Once the Bureau finds out what happened to Hoder, Otto and Hayes, they're going to pull the plug on us.'

'Not if you tell them that you've recovered Nicky Hubbard's fingerprint they won't,' Darby said. 'They're not going to tell us to pack up and leave, not if you dangle the chance of all that great press under their noses.'

'They'll send in new people – senior people – to investigate what happened to the trailer. They'll shake our hands, say thank you, send us packing and go to work. Before any of that goes down, they'll want a full report from me – which will be hard to do, because my cell phone is infected and I can't carry it with me at the moment. But the snow storm will buy us some time.'

'How much time, you think?'

'Forty-eight hours, if we're lucky,' Coop said.

A phone trilled from the corner of the room. Coop got up, fished the phone out of his coat pocket and answered the call.

'Cooper.' He listened for a moment and then he moved the mouthpiece away and said to Darby, 'It's Williams. He's got the warrant.'

Coop turned back to his conversation. Darby sat up again, slowly, and, as she waited for the dizziness to pass and the throbbing to ease to a manageable level, she thought about what had happened last night at the French house, about why the Ripper had gone to such lengths to try to kill them when he could have simply faded back into the woodwork or, better yet, disappeared before the storm. Why stick around when he might be driving through some other state by now?

Darby was getting to her feet when she heard wet shoes squeaking outside her room. Deputy Sheriff Lancaster was storming through the corridor, heading her way.

59

Lancaster's face didn't seem friendly, though it was hard to tell. The right side was swollen, and Darby could see the beginnings of an eggplant-coloured bruise already at work beneath both eyes. The bridge of his nose was covered with a row of stitches.

Coop spoke into the satphone. 'I need to call you back,' he said, and rang off.

Snow lined the brim of Lancaster's hat, and his wet boots squelched until he reached the foot of the bed. He didn't take off his hat or gloves.

Bloodless greetings were exchanged.

Darby had returned to bed, and Lancaster leaned towards her slowly, deliberately, the way you did when you were about to impart a particularly harsh life lesson to a child. His cheeks were smooth, and she saw a small nick along his jawline. Apparently in the midst of all the chaos he had found the time to shave.

'You're goddamn lucky I'm not bringing you up on criminal charges,' Lancaster said to her.

'You had your chance yesterday,' Darby said.

'I'm talking about that interview you and Hoder set up. You deliberately provoked this guy, and for what? Two of your people are dead, one's clinging to life, and I've got another butchered family. Their deaths are on *you*.' Lancaster pointed at her as he said it.

Darby said nothing.

Coop had something to say. 'Chief Robinson signed off on it.'

'Which is exactly why we're having this conversation.'

Darby swore she saw a grin tugging at the corner of Lancaster's mouth.

'Effective immediately, all current and past Red Hill Ripper investigations have been transferred to my office,' Lancaster said. 'That means Red Hill is no longer involved in any way, shape or form. That also includes you two.'

The hospital phone on her bed rang. Darby ignored it.

'Pick it up,' Lancaster said to her. 'It's for you.'

She brought the receiver up to her ear. Her good eye never left Lancaster's face.

'McCormick.'

A deep, rumbling voice spoke on the other end of the line: 'Dr McCormick, my name is Tom Sutherland. I'm the attorney general for the state of Colorado, and this is a courtesy call to let you know that your services, as well as the FBI's, are no longer required in Red Hill. You are not to involve yourself in any investigation. Fail to comply and we'll be forced to file an obstruction of justice charge – and that's just the appetizer. Do we have an understanding?'

'No,' Darby said into the receiver. 'We don't.'

'What did you say?'

Darby hung up. 'Anything else, Teddy?'

'Stay the hell out of my investigation,' Lancaster said. 'The second this storm ends, you two are on the next plane outta here.'

The snow is no longer coming down hard and fast, like a great, white curtain, and the wind has died down considerably. I can actually see more than three feet in front of me, and the major roads are being ploughed, making driving easier. Places like Happy Valley Auto are still covered in a blanket so thick and wet the snow almost comes up to my kneecap, and I can feel water melting inside my boots by the time I reach the payphone.

Sarah answers on the first ring.

'How many minutes are left on your burner?' I ask.

'A little over ten.'

'Is it fully charged?'

'I charged it before I left the house, like you told me to do.'

I had called Sarah last night after I'd taken care of the trailer. 'The suitcases?'

'I have them here with me.'

Her voice is detached, listless; it's as if all the wiring inside her has been yanked from their power supply. She's been this way since I told her the truth about what I did inside the Downes house all those years ago, and about my plan to correct my mistake.

And, just as I feared, the truth has changed her. A man who wants to murder children is a monster, and monsters aren't worthy of forgiveness or redemption. You either put the animal down or you turn your back and run as far and as fast as you can, without looking back.

While I never doubted Sarah's love, I had underestimated her devotion and loyalty. She's still in Red Hill, waiting at the prearranged meeting spot – a good sign.

'Is it done?' she asks meekly.

'Almost.'

'You didn't tell me she was so pretty.'

'What?'

'The FBI consultant. Darby McCormick. She's on the front page of the *Item*'s website. She's beautiful.'

I feel my heart beating in my throat. I didn't tell Sarah about her.

'Is she dead?' Sarah asks.

'Not yet. I'm working on it.'

'That's why you want to stay, isn't it? You want her.'

'No.'

'But you're thinking about it, aren't you?'

'I need to get rid of her and the other one. Once they're dead, we'll be safe.'

'Then let me help you.'

I blink in surprise. 'You'd do that for me?'

'Why would you even ask me that? Baby, I would lay down my *life* for you.'

I feel the trepidation in my heart, and my throat is tight when I say, 'Sarah, honey, I'm so sorry about –'

'Stop. Tell me what I can do to help.'

'I need to do something first. I'll contact you when I'm ready.'

'I love you.'

Once I'm seated back behind the wheel, I reach underneath the seat for the rope. It's sealed inside a clear Ziploc bag. I unzip it and when I press my nose against the bag and inhale the blood and skin and sweat that's seeped into the rope, in my mind's eye I see Darby McCormick, her long, auburn hair spilling over her bare shoulders, every delicious inch of her skin exposed. My loins harden and thicken, and I feel the gates to the kingdom of heaven opening.

60

Eli Timothy Savran lived inside a tiny ranch house painted an awful robin's egg blue. The inside featured mahogany-panelled walls and furniture that had been purchased sometime in the late sixties or early seventies, and the fabrics, curtains, throw pillows and rugs were all depressing shades of brown and dark yellow.

Darby crossed the front door's threshold with Coop and stepped into a living-room with a low ceiling and a soapstone fireplace. The sliding glass door on the other side of the rug had been opened, along with the windows, and, while the air blowing inside the house was cool and clean and carried the pleasant, smoky odour of a nearby woodstove or fireplace, nothing could erase or lessen the permeating, baked-in reek of spoiled meat and fish that hung about the walls like an obscene presence. Her eyes immediately watered, and the food she had grabbed on her way out of the medical centre and eaten during the drive – a banana, instant coffee and an egg sandwich on soggy toast – immediately revolted inside her stomach. When Williams offered her a paper mask, Darby reached for it like it was a life preserver.

Coop gagged and then used the crook of his arm to cover his nose and mouth. 'Jesus,' he said in a muffled voice. 'Maybe we should call a priest and have him perform an exorcism.'

'It's even worse in the bedroom,' Williams said. Rivulets of sweat ran down his face, and, despite the cold air, the underarms of his blue dress shirt were marred with dark wet circles.

'You feeling all right?' Darby asked him.

'I'm operating on zero sleep, and I think I'm coming down with the flu,' Williams replied. 'This way.'

The living-room bled into a small kitchen filled with a dull grey light. A patrolman she didn't recognize, his mouth and nose covered by a mask, opened the cabinets with gloved hands. As she gingerly fitted the mask over her mouth, Darby heard the old refrigerator's motor wheezing what seemed like a death rattle.

She heard movement coming from the hall behind her. She turned and saw the patrolman she'd met last night, Griffin, rooting through a bureau drawer.

'How's your head?' Williams asked her.

'Still on my shoulders,' Darby replied. 'How long have you been inside here?'

'Long enough to know we found our man. This place smells like it was dipped in shit.'

Darby trailed Williams down a hall to the left of the door, the walls decorated with pictures of a stern-looking woman with a dead gaze and a frosted bouffant hairstyle. Darby's head was pounding; she had to concentrate on where she stepped. Coop stuck close to her side.

'I understand you came by to see me this morning,' she said to Williams.

He stopped and looked at her, confused. 'We talked for a few minutes. Don't you remember?'

'No,' Darby said. 'What did we talk about?'

'Teddy. I came to tell you he's taking over the case.'

'He came to see us,' Coop said, and told Williams about Lancaster's visit to the hospital.

'How's Hoder doing?' Williams asked after Coop had finished.

'It's touch and go.'

'I'm sorry. He's a good man. So were the other two. They didn't deserve to go out like that.'

Then she followed Williams into a wallpapered bedroom that looked like it belonged to an adolescent boy. The twin bed had old *Star Wars* sheets and a matching comforter. The bookcase across from it held paperback science fiction novels, action figures and spaceship models, many of which she didn't recognize. Autographed pictures of Captain Kirk and Captain Picard were tacked crookedly to the wall above the bookcase.

On top of a small wooden desk Darby spotted a charging cord. She pointed to it and said, 'Where's the Mac?'

'Don't know. I didn't find a laptop anywhere in the bedroom, so either it's in some other part of the house or he took it with him. How do you know he uses a Mac?'

'The charger at the end of the cord,' Darby replied. 'It's the boxy, magnetic Apple one.'

Williams nodded, then used his forearm to wipe his face. Her attention had drifted up to the wall-mounted shelves above the desk. They were packed with thick computer texts that dwarfed the size of any major metropolitan city phonebook. Futuristic sci-fi weapons encased in clear Plexiglas boxes served as bookends.

'We found a bottle of neomycin in his medicine cabinet,' Williams said. 'Savran gets it from one of those internet pharmacies. Take a look in the closet.'

Darby borrowed a pair of latex gloves from Williams. 'Coop told me you talked to the guy in charge of the cleaning service.'

Williams nodded. 'Ron Gondek,' he said, and again used his forearm to wipe his face. 'Gondek didn't have much to do with Savran, either professionally or personally. Told me Savran was pretty much a loner. Kept to himself and preferred to work by himself. But he was reliable, showed up to the jobs on time and was never a cause for complaint, except for his BO problem.'

Darby opened the closet door. Pressed dress shirts, trousers and khakis hung from the rack, along with two suits. One was black, the other like the one the Tuttle woman had described – dark brown, double-breasted, a J. C. Penney label stitched on the inside.

Coop, standing behind her, pointed to the single shelf above the clothes and said, 'Looky looky.'

To the left of the neatly folded wool sweaters were several rolls of duct tape. Behind them she found a box of tracer ammo and a clear plastic bag stuffed with zip ties.

'Pick up one of those rolls and see if the manufacturer's name's on it,' Coop said. 'Our lab got the duct tape I sent them. They started work on it this morning and, last time I checked in, were still trying to run down the brand.'

Darby pinched a roll between her fingers and read the label printed on the inside cardboard tube. 'It's called "Tough Armour",' she said.

'Never heard of it.' Coop removed the satphone from his pocket.

'Hold up,' Williams said. 'We need to have a talk.'

61

'About what?' Darby asked.

'About Teddy and the call you got this morning from our AG,' Williams said. 'I'm inclined to take their threat seriously. So should you two.'

Darby felt her pulse jump in her throat. 'Two agents are dead, one's in critical condition, Coop and I almost got our heads blown off last night and you're expecting us to, what, go back to the hotel and order room service?'

Williams held up a hand. 'Let me finish,' he said softly. 'Teddy's in charge of this thing now, which means I'm supposed to call the son of a bitch and tell him about Eli Savran. Now, I don't want to do that, but the truth is I have to, because I've got a solid suspect who's currently MIA. The boys and I have been taking turns keeping an eye on this shithole since four, and his vehicle, a '96 forest-green Ford Bronco, wasn't here; nor has it been seen anywhere in town yet. For all we know, Savran bolted after the pyrotechnic display he put on last night at the French house. He could be in another state by now. So, in addition to everything else that's going on, I've got a man-hunt on my hands. I had to put in a call to the state police and the US Marshals Service. I've already got a judge to sign off on Savran's bank statements and credit cards.'

Williams mopped at his face again. 'An APB went out

on Savran and his vehicle, so it's only a matter of time before Teddy finds out and shows up here,' he said. 'My career's already deep-sixed, so Teddy can't hurt me. But if he finds out you two still have your fingers in his pie, I can guarantee he'll lock you up to make sure you're out of the way until Savran's found and arrested. He's never going to let you two get in the way of him and his glory; I'm sure he's already got the reporters lined up.'

Coop said, 'We get it, Ray. Lancaster's a dickhead – the pied piper of assholes. But he's strictly amateur league. He can't compete with the pros Darby and I have played with in the MLD.'

'MLD?' Williams asked.

'Major League Douchebaggery,' Coop said. 'The Bureau's going to want answers for what happened to Hoder, Otto and Hayes, so I'm not about to sit on the sidelines. I don't think you should either.'

'I wasn't planning on it. If we get Savran before Teddy and his men, we'll get credit for the collar, and that'll play well in the press. I'm betting the assholes in Brewster who've been jerking us around ever since this incorporation thing started won't fire or lay off anyone right away because that wouldn't look good, now would it?'

'I agree with your thinking, Ray. To make the case against Savran stick, though, you're going to need all the evidence you can get. The Bureau is currently running down some of it for you right now. This morning we came across something that's a game changer.'

Then Coop moved to the bedroom door, shut it and returned. 'Nicky Hubbard,' he said in a low voice, as

343

though someone were eavesdropping. 'Her name ring any bells?'

'The girl who was kidnapped back in the eighties?'

'That's the one.'

'What about her?'

'The corner of the bedroom the killer cleaned with bleach? We found her fingerprint there. On the skirting board.'

Williams stiffened.

'I got the call this morning,' Coop said. 'Now I can't tell you *when* she was inside the bedroom, but I can tell you she *was* in there at some point because the fingerprint is –'

'Hold it, just hold it,' Williams barked. His mask was soaked with sweat. 'This is the first I've heard about a fingerprint.'

'We didn't think it had anything to do with the Downes case.'

'You just said you found it inside the bedroom.'

'Let me explain. This print was etched in the polyurethane. For that print to be there, she had to have touched the poly while it was in the process of drying. When it hardened, it preserved her print.'

'So it can't be wiped away?'

'No. It'd be like taking a rag to something set in concrete. I don't think the killer knew the print was there; we only found it using an alternative light source. I think he was concerned about wiping down that area to destroy any remaining blood – *Hubbard*'s blood. I think he killed Hubbard there at some point and then, after he finished with the Downes family, he decided to wipe down that area again with bleach so we wouldn't be able to link that blood back to Hubbard. Can you imagine what would happen if the news got out her blood had been found at the scene of a triple homicide more than three decades later?'

Williams stared at the snow-caked window glowing with a dull, grey light. 'This place would turn into a zoo overnight,' he said quietly.

'It'd be a goddamn *stampede*. Hubbard's case would be reopened; Red Hill would be all over the news channels, in every major newspaper. The killer would have nowhere to hide. He'd have to pack up and run, which, as you know, isn't as easy as it sounds.'

'Jesus.' Williams rubbed a gloved hand across the back of his head. 'Jesus,' he said again. 'You're *sure* about the print?'

'Positive. If your guys find Savran first, will they call you or will they get on the horn to Lancaster?'

'Most of 'em don't have any love for Teddy.' Williams's voice had taken on a far-away, almost dreamy tone as he struggled to process the news.

A serial killer who had tortured and killed several families over the course of a year was taxing enough on a small law-enforcement agency. Add to that a fingerprint belonging to one of the greatest crime mysteries of the twentieth century – it was overwhelming.

'Ray?' Coop prompted.

'Sorry. Yeah, I think they'd call me first. That being said, someone might call him thinking Teddy'll give him a job in the sheriff's office once the incorporation goes through. I guess we won't know until it happens.'

'Call me shallow for thinking this, but I don't want a jerk-off like Lancaster to get any credit. A case like this comes around once in a lifetime, if at all.'

Williams's eyes were bright with meaning. Darby saw some dread there – and some excitement too. Finding out what had happened to Hubbard would open up a whole new world of career prospects.

'Small problem,' Williams said. 'Once Teddy finds out, he'll –'

'I can guarantee you he won't. The lab know Hubbard is a hot button, which is why they called me directly instead of putting it out over IAFIS. The only three people who know about it are standing inside this room.'

Inside the bookcase Darby found a picture frame wedged between a pair of hardcover *Star Wars* books. As she removed it, Coop said, 'We need to keep this quiet until you've got Savran in custody.'

'Teddy is going to want his people to process this house,' Williams said. 'I can't stop him from doing that.'

'So let him. All we need to do is to find Savran.'

Darby assumed the picture inside the frame had been taken at a wedding, given the elaborate floral arrangement sitting on a white linen tablecloth set with china and crystal goblets. The table was empty; a tall man and the stern-looking woman Darby had seen in the hallway pictures stood to the left of it, staring into the camera.

Coop said to Williams, 'You want to nail Savran to the wall, you're going to need us to nail down the evidence. I've got to call the lab and tell them about the brand of duct tape, see if it matches what I FedExed them yesterday.'

'You need to stay off Teddy's radar screen.'

'Which is why Darby and I will work out of the chief's office. Once you've got Savran in custody, all I want is to have a run at him.'

'Fair enough,' Williams said.

'We'll keep in touch with these.' Coop handed Williams a satphone. 'I've got Hoder's. I'll write down our numbers.'

Darby looked at the picture. The tall man was bald and jowly and had an egg-shaped face, and he wore the brown suit that was hanging in the closet. He stood shoulder to shoulder with the petite woman who, Darby assumed, was his mother. They held their hands rigidly by their sides, their faces set with the hard and joyless expressions of two people who were about to be greeted by a firing squad.

Williams pointed at the woman and said, 'That's Thelma Savran. She died about two years back.'

'You knew her?'

'I'd bump into her from time to time at the grocery store over on Route Six. She was always one of those lonely women who just liked to talk to people, you know? She told me she had a son but that he couldn't come home to see her because he lived in another state, Texas or Louisiana, I think.'

'What about her husband? He still alive?' Darby was wondering if Savran might be on his way to see his father, to seek refuge. She had been involved in cases where the parent went out of their way to protect their grown child.

'I'll get on it. I'm assuming that's Eli in the photo. Face bears a strong resemblance to his driver's licence photo.'

'Did Rita Tuttle make her flight?'

'No. She's back in Brewster.' Williams took the picture from Darby's hand. 'I'll show this to her. If that's Eli, or Timmy – and I sure as hell hope to God it is, since there isn't a single picture of him inside the house – I'll get the photo out to the news. I'll nail down her statement while I'm there.'

There was a knock at the door. It opened and the patrolman Darby had seen rooting around in the kitchen stepped inside the bedroom, a folded and badly wrinkled brown paper grocery bag pinched between his gloved fingers.

'I found this on top of one of the kitchen cabinets,' the patrolman said.

'What's in there?' Darby asked.

'A whole lot of pervert,' he said. 'Panties and bras of all colours and sizes, lipsticks, you name it, I've got it.'

62

Coop drove. The storm seemed to have tapered off, but the roads weren't well ploughed, and it was slow-going.

'You were awfully quiet back there,' he said.

'I have an Olympic-standard headache.'

Coop drummed his fingers against the steering wheel. The windshield wipers throbbed like a racing heartbeat.

'I think there's another agenda at work here,' he said.

'And what would that be?'

'You really need me to say it?'

Darby didn't answer, just stared out the front window. Everywhere she looked was white and wet; branches sagged from the weight of the snow.

'I think you're disappointed you're not going to be alone in a room with Eli Savran. You want a shot at ripping his skin off,' he said.

'Wrong.'

'For as long as I've known you, you've carried this idea in your head that evil can be extinguished. That if you put down a guy like Savran, it will somehow restore balance to the world. That's what shrinks call "magical thinking", right?'

'Eli Savran is forty-seven,' Darby said. 'That would have made him fifteen or sixteen when Hubbard was abducted.'

'The man who worked at the department store, Fisher, told the police he saw Hubbard walking out of the toy aisle and holding hands with a teenage boy. It fits.'

'Fisher didn't get a good look at the guy's face.'

'True. Not that it would matter if he had at this point. Fisher died eight, maybe ten years ago. Heroin overdose.'

'I remember reading about it,' said Darby.

'Joan Hubbard is still alive, I'm pretty sure. Her husband, though, died. Heart attack or something.'

'Coop, if Savran was fifteen when he took Hubbard, he wouldn't have been old enough to drive.'

'Doesn't mean he *couldn't* drive. He probably had his learner's permit.'

'Either way, why would Savran drive all the way to a mall in Wichita, snatch a seven-year-old girl and then drive all the way to Red Hill to kill her? That's got to be at least five hundred miles each way.'

'You're assuming Savran was living here in Red Hill at the time. According to what Williams said, Savran was living with his old man.'

'Okay, let's say he was living in Wichita. Why would he decide to drive all the way to Colorado to kill her? It doesn't make any sense.'

'Since when do these guys ever think logically? They're locked in a mind-meld with their peckers. And teenagers, even normal ones, do stupid shit and act reckless. You expect a teenager who's also a budding psychopath to be well thought out and rational?'

Darby said nothing.

'We don't know *anything* about this guy yet,' Coop said.

'We haven't dug into his background, we have no idea where he's lived for the past thirty years or how his head's wired.'

'If Savran abducted and killed Hubbard, there'll be a string of other related disappearances in his wake. Guys like this don't stop at one. They keep going until they're caught.'

'We'll be sure to ask him once we have him in custody.'

'The guy shot at us last night. You think he's going to surrender peacefully?'

Coop shifted in his seat, his tongue digging into a back molar.

'We need to find a hardware store,' he said.

'For what?'

'So I can buy a can of pesticide and kill that bug that's crawled up your ass.' He turned to her and said, 'You want to tell me what's really eating at you, or do you want to stay in this foul mood?'

'If Savran who, at fifteen, maybe sixteen, abducted Hubbard and killed her inside the Downes house, why would he return to it some thirty years later to bind, torture and kill an entire family? Why revisit the crime scene?'

'Ted Bundy revisited his killing grounds. All those women in Seattle who disappeared – he later admitted to bringing them all to the same area up in the mountains, where he raped, killed and buried them.'

'That was outdoors. We're talking about a *house*. He killed an entire family and left them there for the police. He had to have known we'd come there and find Hubbard's blood – if it is, in fact, her blood.'

'Which is why he decided to go over it with bleach.'

'The man who killed these families is extremely methodical and careful. He wouldn't kill a family at the same place where he killed a seven-year-old girl who went on to become the world's most famous missing kid. There's no way he'd take a risk like that unless he –'

Darby cut herself off and straightened a little in her seat.

'Unless he what?' Coop prompted.

'Last night at the bar I told you that no one in this town seemed afraid of the Red Hill Ripper. That maybe we were looking at this from the wrong angle, that if we removed sex from the equation we were left with only two possible motives.'

'Power and money.'

'What if the Ripper *had* to kill the Downes family?'

'Then that would mean all the families are linked somehow – that they weren't randomly selected.'

'And he's *only* killing families who live in Red Hill. He hasn't killed a single family in a neighbouring town. It's all focused here in Red Hill.'

Coop's satphone trilled and vibrated inside the dashboard cubbyhole.

The caller was a federal agent named Susan Villa who worked in the lab. She was calling about the duct tape.

'Susan, I'm going to put you on speakerphone. I've got Darby McCormick with me. She's consulting with us on the case.' He handed Darby the phone so he could concentrate on driving. 'Okay, Susan, go ahead.'

'The duct tape samples you sent match a brand called True Armour.'

'All the samples?'

'Every one. Brand's very popular and used mainly for boating and outdoors because the glue is especially water resistant.'

'We found several rolls inside a suspect's home. I'll FedEx out a roll to you hopefully sometime later today. Right now we're still buried in a snowstorm.'

'One other thing,' Villa said. 'That strip of tape you sent us with the piece of latex stuck on it – that spot you found *is* ink. Hayes identified it using the mass spectrometer in your mobile lab. But your mass spec didn't have the proper library loaded on to it, so it couldn't identify the brand.'

The relaxed and breezy way the woman spoke made it clear she hadn't yet found out about what had happened to Hayes, Otto and Hoder.

'It's a black ink called "Magic Moon",' Villa said. 'You can't find it any more, except on places like eBay or on websites that cater to fountain pen and ink enthusiasts. Company that made it, J. D. Humphrey, went out of business in the early seventies.'

'This ink,' Darby said. 'Does it come in a pear-shaped bottle? Is there a picture of a penguin in a tuxedo on the label?'

'Yeah,' Villa replied, surprised. 'I take it you're into pens?'

'No, but I know someone who might be.'

63

Coop dropped her off in front of the Silver Moon Inn and then went to park at the back, where a plough attached to a truck with a blown front suspension was trying to clear away the snow. Her rental, which was still parked across the street, was hidden behind a ploughed wall that was higher than the car's roof.

The hotel lobby was quiet and thick with heat from the fire that cracked and hissed in the hearth. Darby stomped the snow off her boots and went to the reception desk. The scuffed black fountain pen and ledger she'd seen the night she checked in were still on the counter, along with the pear-shaped bottle of ink.

Darby was looking at the label, at the tiny words MAGIC MOON printed underneath the tuxedoed penguin, when the door behind the counter swung open. Laurie Richards stepped out; her gaze fell on Darby and she started, nearly dropping the plastic bucket gripped in her hand.

Darby hadn't called in advance; she had wanted to catch the woman unprepared, didn't want her to have time to rehearse her answers.

'Good *Lord*, you gave me a fright,' Richards tittered. Then she noticed Darby's bandages and her expression turned serious. Bright yellow Playtex cleaning gloves were stretched tightly all the way up to her forearms, and the baggy grey sweatshirt and black leggings she wore were marred with bleach stains.

'I heard about what happened,' Richards said quietly. Her hair was pulled back on her head, and her round, oily face glistened with sweat. 'I'm truly sorry for your loss.'

People who aren't psychopaths or pathological liars reveal themselves in small ways when they're working at trying to conceal the truth. They begin to fidget and sweat, and they have trouble maintaining eye contact. The rush of adrenalin dries up their saliva and they constantly swallow and clear their throats; they breathe faster, their noses itch and they constantly scratch or cover their mouths as if trying to cover the lie. The mouth appears tense, the lips pursed.

Nine times out of ten, their eyes and 'microexpressions' – those fraction-of-a-second facial movements that reveal the true emotion beneath the lie – are what betray them. They act distressed and their eyes are drawn upwards and they blink rapidly. Darby watched for any changes in the woman's expression.

'Who told you?'

'It was on the radio. I listen to the news and NPR while I'm cleaning the rooms.'

'Was Eli on the radio too?'

The woman blinked once, and her brow furrowed in thought. 'Eli?'

'Eli Savran. People call him Tim or Timmy.'

'I don't think I heard anything like that on the radio.'

'Do you know him?'

355

'No.'

'You sure? Guy I'm talking about smells like a human garbage truck.'

The lobby door opened. Richards watched as Coop headed their way.

'Ms Richards?'

'No. No, I don't know anyone like that.'

When a suspect, witness or any ordinary citizen hesitated before answering a question, it meant they were debating whether to hide information or whether deliberately to lie about it. Laurie Richards hadn't paused to think about her responses; she didn't look away and she seemed genuinely confused about who Eli Savran was. Now Darby had a baseline to work with when she asked her next set of questions.

Coop stepped up to the counter. His face was not friendly.

'Would you tell me?' Darby asked Richards.

'Tell you what?'

'If you did know someone like Eli Savran.'

'Of course I would,' Richards replied, indignant. 'My mother didn't raise a liar.'

'Good. So I don't have to explain to you that lying to a police or federal officer is a crime.'

Richards arched her back slightly. After she placed the bucket on the counter, she put her hands on her hips and puffed out her chest a little.

'With all due respect to the both of you, I don't like the way you're treating me. I've been nothing but helpful to you people, I've been nothing but truthful.'

'Then maybe you can explain this,' Darby said. She tapped a finger against the bottle of ink, her eyes never leaving the woman's face.

It was only a fraction of a second, but Darby saw that her words had hit home. And, while her gut said the woman had nothing to do with Eli Savran or the Red Hill Ripper, Darby knew she had stumbled upon something. Richards swallowed and licked her lips. Then she swallowed again.

'That's a bottle of ink.'

'A bottle of ink that's no longer in production,' Darby said. 'It's actually forty years old.'

'So?'

'It showed up on the duct tape wrapped around David Downes's mouth.'

Now Laurie Richards looked distressed. Her eyebrows drew upwards, towards the middle of her forehead, and suddenly she didn't know what to do with her hands.

Coop took out his handcuffs. 'Think real carefully before you answer,' he said, and placed the cuffs on the front counter.

'It was a gift,' Richards said.

'From Eli Savran?' Darby asked.

'No! I told you I don't know who he is. David gave them to me. The ink and the fountain pen.'

'David who?'

'*Downes*. He was really into fountain pens and stuff. He was cleaning out his office closet or something and came across the bottle of ink – it's called "Magic Moon", see? We're the Silver Moon Inn, and David thought the owner would like to use it here on the front desk because it went with the décor. He was kind like that.'

'You didn't tell us you knew him.'

'You didn't ask.'

'But you didn't volunteer the information either. Why? Were you having an affair with him?'

'An *affair*,' Richards said, aghast. 'He was a *married man*.'

'So David Downes just waltzed in here one day out of the blue and decided to give these things to the hotel? That's what you're telling us?'

'No, he did . . . He . . .'

'He *what*?'

'Stop yelling at me! You're getting me all confused.' A sour, unwashed odour rose from Richards, and her breath was rank. 'When my husband, Larry, dropped dead of a heart attack, David helped me with all the probate stuff. Larry was a good man but he wasn't exactly a forward-thinker, so he didn't leave a will. I went to David's office a few times, and during one of them he gave me the pen and the bottle of ink. Why? Because David was a very thoughtful and very kind man. If you don't believe me, I suggest you talk to his secretary, Sally Kelly. She was there the day David gave me the pen and the ink.'

'So explain to me how the ink from that bottle wound up at a crime scene.'

'How the heck should I know? That's *your* job, number one. Number two, who's to say David didn't have a similar bottle inside his office? Or his house?' The woman smiled a greasy, triumphant smile; her eyes roved over them as though she had made a profound observation.

Everything Laurie Richards had said sounded perfectly logical, and Darby sensed the woman was telling the truth. And maybe Darby would have let the whole thing go if it weren't for the smile that had punctuated her last words. It was as if she had swerved at the last moment to avoid a head-on collision and had righted herself, back on course to her destination, no one knowing how close she had come to a fatal accident.

'That's it, the whole big whopping mystery,' Richards said in mocking sarcasm. 'Satisfied?'

Not yet, Darby thought, and moved behind the reception desk.

64

Laurie Richards made gulping sounds as Darby approached.

'I told you the truth,' Richards said.

'Not all of it.' The woman was still holding something back. Darby could sense it the way a bloodhound picks up a scent.

'Yes, I did! Why do you insist on harassing me?'

To get anything more out of Richards, Darby would need a warrant – but both she and the FBI had been booted off the case. So she decided to play the only card she had left, one that would, hopefully, push the envelope.

Darby glared at the woman and said, 'You know why he's killing these families.'

The woman's mouth went slack, and her small eyes were bright with terror.

'You knew all this time and yet you didn't tell us,' Darby said. 'That's called obstruction of justice – and we're talking about a federal-level charge here. Coop, what's the going rate these days for a federal charge?'

'Minimum of ten years,' Coop replied. 'Max of twenty.'

Richards blinked rapidly, and she seemed to have trouble catching her breath.

'Why are you protecting him?' Darby asked the woman.

'I'm doing no such thing,' Richards replied. A steely

resolve had wormed its way into her tone. 'You don't scare me. You don't –'

'Let me tell you what's going to happen, Ms Richards. I'm going to pick up these handcuffs, and then we're going to take a ride down to the station. You can call your lawyer, if you have one, and while you're on the phone with him or her *I'm* going to be on the phone with the reporter from the *Red Hill Evening Item*. I'm going to tell him how Laurie Richards has known all along why the Red Hill Ripper has been torturing and murdering these families –'

'*I don't know who he is!*'

'– and that you didn't come forward with this information.' Darby picked up the handcuffs. 'All these families were murdered because you, Laurie Richards –'

'I'M SICK AND TIRED OF WAITING FOR THEIR SCRAPS AND CRUMBS!'

Darby stood stock still. Her ears rang in the silence and her feet felt as if they had been welded to the floor.

Laurie Richards's face was flushed and heated; tears streamed down her ruddy cheeks. She heaved in great gulps of air and her limbs and voice trembled when she spoke.

'They could've saved us. David and his family, the Connelly family and the others – they could have saved the *entire* town but they kept saying no because they were selfish and greedy. They wouldn't sell their properties to the state. They were offered fair market value for their homes and their land, but no, the money was never good enough, because people like that, no matter how much you give them they're never satisfied, their bellies and bank accounts are never full. They always want more and more while the rest of us are left to fight over the crumbs from their table. *It's their own goddamn fault, what happened to 'em.'*

Darby felt like her heart had stopped beating.

'I'm looking out for *my* family just like they were looking out for theirs and you're here harassing *me*? I had to send my son to live with my bitch of a sister because I can't afford to feed my child or pay rent – I'm barely scraping by and you waltz into town and have the nerve to lecture *me* about what's fair and right?' Some steel had entered the woman's voice. 'I've played by the rules my entire life and for what? What does being nice and thoughtful and fair get you in the end? I'll tell you what. A big, fat whopping nothing.'

Then the woman's expression changed. The neurotic mess of anxiety and fear that lived inside her head like a nest of snakes had shed its skin, giving birth to something else, something . . . darker. Laurie held her head high and proud and said, 'The Red Hill Ripper's a goddamn saint as far as I'm concerned.'

What Darby saw in the woman's eyes scared the shit out of her. Put a gun in Laurie Richards's hand and she'd squeeze the trigger without a moment's hesitation. She'd bitch nonstop about having to clean up the mess but she wouldn't lose any sleep over a murder. She wouldn't kill out of malice or anger or fear or because of twisted psychological wiring. She was no different than a mother lion protecting its cub.

Right then Darby understood what this was about: survival.

'You think I'm the only one who turned their back and decided to look the other way?' Richards snorted. 'Please. It's their own fault what happened to them. *They* decided to be greedy, not me. You think I'm going to put my life in danger because a bunch of greedy pricks are holding out for more money?'

'Tell me why he killed these families,' Darby said.

65

Laurie Richards crossed her arms over her chest and stared defiantly at Darby and Coop.

Darby continued to press her with questions, but Richards refused to answer – refused to speak. When Coop threatened to arrest her, Richards calmly turned around, put her hands behind her back and waited to be handcuffed.

Darby knew as well as Coop that the obstruction of justice charge wouldn't stick; she had thrown it out as a scare tactic to get the woman to talk. But now that Richards was deliberately stonewalling them, refusing to share the reason why the families had been killed and, technically, impeding their investigation, Coop could arrest her, and he did. Darby knew why: the reality of being arrested and placed in a holding cell might jolt the woman out of her self-imposed silence and convince her to co-operate.

They brought her to the station and handed her over to the officer in charge of booking.

Darby went to the break-room for coffee. Coop joined her ten minutes later. He held a small stack of sheets in his hand.

'What'cha got there?' she asked.

'A list of everyone in Red Hill who's logged on to the newspaper's website and watched the video. Savran's name and address aren't on it.' He handed the sheets to her and picked up the coffee pot. 'The computer guys in Denver are handling the traces.'

'You told me.'

'I can't think straight.' Coop picked up the coffee pot.

Darby looked through the pages as she spoke. 'It's got to be tied into the town's incorporation somehow – the reason why the families were killed.'

'Agreed. All this time we've been thinking that the incorporation was just about re-districting town assets. It's also about money, if we believe Richards. My guess? Developers were probably targeting key sites to build on in this town, and these families were holding out because they were offered less than fair market value for their homes. What did she call them again?'

'A bunch of greedy pricks whose bellies and bank accounts were never full.'

'Said – and I quote – "It's their own goddamn fault, what happened to 'em."'

'Called him a goddamn saint.'

'Robin Hood as a serial killer. That's a new one.' Coop drank his coffee. 'Looks like your theory about the town protecting this guy was correct.'

'You don't seem surprised.'

Coop shrugged. 'Like I told you last night, I grew up with that whole town-protects-its-own mentality. Savran gets his rocks off while doing the town a favour.' He rubbed his eyes. 'I'll give Richards an hour or so and then I'll put her in the box. You want to take a run at her first?'

'I want to talk to Sally Kelly.'

'To verify Richards's story about Downes giving her the pen and ink?'

'That, and to find out how the families are connected. Richards said something about how Downes and his family and the Connelly family could've saved the town. Downes was a real estate lawyer. If he was killed because of the incorporation – if he was possibly representing the other families who were killed – Kelly will know.'

'And she may clam up like our friend in the holding cell.'

Darby kept reading through the names of the people who'd logged on to the newspaper's website to watch the video.

'Her name's here,' she said.

'Whose name?'

'Sally Kelly. The other day she gave me this long spiel about how she didn't follow the Ripper case.'

'So?'

'May I keep these?'

Coop nodded. 'I need to make some calls. The SAC for the Denver field office found out what happened last night and left me several messages. I've got to call him back – and he's sending some people up here.'

'Lancaster's going to love that.'

'I've got a couple of officers here running down the information on the Downes house. I've got to sort through that, see if we can find anything that can put Savran inside the house. You want to talk to the Kelly woman, fine, but I don't want you going alone with Savran still on the loose.'

'I'll call Williams and have him meet me there.'

'Look at you, playing nice for a change. After you call him, you *will* have someone here drive you to Miss Kelly's house. Now tell me how much juice you've got left on your phone.'

Darby took it out. Coop propped his arm on the windowsill and glanced out at the back parking lot. The snow was still coming down, but it was as fine as dust. The storm was dying.

'Battery's three quarters full,' she said.

'Fantastic. So you'll have no problem checking in with me when you get there and calling me when you leave.' Coop held up a hand before she could say anything. 'Just do it for me, please, no argument. I need to focus on what's going on here, and I can't do that if I'm worrying about you, okay?'

'Aye, aye, Captain.'

The old stone wall on Route Six is a mile away from the border separating Red Hill from Brewster. It's short in length but wide enough to accommodate two lanes of cars, and even when it's ploughed people tend not to drive across it during the winter. The guardrails are made of stone instead of galvanized steel; you take the corner too fast or if your car slides on ice, chances are you'll hit the wall, go over the side and plunge thirty feet into the river.

The river hasn't frozen over yet. I toss the MacBook holding the videos of the dead families over the side of the bridge and watch it sink into the dark and murky waters. I toss the other items – an external hard drive and several USB keys – and feel a sweet and blessed relief surge through me.

Sarah calls as I'm making my way back to the car.

'McCormick and the other one, the really tall guy with dirty-blond hair, they went to the Silver Moon Inn and arrested her.'

'Arrested who?'

'The woman who works the front desk. They arrested her.'

I slide behind the wheel, thinking.

'You're sure?'

'They handcuffed her,' Sarah replies. 'Is she a problem?'

'I don't know. Maybe. Did they see you?'

'No, absolutely not. I followed their tyre tracks in the snow, just like you told me to. It was easy, there's hardly anyone on the roads.'

I can't back up; the road behind me is too steep and I might get stuck. I put the car in gear and drive across the bridge.

'Where are you?' Sarah asks.

'I just got rid of the MacBook and the other stuff.'

'You sure this is going to work?'

No, Sarah. I'm not sure of anything right now.

I reach the end of the bridge, do a three-point turn and drive back across it.

'Eli Savran is all over the radio,' Sarah says.

'I know. I've been listening.'

'I'm worried.'

I am too. I reassure her everything's going to work out. After I hang up, I stare out the windows, at the roads, and wonder if it's time to disappear. Alone.

66

Ray Williams didn't answer his phone. Darby left him a message about the ink and a quick summary of the Laurie Richards situation; then she told him where she was going, hung up and went outside to the waiting patrol car.

Barry Whitehead, the patrolman who had volunteered to drive her to Sally Kelly's house, had a beard that looked like pubic hair had been glued to his face. He was somewhere in his late twenties and wore a wedding ring, and his patrol car smelled of Copenhagen dipping tobacco. Several tins were stuffed inside the dashboard's cubbyholes. He didn't talk, which Darby appreciated. She used the quiet to sort her thoughts.

Sally Kelly's driveway had recently been ploughed, and her black Honda Accord had been cleaned off. Whitehead pulled in and put the car in park.

'Stay here and leave the motor running,' Darby said. 'I'll be back in a few.'

'Your federal friend told me specially not to let you out of my sight.'

'If I need you, I'll holler.' Darby didn't want him listening in on her conversation. Deputy Sheriff Lancaster, Williams had told her, had spies everywhere. If Whitehead, with his wide, gummy smile, was one of them, she wasn't going to let him give Lancaster a heads-up.

Darby held up her satellite phone. 'Watch this,' she said, and dialled Coop's number. A moment later, she said, 'I'm here, Daddy-o. I'll call you when we leave.'

She hung up and opened the door.

'If you're not out in ten minutes, I'm coming in,' White-head said as she got out. 'I don't need no fed putting my nuts into a meat grinder, know what I'm saying?'

'Got it.'

The roofed porch protected Darby from the snow but not the wind. It slammed into her back as she pressed her thumb to the doorbell and kept it there.

Sally Kelly opened the door a crack. She wore pink slippers and a matching bathrobe over a big wool sweater that went down to her knees. Her red-rimmed eyes looked sleepy.

That sleepy look vanished when she saw Darby's band-aged face.

'The Ripper struck again last night,' Darby said. 'I'm sure you read about it.'

'No. No, I haven't. I've been in bed all day. I've got that nasty stomach bug that's going round.'

'May I come in?'

'I've already told you everything I know about David and his family.'

Not everything, Darby thought. 'I need to talk to you about the Red Hill Ripper.'

'I told you yesterday, I don't have any interest in that business.'

'Then maybe you can tell me why you watched the video interview.'

'I don't know what you're talking about.'

'Of course you do. Your local newspaper, the *Red Hill Evening Item*, posted a video of me on their website. You watched it last night at half past one.'

Sally Kelly stiffened, shooting Darby a look that said *How could you possibly know such a thing?*

'Oh, that. Yes, I saw it.' Kelly nearly choked on her words. 'I decided to check on the storm, and I saw the video and decided to take a look.'

'At half past one in the morning?'

'I told you, I wasn't feeling well.'

'Why would you watch the interview when you don't have any interest in the Red Hill Ripper?'

'Well, I . . . Yesterday, after you left, you got me thinking about this person, so when I saw the video I was . . . I was curious and decided to watch it. I got so upset thinking about David and his family that I stopped watching.'

'You watched it from beginning to end,' Darby said. 'Twice.'

Kelly looked like she'd been hit on the back of the head with a shovel.

'And,' Darby said, 'you watched the video *again* this morning at a few minutes past eight.'

'I need to go back to bed.' Kelly went to shut the door.

Darby's foot prevented it from closing. 'Why did you lie to me, Ms Kelly?'

Kelly bundled the robe around her tightly, like a shield. Once again, Darby was struck by the smallness of the woman. The fragility. If she stepped outside, the wind would blow her off her feet, sending her deep into the woods behind the house, where she wouldn't be found until spring.

'Ms Kelly?'

'I wasn't lying. I must've been – the medication I'm taking for my fibromyalgia, sometimes I have a hard time remembering things.'

'Yesterday you told me you couldn't afford the medication.'

'I get confused – especially when I'm upset, like now.'

'I think I should come in now, so you can tell me the truth,' Darby said.

'I don't think that's a good idea.'

'Telling the truth or me coming in?'

'Coming in. I wouldn't want you to catch this bug. I can't keep food down, water, anything.'

'I'll take my chances.'

'Please remove your foot.'

Darby's head pounded; the staples along the left side of her face felt as though they were tearing into her skin. The Tylenol had made the pain somewhat manageable. She couldn't say the same about her judgement. She shoved the door, and Sally Kelly along with it.

Kelly staggered backwards. Darby entered the house and, slamming the door behind her, went over to the woman, who had collapsed on her plastic-covered couch.

Kelly held up trembling hands, as though trying to ward off a blow. 'Please,' she said. 'I don't –'

'Don't want to get involved?'

'I need to go back to bed. I'm not feeling well, and you're scaring me.'

'Good. Because I know why the Ripper is killing these families. Laurie Richards told us —'

Darby cut herself off; she had seen a shadow jump across the wall opposite her.

But it was too late. He had been standing behind her, behind the door, and within two steps across the carpet he had the barrel of a pistol pressed behind her ear.

'Don't turn around,' Teddy Lancaster said.

67

'Hands on your head,' Lancaster said to Darby. 'Nice and slow, that's it, you know the drill . . . Good girl. Sarah, be a dear and unzip Miss McCormick's jacket for her and remove the handgun inside her shoulder holster.'

Kelly had staggered to her feet. Her fingers trembled as she gripped the zipper of Darby's jacket.

'Careful, Sarah,' Lancaster said. 'This one likes to punch, especially when you're not expecting it.'

Why is he calling her Sarah? Darby wondered. Then she remembered: Sarah was the familiar name for Sally, and vice versa.

'You still got a chance to get out of this alive, Teddy,' Darby said. 'Coop, Williams and the others will be here any moment.'

'What others?'

Darby didn't answer. *Let him stew in it*, she thought.

Kelly had unzipped the coat; Darby could feel the woman's fingers fumbling on the strap for the shoulder holster. Kelly's head smelled of shampoo, and her ratty pink robe reeked of bacon and burned toast.

'I'm sorry,' Kelly said under her breath. 'I didn't –'

'No talking, Sarah,' Lancaster said. 'Darby's got an important decision to make, and I want her head clear so she can focus on the matter at hand, understand?'

Kelly nodded compliantly. For a moment Darby had the distinct impression the woman was going to apologize to him.

Then Lancaster pressed the barrel deeper into the base of Darby's skull. 'I asked you a question, missy.'

'The agents from the Denver office,' Darby said. 'They're here in Red Hill.'

Kelly removed the SIG. She dropped it to the floor and kicked it over to Lancaster.

Lancaster grabbed Darby by the back of the collar. 'Keep your hands on your head, understand? I'm not fooling around here,' he said. 'In fact, I'll prove it to you.'

Then he marched her towards the archway leading into the kitchen. Darby had just crossed the threshold when Lancaster yanked her collar again, forcing her to stop.

Ray Williams sat in the middle of the tiny kitchen, between the stove and the sink, his hands tied behind a rolling wooden desk chair. His mouth was covered in duct tape and his head was slumped forward, against his shoulder; his nose had been broken; his face was swollen and bloody from the cuts along his cheek, temple and forehead.

'Ray?' Lancaster said. 'Wake up, Ray, your sexy lady friend is here.'

Williams moaned behind the tape. His head twitched but he didn't look up.

'That's okay, Ray, you two can talk later. Go ahead and rest.' Then, to Darby: 'Ray was unco-operative, so I had to use this on him.' Lancaster held up a short billy club, the kind patrolmen use, only this one was made of leather instead of wood. 'I can honestly say the rude son of a bitch completely deserved it. Oh, and the patrolman who drove you here, Whitehead? You can forget about a rescue from him. He called to tip me off before you left the station.'

Darby felt her stomach sink. How many people did Lancaster have on his payroll? Did these people know he was the one killing the families? Or did they, like Laurie Richards, simply turn a blind eye to it?

'I've got friends everywhere these days,' Lancaster said, and marched Darby back into the living-room. Kelly sat on the couch, her hands folded on her lap and her head bowed, looking like a woman attending church. 'People do all sorts of things when they need a few extra bucks. Lucky for me it's a buyer's market.'

'That's what all this is about, isn't it? Money.'

'It's what makes life go 'round, darlin'. Get up, Sarah, you're not done working.'

'The families you killed were standing in the way of the incorporation, weren't they?' Darby said. Her clothes were damp with sweat, her mouth and throat as dry as bone. 'I'm guessing they wouldn't sell their properties to the state because they were offered pennies on the dollar, and the state needs their properties to secure developers.'

'Bingo. Hurry up, Sarah.'

'And in order to receive government funding, the state has to find the money to pay for additional infrastructure and additional services. Money has to come from somewhere, and the state can't raise taxes because no one living here can afford to pay more – they can hardly pay now.

The only way the state can meet its costs is through money from developers.'

Lancaster grinned. 'See, it's not that complicated, is it, sweetheart? Now –'

'And when the families said no, you decided to come on in and speed up the process, maybe even encourage the other holdouts. If the incorporation didn't go through, you wouldn't be part of the new regime, now, would you?'

'I don't really want to play the question and answer game any more. Thanks to you, I've got a full plate today. Now keep those hands on that pretty little head of yours, or it'll get messy.'

Lancaster let go of her collar and quickly stepped away, to her right, to gain some distance. His arm was extended, as straight as a board, and Darby could see the silencer attached to the end of what looked like a Glock. His free hand reached into a jacket pocket.

'You staged all the murders to make them look like the work of a sexual sadist,' Darby said. 'You wanted everyone thinking that a deranged psychopath was running all over town, when it was really about money.'

Lancaster came back with a pair of plastic ties. In her mind's eye Darby saw the Downes family bound to the dining-room chairs.

'Once the families are out of the way,' Darby said, 'all the pieces are in place for the incorporation. When that happens, Red Hill PD goes away, and you're the man in charge.'

Lancaster handed the plastic ties to Kelly.

'You set up Eli Savran as your scapegoat,' Darby said.

'You already had him picked out before you started this. You crushed a tablet of neomycin on the floor, knowing we'd find it, and then you had Kelly tell me about a man who smelled like garbage who was possibly stalking Samantha Downes, then you followed it up by having Rita Tuttle tell us all about Timmy.'

'Clever girl. Hands behind your back.'

'Why'd you shoot at us last night?'

'I'm into theatre. That, and I didn't have a clear shot of you in the bedroom. Tie her up, Sarah.'

Darby kept her hands clasped on her head. Something nagged at her, but the thought or feeling or whatever it was had been washed away by surging tides of adrenalin. Her mind, though, was busy cataloguing all the ways the Red Hill Ripper – *Lancaster* – had remained several steps ahead of them: the iPad in the Downes bedroom, the audio bug she found in her hotel room, the GPS tracker on her rental and the USB spy device stuck inside the back of Williams's office computer.

'That was a nice trick with the pictures,' Darby said. 'How'd you manage to pull that off?'

Lancaster smiled, his eyes dancing with a bright and joyful light. Like every garden-variety sadist, not only did he get off on controlling a situation, he loved to showcase just how intellectually superior he was to everyone around him.

'While you and Hoder were educating us backwoods folks on the Ripper, I slipped my hand inside my pocket and hit the send button on the burner I was carrying. Then, while the troops were enjoying your titty pics, I removed the SIM card, placed it in the spare burner I keep in my glove compartment and then left the phone on the front windshield of that fat broad who sleeps in her van.'

'You've thought of everything, haven't you?' Darby said.

'Don't pin this on me, Missy. You were given fair warning at every turn. First the pictures, then the texts – I even had our AG call to tell you to stay away. But did you listen? Nope. A normal person would've packed up and left. But not you. Then you show up here and my Sarah told you to go away – she even tried to close the door on you – but you barged your way in because you're an annoying, meddlesome bitch. What's about to go down now is on your shoulders. Hands behind your back.'

'I don't think so.'

'Look, I'm not going to disrespect you and say I won't hurt you if you do what I say or any of that other bullshit,' he said. 'You know how this is going to go down. If you want, I can blow your brains out right here, right now. I'd prefer not to do that, because it'll complicate things, and, like I said, I've already got a full plate today. You decide.'

Darby slowly lifted her hands off the top of her head. As she placed them behind her back, her gaze dropped to the thick, gold-capped pen sitting in Lancaster's breast pocket.

Lancaster saw where she was looking. 'You like that? It's a Waterman Edson fountain pen.'

Darby placed the back of one hand flat against the other; then she kept squeezing her hands into fists. If

Kelly tied her while her muscles were pumped full of blood, she could relax her hands afterwards and, hopefully, gain the space necessary to free them. During her SWAT training, she'd been taught various methods to free herself from plastic ties. All she needed was the time in which to do it.

'David's wife bought it for him for their tenth anniversary or some shit – she spent almost a *grand* on this stupid thing, can you believe it? I know that because David was always bragging about it. I picked it up from his bedroom nightstand, made sure the greedy bastard saw me stick it in my pocket.'

'I know. Laurie Richards told us.'

Kelly tightened the plastic bindings against Darby's wrists. Lancaster's gaze had narrowed in thought.

'Told you what?'

Darby didn't answer. Smiled back at him.

'You know what? I changed my mind,' Lancaster said, and cocked the pistol's trigger.

68

Some people believe your whole life flashes before your eyes during your final moment. Darby had the opposite experience. She didn't remember her father taking her to her first Red Sox game, how he always smelled of cigars and aftershave; the way his big, callused hand swallowed hers. She didn't think about the man she loved, or maybe was afraid to love, or how she wished she had spent more time away from the office, instead of devoting almost all her energy to finding people who, when you got right down to it, weren't part of the human race – people who should be ground into chum and tossed off the side of a boat. Her final moment would be spent looking at blue-striped wallpaper and a couch covered in plastic; at a black-and-white cat that had popped its head around the corner and then disappeared.

Then the front door swung open to Barry Whitehead. He stepped inside, and his face turned almost as white as the snow stuck to his boots.

'Jesus, Teddy, you didn't say anything about killing a fed.'

'She look dead to you? I need her cuffed, after what the bitch did to my face. Williams is in the kitchen. Put him in the trunk and come back here.'

Whitehead didn't move. His face was bloodless, and he

looked like he had swallowed barbed wire. He had stepped into a new script and he didn't want a part in it.

Darby said to Whitehead: 'He's going to kill you, dumbass. Lancaster's not the type to leave loose ends.'

Lancaster pistol-whipped her against the right side of her face; the gun split open her ear and pain exploded in black and red clouds behind her eyes. Her hands immediately went up to protect her face, but her wrists were tied behind her back. She staggered and her knees gave out. She dropped to the floor, near the couch, falling face first into the plastic-covered cushions.

Kelly screamed. Whitehead's hand had reached the butt of his weapon when Lancaster fired.

The round went through Whitehead's shoulder and the wall behind him exploded in a mist of red. The patrolman's eyes were wide, his mouth a round, wet O; he stared in helpless confusion as he tumbled against a small sideboard, knocking over the Hummel figurines that had been sitting on its top. They smashed against the floor as Kelly screamed again, her hands pressed against her cheeks, staring in horror at what was unfolding.

Darby had moved to her side. There was some give in the restraints. She was getting to her feet and trying to slide out her wrist when Lancaster turned his weapon on Kelly and fired. The round went through her forehead, and she collapsed like a puppet whose strings had been cut.

But Lancaster thought Darby wasn't a problem. Her hands were tied behind her back, and he had to deal with a more immediate problem: Whitehead, who had managed to remove his side-arm. The patrolman lay sideways on the floor, his shoulder gushing blood from a severed artery. He clicked off the safety just as Lancaster fired a round into his stomach.

Lancaster was about to charge forward, most likely to plant a final round into the patrolman's skull. Darby saw her opportunity: she swung her leg and felt it connect with his shin. He tripped, and his forward momentum knocked him off balance. He pinwheeled, and by the time he had tumbled against the floor she was already on her feet and moving.

Lancaster had landed face first on the carpet. But he wasn't injured, and he could attack. He threw himself on to his side, pointed the Glock at the couch and fired. Darby, who had already placed herself behind him, kicked Lancaster in the back of his head. She heard a crunching sound and his arm faltered. She raised her foot and brought the heel crashing down on his temple and he went limp.

She was about to kick him again when a voice said, *If you kill him, you'll never know what happened to Nicky Hubbard.*

Darby kicked his gun across the floor. Her head was pounding, her stomach roiling; she gulped in air, trying to clear her head, trying to keep the sour mash of breakfast from coming up. The room smelled of cordite and blood, and she could hear Williams moaning in the kitchen. She sat on the floor, leaning back against the carpet and working her cuffed hands over her rump and the back of her legs.

Her wrists were still bound, but her hands were in front of her now. Kneeling, she found Lancaster's handcuffs, then she pulled his hands behind his back and cuffed him. She got to her feet, dizzy and nauseous, and entered the kitchen.

Ray Williams's head bobbed up, and he made a sick, wheezing sound.

'Give me a minute and I'll have you outta there,' she panted, and removed a knife from the butcher's block next to the stove.

Darby sat at the breakfast nook where Sally Kelly had served tea to her yesterday and propped her arms on the table. Because of the way her hands were bound, it took her a moment to angle the blade correctly so she could saw through the plastic without slitting a wrist in the process.

It was slow going. Her hands were not steady, shaky from the adrenalin, and the pounding in her head made it difficult to concentrate.

Finally, her hands were free. Darby made quick work of Williams's bindings. He slumped back against the chair as his fingers scratched at the duct tape plastered across his mouth. She helped him to peel it off.

'My ribs,' Williams wheezed. 'I think he broke them.'

He needed to stand to reduce the pressure and strain. Darby threw his heavy arm around her shoulder, and when she helped him to his feet he locked her in a chokehold.

To perform a standing rear-chokehold correctly, you need to wrap one arm around the victim's throat. You place your other hand squarely on the back of the head and, gripping the hair, push the head forward while cutting off the airway. All it takes is five pounds of pressure; it takes more force to crack an egg. Almost always, the victim is immediately subdued.

But Darby McCormick is no ordinary victim. She's a cop and, like me, she has not only been trained in the art of the chokehold, she knows how to break out of one. She knows to sink her chin against the crook of my elbow and hold on to my arm while she crouches forward. She knows she needs to wrap one of her legs around the back of my calf to trap my leg, then turn a sharp 180 degrees to break out of the hold – and she needs to do it fast, because the blood flow to her brain has already been cut by 13 per cent.

Which is why I immediately launch myself backwards while I hold on to her, squeezing. I pull her out of the kitchen and into the hall, where I press my back against the wall. Now she has no way to free herself. She's trapped, thrashing against my chest, using her elbows to deliver sharp blows against my ribs. But my ribs are fine; I lied to get her to help me up so I could easily grab her.

Six seconds later, her vision fails.

In eight seconds her frontal cortex shuts down.

Nine seconds in, and she slumps in my arms, completely unconscious. I could keep squeezing and kill her right now and be done with it all; or I could take advantage of this tremendous blessing.

I release my grip and carry her into the living-room. Not wanting to cause any further trauma to her face, I lay her down against the couch. Her face will heal in time, and then she'll look as radiant and beautiful as the day when she stepped inside the entryway of the Downes home. God willing, we'll have plenty of adventures together, she and I.

But I have to act quickly.

I push her hands behind her back and secure her wrists with the steel handcuffs from my belt. Sally Kelly has a pair of decorative Christmas dish-rags hanging from the stove handle. I retrieve them and stuff one in Darby's mouth. The other I use as a makeshift blindfold.

Then I notice Teddy Lancaster is watching me. His eyes are open, blinking; he either can't or won't move. A deep, gurgling sound escapes his bloody lips as I pick up his silenced Glock. He tries to raise a hand, about to speak, when I park a round into his brainpan, the gunshot as loud as a balloon popping. I toss the nine on the floor and my head throbs in what feels like hundreds of different places. It's difficult to concentrate, and the floor doesn't feel stable underneath my boots.

The burner is still tucked inside my jacket pocket. I take it out and call Sarah as I step into the bathroom off the hall. The window facing me is dark; night has fallen. Another blessing.

'I was getting worried,' she says.

'You still parked down the street?' I've asked Sarah to shadow me, to stick close by, in case we need to run together.

'I'm still there, like you asked,' Sarah says. 'What's wrong with your voice?'

I yank down a pink bath towel hanging on a rack. 'Teddy hit me in the face with a billy club and split my lips open.'

'Teddy who?'

'I'll explain later,' I say, and march back towards the living-room. 'I need you to come here. Now.'

'There's a police car parked in the driveway. I'm looking at it through the binoculars.'

'They're all dead. Hurry – and bring my kit. Make sure no one sees you.'

I hang up, not knowing why I said that last part, as Kelly, like everyone else who lives in Red Hill, doesn't have any nearby neighbours. The advantage of hunting in a town like this instead of a city is that you don't have to worry as much about potential witnesses.

But I've never hunted in Red Hill or in any of the other nearby towns. I've always abducted my women either from out of state or from someplace very far away from Red Hill, which is how I've managed to hunt all these years without getting caught. When the Red Hill Ripper started killing here, though, I saw it as an opportunity to take women closer to home – women like Tricia Lamont – and blame it on the Red Hill Ripper.

Is there time to take Tricia today? I've never had two women at once. The possibilities are ... No. No, I'm being greedy. The McCormick bitch is my prize.

Darby moans as I use the towel to tie her ankles together. The knot won't hold for long, but it will prevent her from kicking. I sit next to her and use my weight to pin her face and chest against the back of the couch. I pat down her pockets but I don't find her satellite phone. Did she leave it out in the patrol car? No, there it is, lying on the bloodied carpet.

Darby has come back to life; I can feel the muscles in her back tensing just as Sarah's SUV pulls into the driveway. Seconds later, the front door opens. Sarah no longer flinches or pales at the sight of the blood and carnage; she's seen it before, many, many times. The small black leather case is gripped in her gloved hand.

'Don't come inside,' I say. I don't want her footprints to be discovered inside the house. 'Just toss me the kit.'

Sarah is staring at Lancaster's body.

'That's Teddy,' I say. 'Teddy Lancaster. He's the Red Hill Ripper.'

'So he's the one who recorded you inside the bedroom?'

I nod. 'The video was on Savran's MacBook, along with all the others. The laptop is now at the bottom of the river. Now toss –'

'What if he made copies?'

'One thing at a time, Sarah. Now hurry up and toss me the kit.'

She does. I use my teeth to unzip it, then take out a preloaded syringe. Sarah watches me with a strange mixture of anger, fear and, I think, jealousy, as I sink the needle into Darby's neck and inject her with Etorphine. The opioid is several thousand times more potent than morphine, and I need only a small amount to send her off into the valley of sweet dreams.

'You said this wasn't about her.'

'It isn't,' I say. 'It just worked out this way. You got the latex gloves in your pocket, like I asked?'

Sarah nods. Looks disappointed. Hurt.

'I need this. The next few weeks, I'm going to be under a lot of stress. You know what happens when I get stressed.'

'I can satisfy you,' Sarah says, blinking back tears. 'I know how to satisfy you.'

'Is there anyone outside?'

Sarah looks, begrudgingly.

'No,' she says. 'No one's coming.'

'Keep watching – and put on those gloves.'

The drug has taken effect; Darby has gone limp, sliding into unconsciousness. Head pounding, I move off the couch and crawl towards Lancaster. I find his key fob inside his jacket pocket and toss it to Sarah. Then I get to my feet, collect Darby's satellite phone and the Glock, and hand them to Sarah.

In my present physical condition, it takes what feels like

an hour to pick up Darby and sling her over my shoulder. Sarah holds the door open for me as I carry her outside and lay her gently across the SUV's backseat.

As we return to the house, I tell Sarah what she needs to do next. She listens and doesn't ask any questions.

'I've got to shut off my phone,' I tell her. 'I won't be able to call you for a while.'

'Are we safe?'

'As long as you do what I said. We'll have to lay low for a bit – the FBI will have all sorts of questions about Nicky Hubbard, but –'

'They *know* about her?' Her face is bloodless.

I gently cup her face in my hands. 'The FBI found one of her fingerprints in the bedroom – that's *all* they know and that's all they'll ever know.' I step inside the house. 'Slip out of your boots. Follow me – and watch where you step.'

'What about Sherrilyn O'Neil?' she asks, referring to the woman I had accidentally killed before the arrival of the FBI. She lasted a good eight months before the fight left her. Darby, I'm sure, will last longer – a year, maybe even two.

'They don't know about Sherrilyn,' I say, 'or about any of the other ones.' I pick up the severed bindings from the floor and stuff them in her jacket pocket. Sarah looks panicked. 'Sarah, there's nothing to link Nicky to the other girls.'

'What about Teddy Lancaster? He recorded you, so he knows about Nicky –'

'He doesn't,' I say, but I have no way of knowing that for sure. Teddy never mentioned Hubbard while he had me tied down to the chair. Sure, he knew *something* had happened inside the Downes bedroom – he had recorded a video of me on my hands and knees scrubbing away, trying to destroy any trace of Nicky's blood. But I refused to tell Teddy what I was doing, or why I was doing it. He thought he could beat the truth out of me, but he was wrong. He had finally given up when Darby McCormick rang the doorbell. He said he would find out. The truth would come out, and, whatever it was, he said, he would expose me.

And now I'm safe again, and there's only one last thing to do.

'Nicky can't hurt us,' I tell her as I sit down on the desk chair. 'She's dead. They all are.' I point to the small bag of plastic zip-ties Kelly had placed on the counter and say, 'Grab a couple of those. I need you to tie me up.'

Sarah returns with the bindings. 'Everyone on the planet is looking for Hubbard,' she says as she ties my wrists together. 'The FBI aren't going to go away. They'll stay here and look for her.'

'They won't. Grab the tape from the floor.'

She does, and I say, 'The Hubbard stuff will die down, I promise. After that, we'll be free to go wherever we want, together.'

Sarah kisses me deeply. Smiling and grateful, she secures the tape over my mouth.

Then she's gone, and I'm alone inside the house, tied up and gagged, another unfortunate victim of the Red

Hill Ripper. The air reeks of blood and gun smoke and, as I close my eyes, I think about the way Sarah stiffened when I touched her. I'm not worried. She loves me. She always does what she's told.

69

Coop sat back down in Chief Robinson's office chair, about to have another go at the property records for the Downes home, when from down the hall he heard the dispatcher's alarmed voice say, 'Dead. They're all dead.'

Coop was suddenly on his feet and moving into the hall, which was practically desolate. Red Hill PD had been called in to help with the manhunt for Eli Savran. His Ford Bronco hadn't been sighted anywhere in Red Hill, Brewster or the surrounding towns. The Colorado state police had started reviewing the security-camera footage for all their nearby tollbooths, looking for the Bronco, but Coop was willing to bet a week's salary that the guy had changed it for a stolen car and left town. By now, he was probably already out of the state.

Inside the communications room, Betty the dispatcher was talking to a patrolman Coop hadn't seen before, a tall, skinny guy with a slight overbite who looked like he had just graduated from puberty. They saw Coop approaching and visibly stiffened.

Darby, he thought, a cold pit forming in his stomach.

She's dead, he thought as he jogged towards them, rubber-legged. An hour and fifteen minutes had passed since Darby had called to tell him she'd arrived at Sally Kelly's house. Then she had gone into radio-silence mode and refused to answer her satellite phone. No big surprise there. When it came to working a case, Darby always did things in her own way and in her own time, which was why he had sent the patrolman with the gummy smile, Whitehead, to chaperone her. There had been no reason to worry, he had told himself, throwing his attention back into the property records.

Coop didn't need to ask the question. Betty, face ashen and voice tight, answered it for him. 'Doug's there right now. He just called.'

'Doug who?'

'Freeman. He's one of ours.' The look in the woman's eyes made Coop want to turn away and block his ears, just as he did when he was a boy, when his parents were fighting. *If don't see it or hear it that means it didn't happen.*

The dispatcher licked her lips and her body trembled as she spoke. 'Sally Kelly, Lancaster and Whitehead – Doug Freeman says they're all dead. Gunshots. Blood everywhere, he said.'

Coop had his keys in his hand. 'Dr McCormick?'

'He didn't say anything about her. He had just radioed to say he was entering the house. I'll call him right now.'

But Coop was already running down the hall.

The snow had stopped. It was a few minutes shy of 5.30, and the sky was pitch black. He couldn't hold his hand steady when he dialled the number for the computer guys in Denver to trace the signal for Darby's satellite phone. After he hung up, he drove with both hands gripping the wheel to stop his arms from shaking.

Dead, the dispatcher had said.

The wind howled and slammed against his car, and it occurred to him, again, how a good portion of his adult life had been spent caged with anxiety, worrying about the moment when he received the call that Darby had finally died.

They're all dead, Betty had said.

For as long as he'd known her, she had been attracted to darkness – and attracted too much darkness. And yet wasn't that the reason why he had fallen in love with her in the first place? He had tried to disconnect himself from her, to gain some distance, by dating a string of women who had the intelligence, emotional depth and career ambition of a cucumber. Why? They were a distraction, sure, but more importantly they were uncomplicated, easy to be with and, emotionally, easy to manage. The moment one of them wanted more, he picked another living Barbie doll.

Darby was dangerous to him – to everyone, really, when he thought about it. Inviting her into his life on a full-time basis meant subjecting himself to a purgatory of anxiety and aggravation, waiting for the inevitable call that she had been killed. Naively – maybe even stupidly – he thought he could spare himself the full impact of that moment by refusing to allow himself to be emotionally entangled with her. That decision, he thought, would give him some much-needed distance. A possible buffer. And yet here he was, sinking, his lungs and stomach filling with what felt like wet cement.

His satphone rang. As he reached for it, he knew it was the dispatcher, Betty, calling to tell him Darby was dead.

But the caller-ID said 'Harold Scott'. Who was that? It sounded familiar, but he couldn't remember why, and then suddenly he did: Scott was the special agent in charge of the Denver field office. He was due to arrive at the Red Hill station at six.

Coop answered the call.

Scott got right to it. 'What happened last night, Eli Savran – the cat's out of the bag,' he said. 'Story's all over the local and national news, the internet and Twitter. You got anything new on your end?'

Coop told him about Sally Kelly's house. 'I don't know much,' he said. 'I'm on my way there right now.'

'So Savran is still in Red Hill.'

'It looks that way.'

'Give me the address.'

Coop did, reading it off the GPS. He was ten minutes away – probably more, because of all the snow packing the barren roads.

'I'll meet you there,' Scott said. 'Take control of the scene, make sure no one tramples on anything.'

'Understood.' Scott hadn't mentioned anything about Nicky Hubbard's fingerprint. It was possible he didn't know yet. That, or he had been told by the lab's fingerprint people and was sitting on it for the moment. Either way, Coop knew he couldn't sit on it any longer. 'Sir, are you someplace where you can talk freely? I have some sensitive information I need to share with you.'

'I'm alone in my car.'

Coop told him about finding Nicky Hubbard's fingerprint and about what he'd found out earlier in the property records – that before the Downes family moved into their home, it had been vacant for nearly a year. The original owners, Robert and Alice Birmingham, were dead – Robert of a stroke in '79; the wife following four years later, of a heart attack in her sleep, during the spring of 1983, the same year Nicky Hubbard had been abducted. During the time the home was vacant, their only child, Stephen Birmingham, who had been living in San Diego when his mother died, hired contractors to renovate the house – new roof, new carpeting, the walls and floor-boards in all the rooms stripped down to the bare wood and freshly painted and stained. At some point during that time, Savran had brought Nicky Hubbard there and she had touched the floorboard while it was still drying, her fingerprint forever sealed in the poly.

'You're sure about this?' Scott asked. 'About Hubbard's fingerprint?'

'There's no question.'

'Jesus H. Christ.'

In the silence that followed, Coop's mind swung back to Darby, to the dead waiting for him inside Sally Kelly's house. As he glanced again at the GPS, he pictured the patrolman navigating his way through a house of blood and gun smoke.

'We're going to need a list of the contractors, painters – whoever was working on the house during that time, I want their names,' Scott said. 'One of them might've seen Savran there at some point.'

'We can ask Savran when we find him.'

'*If* we find him. A mook like Savran isn't going to

surrender. Guys like him exit the planet one of two ways: a blaze of glory or the noose route. We'll need to establish a timeline for when he was inside the house with Hubbard.'

Then Scott was gone, and Coop was alone with his thoughts again. As he drove down yet another cold and bone-white tunnel, thinking about Darby and all the blood waiting for him, the wind whipped against his car as if wanting to shove him in another direction, any direction but the one in which he was heading.

A pretty EMT named Leila is stitching up the laceration near my mouth when the back of the ambulance door swings open, letting in a blast of cold air and the blinking merry-go-round of police and emergency lights.

Agent Cooper's hair is windblown, and his cheeks look sunken and hollow.

'Could you please give us a minute?' he asks Leila, yelling over the outside voices shouting orders to one another through the wind and crackle of handheld radios.

After she leaves, Cooper sits on the gurney across from me, elbows on his knees, his satellite phone gripped in one hand. When I see the crushing terror in his face, I can't conceal my delight. Fortunately, my face and lips are swollen and numbed by Novocain, so my true expression and emotions are withheld from him.

His gaze roves over the various cuts and lacerations, the stitches and Steri-Strips.

'Savran did that to you?' he asks.

I nod, slowly. 'He was waiting behind the front door.'

The words come out in a slurred, wet mess. Cooper doesn't understand me. I use the pad pinched between my fingers to gently wipe at my lips. They feel as thick as a bicycle tyre.

Cooper leans closer, straining to hear.

'The front door was unlocked,' I tell him. 'I stepped inside and saw Kelly and Lancaster dead on the floor. But it was too late. Savran must've been standing behind the door, because that's when he attacked me. I didn't see him.'

I feel myself drooling and wipe at my mouth again. 'When I woke up, he had me tied down to the chair in the kitchen. He wanted to know how we found him. Savran. Wanted to know what we knew. He was using a billy club on me when we heard someone pull into the driveway. Then he hit me again and I was out. Next thing I know, patrol is inside the house, cutting me from the chair.'

'And Darby, where was she?'

'I'm not following.'

'Did you see her come inside the house?'

'No. What's going on?'

'I think Savran took Darby.'

He didn't, Agent Cooper. I did. And after I'm done playing with her, Sarah and I are going to move far, far away and start a new life together.

'Did you hear Savran say anything?'

'No,' I say. 'Nothing.'

Cooper looks like a man who has been forced out of a plane without a parachute. I want to smile. Instead, I stare at him blankly, pretending to be horrified.

'We'll find her,' I say.

'What were you doing at Kelly's house?'

'Teddy called me.'

Which is entirely true. Teddy *did* call me while I was on my way to the river. Up until that moment, I too believed Eli Savran was, in fact, the Red Hill Ripper. I knew that the Red Hill Ripper had surreptitiously recorded himself killing the families – had, in all probability, recorded me down on my hands and knees, wiping down the wall and floor in the corner of the Downes bedroom. When I tossed Savran's MacBook and computer paraphernalia into the water, I truly believed I was halfway home to saving myself. All I had to do was to find Savran before anyone else did and, God-willing, kill him – a definite long shot, which was why I had Sarah shadowing me in case we needed to run. I had finally shared with Sarah the horrible truth of the mistake at the Downes house that morning.

'Teddy wanted me to talk to Kelly,' I say.

'About what?'

'Kelly said she had something on Savran, but she would talk only to me.'

This too is true. Teddy called and used those exact words. When I arrived at Kelly's house, I had no idea Teddy Lancaster was the Red Hill Ripper – that it was he, and not Savran, who had been recording the families. Teddy greeted me warmly at the door, and when I entered, on my way to the kitchen to talk to Sally Kelly, he smacked me over the head with his billy club. Kept hitting me until I blacked out. It wasn't until after I woke up and found myself bound to the chair that I learned of the monster living inside Teddy Lancaster.

'I walked inside and then this happened,' I say, and point to my face. 'That's all I remember.'

'Think for a moment. Maybe you thought you heard Darby or Savran talking.'

I heard all sorts of things, Agent Cooper. I can tell you

that Teddy Lancaster killed the families because they were standing in the way of the town's incorporation. The state had developers all lined up, but the families refused to sell their properties for well below fair market value, and unless they sold the incorporation wouldn't go through. The state was in thrall to the developers, who would help it to meet all its costs – and line any number of individuals' pockets as well of course. Teddy's power base would expand as a result, and he and his state cronies – the ones who had made all the financial arrangements – would receive kickbacks galore. Teddy disguised the murders to look like the work of a serial killer, so he and his politician friends could get rich turning Red Hill into a strip mall. Oh, and Eli Savran is dead. Teddy killed him, and I heard him say where Eli's body is.

'Can you tell me anything?' Cooper asks. He's barely able to conceal the beautiful hopelessness in his voice. 'Anything at all?'

Yes, Agent Cooper. I can tell you I made a mistake that morning. I fully admit that. When I stepped inside the Downes bedroom and found them all dead, my first thought was to protect Sarah. I couldn't risk your finding any lingering traces of Nicky Hubbard's blood because you and I both know that forensic DNA identification has evolved light years since 1983.

'Ray?'

Teddy doesn't know about Nicky Hubbard or what I did to her in that bedroom a long, long time ago. About how, when I was strangling her, she cut her head and started to bleed everywhere – you know how cuts on the head are. But Teddy knew I was up to something, because he had recorded me cleaning up that area – which is why he wanted me to go to Kelly's house, why he tied me up to the chair. He wanted to know all about the fingerprint because he had run out of time – because you and the FBI refused to leave, and Teddy didn't want to leave any loose ends. I refused to tell him, which is why he tried valiantly to redecorate my face. He doesn't know about Nicky Hubbard or any of the others – and neither will you, Agent Cooper – neither will you.

'I've told you everything I know,' I say.

His crestfallen expression makes my heart surge. I can smell the fear and desperation bleeding from his pores.

I grab his wrist and squeeze. 'We'll find her.'

His satellite phone rings. As he answers the call, he removes a pen from his shirt pocket.

'Go ahead,' he says into the phone. He's patting down his pockets, searching for his notebook, when I hand him mine. He writes down an address and then hangs up.

'Did you find her?' I ask.

'Maybe. The guys in Denver traced the signal on her satellite phone.'

I make a show of trying to stand.

'No,' Coop says. 'You're still bleeding.'

'I'm coming with you.'

'You've suffered a major concussion, Ray.'

'I want to help. Darby, I don't want anything to happen to her.'

70

Darby's satellite signal was coming from Route Six, near the Red Hill/Brewster line, a no man's land of endless forest and cliffs known as Dead Man's Curve. The patrolman who was driving Coop said the area had been named that because it was packed with so many roadside crosses it resembled a cemetery.

Then, for a reason Coop didn't understand, the patrolman added how Red Hill had lost count of the number of cars that had spun out of control every time the road was wet or icy; how they would crash into each other and into trees, some tumbling down the steep slopes on either side of the road, never to be found again, some having to be lifted out by a crane.

Coop saw the road ahead of them turn sharply to his left, no guardrail there, and when the road dipped steeply, like the first steep plunge of a rollercoaster, he felt his stomach drop. Drenched in sweat, his clothes stuck to his skin. His mouth and throat were parchment-dry, his chest tight, and his heart felt like it had been dunked in ice water.

She's not dead, he kept telling himself. *She's a fighter. She knows I'm looking for her, she'll be okay.*

Coop brought the phone back up to his ear. He had a guy named Lee from RCFL on the line, who was tracking Darby's signal – and his.

'There's nothing out here but woods,' he told Lee.

'That's where the signal's coming from. You're right on top of it.'

Coop told the driver to pull over. He got out of the car and heard the roar of water. Dread swam through him as he spoke into the phone: 'Tell me where to go.'

'North-east, about 500 yards.'

Coop made his way up an embankment of ploughed snow. An ambulance and uniformed deputies from the Brewster sheriff's office had just pulled on to the road and parked, their lights cutting through the dark, cold air. He could see, directly below, a river bursting with rapids.

'DARBY!'

He made his way into the woods. Because of the tree cover, the snow wasn't as deep here. But it came up his boots, thick and wet, soaking his trousers. He ran as fast as he could with the flashlight gripped firmly in his hands, the beam zigzagging everywhere, searching for her.

'DARBY!'

His voice echoed and died.

She's alive, Coop told himself. He kept screaming out her name, knowing she would answer him any second now. She couldn't hear him and he couldn't hear her, because their voices were drowned out by the roars of wind and water.

He brought the phone back up to his ear. 'I don't see her.'

There was a slight pause, and then Lee said, almost sadly, 'You're right on top of her signal.'

Which meant the satellite phone he had given her was

buried somewhere in this snow. Not Darby, just the phone. Savran must have tossed it out the window.

The woods took on a surreal, dreamy quality, as though this were a nightmare from which he would wake up at any moment, the normal flow of life restored.

Or she dropped it, Coop thought. *She fought off Savran and escaped: she was running through these woods and she dropped the phone. She's alive. All I've got to do is find her.*

Coop moved more deeply into the woods, screaming out her name.

71

He put me in a chokehold. Ray Williams.

The words ran through Darby's mind as she fluttered awake.

Ray Williams, the lead detective on the Ripper case, had put her in a chokehold. She remembered that, and she remembered how she had helped him to his feet – and then he had put her in a chokehold until she passed out. Next came a foggy memory of waking up on Kelly's couch with her hands cuffed behind her back and Williams pressing her against the plastic-covered cushions. Williams had been talking to someone. A woman. Darby couldn't remember what they had said or the content of their conversation, but she remembered he had stuck a needle into her neck, and whatever he had injected into her had burned. Then the drug kicked in and she had blacked out and she was . . . where? Where was she?

Her good eye blinked open to a darkness as thick as paint and she felt cold all over. Fear seized her, but her heart continued to beat at its normal resting rate.

The drug, she thought. *Whatever drug he used is still in my system.* She couldn't feel the pain from the stapled wound on the left side of her head or on the split ear where Lancaster had pistol-whipped her. She couldn't, in fact, feel anything, but the voice in her mind was awake, and it was telling her about Lancaster, how he had admitted to being the Ripper, how he had been killing families who had been standing in the way of the incorporation. And then Ray Williams had put her in a chokehold.

Had they been working together? If so, why had Lancaster tied Ray to the chair? And who was the woman who had entered the house to help Williams?

Darby saw that she'd been placed on her right side, on top of something soft, her head on a pillow and her hands tied behind her back not with metal handcuffs but something thin and hard that bit into her wrists. Plastic cuffs. She tried to move her arms and legs, but they wouldn't respond. She couldn't move anything.

Her ankles too had been bound with plastic cuffs. She managed to wiggle her toes – it seemed to take an enormous effort – and she felt the sole of her foot. Her socks were gone, which meant her boots had been removed, and right then she realized why she felt cold all over: Ray Williams had removed her clothes.

And he had placed something thick and tight around her neck.

Fear exploded through her and then vanished behind the drug, her heart still oblivious to her predicament, still snoozing. She could breathe and she had no problems swallowing, not yet. She knew she should be terrified but she wasn't, because she was doped up to the gills. She felt herself sinking, her good eye fluttering shut as part of her said, *That's it, go back to sleep.*

Darby didn't want to go back to sleep. Knew it was stupid and foolish.

If you're asleep, he can't hurt you. Go back to sleep and —

A dim light came on. Darby forced her eye back open. The dim light came from a battery-operated camp light made of plastic. It sat a few feet away, on a concrete floor.

She couldn't move her body, but she could move her eye, and she saw that she was lying sideways on a bare mattress. Then she heard what sounded like soft footsteps, and when they stopped in front of her she saw a pair of fuzzy pink slippers.

The person set a plastic bucket on the floor. Darby couldn't see the woman's face yet – but it was a woman because the hands that were wringing out the wet facecloth were feminine. The woman set the facecloth on the edge of the bucket. Darby licked her dry lips, wanting to speak, but the woman stood and moved away, out of the cell.

I'm inside a prison cell, Darby thought, staring at the iron bars. This wasn't a jail cell but someone's personal holding tank. Ray Williams's personal holding tank. He had brought her here and tied her up and she had no idea why, not yet.

Then she caught a flash of khaki and polished loafers clicking across the floor, heading her way. Ray Williams picked up the facecloth and, kneeling, rubbed Darby's bare arms, the cloth warm and wet against her skin.

'You're so beautiful,' Ray said. 'But you already know that.'

Again, Darby licked her dry lips. When she spoke, her

throat raw, the words came out sounding dry and brittle, like paper crackling. 'I saved your life.'

'And I thank you for that,' Williams replied. He kissed her gently on the forehead and went back to washing her.

Darby moved her good eye to track the other woman but she couldn't see her. Where did she go? Was she a part of this – and who was she? Then Darby's gaze dropped to the concrete floor, to the dried, jagged lines of blood and the fragments of torn skin and broken fingernails. Someone had clawed at the floor.

Ray saw where she was looking and said, 'Sherrilyn gave up too quickly.'

'Sherrilyn?' Darby's eye darted back to him.

'Sherrilyn O'Neil, the previous occupant. From Utah,' Ray said, dipping the facecloth back in the bucket. 'I only hunt in other states.'

Nicky Hubbard's fingerprint, how Darby had told Coop that the Red Hill Ripper wouldn't return to a previous crime scene – it all swam through her. The Red Hill Ripper hadn't killed Hubbard inside the Downes bedroom; someone else had.

'Nicky,' Darby croaked.

'Dead. Gone. You don't need to worry about her any more.'

Ray ran the washcloth over her chest, paying close attention to her breasts.

'You,' Darby said, voice barely above a whisper. She so badly wanted to go back to sleep. 'It was you who washed down that area. Lancaster filmed you.'

'It's all over now.'

There were two serial killers here in Red Hill: Teddy Lancaster, who had been killing families standing in the way of the town's incorporation; and Detective Ray Williams, who had just admitted to hunting in other states.

'Women,' Darby said, voice coarse. 'How many?'

'Shh. You need to rest.' Ray wrung out the washcloth again. 'Go to sleep.'

'How many?'

Ray Williams tossed the washcloth into the bucket. 'I killed her there, in the bedroom. Nicky,' he said. 'I was the one who washed down the area that morning, before you arrived. And Lancaster caught me. Lancaster had no idea why I'd done it. He didn't say anything to me because he was waiting to see if you guys found out anything before he made his move. Now he's dead, and my secret is safe.

'As for the other women I've hosted here, it doesn't matter. What matters is that you and I are together. You're my special girl. I only have eyes for you.'

Ray Williams placed his hands on either side of her hand and then his lips were mashed against hers, breath stale and tongue probing, and he inhaled deeply as if trying to draw something out of her.

Then, mercifully, it was over. He stood and she watched him move past the iron door and out of the cell. The woman was waiting by a ladder. Ray was about to go to it when she grabbed him by the back of the head and pulled him towards her, kissing him deeply, one hand massaging his crotch as she glared at Darby like a hungry wolf protecting its food supply.

When Ray Williams finally pried himself away from the woman's grasp, he turned to the ladder.

'I love you, baby,' the woman said to him. 'Forever.'

'I love you too, Sarah.'

As Ray climbed the ladder, Sarah entered the cell.

72

'Relax,' the woman said, as she picked up the washcloth. 'I'm not going to hurt you.'

Darby tried to speak, but the words dissolved in her throat.

'It's okay,' the woman cooed as she cleaned Darby. 'It's okay. Go ahead and close your eyes and sleep.'

The woman hummed as she worked. Several minutes later, the woman gently rolled Darby on to her back. Darby, still immobilized from the drugs, couldn't do anything but lie on her back with her wrists tied behind her and her midsection exposed. If the woman wanted to kill her, there was nothing she could do to prevent it. She was helpless.

'Just remember,' the woman said, 'he's mine.'

Darby wasn't listening, her attention locked on the plastic-wrapped steel wire that ran from whatever was on her neck to a hole in a steel ceiling.

The woman saw Darby looking at it but said nothing.

Darby blinked, concentrating on the round, pale face hovering just inches away. The woman's dark brown hair was greying at the roots, and cut short; her dark blue eyes were bloodshot, damp and puffy from crying. Her front teeth were crooked and gapped.

The woman noticed Darby staring and, self-conscious,

clamped her lips shut and turned her attention back to the bucket.

I know who you are, Darby wanted to say. *You'd go unrecognized on the street, because you're a middle-aged woman now. Your face has filled out, and you're wearing glasses and your hair is a different colour, but you've got the same eyes, the same nose and lips.*

'Nicky,' Darby croaked. 'You're Nicky Hubbard.'

The woman paid no attention. She wrung out the washcloth and said, 'Ray loves me and only me. Remember that. And fight back. Ray really loves it when you fight back. It makes us both so happy.'

Day Ten

73

It was a shock collar, the kind used to train dogs; but Ray Williams had modified it for human use, and there was no way to remove it.

Darby had tried. She couldn't see the collar – there was no mirror in here – but she could touch it any time she wanted to. The obedience collar, as it was called, was made of thick steel and had a small padlock on the back, along with an O-ring. The inside of the collar was lined with fleece so it wouldn't cut or irritate the wearer's neck. Every time Darby swallowed, she could feel the four metal prongs that delivered the shock digging into her skin.

The collar's O-ring was attached to a heavy steel-mesh wire encased in clear plastic – the kind of cable used in dog leads to prevent the animal from running away. The cable ran up through a hole in the ceiling, which was, along with the floors and walls, made of galvanized steel; it was attached to a pulley, and it allowed her to roam freely about her homemade six-by-eight cell, with its chemical toilet and mattress.

But the wire prevented her from getting anywhere near the cell's steel door and iron bars, which separated her cell from a room that offered more creature comforts: a twin bed, which at the moment was neatly made and decorated with throw pillows; a nightstand and lamp; a small flat-screen TV and a Blu-Ray player; a high-backed chair, toilet and a small refrigerator stocked with bottles of water and cans of soda. The shelves above the bed held boxes of meal-replacement bars, toilet paper and an assortment of paperback books, the majority of which, as far as she could tell, were romance novels.

The adjoining room also held a ladder that led to what Darby guessed had to be some sort of trapdoor. She couldn't see it from her cell, but she always heard it when it was opened, and it was being opened right now.

Darby sat up on her mattress and threw back the wool blanket and comforter. At the moment her cell was bathed in a complete and total darkness. Her facial swelling had disappeared; she was able to see out of both eyes; and the staples along her incision itched furiously. She had been given Tylenol with each meal, and she had been provided with ill-fitting but warm clothes: thermal underwear, fleece-lined sweatpants and a woollen sweater. No shoes, though, just two pairs of woollen socks. Williams was smart enough to know that a shoe could be turned into a weapon.

At least that was what Darby assumed; she hadn't seen Williams since the day he had washed her. Darby figured he was tied up with Coop and the other federal agents who were avidly questioning him about what had happened at Sally Kelly's house. What had Williams told them? That Savran had killed everyone inside the house and then taken her as his hostage? Was Savran alive or dead?

And how many women had been brought here to this

private torture chamber, which was, she suspected, buried underground? She had a solid idea about the purpose this place served. There was no question in her mind about what Williams was going to do to her after the heat died down. Williams, she figured, could afford to wait them out.

Were the FBI still in Red Hill? Were they looking for her or did they assume Savran had killed her?

Her stomach dropped and her muscles tensed when she heard the trap door shut, followed by a padlock clicking into place. Then footsteps continued down the rungs, and a moment later she heard the click of a light switch, and the pair of lamps in the adjoining room came to life.

74

Once her eyes had adjusted to the sudden brightness, Darby saw the woman Williams called Sarah slipping out of her boots. They were wet with snow. Wherever Darby was, she wasn't inside Williams's house. Was she on his property or had he tucked her away somewhere else?

Darby didn't know, but one thing was clear: Williams had designed this place with care and detail to prevent anyone from escaping.

Sarah wore a pink fleece top with matching sweatpants. 'It's time for your feeding,' she said, slipping her stockinged feet into a pair of slippers.

That was what she called Darby's meals: feedings. Like she was some sort of caged pet. *That's exactly what I am.*

Sarah smiled brightly. 'Did I tell you Ray belongs to Netflix?'

Darby said nothing, looking at the neatly made bed outside her cell. The woman slept here almost every night, and she spent the majority of the day down here too, reading her Victorian romance novels and watching TV series and movies on DVD. She left for a couple of hours at a time and always came back with supplies – at least Darby assumed it was a couple of hours. She had no idea. There was no clock down here; no windows to tell here whether it was day or night; no calendar to mark off the passage of days. She was buried underground, trapped inside the waiting room to hell.

'Ray allowed me to get the first season of *The Tudors*. If you're nice to me –'

'How many women?' Darby asked.

'We're not doing this again. I told you, no questions.'

'I know who you are. Why do you keep denying it?'

'Please, I want to have a nice day today. Please.'

'Your name is Nicky Hubbard.'

'Nicky Hubbard is dead. Ray killed her.'

She repeated the same words every time Darby brought up the subject.

'No, he didn't. You're Nicky Hubbard,' Darby said. The woman could deny it all she wanted, but there was no doubt in Darby's mind. 'That's why he's hiding you down here with me. Red Hill's swarming with the FBI, and other cops –'

'Wrong.'

'Ray can't afford to have someone stop by the house during the day and see you,' Darby said. She felt sure the news about Hubbard's fingerprint had been released. 'Someone would recognize you if they looked carefully enough.'

'Wrong.'

'You have Nicky Hubbard's eyes. Her nose and lips.'

The woman kept shaking her head. 'I'm getting real tired of you –'

'You have her ears too,' Darby said. 'You're Nicky Hubbard.'

'Enough!'

For the past few days, Darby had been playing around with numbers. Ray Williams had abducted Nicky Hubbard thirty-one years ago; Darby didn't know the how and why, because the woman kept refusing to answer Darby's repeated questions on the subject. And Darby knew Williams had abducted another woman not that long ago, the previous occupant of this cell, a woman named Sherrilyn O'Neil. If Ray had been abducting a woman every year, that meant he was responsible for disappearances of thirty other women.

And that was just a conservative estimate. It was more than likely he had been taking two women a year, which brought his lifetime record up to sixty. The frightening thing was that sixty was in all probability still too low a number. How many had he abducted and killed? Darby felt sure Nicky Hubbard knew. But did the woman know where Williams had buried the remains?

The woman who called herself Sarah had collected herself. 'If you behave, I'll turn on the TV so we can watch *The Tudors*. We can have a nice, enjoyable day together.'

As the woman got down on one knee and reached inside the big plastic bucket she'd brought down with her, Darby launched into the same script she'd been using day after day, hoping that it would release the memories buried somewhere inside this meek middle-aged woman who had been brainwashed into believing Ray Williams loved her.

'You were seven years old when your mother brought

you to the Carter & Sullivan department store,' Darby said. 'You were looking at Cabbage Patch dolls when Ray Williams kidnapped you. He was a teenager. He –'

'I'm not listening to you any more.' The woman began to transfer the contents of the bucket to a small cardboard box: clean clothes, a bottle of water and a meal-replacement bar.

'Your mother's name is Joan,' Darby said. 'She misses you and loves you, Nicky. She wants you to come home.'

The woman who called herself Sarah Williams stood abruptly. She reached inside her pocket and came back with a small handheld remote with a thick rubber antenna.

'Your mother is alive,' Darby said, struggling to keep her gaze locked on the woman. 'I can take you to her.'

'Say my name – my *real* name. You say it right now or you'll force me to press the button.'

Darby had been repeating the script for God only knew how many days, but this was the first time she had seen the woman who believed her name was Sarah with the remote.

'Let me help you,' Darby said. 'I want to help you.'

'Say it. Say my name or I'll do it.'

Darby had an idea of what was coming. Her muscles tensed, and she broke out in a cold sweat.

'*Say it!*'

'Nicky Hubbard. Your name is Nicky Hubbard.'

The woman pressed the remote's side button.

Darby had been Tasered before, but this was a thousand

times worse. Hundreds of electrified razors tore through her neck and limbs and exploded through the meat of her brain. She clutched the steel collar frantically, uselessly, trying to tear it off. Her legs gave out and then she fell against the floor, writhing. Screaming.

75

When it was over, Darby lay on the floor, quivering and gasping. As her vision finally returned, she saw that Hubbard had moved the cardboard box inside her cell.

Nicky Hubbard – and that's who she was, Nicky Hubbard, not Sarah – Nicky Hubbard pressed her face against the bars. She looked sad. Apologetic.

'That was the number seven setting.'

'Nicky,' Darby croaked.

'I don't want to hurt you again. Please, I'm begging you, stop calling me that. You're wrong about Hubbard. She's dead.'

'It's not . . . your fault. Battered women, abused children and cult members – they all undergo a very traumatic bonding process. Victims become loyal, even protective of the perpetrators.'

'I am *not* a victim. I told you that before.'

'Victims go on to develop their abuser's beliefs, values and –'

'Stop or I'll press the button again.'

Darby was breathing hard, but she managed to keep her voice calm and empathetic. 'You're scared,' she said, forcing herself on to her side. 'I don't blame you. I would be scared too.'

'I'm not scared. You don't know what you're talking about.'

Darby remained quiet for a moment, waiting to see if Hubbard would retreat to her bed, pick up her noise-cancelling headphones and watch TV. The first few times she had confronted Hubbard, the woman was too terrified to speak. Then Hubbard tried to ignore her. When Darby refused to stop talking, to stop asking questions, Hubbard became angry. She shouted at Darby to shut up.

But Hubbard was still standing at the bars, looking down at her, like she was waiting for an explanation.

Good, Darby thought. *Definite progress.* 'If I don't know what I'm talking about, explain to me why he tried to kill you inside that bedroom.'

'Why do you care?'

'Why are you afraid to tell me?'

Hubbard held her head high. 'I am *not* afraid,' she said. 'And Ray apologized for what he did. It was an accident. His mother had always wanted a girl.'

Darby remained quiet. This was new information.

'Mother Sarah didn't like boys. She'd always wanted a girl, and when Ray brought me to her car, she was so excited. She was very kind to me. Very, very nice. She named me after herself, you know.'

'And Ray? Was he nice and kind to you?'

'Of course he is.'

'Then why did he try to kill you?'

'I don't want to talk about this any more. You're upsetting me, and I'm very tired.'

'We found your fingerprint in the bedroom.'

'I know. Ray told me. He tells me *everything*.' She smiled in sour triumph.

'The FBI will find you,' Darby said.

Hubbard said nothing. She didn't have to; her fearful expression confirmed Darby's suspicion.

'Everyone in the world has been looking for you,' Darby said. 'Your mother –'

'My mother is dead.'

'She's alive. If you don't believe me, go on the internet and look.'

'Ray doesn't let me use it.'

Of course he doesn't, Darby thought. 'Tell me what happened and I promise I'll be good,' she said. 'Then we can watch *The Tudors* together, just like you wanted. We'll have a nice day together.'

'You promise?'

Darby nodded.

Hubbard composed herself. When she spoke, the words came out in a rush, as though they were poisoned and she had to get them out of her throat or she'd die. 'Ray told me he was jealous of all the attention his mother was giving me, so one night he brought me to that house so we could play hide-and-seek, okay? And then he got . . . got mad and shoved me and I must've split my head on the floor or something. And he said I was bleeding everywhere and when I wouldn't stop crying he started to . . . He just got really, really mad, and he started . . . He had to make me be quiet.'

'Did he strangle you? Hit you? What?'

'It doesn't matter. What matters is he *stopped*. He stopped because he loves me, and I love him.'

'If he loves you so much, why does he bring women here and strangle them?'

'I answered your question.' Hubbard's voice trembled, and her eyes threatened tears. 'Now, you promised to be good. No more talking.'

'You didn't answer my question.'

'I just did!'

'You told me Ray's version of what happened. I want to hear *your* version. I want to hear *you* tell me what happened.'

'I don't remember. I was too young to remember.'

Darby wondered if that was true. Had Hubbard managed to bury that traumatic event in order to function? To survive living with a sadist?

'I study people like Ray for a living,' Darby said. 'He's a psychopath – a very smart one.'

'No. More. Talking.' Her voice trembled and her eyes threatened tears. 'You promised.'

'The FBI are looking for you. They're going to find you – and him.'

Hubbard brought the remote up to Darby's face. Her hand shook in anger – or was it fear?

Darby knew she had to keep pressing her. 'Ray is going to kill you.'

'I'm turning the dial up to eight.'

'He has to kill you because everyone in the world will be looking for you. You're going to die, and he's going to escape. He's going to –'

'You think you're so special because you're pretty and have a beautiful body. But whores like you are a dime a dozen. That's why he always comes back to me. He loves me. *Only* me. I share his bed because I'm the only one who knows how to satisfy him.'

'I know he doesn't love you,' Darby said. 'If he did, I wouldn't be here, would I?'

Darby saw that her words had hit home. She braced herself for another shock, but Hubbard, red-faced with anger and her eyes bright with tears, had turned to the ladder.

Hubbard stormed up the rungs. When Darby heard the trapdoor slam shut, she moved the steel cord to the front of her face. She curled it around a fist and climbed a foot; she didn't need to reach the top. She swung back and forth a couple of times to get some momentum, the cord digging into her skin; and then she raised her knees to her chest and pushed her legs up until the soles of her bare feet landed on the rough concrete ceiling.

Now she had leverage. Now she was standing on the ceiling, blood rushing into her head. Now, just as she had done every time she was alone in her cell, she wrapped both hands around the cord and pulled, muscles straining, hoping that this time she would somehow manage to break it, and have a fighting chance of defending herself.

76

Like most men, Coop had a complicated relationship with emotions. His father, when the guy was actually around and pretending to be a parent, his uncles and his male older cousins all attacked life's emotional turbulences and soul-crushing losses in the way that Clint Eastwood did in his Westerns: keep your cool, shoot straight and if you go down, go down swinging. And never, under any circumstances, let them see you sweat or give the slightest indication that you're hurting.

Coop was worried sick about Darby, a woman he had worked with since he was twenty-five. Not only did he admire her, he loved her. Darby was honest and loyal and never afraid.

And now she was missing – *missing* being the operative word. Missing didn't mean dead. Missing meant there was still hope.

Denver's FBI office had taken over the Savran investigation. Special Agent in Charge Howard Scott and his agents had commandeered Red Hill PD's squad room, transforming the former Ripper task force centre into a hybrid hotline/command post. Additional phone lines had been installed for the tip lines. Savran, a fugitive who had murdered two federal agents, had gone platinum. The federal government had ponied up $100,000 for information leading to his capture and arrest, an increase of fifty grand on the original reward money. The US Marshals Service was involved in the manhunt, and Savran's name and face had been forwarded to every national news outlet, state police headquarters and law enforcement agency. Everyone in the world was looking for him right now.

So where was he?

Coop thought the answer was hidden in the thick stacks of papers scattered on his desk. He sat in a corner of the room, sifting through Savran's background information while trying to drown out the ringing telephones and the noise of agents, marshals and troopers who, along with Red Hill PD and uniformed deputies from Brewster, kept trekking in and out of the room, talking to each other on their cell and land-line phones.

Eight days had passed since Savran had shot and almost killed Hoder, and still no one had seen him or his Ford Bronco. The last time Savran had used his credit card was during the beginning of the month, a $48.45 purchase at Amazon. He had $62,345.23, courtesy of his mother's estate, parked in a current account at the local bank. He hadn't touched a cent of it since his Amazon purchase.

So why would a skilful, organized killer who had murdered five – no, make that six families – why wouldn't he clean out his account when he might have to blow Dodge at a moment's notice?

Answer: You couldn't apply logical thinking when it came to a psychopath. Doing so, Darby had once told him, was about as useful as sticking your hand inside a clogged toilet.

Here's what he *did* know. Savran's medical records confirmed the 47-year-old had been born with the rare metabolic condition known as trimethylaminuria. People who suffer from TMAU have an impaired FMO 3 enzyme; the odorous TMA can't be oxidized into the non-odorous TMA-oxide. The TMA builds up in the person's system, causing a fishy or garbage-like odour that is secreted through the person's sweat, urine and breath. For the past four and a half years, Savran had been trying to mitigate the intensity of the smell by using the oral antibiotic neomycin.

A victim of bullies and merciless teasing from classmates because of his fish odour syndrome, Eli Savran, unsurprisingly, had a long and well-documented history of anger issues. Thelma and Douglas Savran had officially divorced when Eli was six. At thirteen, he had been expelled from Red Hill High School for breaking a classmate's nose and jaw. He went to live with his father, who was working on oil rigs in New Orleans, for the next year and got into several scrapes, one of which, an assault and battery charge, had landed him a six-month stint in a juvenile detention centre. He bounced back and forth between his childhood home in Red Hill and wherever his father was working at the time. Eli dropped out of high school and took up menial work and odd jobs, mostly at night, when he could keep interaction with people to a minimum. At twenty-four, he had nearly beaten a man into a coma, earning Eli a level-3 A & B charge. The victim, for reasons unknown, later dropped the charge, and Eli was sentenced to community service.

Reports from therapists and his former high school guidance counsellor indicated a bright student who, if it weren't for the rage he felt because of his condition, could have gone on to a promising career in engineering or computer science. He got his high school equivalency diploma and at times flirted with the idea of getting a degree in computer programming.

But what was Savran's motive for killing the families?

It took all the weight of the FBI to find out that the state of Colorado had approached a good number of Red Hill families, secretly and individually, to sell their properties for what pretty much amounted to pennies on the dollar. The state had them over a barrel: sell or don't sell, the state could afford to wait. Their town was dying; there were no jobs or social services. Some families took the state's offer. Others had the financial means to play hardball, but the state wouldn't buckle. The families who had been murdered were holdouts.

The people with meagre jobs who were barely hanging on were the lucky ones. The vast majority were poor and scared and mostly uneducated. They were praying to God there'd be an influx of state aid, jobs and other relief measures once the incorporation went through – and the killer was paving the road for this. Why should they tell the police what they might have suspected about the Red Hill Ripper, when the state had offered these families good money for their properties? What had happened to them was their own fault.

The other factor at work was Red Hill's small-town mentality. The people operated in the same way as the blue-collar Irish Catholics who lived in Charlestown when he was a kid: you didn't volunteer information to the police. If you did, you'd wake up one day and find your car missing or, worse, you'd come home from work to discover your house had been burned down. And then there was always a chance that a group of people would take it upon themselves to corner you in a bar or on the street, or grab you and drive you somewhere where they would make their feelings known with baseball bats.

'Agent Cooper.'

Coop looked up from his papers and saw Denver SAC Harold Scott. He got up and shook the man's hand.

'I need to have a word with you,' Scott said. He had a deep baritone Barry White voice that immediately made him the centre of attention. 'In private.'

77

Coop followed him to Robinson's office, where it was safe to talk. The entire station had been swept for bugs. The USB device Darby had discovered inside Williams's office was the only one that had been found.

'Couple of things,' Scott said as he shut the door. He had dark skin and dark brown eyes; he was bald on top, with the hair on the sides of his head as white as snow. 'First is Hubbard's fingerprint. The DD assured me it's still locked down, so, thankfully, no one on the outside knows we found it.'

The DD was FBI Deputy Director Lou LaRoca – Scott's boss. The two men had decided to keep the information about Hubbard's fingerprint secret until Savran was in custody. If word about her print got out, Red Hill would turn into a free-fire zone.

'Second is Savran's Bronco,' Scott said. 'There's an abandoned coal-burning power plant in a town fifty or so miles from here, place called Leadville. They found the Bronco parked inside. We've got the rifle with a thermal scope and tracer ammo – and a backpack stuffed with duct tape and zip ties. Forensics is over there working on it right now. They've found plenty of blood samples.'

'You want me to head over?'

'No, we've got it covered.'

Coop sensed a shift in the man's tone that reminded him of the way the temperature suddenly drops before a thunderstorm. 'I've been looking through Savran's background info,' he said, and filled Scott in on the man's bank and credit card record.

Harold Scott listened attentively. He remained standing and did not ask Coop to sit.

'Hoder's profile said this guy was a planner,' Scott said, after Coop had finished. 'Speaking of Hoder, he's out of the woods. He woke up from his coma, but he's still having problems breathing on his own.'

'Good. That's good. Sir, if Savran was so meticulous, why would he leave all that cash parked in his bank account?'

'Because these jerkoffs never think they're gonna get bagged, that's why. What about the background on the murdered families? Anything new?'

'Lancaster went to school with both Eli Savran and David Downes.'

Scott nodded and stole a glance at the wall clock. 'Anything else?'

'Did you read my report on the burglary?' Coop asked.

Scott straightened a little, his starched shirt tightening against his chest, a tired look washing across his features.

After Teddy Lancaster was killed, it was discovered that his keys were missing. Coop had searched the man's pockets, his car and Kelly's house, but he couldn't find them. He believed Savran had taken Lancaster's keys.

Scott scratched the corner of his lip. 'We talked about

this. You don't have any proof or evidence Savran was inside Lancaster's house.'

'You're right, sir, I don't. But I went through Lancaster's home, and I didn't find a single computer anywhere. And why would Savran take Lancaster's keys?'

'You're assuming Lancaster had a computer in his house. My father's eighty-two, and he doesn't have a computer or a cell phone. No interest. Some people are like that. Besides, Lancaster didn't need one. He had an iPhone, which is pretty much a portable computer.'

Coop didn't know about the iPhone. 'You're sure?'

'Positive. Lancaster got a bill from AT & T in yesterday's mail.' Scott saw the suspicion lingering in Coop's gaze and added, 'When you searched Lancaster's house, did you find any computer equipment? CDs, disk keys, backup drives, books, anything like that?'

'No. I didn't.'

'Now, next item. Anything new on Savran?'

'During the summer of '83, he was sixteen and living with his father in New Orleans. He was working at the Dairy Queen the day Hubbard was abducted – his time sheet for that week was faxed this morning.'

'I read the fax,' Scott said, and stole a glance at the wall clock. 'It was probably a mistake, you know. It happens. The manager at the time was, what, nineteen?'

'Eighteen.'

'High school kids aren't exactly what you'd call responsible.'

'True,' Coop conceded, 'but the timing of the Hubbard kidnapping doesn't jibe with me. Driving from New

Orleans to Wichita would take roughly five and a half hours. Then, to go from Wichita to Red Hill, you're talking nine hours.'

'Again, we're talking about a high school kid – one who was a budding psychopath. It might not have been thoroughly thought out, especially if Hubbard was an impulse kidnapping. If it was, he probably wanted to bring her someplace where he felt safe, like his home turf.'

'I'm looking to see if Savran had any relatives in Wichita. I'm also still going through that list of contractors and painters who worked on the Downes house the summer before they moved in.' Coop turned to the door.

'Hold up.' Scott's lips were pursed tight, and his tone changed when he said, 'There's something I need to tell you.'

78

'Everyone here appreciates your dedication and hard work,' Scott said.

Coop stared at him stupidly. 'Are you giving me the bounce?'

Scott looked uncomfortable. 'The place where we found the satellite phone,' he said. 'That river is a class-three rapid. It merges with another one about a quarter of a mile away.'

'The Wild Straits,' Coop said distantly. He had an idea where Scott was leading him.

'And that one's a class-five rapid, nasty as hell.'

Coop had searched the areas well into the night. It had been an excruciatingly perilous affair for everyone involved. Not only was the bumpy and uneven terrain strewn with hidden rocks, boulders and downed tree limbs – most of which were obscured underneath at least a good six inches of crusted snow – but the ground was covered in ice. Despite his caution, every step had proved to be a roll of the dice; he had slipped and tripped more than once. One uniform had taken the worst spill, falling ass over elbow and almost rolling straight into the rapids. Fortunately, he walked away with only a sprained ankle and a couple of nasty bruises.

'I know you and Dr McCormick were very close.'

Were.

'Sir, I understand –'

'I don't think you do,' Scott said. His voice was quiet. Respectful. 'We put birds in the sky equipped with thermal imaging. We didn't find a heat signature anywhere in the woods. If Savran . . . people who get caught in those rapids, sometimes they're never found.'

'That doesn't mean she's dead. What if Savran took her as a hostage?'

'Then why hasn't he contacted us?'

Coop didn't have an answer. The feeling of dread that he woke up with each morning gripped him, but he said the words anyway: 'She could still be alive.'

Scott tried to keep his face empty. 'DD wants you on the next flight home.'

'Why?'

'He thinks you're too close to this – conflict of interest and all that.'

'And you? What do you think?'

Scott didn't have a chance to answer; his satellite phone started ringing.

As Scott took the call, Coop saw himself walking back to the main road as the dawn broke. Darby wasn't anywhere in those woods. And yet he had refused to get back into the car and pack it in because it felt like a betrayal. As if he were turning his back on her. Because if the roles had been reversed, she'd have moved heaven and earth to find him, dead or alive, it wouldn't have mattered.

Then his mind snapped back to the present, back to Lancaster's missing keys and the fact that he hadn't found a computer or any computer-related equipment inside the man's house. Maybe Lancaster was one of those people, like Hoder, who disliked computers, or maybe Lancaster thought his iPhone was all the technology he needed.

So why was it nagging at him?

Scott hung up, his face and tone grave when he said, 'They found Savran. He's dead.'

79

Darby heard the trapdoor open and saw a glint of sunlight on the ladder's rungs.

Nicky Hubbard wasn't alone this time; Ray Williams had come with her. She stood slightly behind him, arms crossed over her chest and pouting, eyes flaring with hatred.

Williams had the put-out expression and demeanour of a parent summoned to the principal's office to discuss an argument between his child and another student. 'My Sarah says you –'

'Nicky,' Darby said. 'Her name is Nicky Hubbard.'

A dangerous light came into his eyes, one that for some reason brought to mind video images she'd seen of Nazi soldiers. It made her skin crawl.

'Her name is Sarah,' Williams said.

Nicky Hubbard's wide smile glowed with satisfaction.

Williams stuffed his hands deep in his trouser pockets. 'Her name is Sarah,' he said again. 'You will not ask my Sarah any more questions. You will do what she says, when she says it. If you don't, when I come for you, I'll punish you like this.'

Darby heard a new sound, a whining squeak, above her; then whiplash-quick the lead connected to her steel collar yanked her off her feet. A split-second later her head slammed against the ceiling and she dangled in the air, choking, legs scissoring and her torso jerking wildly, her weight strangling her to death. Her brain screamed like a fire alarm as she clawed desperately at the steel collar. Her face burned, and the pressure in her head threatened to explode unless she could draw a breath and she couldn't draw a breath. Her legs kept kicking, the oxygen was dying, and her brain and blood howled in protest, fighting to survive. Black and red spots like drops of pain appeared in her vision, bleeding together, and she couldn't see anything, and she couldn't breathe.

Then the tension in the cord suddenly gave way, and Darby crashed against the floor, gasping. Her legs had no strength in them, they had turned to liquid. She couldn't breathe – she tried, but it was as if her lungs had quit working. When they finally, mercifully, roared back to life, she sucked in great gulps of precious air. Her vision cleared, and she could see Williams next to Hubbard, rubbing her back as he whispered words of comfort into her ear.

Then Williams kissed the top of her head and turned back to the ladder. Nicky Hubbard remained standing, hatred still glowing in her eyes as she slammed her thumb against the remote button for the shock collar and kept it there.

This time the shock was a hundred times stronger; it was as if she'd stepped on to a high-voltage wire. Her eyes slammed shut and she saw a supernova of white stars explode and scream through her skull as her limbs flapped uselessly, banging against the concrete. Darby kicked and thrashed, spittle flying from her mouth, and an inner voice said, *I'm going to kill him. I'm going to kill him the first chance I get, and if you get in my way, Nicky, I'm going to kill you too.*

'My vision's getting better each day,' I say into the phone.

'That's good,' Griffin replies. It's coming up on 10 p.m. and I can tell he's slightly drunk. He feels the need to call me each day, to check up and see how I'm faring – which is good. I can also get information on the progress of the Savran manhunt.

'What about the headaches?' Griffin asks.

'Awful.' Which is completely true. Lancaster treated me to a hairline fracture. 'They've got me on this migraine-level medication. Guess who has to pick up the tab for it?'

Griffin chuckles. He knows our health insurance is for shit.

'If I were you, I'd ride the disability and workman's comp into the sunset. I bet you're making more on those two than you do on your regular pay.'

'You're right.'

'I'm telling you, go out on a permanent disability.'

'I'm seriously thinking about it.'

'Good. Because guys like us who actually give a shit and play by the rules? We're suckers. And I'm sick and tired of being a sucker, Ray. Tomorrow morning I think I'm gonna slip on a sheet of ice on my way into the station.'

I laugh. 'What's going on with Savran?'

'You haven't heard?'

'Heard what?'

'They found his Bronco at the old coal plant in Lead-ville earlier today – and Savran lying in a ditch about a mile away. ME said it's a suicide.'

I close my eyes, sweet and blessed relief flooding through me. Lancaster had told me the truth about Savran being dead.

'Blew his brains out,' Griffin says.

'When did they find him?'

'Couple of hours ago.' Griffin takes a sip of his drink. I hear a rattle of ice cubes and then, in the background, a man who sounds like Billy O'Reilly shouting something about immigrants. 'I don't have any idea about the McCormick broad. My guess is he dumped her body in the rapids where they found her phone, which means we'll never find her.'

You got that right, I add silently.

'That fed there, what's-his-name, Cooper, he thinks Savran took Lancaster's keys and went through Teddy's house and took a whole bunch of his computer stuff.'

I had given Teddy's keys to Sarah. She drove to Lancaster's house to remove any computers, programming books and computer equipment – CDs, USB keys, anything that could be used to store copies of the videos – anything that would suggest that Lancaster knew his way around computers.

Later that same night, when I returned home from the hospital, I looked through Teddy's laptop and discovered he had kept copies of the videos. He wasn't in any of them, of course, because he had to use the videos to frame Savran.

'Did the feds find any evidence suggesting Savran stole Lancaster's laptop or whatever he used?'

'No,' Griffin said. 'If Savran did it – why he did it – well, we're not going to know now, are we?'

'What's Brewster saying?'

'Nothing. Everyone knows the feds like to invent shit to keep themselves busy. It's how they justify their pay cheques to the taxpayers.'

After I get Griffin off the phone, I pick up the walkie-talkie, call Sarah and tell her to come to the house. Then I stand by the window. Several minutes later, I see the shed door open under the moonlight.

I've been having her spend her days inside the chamber with Darby; federal agents and marshals have been stopping by the house at all hours, asking questions about the massacre inside Sally Kelly's house. Having suffered a skull fracture and a major concussion, I'm able to use the 'I don't remember' defence. I squirreled her away, anticipating the news about Nicky Hubbard's fingerprint to break at any second.

I grew up in Red Hill and have lived here all my life. My mother had a sister who lived in Wichita. We'd visit her sometimes. During one of those trips I went to the mall and found her a daughter, just like she asked. We brought Nicky home and we called her Sarah. Sarah lived in the basement and was home-schooled. We loved her and fed her and cared for her. I loved her and fed her and cared for her, yet the FBI could take all that away at a moment's notice.

Nobody knows about Sarah – no one has ever seen her. My new Sarah now lives a comfortable and peaceful life right here inside our home. She has never left the house without my permission (she knows better), and as I watch her trundle through the snow, I wonder again about Lancaster – if the man had told someone about the video of me scrubbing down the corner inside the Downes bedroom. It's still a possibility; Teddy did, after all, have people helping him – Whitehead and Nelson, to name two.

No, I remind myself again. Had Teddy told anyone, something would have happened by now. Seven days have passed and nothing has changed. But if Cooper or any other fed starts digging into my background, there's a chance they might be able to connect me to Hubbard . . .

'What is it, baby?' she asks, rubbing the sleep from her eyes.

'Where do you want to go?'

Anywhere but prison, Sarah. I'll die before I let that happen.

'I don't care,' she says, 'as long as I'm with you.'

She hugs me fiercely. I'm staring at her neck, thinking about how easy it would be to snap it. One swift tug and pull and it's over. *If you're dead, Sarah, no one can find you. If you're dead, I'm safe. Free.* I can dump her body in my room underneath the shed. No one will find her – or Darby. Kill them both and run.

'I'm hungry,' I say.

'I'll make us a nice dinner, then.'

That's not what I meant, but I don't tell her. I want her happy and occupied. 'That sounds wonderful,' I tell her, smiling. 'Go ahead and do that. I've got to take care of something first.'

Sarah knows I'm thinking of Darby McCormick – knows I've been wanting to spend time with her alone for days now.

She looks wounded. 'You don't need her,' she says. 'You can play with me.'

I sigh, pinching my temples. I close my eyes, wishing that I could open them and find myself in another state or city or country, anywhere but here.

'Sarah, I –'

'I know what you like, baby. I know how to make you feel good, you've taught me how to make you feel good in all sorts of different ways.'

'I'm not going to play with her.'

Sarah stares at me for a beat, confused, a dog which has failed to understand a command.

'Then why are you going to –'

'To kill her,' I say. 'I'm going to kill her.'

Sarah stands as motionless as a statue.

'I don't want her,' I say. 'I want you.'

'Don't take too long. I have something real special planned for you.'

Sarah bites her bottom lip, her eyes twinkling with a mischievous, almost diabolical light. Then she stands on her tiptoes and kisses me deeply, like she's trying to draw a secret from my heart. Like she knows I'm going to kill her.

80

Solve the problem, Darby.

Her father's voice, his words. When she was a kid, 'Big Red' McCormick would listen patiently to whatever gripe or troublesome situation she laid before him, and then, when he was sure she was done, he'd calmly deliver the same three words he always said to her during their very short life together: *Solve the problem, Darby. You're the only one who can.* Sometime during her senior year in high school, and years after he'd died, she'd had a small epiphany, her brain finally accepting the wisdom he'd been drilling into her when he was alive: bitching and complaining and venting about it got you absolutely nowhere in life. Either solve the problem or shut up. Like the gladiators who were forced to fight in the ancient coliseums, you could lay down your sword and shield and surrender to your fate – or you could fight.

For days now, every time she was alone, she had tried to tear the lead from Williams's hanging contraption, and each time she had gotten nowhere. There was no way to break it off, but that didn't mean she had to give up. She kept at it, thinking – hoping – that all the pulling that left her muscles depleted might weaken, if not damage, Williams's personal torture porn device.

But she wouldn't know until he used it on her again, and that scared her.

Darby heard the trapdoor open. No light cascaded down the rungs. *It must be night*, she thought, standing upright in the pitch-black darkness, the soles of her bare feet cold and damp against the rough concrete. She tried to empty her mind of fear, but that was about as useful and productive as using a paper cup to bail out a sinking ship. She knew what was coming.

Lancaster was power hungry; he had staged the crime scenes to look like the textbook handiwork of a sexual sadist. Williams, however, was the real deal, a creature who fed off human pain and suffering. Deny the monster its food, and it became enraged. And even more irrational.

At least that had been her experience. Darby had no idea how Williams would act.

I'm going to find out, she thought as the interior lights came on. What had Nicky Hubbard told her about Williams? *Fight back. Ray really loves it when you fight back. It makes us both so happy.*

Us, Darby thought, her eyes finally adjusting to the brightness.

Ray Williams stood on the other side of the bars. The swelling had disappeared from her face, and she had the use of both eyes now. He was dressed like a man who was about to spend a summer afternoon out on his boat: white tee, khakis and penny loafers without socks. His bruised face had turned a dark violet, and dozens of stitched lacerations covered his face, scalp and ears.

He reached through the bars and dropped a pair of black lace panties and a bra on the floor.

'Put them on,' he said.

Darby didn't move.

She broke out in a slick and greasy sweat when she saw Williams remove the remote for the shock collar from his trousers pocket. His eyes were as dead and lifeless as marbles.

'I've adjusted the setting to ten,' he said. 'Put on the clothes or I'll shock you.'

'No,' she replied, and her stomach turned to ice.

Williams's eyes were busy with thought, and a grin tugged at the corner of his mouth. Darby swallowed, bracing herself for what was about to come.

But he didn't shock her. Instead, he placed the remote on the edge of one of the bars. Then he reached into his pocket again and came back with a new item: another remote, this one smaller, like a car-key fob.

The remote for his hanging contraption, she thought, her muscles tensing as her hands flew up to grab the lead.

Williams pressed the button. Again, Darby was yanked off her feet, but the motor sounded different, like it was struggling to complete the task. Williams didn't seem to notice, or didn't care. Keys in hand, he unlocked the door and moved inside her cell.

Darby had managed to wrap the lead around her fists. The plastic-encased metal dug into her skin and callused palms as she hoisted herself up to relieve the pressure on her neck. Williams stepped closer and, tilting his head to

455

the side, looked up at her, curious, like an art collector admiring a prized painting.

Sweat popped all over her skin, and she gulped air to stave off the burning in her muscles. She was only buying herself seconds, though, and Williams knew it. At any moment she'd use up the limited glycogen stored in her muscles. The strength would leave her arms, shoulders and back, and then gravity would take over and she'd fall and hang from the ceiling, body twisting and swaying and suffocating, her fingers desperately clawing at the collar.

Williams must have pressed the button, because the next thing she knew she had crashed against the floor. Her skin and brain on fire, she rolled on to her side, gasping, and saw Williams staring down at her. Black gloves covered his hands now, and he held two new items: a pair of steel handcuffs and a hunting knife with a long, curved, sickle-like blade.

Don't let him cuff you, she thought, gasping in mouthfuls of much-needed air. *If he cuffs you it's over.*

Williams swung his foot back. Darby knew he was going to kick her, knew that if she tried to protect her stomach with her arms and hands, he might break her fingers. She tried to turn away, but his shoe slammed into her stomach. Air exploded past her throat and bright stars exploded across her vision. She curled into a foetal position and she used her arms to protect her face. She couldn't fight him if he broke her nose or, worse, delivered a kick that would swell her eyes shut.

But he didn't kick her. Instead, he dropped the handcuffs to the floor, grabbed a fistful of hair from the back of her head and pulled her up, no doubt wanting to smash her face on the floor.

Mistake. Darby wasn't afraid to fight, knew how to fight. She braced an arm against the floor and then, using all of her strength, spun around to face him. Williams, still clutching her hair, was knocked off balance; he didn't let go, and, as he fell sideways, towards the wall, his right hand, the one holding the knife, reached out to brace his fall. The blade scrapped against the concrete wall, twisting his wrist at an odd angle, and he screamed.

Darby screamed as she rose to her knees. Screaming meant delivering oxygen to her bloodstream. She had him pinned against the corner, and with her hands gripping the wrist holding the knife she screamed again and slammed her knee into his groin. She felt him buckle and his strength left him.

But not his fight; he still had plenty of that in him, and she swore she saw him smile as he knocked her back against the wall. Her head was slammed against the concrete, pain and terror exploding through her skull; but her eyes were pinned on the knife lying on the floor. *Go for it or you'll die down here.* She did so, the concrete scraping her knees and palms, and had reached its hilt when Williams grabbed her by the ankle and pulled.

Darby turned and moved towards him. Swung the knife and saw the curved blade slice through his cheek and slash his left eye.

The howl that escaped his lips exploded off the walls and drilled into her head. His hands clutched at his face, blood and spittle spraying from his gloved fingers as he screamed again, and Darby felt something inside her break away and soar like a bird being released from a cage and given a chance to fly. He rolled on the floor, clawing at his face, kicking his feet. She moved to him, ready to put an end to this, when she heard the whine of the motor hidden somewhere inside the ceiling.

How? She had assumed he'd put the remote in his pocket. Then an inner voice screamed *Whatever you do, don't let go of the knife.* Darby clutched the hilt as she was yanked backwards, her feet scraping against the floor. Williams howled again, and as she was pulled up to the ceiling Darby reached around the back of her head and grabbed the lead, catching sight of the remote on the floor just before her head slammed into the ceiling.

But she didn't let go of the knife. She sawed at the lead wildly, the blade cutting her fingers, as Williams staggered to his feet. His face was buried in his shaking hands, and he screamed through his bloody fingers. *Blinded him*, she thought. *Please let him be blind.* The pressure on her neck was immense. She gasped desperately for air and kept sawing and sawing as Williams stumbled blindly towards the cell door. He had left it open – and he had left the remote for the shock collar on one of the bars.

The pain in my left eye is unlike anything I've ever experienced. It feels like hot shrapnel is buried deep in the socket. The only way I can save my eye is to keep the heel of my palm mashed up against it, no matter how agonizing it feels.

The door for the cell is open. I'm staggering over to it when I hear a thud, and I turn and see the McCormick bitch on the floor. She's on the floor because she's severed the lead. The bitch managed to cut through it because she has my knife, it's still gripped in her hand. I reach out to grab the shock collar remote and end up knocking it off the bar. The remote lands somewhere on the floor outside the cell, and there's no time to reach it and there's no time to lock her up in here because the bitch has gotten to her feet, she's holding the knife and she's coming for me.

I have to use both hands to climb the ladder. I can't see out of my ruined eye, can't close it to prevent the blood and whatever else from spilling down my cheek. As I look up at the opening, all the women I brought down here race through my mind. They all fought back – I *wanted* them to fight back, it's what makes life worth living – and the McCormick bitch was supposed to act just like the rest of them, scratching and clawing and kicking the way women do. I underestimated her, but it's not my fault. I didn't know she was inhuman. A monster.

I move past the opening and crawl out, on to the shed floor. All I have to do is slam the trapdoor on her and lock it. I've spun around, on to my side, and grabbed the trapdoor when the bitch pops out of the opening like a jack-in-the-box. I try to push the trapdoor down, but the top part of her body is already out and she's pushing against the door with her shoulder. Her other arm wiggles out and I see she's holding my knife and she slashes at my arm and wrist until I let go.

But there's still hope. I throw open the doors and scramble away. The backyard's sensor lights are off at the moment, but there's a full moon, the sky is packed with bright stars, and I can make out the path that's been shovelled in the snow.

I wipe the blood away from my good eye and then I see her, my precious Sarah, standing at the window overlooking the backyard. The lights inside the kitchen are on, and as I run to her I can see her washing something in the sink, her pink bathrobe open, revealing the special lingerie she wears for me. Her body is much plumper now, her thighs are riddled with cellulite and her skin is beginning to sag, but I don't care because she is my precious Sarah, my beautiful Sarah, and I love her.

'SARAH!'

I hear feet running behind me and I see Sarah walk away from the window. I'm about to call out again when I'm tackled around the waist and thrown against the hard-packed snow. I'm screaming for my Sarah when the

McCormick bitch, this creature sent from hell, clenches her right hand and drives it into my throat.

And then she is all over me. She hits me full in the face with her other hand and the next blow shatters my nose. I throw up my arms to protect myself, but this succubus is too strong and too powerful, with fists like concrete. She hits me again and again in a demonic fury and I beg her to stop.

'Shut up,' McCormick hisses, and the next blow to my skull makes my arms go limp and fall uselessly by my sides. I'm defenceless, at her mercy, and yet her fists keep raining down on my face and skull, and through the blood and pain I see her smile. 'Shut up and bleed.'

Again I beg her to stop and then I realize she can't hear me because I'm choking on blood and teeth – *my* blood, *my* teeth – and I can't see or hear Sarah oh please help me baby I love you so much –

81

Darby was straddling Williams when the back door flew open.

At first she couldn't take in the situation. The backyard sensor lights clicked on as Nicky Hubbard, dressed in a pair of snow boots and a pink bathrobe, rushed out on to the path. Beneath the robe she wore a black halter fishnet body stocking, and she had a shotgun gripped in her hands.

Hubbard pumped the action. The bitter night wind blew her hair wildly about her face as she brought up the shotgun. Darby had no cover, but she had some distance. She had rolled off Williams, and into a bank of fresh snow, when Hubbard pulled the trigger.

The report echoed but Darby knew she hadn't been hit – not yet. Nicky Hubbard screamed as Darby scrambled to her feet, and when she broke through a crust of snow, her face, hair and ears covered in white and burning from the freezing cold, she realized she had made a tactical terror. Wading through waist-high snow was about as productive as running through water: slow and laborious. Useless. She'd be a target.

But there was no need to run. Hubbard had dropped the shotgun; Darby saw it lying on the ground, smoking, before the backyard's sensor lights clicked off.

She also saw what was left of Ray Williams. Hubbard had blown apart most of his chest.

Darby moved on to the path. She wasn't wearing any gloves, and her feet and legs were bare. The woman who believed her name was Sarah – who believed that the man named Ray Williams loved her – sat in the bloody snow, cradling his ruined face against her chest, her wails of loss echoing through the dark woods, her torn soul searching for answers.

82

A nurse was standing inside Terry Hoder's room in Brewster General, checking on the man's various monitors and tubes, when the tall, good-looking FBI agent visiting him received a call on his satellite phone. The nurse, whose name was Maura, would later tell her friends that she had never witnessed such a transformative expression on another person's face – one that started with the euphoric ecstasy of someone who appeared to have been granted a wish by God Himself and then ended with the tall man's face stretched tight with fear.

The man hung up and seemed to sway on his feet.

Stroke, the nurse thought, moving around the bed as FBI Agent Hoder eyed him curiously. *He's going to have a stroke or a heart attack.*

'Sir? Sir, are you okay? Take that chair right next to you.'

'I'm fine. Honest,' the man replied. He had blond hair and differently coloured eyes, and he looked like he had slept in his clothes. 'Would you please excuse us for a moment? I need to talk with Agent Hoder privately.'

The nurse left to find a doctor; she didn't like the man's colouring. Just as the door shut, she thought she heard him cry in relief, or possibly sadness, she wasn't sure which.

*

By the time Denver SAC Scott called back, Coop had already made the necessary arrangements with Brewster General. As he climbed into the back of the ambulance, he told Scott about his short conversation with Darby and the few details he knew about what had happened at Ray Williams's home.

An hour later, as the ambulance was slowing to a stop near the end of Williams's driveway, Coop opened the back door, jumped out and started running. All the house lights were on, including the outdoor ones; he saw shadows moving behind the windows. There were three federal cars parked in the driveway; because kidnapping is a federal crime, the FBI had taken charge of the case. But Coop was sure the news about Ray Williams was burning its way through Red Hill, Brewster and the surrounding towns.

An agent met him at the front door. 'She's upstairs,' the man told Coop, stepping aside to let him into the foyer. 'Door to the left of the stairs.'

'How is she?' Coop asked. Darby, naturally, had dodged the question on the phone. *Just hurry up and get here*, she had said and hung up.

'She looks fine – although I can't say that for sure, because she won't let anyone get near her – and she refused to let us take her to the hospital until you got here.'

The foyer hall ran into the kitchen. Coop saw SAC Scott sitting at a small table with a shell-shocked blonde-haired woman dressed in a ratty pink bathrobe, her arms wrapped around her chest as though she were struggling to keep warm. She rocked back and forth, humming to herself, eyes puffy from crying and black from smeared mascara. Scott was the only one with her, but her gaze darted frantically around the kitchen, as though multiple voices were shouting at her.

The agent saw Coop looking at the woman and said, 'Her name's Sarah.'

No, it's not, Coop thought, recalling the contents of Darby's phone call.

'Says she's his wife, but people at the station are saying Williams isn't married or was never married. It's gets even weirder, if you can believe it. She's in here cooking him a steak dinner, dressed in lingerie and heels, while *he*'s torturing broads out in the shed.

'Sarah here told us she shot at McCormick because she was beating the shit out of her man. McCormick dodged the bullet and the lug ripped apart Williams's chest, but I'm willing to bet he was already dead at that point, or well on his way to it.'

Then the agent scratched the corner of his eye. 'McCormick did a real number on him first.' He swallowed, grimacing when he said, 'The guy's face is unrecognizable, if you catch my drift.'

Upstairs, another federal agent stood by the bedroom door. It was open, and Coop saw Darby sitting on the floor in the corner and hugging her knees against her chest. The only thing she wore was an oversized wool sweater that barely covered her rump. Her legs and feet were bare, smeared with dried blood.

It's her, Coop thought, suddenly afraid to move. *It's really her*. When she called him at the hospital, he hadn't believed

466

it was her – thought that he was possibly talking to a recording. That someone was playing a sick joke. She had been missing for over a week, and his mind had already begun to accept that her body had been dumped in the rapids, never to be found.

But here she was, alive, and the relief and joy he felt was almost powerful enough to bring him to his knees.

Darby didn't get up as he approached – didn't look up either. Her gaze was riveted on the neatly made bed.

'Hey,' he said gently, balancing himself on the balls of his feet. 'It's me.'

Darby still didn't look at him. He was about to touch her shoulder when she pulled away. 'Don't,' she said, her voice cracking. 'Not now.'

'Okay. I'm just going to sit beside you. We don't have to talk. I'm just going to sit here with you.'

Coop glanced at the federal agent by the door; he was whispering to one of the paramedics. Coop shook his head and motioned for them to leave. The agent nodded and had the good sense to shut the door to give them some privacy.

He sat next to Darby. Her hands and fingers were swollen, cut and caked with blood, and he wondered how many times she had hit Williams with her fists. The wind roared past the house, shaking it, and, as he looked around the bedroom, everything he saw was clean and meticulously organized. No pictures on the walls or bureaus. It looked like a single man's bedroom, cold and sterile, not a feminine touch anywhere. Nothing to indicate that he had shared a bed with a woman night after night.

For thirty-one years, Coop thought, and the picture of Nicky Hubbard at seven, Nicky with her gap-toothed smile and T-shirt stained with spaghetti sauce, flashed through his mind. He compared the photograph with the pale and haggard woman he'd seen downstairs, and his mind couldn't reconcile the two. But on the phone Darby had told him Nicky Hubbard was alive. Williams had abducted her and his mother had changed Hubbard's name to Sarah, and Sarah had shared this home with him.

'The shed,' Darby said. 'He brought them there.'

Coop turned to her. She still wouldn't look at him.

'There's a trapdoor there. He did this to them,' Darby said, and with her eyes locked on the bed she grabbed the sweater's collar and pulled it down.

Her neck was covered with raw, red rings, the skin full of cuts and abrasions. Coop felt his face tighten and his stomach roil in anger and fear, as he conjured up grisly possibilities of how Williams had injured her. Coop wanted to say something but there was nothing to say, and he fought the urge to comfort her. He wanted to touch her – needed to, a part of him still believing that this was a dream, that the only way he could prove it wasn't was to put a hand on her shoulder and pull her close to him. But trying to comfort her or to hold her, he knew, would be a mistake, because she'd shut down on him.

'He told me one name,' Darby said. 'Sherrilyn O'Neil, from Utah.'

Coop recorded it to memory. He didn't write it down; there would be plenty of time for that later. Right now, all he needed to do was to sit here and listen, just listen.

'I don't know where he buried them. Or their names or how many were tortured down there. We may never know.' Darby's gaze remained locked on the bed, and her voice sounded hollow. *She's still in shock*, Coop thought.

'I'm sure Hubbard knows things that'll help us.'

'She shot him. Hubbard. Blew a hole the size of a basketball through his chest. But I killed him, Coop.'

Darby started to tremble. She opened her mouth, then closed it.

Coop stared down at her cut, bloody and swollen hands. *Wait*, he reminded himself. *Don't force it.*

'Like a dog,' Darby said, her voice raw. 'He made her sleep on the floor next to the bed, like a dog.'

Coop didn't know what to say, but felt he had to say something. He was searching for the right words when Darby hugged her legs fiercely against her chest. She placed her forehead on her knees and began rocking back and forth, fighting tears.

Day Eleven

83

The following morning, at 11 a.m., Darby walked into Chief Robinson's office and found Terry Hoder waiting for her. She was freshly showered and dressed, the knuckles of both hands wrapped in gauze and compression bandages. He wore a rumpled suit and a cannula that was connected to an oxygen tank strapped to the back of his wheelchair.

A tense moment followed as Hoder studied her face and hands. Then his gaze landed on the raw, torn circles of skin around her neck. Darby had made no attempt to hide her injuries.

'Well, don't you look like shit,' he said in a dry, raspy voice.

'You're not looking so hot yourself, Terry.'

'It's that damn hospital food. See what you look like when you're forced to eat puréed spaghetti and meatballs.'

Darby moved behind the wheelchair. She gripped its handles, and was about to roll him out when he tilted back his head, his face turning serious as his rheumy eyes looked up at her.

'Coop didn't get into the specifics of what happened to you down in that . . . place. I'm not asking you to do so now. But if you need to talk, I'm here.'

Darby said nothing.

'And I'm sorry,' Hoder said.

'For what?'

'For what you had to endure. No human being should ever –'

'Come on, we need to get going,' Darby said as she pushed him into the hall. 'I was told you only have an hour. I don't want you to miss your next puréed lunch.'

'You're going to dine with me today. But you're going to hit a liquor store on the way, buy me a bottle of Knob Creek bourbon, and sneak it into my hospital room. That's an order.'

'Ten-four on that.'

Darby wheeled him past the station's front doors. Outside, she spotted the Brewster General ambulance that had delivered Hoder – and a pair of news vans from Boulder and Denver. The Ray Williams story was out, but nobody knew about Nicky Hubbard, not yet.

But they would, maybe even by the day's end. The FBI wouldn't be able to contain the story much longer.

Darby pushed Hoder through the hall until they reached Coop standing in a doorway. The room they entered was fitted with an observation mirror that looked on to Nicky Hubbard, who was sitting alone at a table. A breakfast tray of eggs and toast remained untouched, and the famous photograph of Hubbard at age seven had been overturned. Darby had taken the picture into the room with her, hoping it would get the woman to open up and talk. So far, she hadn't had much luck.

Hubbard, dressed in a sweatshirt and jeans, her hair

unkempt and face puffy from crying and lack of sleep, worked a paper towel over her ink-stained fingers.

'My God,' Hoder whispered. 'Is it really her?'

Coop said, 'The fingerprints match. Each and every one. But she keeps insisting her name is Sarah, that Nicky Hubbard is dead.'

'And no one who saw her ever knew?'

Darby answered the question. 'Williams never went anywhere with her – never allowed her outside the house. The few times people went round, he made Nicky hide in that area underneath the shed. She had her own bed there.'

'The women Williams abducted – do we have any idea about the number?'

'Nicky told me she stopped counting after twenty.'

Hoder closed his eyes. 'Jesus,' he said under his breath.

'Williams's last victim, Sherrilyn O'Neil, was from a small town in Utah.' Darby felt cold all over as she thought about the O'Neil woman trapped inside that cold, concrete cell with the shock collar tied around her throat, and the terror the woman must have felt when Williams hit the button for the hanging contraption. 'He abducted her last year, in March.'

'Any other names?'

'No,' Darby said. *And we'll probably never know because I killed him*, she thought.

Coop said, 'Williams had a home computer and we found surveillance notes and pictures of women in the surrounding towns,' he said. 'But they're all alive. My guess is he was staking them out, perhaps with the idea of blaming their disappearance on the Red Hill Ripper. But Williams never went through with it.'

'We also spoke with Rita Tuttle. In exchange for immunity, she told us Lancaster coerced her into coming forward with that story of Eli Savran being one of her clients. She'd never met him.'

'And Lancaster was the one who recorded Williams scrubbing down that corner of the Downes bedroom. Williams didn't want us to find her blood.'

'I don't think he knew about the fingerprint.'

'I wonder why Lancaster didn't make a move on Williams sooner.'

'Darby and I talked about this, and our theory is that Lancaster was waiting until he found out more about what Williams was up to. Once the news broke about Hubbard's fingerprint –'

'He could swoop in and solve one of the greatest mysteries of the modern century,' Hoder said. His gaze was locked on Hubbard the entire time. 'That poor girl.'

'We think Williams was getting ready to run, probably that night. We found a packed suitcase in the trunk of his car, and a briefcase with cash and fake IDs to give him a new life.'

'What about Hubbard? Did he have a new ID for her?'

'No. And we found her suitcase in the basement. Maybe he was going to take her, I don't know. Darby thinks Williams felt the walls closing in on him, might've been thinking of killing Hubbard before he left town.

'We also found a trunk,' Coop said. 'It was packed with

dynamite, grenades, ammo, you name it. And he had weapons stashed all over the house.'

The door opened and SAC Scott poked his head inside. 'You ready to take another run at her?' he asked Darby.

Darby nodded. Hubbard glanced at the mirror, as if she had heard their voices. As Darby left the room, her mind flashed back to the moment when the woman had raised the shotgun, a Mossberg with ghost-ring sights that had been loaded with 12-gauge slugs – which is why Darby hadn't been hit. If the shotgun had been loaded with buckshot, the wide blast radius would have torn through her viscera, and her body would've been lying next to Williams's at the morgue.

Her feelings about Ray Williams were pretty simple: he had gotten what he deserved. His victims, though, deserved better. Instead of arresting him so he could tell them where he had buried the bodies, she had satisfied her own bloodlust, and it ate at her. Darby had to do right by his victims – had to do whatever it took to find their remains and bring them home.

Epilogue

Darby started awake, torn from a nightmare where she was again yanked from her feet to the ceiling, only this time the steel collar snapped her neck. Her eyes flew open, the scream already rising in her throat, when she saw Coop leaning over the front seat, his hand on her arm.

'We're here,' he said.

Heart still tripping with fear from the dream, Darby sat up and swallowed back the scream. She touched her throat to make sure the collar wasn't there and then took off her sunglasses and rubbed her eyes, head pounding with exhaustion and the dream still vivid in her mind, screwing into her head like a drill bit.

Whitlow, the agent with the thick, curly hair who had picked them up at the airport, was driving across a long gravel driveway, rocks pinging underneath the car and the air-conditioning on full blast. She glanced out the back window and saw that the pair of Chevy Impalas hadn't followed, Coop already having told them to hang back at the main road to watch for reporters.

Coming into view through the front window was the Canterbury Retirement Community, a series of connected ranch-style stone buildings with red clay roofs built around the kind of opulent fountain commonly seen in the estates of the rich and famous. The cherry trees and weeping willows, some of them so old they looked like they had been there since the beginning of time, offered shade from the unrelenting Texas sun. The owners had put a lot of time and money into the landscaping, wanting to give the assisted living centre a feeling of vibrant health and activity instead of a way station on the route to death.

Darby was relieved to see everything business-as-usual quiet. For the past forty-eight hours she had lived in fear that someone at Brewster General would recognize Nicky Hubbard and call a reporter or tabloid. Darby didn't want the news to get out before she'd had a chance to speak with Nicky's mother.

Darby was also relieved that the FBI had allowed her to be the one to approach Joan Hubbard.

The car pulled up to the front and parked. As Darby got out of the back, she heard Coop ask Whitlow for his cell phone. She shut the door and was unable to hear what was said as they walked back and forth until Whitlow handed over his cell.

She followed Coop into the assisted living centre, with seascape watercolours hanging on the walls and Lysol hanging in the air-conditioned air, trying to disguise the atmosphere of death and decay. At the reception desk, he had a quiet conversation with a blonde-haired woman with an overbite. The woman got up and opened the door behind her. Several minutes passed, and then Coop was invited into the room.

When Coop emerged a few minutes later, he went over to Darby and said, 'She's out back, in the garden.'

An orderly escorted them through a maze of rooms

fragrant with coffee and the cellophane-baked smell of reheated eggs and potatoes, and everywhere Darby looked she saw elderly people hunched at tables playing cards or doing puzzles; gnarled limbs planted in wheelchairs and dull eyes staring blankly at TVs playing *Good Morning America*.

Then she was standing outside, breathing in fresh air and feeling the morning sun warm against her face. Darby put on her sunglasses as the orderly left.

Coop turned to her and said, 'She's straight ahead.'

A path was carved through the overflowing gardens. Darby was making her way across it when she noticed that Coop wasn't beside her. She stopped, turned and saw him standing near the door leading back to the activity room.

'You coming?' she asked.

'I want you to do it.'

'She's going to have questions about her daughter and –'

'I'll be right here.' He smiled. 'You've earned it. Go.'

Darby carried on across the path, slowing when she saw a small, fair-skinned woman kneeling in the dirt and pressing the earth with a trowel. She wore jeans, a long-sleeved grey T-shirt, a big floppy straw hat that tied underneath her chin and gardening gloves that went up past her wrists.

Aside from the cacti, Darby didn't recognize any of the flowers. Gardening had been her mother's thing, Darby never having had any interest in it, unable to understand the point of all that hard work when winter and animals would come along and destroy everything you had spent so much time and money on. And yet her mother kept doing it year after year, right up until the day she died.

Just as I keep doing what I do, Darby thought. And, in her own way, wasn't she a gardener too? A gardener for lost souls?

The whole flight here, Darby had rehearsed what she would say to Nicky's mother. When Joan Hubbard looked up from her work, smiling warmly, Darby was struck by how frail the woman was, and the words died in her throat.

But there was nothing frail about the woman's voice. It was strong, like a fist: 'Can I help you?'

'My name is Darby McCormick.'

Joan Hubbard's gaze narrowed, alarmed at the bruising and cuts on Darby's face.

Darby licked her lips nervously. 'I'd like to speak to you about your daughter.'

Joan Hubbard held up a hand and said, 'Stop right there.'

'I'm not a reporter. I'm working with –'

'Stop. Please, just stop.' Nicky's mother got to her feet. She dropped her trowel and looked at Darby, a hardscrabble, no-nonsense woman who knew how to fight with her fists and her mouth. 'I don't care who you are, and I don't know how you got in here. But I want you to leave, now.'

'Nicky's alive. I –'

'Whatever service you're trying to sell me, I'm not interested. I've had the top private investigators and even a few retired policemen who believed they could find my daughter. They couldn't, and neither can you. My daughter is dead, God rest her soul. Now, please, leave me in peace.'

'I found her,' Darby said. 'She's alive.'

Joan Hubbard made her hands into fists by her sides. Her mouth worked but no sound came out. Birds chirped from a nearby tree.

'I'm working with the FBI,' Darby said. 'They're here. Nicky is waiting for you in Colorado. She's –'

'How *dare* you sneak in here and say such a thing to me, you sick –'

'Nicky is alive,' Darby said again. 'Your daughter is alive, and I'm here to take you to her.'

Joan Hubbard looked over her shoulder, at the hard Texas sun beating down on her and on the flat, sprawling land, the heat already so strong it could melt bones. She looked up at the trees and then at the flowers, as though they were going to confirm what she had hoped for, prayed for and dreamed about every night for decades.

'My daughter is dead. She's been missing for more than thirty years. There must be some mistake.'

'There's no mistake,' Darby said gently. 'We found her.'

Joan Hubbard glared at her, wanting more. Darby wondered where to start, how much to tell her. *Your daughter wasn't harmed, at least not physically. The teenager spotted with your daughter that day in the store? His name was Ray Williams. He was a teenager when he abducted your daughter because his mother had always wanted a girl. They cared for her in their own way, and he loved her in his own way. He abducted women from other states for many, many years. Your daughter is doing her best to provide us with their names and, hopefully, the places where he buried them – but she's mourning his death. I know it sounds odd, almost incomprehensible, but victims in these sorts of situations are often bound up with their abusers. It's going to take a long, long time for your daughter to heal – and she may never heal psychologically. But the important thing right now is that Nicky is alive and she's safe. Your daughter is alive and safe and you two will have time together. You have time.*

'You're lying,' Joan Hubbard said, her voice catching on her tears.

'There's an FBI agent here with me. His name is Jackson Cooper. He has a phone with him. You can call and talk to her.'

The woman stared at the ground as if she'd dropped something precious.

'After you speak to Nicky,' Darby said, 'we'll take you to see her. The Bureau has a private plane, they've already made preparations –'

Joan's legs buckled. Darby ran to her.

'She's alive,' Darby said, holding Nicky's mother in her arms. Joan Hubbard felt as light and frail as a bird. 'Your daughter is alive.'

And as Joan Hubbard wailed tears of joy and relief and sadness and heartbreak and loss, Darby thought, *This is why you do this. This is why you travel through the dark and put yourself at risk. You do it for these moments: to bring lost souls home.*

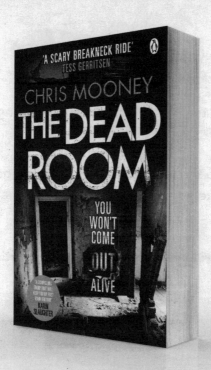

A mother and her son have been executed in their home and fingerprint matches show their attacker died twenty years ago.

But how can dead serial killers return to haunt the present?

The answers lie in the darkest shadows of *The Dead Room*.

When CSI Darby McCormick is called to the crime scene, it's one of the most gruesome she's ever seen. But the forensic evidence is even more disturbing: someone watched the murder unfold from the woodland behind the house – and the killer died in a shoot-out two decades earlier.

The deeper Darby digs, the more horrors come to light. Her prime suspect is revealed as a serial killer on an enormous scale, with a past that's even more shocking than his crimes, thanks to a long-held secret that could rock Boston's law enforcement to its core.

Is it possible to steal an identity? Or are dead men walking in Darby's footsteps? The line between the living and the dead has never been finer.

Behind every door
death awaits you . . .

THE KILLING HOUSE

CHRIS MOONEY

'Scary voice, scary talent. Mooney is one of the
best thriller writers working today' LEE CHILD

RULE #1: DON'T SCREAM

Four years ago, Theresa Herrera's ten-year-old son Rico was abducted. The
police found little evidence and the case went cold. Theresa's husband has
told her to move on, but she won't give up hope.

RULE #2: DON'T CALL THE POLICE

A mysterious woman invades Theresa's home and tells her that Rico is alive.
Theresa talks on the phone to a young man who is, without question, her son.

RULE #3: DON'T RUN. DON'T FIGHT

The woman promises to reunite Theresa with Rico only if she will follow the
rules. But it is the last rule that fills Theresa with horror . . .

RULE #4: KILL YOUR HUSBAND AND YOUR SON WILL LIVE

Malcolm Fletcher – a former FBI profiler and now the nation's Most Wanted
fugitive – arrives in Colorado to help Theresa and her husband find their son.
But his arrival coincides with a dangerous and shocking twist in the case.

Barely surviving his first encounter with a suspect, Fletcher embarks on his
own secret investigation, with the police just behind him every step of the way.

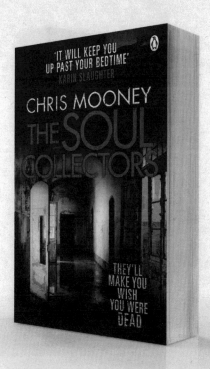

Ten years ago CSI Darby McCormick investigated a sinister child abduction case.

Today, the missing child is back from the dead and holding his family hostage.

He makes only one demand. Bring me Darby McCormick . . .

Charlie Rizzo has his family at gunpoint and when Darby arrives to defuse the scene, she finds him horrifically mutilated, with a mask of human skin sewn in place over his own face. Within minutes, a group of men disguised as SWAT officers bursts in and releases deadly Sarin gas, killing the Rizzo family outright and leaving Darby herself barely alive.

Where has Charlie Rizzo been held all these years? Who are The Twelve who have been executing this gruesome torture? And why are the FBI running scared in the face of this particular, chilling episode? Darby is facing the toughest case of her career . . . and, as the body count rises, one that will bring her into great personal danger and leave her in fear of losing her mind, if not her soul.

For the Soul Collectors are the monsters from your worst nightmares.

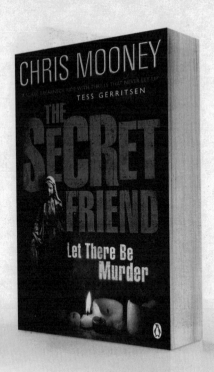

CHRIS MOONEY

A SAME BREAKNECK RIDE WITH THRILLS THAT NEVER LET UP'
TESS GERRITSEN

THE SECRET FRIEND

Let There Be Murder

Two dead girls in the water.

Two tiny statues of the Virgin Mary concealed in their clothing.

One CSI on the hunt for their killer.

When Judith Chen is found floating in Boston's harbour, links are made with the murder of Emma Hale, a student who vanished without trace, only for her body to wash up months later.

CSI Darby McCormick is assigned to the case and uncovers a piece of overlooked evidence from the Hale investigation – which brings her into contact with Malcolm Fletcher, a former FBI agent now on the Most Wanted list after a string of bloody murders. And when a third student goes missing, Darby is led into a dangerous game of cat-and-mouse with deadly links to the past – and a man who speaks to the Blessed Virgin. A man who wants to be a secret friend to the girls he abducts.

'A SCARY, BREAKNECK RIDE WITH
THRILLS THAT NEVER LET UP'
TESS GERRITSEN

THE MAN
WITH NO FACE
IS COMING

THE
MISSING

CHRIS
MOONEY

A CSI Darby McCormick thriller

The woman missing for five years.

The Crime Scene Investigator who finds her.

And the serial killer who wants them both dead . . .

When Boston CSI Darby McCormick finds a raving and emaciated woman
hiding at the scene of a violent kidnap, she runs a DNA search to identify the
Jane Doe. The result confirms she was abducted five years earlier and has
somehow managed to escape from the dungeon in which she's been caged.

With a teenage girl also missing and the Jane Doe seriously ill, the clock is
ticking for Darby as she hunts for the dungeon before anyone else disappears
or dies. And when the FBI takes over the investigation, it becomes clear that
a sadistic serial killer has been on the prowl for decades – and is poised to
strike again at any moment. A killer with links to horrors that Darby has tried
desperately to bury in her past . . .

dead good

*For all of you who find
a crime story irresistible.*

Discover the very best crime and thriller books on our dedicated website – hand-picked by our editorial team so you have tailored recommendations to help you choose what to read next.

We'll introduce you to our favourite authors and the brightest new talent. Read exclusive interviews and specially commissioned features on everything from the best classic crime to our top ten TV detectives, join live webchats and speak to authors directly.

Plus our monthly book competition offers you the chance to win the latest crime fiction, and there are DVD box sets and digital devices to be won too.

Sign up for our newsletter at
www.deadgoodbooks.co.uk/signup

Join the conversation on: